Praise for the authors of *Cravings*

Laurell K. Hamilton

"[A] sexy, edgy, wickedly ironic style . . . red-hot entertainment."
—*Jayne Ann Krentz*

"I've never read a writer with a more fertile imagination."
—*Diana Gabaldon*

MaryJanice Davidson

"Delightful wicked fun!"
—*Christine Feehan*

"Chick lit meets vampire action in this creative, sophisticated, sexy and wonderfully witty book."
—*Catherine Spangler*

Eileen Wilks

"Eileen Wilks writes what I like to read." —*Linda Howard*

Rebecca York

"[Her] books . . . deliver what they promise: excitement, mystery, romance." —*The Washington Post Book World*

CRAVINGS

Laurell K. Hamilton
MaryJanice Davidson
Eileen Wilks
Ruth Glick writing as Rebecca York

JOVE BOOKS, NEW YORK

CRAVINGS

A Jove Book / published by arrangement with the authors

PRINTING HISTORY
Jove edition

ISBN: 0-7394-4433-6

Contents

BLOOD UPON MY LIPS

Laurell K. Hamilton

IT was an October wedding. The bride was a witch who solved preternatural crimes. The groom raised the dead and slew vampires for a living. It sounded like a Halloween joke, but it wasn't.

The groom's side wore traditional black tuxedos with orange bow ties and white shirts. The bride's side wore orange formals. You don't see Halloween-orange prom dresses all that often. I'd been terrified that I was going to have to shell out three hundred dollars for one of the monstrosities. But since I was on the groom's side I got to wear a tux. Larry Kirkland, groom, coworker, and friend, had stuck to his guns. He refused to make me wear a dress, unless I wanted to wear one. Hmm, let me see. Three hundred dollars, or more, for a very orange formal that I'd burn before I'd wear again, or less than a hundred dollars to rent a tux that I could return. Wait, let me think.

I got the tux. I did have to buy a pair of black tie-up shoes. The tux shop didn't have any size seven in women's. Oh, well. Even with the seventy-dollar shoes that I would probably never wear again, I still counted myself very lucky.

As I watched the four bridesmaids in their poofy orange dresses walk down the aisle of the packed church, their hair done up on their heads in ringlets, and more makeup than I'd ever seen any of them wear, I was feeling very, very lucky. They had little round bouquets of orange and white flowers with black lace and orange and black ribbons trailing down from the flowers. I just had to stand up at the front of the church with my one hand holding the wrist of the other arm. The wedding coordinator had seemed to believe that all the groomsmen would pick their noses, or something equally embarrassing, if they didn't keep their hands busy. So she'd informed them that they were to stand with their hands clasped on the opposite wrist. No hands in pockets, no crossed arms, no hands clasped in front of their groins. I'd arrived late to the rehearsal—big surprise—and the wedding coordinator had seemed to believe that I would be a civilizing influence on the men, just because I happened to be a girl. It didn't take her long to figure out that I was as uncouth as the men. Frankly, I thought we all behaved ourselves really well. She just didn't seem very comfortable around men, or around me. Maybe it was the gun I was wearing.

But none of the groomsmen, myself included, had done anything for her to complain about. This was Larry's day, and none of us wanted to screw it up. Oh, and Tammy's day.

The bride entered the church on her father's arm. Her mother was already in the front pew dressed in a pale melon orange that actually looked good on her. She was beaming and crying, and seemed to be both miserable and deliriously happy all at the same time. Mrs. Reynolds was the reason for the big church wedding. Both Larry and Tammy would have been happy with something smaller, but Tammy didn't seem to be able to say no to her mother, and Larry was just trying to get along with his future in-law.

Detective Tammy Reynolds was a vision in white, complete with a veil that covered her face like a misty dream. She, too, was wearing more makeup than I'd ever seen her in, but the drama of it suited the beaded neckline, and full, bell-like skirt. The dress looked like it could have walked down the isle on its own, or at least stood on its own. They'd done something with her hair so that it was smooth and completely back from her face, so that you could see just how striking she was. I'd never really noticed that Detective Tammy was beautiful.

I was standing at the end of the groomsmen, me and Larry's three brothers, so I had to crane a little to see his face. It was worth the look. He was pale enough that his freckles stood out on his skin like ink spots. His blue eyes were wide. They'd done something to his short red curls so they lay almost smooth. He looked good, if he didn't faint. He gazed at Tammy as if he'd been hit with a hammer right between the eyes. Of course, if they'd done two hours' worth of makeup on Larry, he might have been a vision, too. But men don't have to worry about it. The double standard is alive and well. The woman is supposed to be beautiful on her wedding day, the groom is just supposed to stand there and not embarrass himself, or her.

I leaned back in line and tried not to embarrass anyone. I'd tied my hair back while it was still wet so that it lay flat and smooth to my head. I wasn't cutting my hair so it was the best I could do to look like a boy. There were other parts of my anatomy that didn't help the boy look either. I am curvy, and even in a tux built for a man, I was still curvy. No one complained, but the wedding coordinator had rolled her eyes when she saw me. What she said out loud was, "You need more makeup."

"None of the other groomsmen are wearing makeup," I said.

"Don't you want to look pretty?"

Since I'd thought I already looked pretty good, there was only one reply. "Not particularly."

That had been the last conversation the wedding lady and I had had. She positively avoided me, after that. I think she'd been mean on purpose, because I wasn't helping her keep the other groomsmen in line. She seemed to believe that just because we both had ovaries instead of balls that we should have joined forces. Besides, why should I worry about being pretty? It was Tammy and Larry's day, not mine. If, and that was a very big if, I ever got married, then I'd worry about it. Until then, screw it. Besides, I was already wearing more makeup than I normally did. Which for me meant any. My stepmother Judith keeps telling me that when I hit thirty I'll feel differently about all this girl stuff. I've only got three years to go until the big 3-0; so far panic has not set in.

Tammy's father placed her hand in Larry's. Tammy was three inches taller than Larry; in heels, she was more. I was standing close enough to the groom to see the look that Tammy's father gave Larry. It was not a friendly look. Tammy was three months, almost four months pregnant, and it was Larry's fault. Or rather it was Tammy and Larry's fault, but I don't think that's how her father viewed it. No, Mr. Nathan Reynolds definitely seemed to blame Larry, as if Tammy had been snatched a virgin from her bed and brought back deflowered, and pregnant.

Mr. Reynolds raised Tammy's blusher on her veil to reveal all that carefully made-up beauty. He kissed her solemnly on the cheek, threw one last dark look at Larry, and turned smiling and pleasant to join his wife in the front pew. The fact that he'd gone from a look that dark, to pleasant and smiling when he knew the church would see his face bothered me. I didn't like that Larry's new father-in-law was capable of lying that well. Made me wonder what he did for a living. But I was naturally suspicious; it comes from working too closely with the police for too long. Cynicism is so contagious.

We all turned towards the altar, and the familiar ceremony began. I'd been to dozens of weddings over the years, almost all Christian, almost all standard denominations, so the words were strangely familiar. Funny, how you don't think you've memorized something until you hear it, and realize you have. "Dearly, beloved, we are gathered here today to join this man and this woman in Holy Matrimony."

It wasn't a Catholic or Episcopalian wedding, so we didn't have to kneel, or do much of anything. We wouldn't even be getting communion during the ceremony. I have to admit my mind began to wander a bit. I've never been a big fan of weddings. I understand they're necessary, but I was never one of those girls who fantasized about what my wedding would be like someday. I don't remember ever thinking about it until I got engaged in college, and when that fell through, I went back to not thinking about it. I'd been engaged very briefly to Richard Zeeman, junior high science teacher, and local Ulfric, Wolf-King, but he'd dumped me because I was more at home with the monsters than he was. Now, I'd pretty much settled into the idea that I would never marry. Never have those words spoken over me and my honeybun. A tiny part of me that I'd never admit to out loud was sad about that. Not the wedding part. I think I would hate my own wedding just as much as anyone else's, but not having one single person to call my own. I'd been raised middle-class, middle America, small town, and that meant the fact that I was currently dating a minimum of three men, maybe four, depending on how you looked at it, still made me squirm with something painfully close to embarassment. I was working on not being uncomfortable about it, but there were issues that needed to be worked out. For instance, who do you bring as your date to a wedding? The wedding was in a church, complete with holy items so two of the men were out. Vampires didn't do well around holy items. Watching Jean-Claude and Asher burst into flames as they came through the door would probably have put a damper on the festivities. That left me with one official boyfriend, Micah Callahan, and one friend, who happened to be a boy, Nathaniel Graison.

They'd come to the part where the rings were exchanged, which meant the maid of honor and the best man had something to do. The woman got to hold Tammy's huge spill of white flowers, and the man got to hand over the jewelry. It all seemed so terribly sexist. Just once I'd like to see the men have to hold flowers and the women fork over the jewelry. I'd been told once by a friend that I was too liberated for my own good. Maybe. All I knew was that if I ever did get engaged again I'd decided either both of us got an engagement ring, or neither of us did. Of course, again, that not getting married part meant that the engagement was probably off the board, too. Oh, well.

At last, they were man and wife. We all turned and the reverend presented them to the church as Mr. and Mrs. Lawrence Kirkland, though I knew for a fact that Tammy was keeping her maiden name, so really it should have been Mr. Lawrence Kirkland and Ms. Tammy Reynolds.

We all fell in to two lines. I got to offer my arm to Detective Jessica Arnet. She took the arm, and with her in heels, I was about five inches shorter than she was. She smiled at me. I'd noticed she was pretty about a month ago, because she was flirting with Nathaniel, but it wasn't until that moment that I realized she could be beautiful. Her dark hair was pulled completely back from her face, so that the delicate triangle of her cheeks and chin was all you saw. The makeup had widened her eyes, added color to her cheeks, and carved pouting lips out of her thin ones. I realized that the orange that made most of the bridesmaids look wan brought out rich highlights in her skin and hair, made her eyes shine. So few people look good in orange, it's one of the reasons they use it in so many prisons, like an extra punishment. But Detective Arnet looked wonderful in it. It almost made me wish I'd let the wedding lady talk me into the extra makeup. Almost.

I must have stared, because she frowned, and only then did I start forward, and take our place in line. We filed out like good little wedding party members. We'd already endured the photographer for group shots. He'd be hunting the bride and groom for those candid moments: cutting the cake, throwing the bouquet, removing the garter. Once we got through the receiving line, I could fade into the background and no one would care.

We all stood in a line as we'd been drilled. Bride and groom at the front of the line, because, let's face it, that's who everyone is really here to see. The rest of us strung out beind them along the wall, waiting to shake hands with mostly strangers. Tammy's family were local, but I'd never met any of them. Larry's family were all out-of-towners. I knew the policemen that had been invited; other than that, it was all nod and smile, nod and smile, shake a hand, or two, nod and smile.

I must have been concentrating very hard on the people I was meeting, because it surprised me when Micah Callahan, my official date, was suddenly in front of me. He was exactly my height. Short for man or woman. His rich, brown hair was nearly as curly as mine, and today his hair fell around his shoulders loose. He'd done that for me. He didn't like his hair loose, and I understood why. He was already delicate looking for a man, and with all that hair framing him his face was almost as delicate a triangle as Detective Arnet's. His lower lip was fuller than his upper lip, which gave him a prepetual pout, and though wider than a woman's mouth, that didn't really help. But the body under his black tailored suit, that definitely helped make it clear he was a man. Wide shoulders, slender waist and hips, a swimmer's body, though that wasn't his sport. From the neck down you'd never mistake him for a girl. It was just the face, and the hair.

He'd left his shirt open at the neck so that it framed the hollow in his throat. I could see myself reflected darkly in his sunglasses. It was actually a little dim in the hallway, so why the sunglasses? His eyes were kitty-cat eyes, leopard, to be exact. They were yellow and green all at the same time. What color predominated between the two depended on what color he wore, his mood, the lighting. Today, because of the shirt, they'd be very green, but with a hint of yellow, like dappled light in the forest.

He was a wereleopard, Nimir-Raj of the local pard. By rights he should have been able to pass for human. But if you spend too much time in animal form sometimes you don't come all the way back. He didn't want to squeak the mundanes, so he'd worn the glasses today.

His hand was very warm in mine, and that one small touch was enough, enough to bring some of the careful shielding down. The shielding that had kept me from sensing him all through the ceremony like a second heartbeat. He was Nimir-Raj, to my Nimir-Ra. Leopard King and Queen. Though my idea of the arrangement was closer to queen and consort, partners, but I reserved presidential veto. I'm a control freak, what can I say?

I was the first human Nimir-Ra in the wereleopards' long history. Though since I raise the dead for a living and am a legal vampire executioner, there are people who'll argue the human part. They're just jealous.

I started to pull him in against me for a hug, but he gave a small shake of his head. He was right. If just holding his hand sped my pulse like candy on my tongue, then a hug would be bad. Through a series of metaphysical accidents, I held something close to the beast that lived in Micah. That beast and Micah's beast knew each other, knew each other in the way of old lovers. That part of us that was not human knew each other better than our human halves. I still knew almost nothing about him, really. Even though we lived together. On a metaphysical level we were bound tighter than any ceremony or piece of paper could make us; in real everyday life, I was wondering what to do with him. He was the perfect partner. My other half, the missing piece. He complemented me in almost every way. And when he was standing this close, it all seemed so right. Give me a little distance and I would begin to wonder when the other shoe would drop and he would stop being wonderful. I'd never had a man in my life yet that didn't spoil it somehow. Why should Micah be different?

He didn't so much kiss me as lay the feel of his breath against my cheek. He breathed, "Until later." That one light touch made me shiver so violently that he had to steady me with a touch on my arm.

He smiled at me, that knowing smile that a man gives when he understands just how much his touch affects a woman. I didn't like that smile. It made me feel like he took his time with me for granted. The moment I thought it, I knew it wasn't true. It wasn't even fair. So why had I thought it at all? Because I am a master at screwing up my own love life. If something works too well, I've got to poke at it, prod it, until it breaks, or bites me. I was trying not to do that anymore, but old habits, especially bad ones, die hard.

Micah moved off down the line, and Detective Arnet gave me a questioning look out of her heavily painted but lovely eyes. She opened her mouth as if to ask if I were alright, but the next person in line distracted her. Nathaniel was distracting, no doubt about that.

Jessica Arnet was a few inches taller than Nathaniel's 5' 6", so she had to look down to meet that lavender gaze. No exaggeration on the color. His eyes weren't blue, but truly a pale purple, lavender, spring lilacs. He wore a banded-collar shirt that was almost the same color as his eyes, so the lavender was even more vibrant; drowningly beautiful, those eyes.

He offered his hand, but she hugged him. Hugged him, because I think for the first time she was in a public situation where no one would think it was strange. So she hugged him, because she could.

There was a fraction of a moment's hesitation, then he hugged her back, but he turned his head so he could look at me. His eyes said clearly, Help me.

She hadn't done that much yet, just a hug where a handshake would have done, but the look in Nathaniel's eyes was much more serious than what she'd done. As if it bothered him more than it should have. Since in his day job he's a stripper, you'd think he'd be used to women pawing him. Of course, maybe that was the point. He wasn't at work.

She stayed molded to his body, and he stayed holding, with only that mute look in his eyes to say he was unhappy.

His body seemed happy and relaxed in the hug. He never showed Jessica Arnet his confused eyes.

The hug had gone on longer than was polite, and I finally realized what part of the problem was. Nathaniel was the least dominant person I'd ever met. He wanted out of the hug, but he could not be the first one to pull back. Jessica had to let him go, and she was probably waiting for him to move away, and getting all the wrong signals from the fact that he wasn't moving away. Shit. How do I end up with men in my life who have such interesting problems? Lucky, I guess.

I held out my hand toward him, and the relief on his face was clear enough that anyone down the hall would have seen it, and understood it. He kept his face turned so Jessica never saw that look. It would have hurt her feelings, and Nathaniel didn't want to hurt anyone's feelings. Which meant that he didn't see her shining face, all aglow with what she thought was mutual attraction. Truthfully, I'd thought Nathaniel liked her, at least a little, but his face said otherwise. To me, anyway.

Nathaniel came to my hand like a scared child who's just been saved from the neighborhood bully. I drew him into a hug, and he clung to me, pressing our bodies tighter than I would have liked in public, but I couldn't blame him, not really. He wanted the comfort of physical contact, and I think he'd figured out that Jessica Arnet had gotten the wrong idea.

I held him as close as I could, as close as I'd wanted to hold Micah. With Micah, it might have led to embarrassing things, but not with Nathaniel. With Nathaniel I could control myself. I wasn't in love with him. I caressed the long braid of his auburn hair that fell nearly to his ankles. I played with the braid, as if it were other more intimate things, hoping that Jessica would take the hint. I should have known that a little extra hugging wouldn't have done the job.

I drew back from the hug first, and he kept his gaze on my face. I could study his face and understand what she saw there, so handsome, so amazingly beautiful. His shoulders had broadened in the last few months, from weight lifting, or just the fact that he was twenty and still filling out. He was luscious to look at, and I was almost certain he would be nearly as luscious in bed. But though he was living with me, cleaning my house, buying my groceries, and running my errands, I still hadn't had intercourse with him. I was really trying to avoid that, since I didn't plan on keeping him. Someday Nathaniel would need to find a new place to live, a new life, because I wouldn't always need him the way I did now.

I was human, but just as I was the first human Nimir-Ra the leopards had ever had, I was also the first human servant of a master vampire to aquire certain . . . abilities. With those abilities came some downsides. One of those downsides was needing to feed the ardeur every twelve hours, or so. *Ardeur* is French for flame, roughly translates to being consumed, being consumed by love. But it isn't exactly love.

I stared up into Nathaniel's wide lilac eyes, cradled his face between my hands. I did the only thing I could think of that might keep Jessica Arnet from embarrassing them both at the reception to follow. I kissed him. I kissed him, because he needed me to do it. I kissed him because it was strangely the right thing to do. I kissed him because he was my *pomme de sang*, my apple of blood. I kissed him because he was my food, and I hated the fact that anyone was my food. I fed off Micah, too, but he was my partner, my boyfriend, and he was dominant enough to say no if he wanted to. Nathaniel wanted me to take him, wanted to belong to me, and I didn't know what to do about it. Months from now the ardeur would be under control and I wouldn't need a *pomme de sang*. What would Nathaniel do when I didn't need him anymore?

I drew back from the kiss and watched Nathaniel's face shine at me the way Jessica Arnet's face had shone at him. I wasn't in love with Nathaniel, but staring up into that happy, handsome face, I was afraid that I couldn't say the same for him. I was using him. Not for sex, but for food. He was food, just food, but even as I thought it, I knew it was partly a lie. You don't fall in love with your steak, because it can't hold you, can't press warm lips in the bend of your neck, and whisper, "Thank you," as it glides down the hallway in the charcoal gray slacks that fit its ass like a second skin and spill roomy over the thighs that you happen to know are even lovelier out of the pants than in. When I turned to the next smiling person in line, I caught Detective Jessica Arnet giving me a look. It wasn't an entirely friendly look. Great, just great.

THE Halloween theme continued into the reception hall. Orange and black crepe paper streamers dangled everywhere; cardboard skeletons, rubber bats, and paper ghosts floated overhead. There was a fake spiderweb against one wall big enough to hang someone from. The table centerpieces were realistic looking jack-o'-lanterns with flickering electric grins. The fake skeletons were long enough to be a hazard to anyone much taller than I was. Which meant most guests were having the tops of their hair brushed by little cardboard skeleton toes. Unfortunately, Tammy was 5' 8" without heels; with heels she got her veil tangled with the decorations. The bridesmaids finally got Tammy's veil unhooked from the skeletal toes, but it ruined the entrance for the bride and groom. If Tammy had wanted the decorations safe for the tall people she shouldn't have left it to Larry and his brothers. There wasn't a one of them over 5' 6". Don't blame me. Groomsman or not, I hadn't helped decorate the hall. It was not my fault.

There were other things that I was going to get blamed for, but they weren't my fault either. Well, mostly not my fault.

I'd escorted Jessica Arnet into the room. She hadn't smiled at me at all. She'd looked way too serious. When Tammy's veil was safely secure once more, Jessica had gone to the table where Micah and Nathaniel were sitting. She'd leaned into Nathaniel, and when I say leaned, I mean it. Like leaned on him, so that the line of her body touched his shoulder and arm. It was bold and discreet at the same time. If I hadn't been watching for it, I might not have realized what she was doing. She spoke quietly to him. He finally shook his head, and she turned and wove her way through the small tables full of guests. She took the last empty seat at the long table where the wedding party was trapped. The last empty chair was beside me. We got to sit down in the order we'd entered. Goody.

In the middle of the toasts, after Larry's brother had made the groom blush, but before the parents had had their turn, Jessica leaned over close enough that her perfume was sweet and a little too much.

She whispered, "Does Nathaniel really live with you?"

I'd been afraid the question would be hard. This one was easy. "Yes," I said.

"I asked if he was your boyfriend, and he said that he slept in your bed. I thought that was an odd way to answer." She turned her head so I was suddenly way too close to her face, those wide-searching eyes. I was struck again by how lovely she was, and felt stupid for not noticing sooner. But I didn't notice girls, I noticed boys. So sue me, I was heterosexual. It wasn't her beauty that struck me, but the demand, the intelligence, in her eyes. She searched my face, and I realized that no matter how pretty she was, she was still a cop, and she was trying to uncover the lie here. Because she had smelled one.

She hadn't asked me a question, so I didn't answer. I rarely got in trouble by keeping my mouth shut.

She gave a small frown. "Is he your boyfriend? If he is, then I'll leave it alone. But you could have told me sooner, so I wouldn't have made a fool of myself."

I wanted to say, You didn't make a fool of yourself, but I didn't. I was too busy trying to think of an answer that would be honest, and not get Nathaniel and me in more trouble. I settled for the evasion he'd used. "Yes, he sleeps in my bed."

She gave a small shake of her head, a stubborn look coming over her face. "That isn't what I asked, Anita. You're lying. You're both lying. I can smell it." She frowned. "Just tell me the truth. If you have a prior claim, say so, now."

I sighed. "Yeah, I have a prior claim, apparently."

The frown deepened, putting frown lines between the pretty eyes. "Apparently? What does that mean? Either he's your boyfriend, or he's not."

"Maybe boyfriend isn't the right word," I said, and tried to think of an explanation that didn't include the words *pomme de sang*. The police didn't really know how deeply involved with the monsters I was. They suspected, but they didn't know. Knowing is different from suspicion. Knowing will hold up in court; suspicion won't even get you a search warrant.

"Then what is the right word?" she whispered, but it

held an edge of hiss, as if she were fighting not to yell. "Are you lovers?"

What was I supposed to say? If I said, yes, Nathaniel would be free of Jessica's unwanted attentions, but it would also mean that everyone on the St. Louis police force would know that Nathaniel was my lover. It wasn't my reputation I was worried about; that was pretty much trashed. A girl can't be coffin-bait for the Master of the City and be a good girl. Most people feel that if a woman will do a vampire, she'll do anything. Not true, but there you go. No, not my reputation at stake, but Nathaniel's. If it got out that he was my lover, then no other woman would make a play for him. If he didn't want to date Jessica, fine, but he needed to date someone. Someone besides me. If I wasn't going to keep Nathaniel forever, like almost death-do-you-part ever, then he needed a bigger social circle. He needed a real girlfriend.

So I hesitated, weighing a dozen words, and not finding a single one that would help the situation. I didn't know how to answer Arnet's question so I used the old excuse of needing to go to the ladies' room. I wanted to avoid her, if I could. And Micah, too. Micah had made me promise I'd dance with him. I hated to dance. I didn't think I was good at it. In the privacy of our home, Micah, and Nathaniel, and hell, Jason, had told me I was wrong. That I actually danced very well. I did not believe them. I think it was a throwback to a rather horrible junior high school dance experience. Of course, it was junior high, is there any experience except horrible for those few years? In Hell, if you're really bad, you must be fourteen forever, and be trapped in school, and never get to go home.

When I came out, Nathaniel was still at the table, but it was Jason with him, not Micah. Jason and Nathaniel were leaning so close together that their heads nearly touched. Jason's short blond hair seemed very yellow against Nathaniel's dark auburn. Jason wore a blue dress shirt that I knew was only a shade or two bluer than his own eyes. His suit was black, and I knew without seeing him standing that it was tailored to his body, and probably Italian in cut. Jean-Claude had paid for the suit, and he was fond of Italian-cut designer suits for his employees. When he wasn't dressing them like they were extras in a high-class porno movie, anyway. For a mainstream wedding, the suit worked. Jason also worked at Guilty Pleasures as a stripper, and Jean-Claude did own the club, but it wasn't that type of employment that let Jason rate designer clothes tailored to his body. Jason was Jean-Claude's *pomme de sang*. Jean-Claude did not think I treated Nathaniel with enough respect for his position as *my pomme de sang*. I had let Micah and Nathaniel go shopping with Jason for dress clothes, and I footed the bill for my two boys. It had been outrageous, but I couldn't let Jean-Claude be nicer to his kept man than I was to mine. Could I?

Technically, Micah wasn't a kept man, but the salary he drew from the Coalition for Better Understanding Between Furred and Non-Furred didn't cover designer suits. I made enough money to pay for designer suits, so I did.

I had time to wonder what Jason and Nathaniel were up to, talking so close together, like conspirators. Then I felt, more than saw, Micah. He was across the room talking to a group of men, most of them cops. He shook his head, laughed, and started across the room, toward me. I didn't get much chance to see Micah from a distance. We were always so close to one another, physically. Now I was able to watch him walk towards me, able to admire how the suit clung to his body, how it flattered the broad shoulders, the slender waist, the tightness of his hips, the swell of his thighs. The suit fit him like a roomy glove. Watching him move towards me, the suit was suddenly worth every penny.

The music stopped before he reached me, some song I didn't recognize. He joined me at the table. Jessica Arnet was gone.

NATHANIEL sat on the other side of me, putting me in the middle. He sat so that the line of his body touched mine as much as possible. There was a time when I'd have made him give me breathing space, but I understood the shapeshifter's need for physical contact now. Besides, making Nathaniel move over an inch when he slept mostly naked in my bed nearly every night would have been silly. Jason just stood and looked down at all of us. He looked unnaturally solemn, at least for him, then suddenly he broke into a grin. Now he looked like himself.

"It's after midnight, we thought you'd be outside feeding the ardeur." His grin was way too wicked to match the mildish words.

"I'm able to go longer between feedings," I said, "sometimes fourteen, or even sixteen hours."

"Oh, pooh," he said, and stamped his foot, pouting. It was a wonderful imitation of a childish snit, except for the devilish twinkle in his eye. "I was hoping to take another one for the team."

I frowned at him, but couldn't make it go all the way up to my eyes. Jason amused me, I don't know why, but he always had. "I don't think we'll be needing your services tonight, thanks for offering though."

He gave an exaggerated sigh. "I am never going to get to have sex with you again, am I?"

"Don't take this wrong, Jason, but I hope not. The sex was amazing, but what put you in my bed was an emergency. If I can't control the ardeur better than that, then I'm not safe to be out in public alone."

"It was my fault," Nathaniel said, voice soft.

I turned my head and was close enough to the side of his face to have kissed his cheek. I wanted to make him move, to give me more room, but I fought the urge off. I was just being grumpy. "It was my fault if it was anyone's, Nathaniel."

Micah's so-calm voice came from my other shoulder, "It was Belle Morte's fault, the wicked, sexy vampire of the west. If she hadn't been messing with Anita, trying to use the ardeur to control her, then it wouldn't have risen hours ahead of schedule." Belle Morte, Beautiful Death, was the creator of Jean-Claude's bloodline. I'd never met her in physical person, but I'd met her metaphysically, and that had been bad enough. Micah laid a hand across my shoulders, but managed to put his hand on Nathaniel's shoulder, too. Comforting us both. "You haven't collapsed since Anita's been able to stretch the feedings out more."

Nathaniel sighed so heavily that I felt the movement against my body. "I haven't gotten stronger, she has." He sounded so sad, so disappointed in himself.

I leaned in against his shoulder, enough that Micah was able to literally hug us both at the same time. "I'm your Nimir-Ra, I'm supposed to be stronger, right?"

He gave me a faint smile.

I laid my head on his shoulder, curving my face into the bend of his neck, and getting that whiff of vanilla. He'd always smelled like vanilla to me. I'd thought once it was shampoo, or soap, but it wasn't. It was his scent for me. I hadn't had the courage yet to ask Micah if Nathaniel's skin smelled like vanilla to him, too. Because I wasn't sure what it would mean if I was the only one who found Nathaniel's scent so very sweet.

"You want to ask Anita something," Jason said.

Nathaniel tensed against me, then in a small voice, he asked, "Do I still get my dance?"

It was my turn to tense. I couldn't control it, it was involuntary. Nathaniel got very still beside me, because he'd felt it, too. I didn't want to dance, that was true, but I had promised Micah and Nathaniel. "Sure, dancing sounds great."

That made Micah and Nathaniel pull back enough to look at me. Jason was just staring down at me. "What did you say?" Nathaniel said.

"I said, dancing sounds great." Their astonishment almost made it worthwhile.

"Where is Anita, and what have you done with her?" Jason asked, face mock serious.

I didn't try and explain. I just stood, and offered my hand to Nathaniel.

After a second of staring at it, and me, he took it, almost tentatively, as if he were afraid I'd take it back. I think he'd come ready for an argument about the dancing, and not getting one had thrown him.

I smiled at the surprise on his face. "Let's dance."

He gave me one of his rare full-out smiles, the one that made his entire face light up. For that one smile, I'd have given him a lot more than just a dance.

Of course, my good intentions lasted about as long as it took to be escorted onto the dance floor. Then suddenly I was expected to dance. In front of people. In front of people that were mostly cops. Cops that I worked with on a regular basis. No one is as merciless if you give them amunition, no pun intended, as a bunch of policemen. If I danced badly, I'd be teased. If I danced well, I'd be teased worse. If they realized I was dancing well with a stripper, the teasing would be endless. If they realized I was dancing badly with a stripper, the jokes would be, well, bad. Either way you cut it, I was so screwed.

I felt fourteen again, and awkward as hell. But it was almost impossible to be awkward with Nathaniel as your partner. Maybe it was his day job, but he knew how to bring out the best in someone on the dance floor. All I had to do was let go of my inhibitions and follow his body. Easy, maybe, but not for me. I like the few inhibitions I have left, thank you, and I'm going to cling to them as long as I can.

What I was clinging to now was Nathaniel. Not much scares me, not really, but airplane rides and dancing in public are on that short list. My heart was in my throat, and I kept fighting the urge to stare at my feet. The men had spent an afternoon proving that I could dance, at home, with only people who were my friends watching. But suddenly, in public in front of a less than friendly audience, all my lessons seemed to have fled. I was reduced to clinging to Nathaniel's hand and shoulder, turning in those useless circles that have nothing to do with the song, and everything to do with fear, and the inability to dance.

"Anita," Nathaniel said.

I kept staring at my feet, and trying to not see that we were being watched from around the room.

"Anita, look at me, please."

I raised my face, and whatever he saw in my eyes, made him smile, and filled his own eyes with a sort of soft wonderment. "You really are afraid." He said it like he hadn't believed it before.

"Would I ever admit to being afraid, if I wasn't?"

He smiled. "Good point." His voice was soft. "Just look at my face, my eyes, no one else matters but the person you're dancing with. Just don't look at anyone else."

"You sound like you've given this advice before."

He shrugged. "A lot of women are uncomfortable on stage, at first."

I gave him raised eyebrows.

"I used to do an act in formal wear, and I'd pick someone from the audience to dance with. Very formal, very Fred Astaire."

Somehow, Fred Astaire was not a name that came to mind when I thought of Guilty Pleasures. I said as much.

His smile was less gentle and more his own. "If you ever came down to the club to watch one of us work instead of just giving us a ride, you'd know what we did."

I gave him a look.

"You're dancing," he said.

Of course, once he pointed out that I'd been dancing, I stopped. It was like walking on water; if you thought about it, you couldn't do it.

Nathaniel pulled gently on my hand, and pushed gently on my shoulder, and got us going again. I finally settled for staring at his chest, watching his body movements as if he'd been a bad guy and it was a fight. Watch the central body for the first telltale movements.

"At home you moved to the rhythm of the song, not just where I moved you."

"That was at home," I said, staring at his chest, and letting him move me around the floor. It was damn passive for me, but I couldn't lead, because I couldn't dance. To lead you have to know what you're doing.

The song stopped. I'd made it through one song in public. Yeah! I looked up and met Nathaniel's gaze. I expected him to look pleased, or happy, or a lot of things, but that wasn't what was on his face. In fact, I couldn't read the expression on his face. It was serious again, but other than that . . . We stood there, staring at each other, while I tried to figure out what was happening, and I think he tried to work up to saying something. But what? What had him all serious-faced?

I had time to ask, "What, what's wrong?" then the next song came on. It was fast, with a beat, and I was so out of there. I let go of Nathaniel, stepped back, and had turned, and actually gotten a step away, before he grabbed my hand. Grabbed my hand and pulled me in against him so hard and so fast that I stumbled. If I hadn't caught myself with one arm around his body, I'd have fallen. I was suddenly acutely aware of the firmness of his back against my arm, the curve of his side cupped in the hollow of my hand. I was holding him so close to the front of my body that it seemed every inch of us from chest to groin pressed against one another. His face was painfully close to mine. His mouth so close it seemed a shame not to lay a kiss upon those lips.

His eyes were half-startled, as if I'd grabbed him, and I had, but I hadn't meant to. Then he swayed to one side and took me with him. And just like that we were dancing, but it was different from any dancing I'd ever done. I didn't follow his movements with my eyes, I followed them with my body. He moved, and I moved with him, not because I was supposed to, but for the same reason a tree bends in the wind, because you must.

I moved because he moved. I moved because I finally understood what they'd all been talking about; rhythm, beat, but it wasn't the beat of the music I was hearing, it was the rythymn of Nathaniel's body, pressed so close that all I could feel was him. His body, his hands, his face. His mouth was temptingly close, but I did not close that distance. I gave myself over to his body, the warm strength in his hands, but I did not take the kiss he offered. For he was offering, he was offering himself in the way that Nathaniel had, no demand, just the open-ended offer of his flesh for the taking. I ignored that kiss the way I'd ignored so many others.

He leaned into me, and I had a moment, just a moment, before his lips touched mine, to say, No, stop. But I didn't say it. I wanted that kiss. That much I could admit to myself.

His lips brushed mine, gentle, then the kiss became part of the swaying of our bodies, so that as our bodies rocked, so the kiss moved with us. He kissed me as his body moved, and I turned my face up to him, and gave myself to the movement of his mouth as I'd given myself to the movement of his body. The brush of lips became a full-blown kiss, and it was his tongue that pierced my lips, that filled my mouth, his mouth that filled mine. But it was my hand that left his back and traced his face, cupped his cheek, pressed my body deeper against his, so that I felt him stretched tight and firm under his clothes. The feel of him pressed so tight against my clothes and my body, brought a small sound from my mouth, and the knowledge that the ardeur had risen early. Hours early. A distant part of me thought, Fuck. The rest of me agreed, but not in the way I meant it.

I drew back from his mouth, tried to breathe, tried to think. His hand came up to cup the back of my head, to press my mouth back to his, so that I drowned in his kiss. Drowned in the pulse and beat of his body. Drowned on the rhythms and tide of his desire. The ardeur allowed, sometimes, a glimpse into another's heart, or at least their libido. I'd learned to control that part, but tonight it was as if my fragile control had been ripped away, and I stood pressed into the curves and firmness of Nathaniel's body with nothing to protect me from him. Always before he'd been safe. He'd never pushed an advantage, never gone over a line that I drew, not by word or deed; now suddenly, he was ignoring all my signals, all my silent walls. No, not ignoring them, smashing through them. Smashing them down with his hands on my body, his mouth on mine, his body pushing against mine. I could not fight the ardeur and Nathaniel, not at the same time.

I saw what he wanted. I felt it. Felt his frustration. Months of being good. Of behaving himself, of not pushing his advantage. I felt all those months of good behavior shatter around us, and leave us stripped and suffocating in a desire that seemed to fill the world. Until that moment I hadn't understood how very good he'd been. I hadn't understood what I'd been turning down. I hadn't understood what he was offering. I hadn't understood . . . anything.

I pulled back from him, put a hand on his chest to keep him from closing that distance again.

"Please, Anita, please, please," his voice was low and urgent, but it was as if he couldn't bring himself to put it into words. But the ardeur didn't need words. I suddenly felt his body again, even though I stood feet apart. He was so hard and firm and aching. Aching, because I'd denied him release. Denied him release for months. I'd never had full-blown sex with Nathaniel, because I could feed without it. It had never occurred to me what that might mean for him. But now I could feel his body, heavy, aching with a passion that had been building for months. When last I'd touched Nathaniel's needs this completely, he'd simply wanted to belong to me. That was still there but there was a demand in him, a near screaming need. A need that I'd neglected. Hell, a need that I'd pretended didn't exist. Now, suddenly, Nathaniel wasn't letting me ignore that need anymore.

I had a moment of clear thinking, because I felt guilty. Guilty that I'd left him wanting for so long, while I had my own needs met. I'd thought that having real sex with him would be using him; now suddenly that one glimpse into his heart let me understand that what I'd done to him had used him more surely than intercourse. I'd used Nathaniel like he was some kind of sex toy, something to bring me pleasure, and be cleaned up and put back in a drawer. I was suddenly ashamed, ashamed that I'd treated him like an object, when that wasn't how he wanted to be treated.

The guilt hit me like a cold shower, the proverbial slap in the face, and I used it to pack the ardeur away, for another hour or two, at least.

It was as if Nathaniel felt the heat spill away from me. He gave me those wide lavender eyes, huge, and glittering, glittering with unshed tears. He let his hands drop from my arms, and since I'd already dropped my hands away, we stood on the dance floor with distance between us. A distance that neither of us tried to close.

The first shining tear trailed down his cheek.

I reached out to him, and said, "Nathaniel."

He shook his head, and backed away a step, another, then he turned and ran. Jason and Micah tried to catch him as he rushed past them, but he avoided their hands with a graceful gesture of his upper body that left them with nothing but air. He ran out the door, and they both turned to follow. But it wasn't either of them who had to chase him down. It was me. I was the one who owed him an apology. The trouble was, I wasn't exactly clear on what I would be aplogizing for. For using him, or for not using him enough.

I caught up with the men in the parking lot.

"Nathaniel says you didn't want to dance with him," Micah said.

"Not true," I said, "I danced, twice. What I didn't want to do was play kissy-face in front of the cops."

Micah looked at Nathaniel. Nathaniel looked at the ground. "You kissed me earlier in front of Detective Arnet. Why was this different?"

"I kissed you to give Jessica the clue to stop hitting on you, because you wanted me to save you from her."

He raised his eyes, and they were like two pretty wounds, so pain-filled. "So, you only kissed me to save me, not because you wanted to?"

Oh, hell. Out loud I tried again, though the sinking feeling in the pit of my stomach told me that I was going to lose this argument. Lately, around Nathaniel, I always felt like I was doing something wrong, or at least not right. "That isn't what I meant," I said.

"It's what you said." This from Micah.

"Don't you start," I said, and I heard the anger in my voice before I could stop it. The anger had been there already, I just hadn't been aware of it. I was angry a lot, especially when I wasn't comfortable. I liked anger better than embarrassment. What's a girl to do if she can't get angry and she can't run away from the problem? Hell if I know. Some of my wise friends encouraged me to be honest, emotionally honest with myself and those closest to me. Emotional honesty. It sounds so harmless, so wholesome; it's neither.

"I don't want to fight," I said. There, that was honest.

"None of us do," Micah said.

Just hearing him be so calm helped the anger ease away. "Nathaniel pushed it on the dance floor, and the ardeur rose early."

"I felt it," Micah said.

"Me, too," Jason said.

"But you don't feel it now, do you?" Nathaniel said. His

eyes were almost accusing and his voice held its own thin edge of anger. I wasn't sure if I'd ever heard him that close to being angry.

"Anita is getting better control over the ardeur," Micah said.

Nathaniel shook his head, hugging himself tight. "If it had been you, she would have just come out into the parking lot and fed."

"Not willingly," I said.

"Yes, you would," he said, and his eyes held the anger his voice had held. I'd never seen those lavender eyes angry before. Not like this. It was strangely unnerving.

"I would not have sex in the parking lot of Larry and Tammy's wedding reception, if I had a choice."

That angry gaze searched my face as if trying to find something. "Why not feed here?"

"Because it's tacky."

Jason patted his arm. "See, it isn't you she turned down, it's that she doesn't want to fool around at Larry's wedding. Just not her style."

Nathaniel glanced at Jason, then back at me. Some strange tension that I didn't quite understand seemed to flow away from him. The anger began to fade from his eyes. "I guess you're right."

"Well, if we don't want to be fooling around in the parking lot, then we need to get going," Micah said. "The ardeur doesn't like being denied. When it does come back tonight, it won't be gentle."

I sighed. He was right. That bit of metaphysical bravado on the dance floor would have all sorts of consequences later tonight. When the ardeur rose again, I would be forced to feed. There would be no stuffing it back into its box. It was almost as if, being able to stop the ardeur in its tracks, to completely turn it off once it had filled me, pissed the ardeur off. I knew it was a psychic gift, and that psychic gifts don't have feelings and don't carry grudges, but sometimes, it felt like this one did.

"I'm sorry, Anita, I wasn't thinking." Nathaniel looked so discouraged that I had to hug him, a quick hug, more sisterly than anything else, and he responded to my body language and didn't try and hold me close. He let me hug him, and step away. Nathaniel was usually almost painfully attuned to my body language. It was one of the things that had allowed him to share my bed for months without violating those last few taboos.

"Let's go home," I said.

"That's my cue to part company," Jason said.

"You're welcome to bunk over if you want," I said.

He shook his head. "No, since I'm not needed to referee the fight, or for sage advice, I'll go home, too. Besides, I couldn't stand listening to the three of you get all hot and heavy and not be invited to play." He laughed and added, "Don't get mad, but having once been included, it's harder to be excluded."

I fought the blush that burned up my face, which always seemed to make the blush darker and harder.

Jason and I had had sex once. Before I realized it was possible to love someone to death with the ardeur, Nathaniel had collapsed at work and been off the feeding schedule for a few days. Micah hadn't been in the house, and the ardeur had risen early. Hours early. It had been interference from Belle Morte, the originator of Jean-Claude's bloodline, and the first, to my knowledge, possessor of the ardeur. It only ran through her line of vamps, nowhere else. The fact that I carried it had raised very interesting metaphysical questions. Belle had wanted to understand what I was, and she had also thought it would raise some hell. Belle was a good business-y vampire, but when she could take care of business *and* make trouble, all the better. So it hadn't been my fault, but my choices had been limited to taking Nathaniel and possibly killing him, or letting Jason take one for the team. He'd been happy to do it. Very happy. And strangely our friendship had survived it, but every once in a while I couldn't pretend it hadn't happened, and that made me uncomfortable.

"I love the fact that I can make you blush now," he said.

"I don't."

He laughed, but there was something in his eyes that was more serious than laughter. "I need to tell you something, in private, before you go running off, though."

I didn't like how suddenly serious he was. I'd learned in the last few months that Jason used his teasing and laughter as a shield to hide a rather insightful intelligence that was sometimes so preceptive it was painful. I didn't like his request for privacy either. What couldn't he say in front of Micah and Nathaniel? And why?

Out loud I said, "Okay." I started off to the far side of the parking lot away from the Jeep.

When the shade of the trees that edged the church parking lot lay cool above us, I stopped and turned to Jason. "What's up?"

"The thing on the dance floor was sort of my fault."

"In what way, your fault?"

He actually looked embarrassed, which you didn't see much from Jason. "He wanted to know how I got to have sex with you, real sex, the very first time I helped feed the ardeur."

"Technically, it was the second," I said.

He frowned at me. "Yeah, but that was when the ardeur was brand new and we didn't have intercourse, and there were three other men in the bed."

I turned away so the dark would help hide the blush,

though truthfully he could probably smell it hot on my skin. "Sorry I brought it up. You were saying?"

"He's been in your bed for what, five months?"

"Something like that," I said.

"And he's not had intercourse yet. Hell, he's not had orgasm, not real orgasm with like release and everything."

I couldn't blush harder or my head would explode. "I'm listening."

"Anita, you can't keep pretending that Nathaniel isn't real."

"That's not fair."

"Maybe not, but I had no idea that you weren't at least doing him orally or by hand, or watching him do himself. Something, anything."

I just shook my head and looked at the ground. I couldn't think of anything good to say. If I hadn't just had my metaphysical peek inside Nathaniel's head, I would probably have gotten angry, or rude. But I'd seen too far into Nathaniel's pain, and I couldn't pretend anymore. Couldn't ignore it.

"I thought that by not doing the final stuff that it would make it easier for him when the ardeur gets under control and I don't need a *pomme de sang* anymore."

"Is that still your idea, to just dump him when you have enough control that you don't need to feed?"

"What am I supposed to do with him? Keep him like a pet, or a really big child?"

"He's not a child, and he's not a pet," Jason said, and the first hint of anger was in his voice.

"I know that, and that's the problem, Jason. If the ardeur hadn't come up I'd have been Nathaniel's Nimir-Ra, and his friend, and that would have been it. Now, suddenly he's in this category that I don't even have a name for."

"He's your *pomme de sang* like I'm Jean-Claude's."

"You and Jean-Claude aren't fucking, and nobody gets upset about that."

"No, because he lets me date. I have lovers if I want them."

"I've been encouraging Nathaniel to date. I want him to have girlfriends."

"And your not-so-subtly encouraging him to look at other women made him turn to me for advice."

"What do you mean?" I asked.

"He doesn't want to date other people. He wants to be with you, and Micah, and the vampires. He doesn't want another woman in his life."

"I am not the woman in his life."

"Yes, you are, you just don't want to be."

I leaned against one of the narrow tree trunks. "Oh, Jason, what am I going to do?"

"Finish what you started with Nathaniel, be his lover."

I shook my head. "I don't want that."

"The hell you don't. I watch the way you react around him."

"Lust isn't enough, Jason. I don't love him."

"I'd argue that, too."

"I don't love him the way I need to."

"Need to, for what, Anita? Need to for your conscience? Your sense of morality? Just give him some of what he needs, Anita. Don't break yourself doing it, but bend a little. That's all I'm asking."

"You said the thing on the dance floor was sort of your fault. You never explained that."

"I told Nathaniel you don't like passive men. You like a little dominance, a little pushiness. Not much, but enough so that you aren't the one that says, Yes, we'll have sex. You need someone to take a little of the responsibility off your shoulders."

I stared at him, studied that young face. "Is that all it is for me, Jason? I just need someone else to help me spread the guilt around so I can fuck?"

He winced. "That isn't what I said."

"Close enough."

"Get mad, if you want, but that isn't what I said, or what I meant. Get mad at me, but don't take it out on Nathaniel, okay?"

"I was raised that if you had sex it was a commitment. I still believe that."

"You don't feel committed to me." He said it as if it were just a fact, nothing personal.

"No, we're friends, and I was sort of a friend in need. But you're a grown-up and you understood what it was. I'm not sure Nathaniel is enough of a grown-up to understand that. Hell, he can't even say no to women who are almost strangers."

"He turned down at least three dance offers while we were talking, and I know for a fact that he turned down the beautiful Jessica Arnet for a date."

"He did, really?"

Jason nodded. "Yep."

"I didn't think he'd be able to say no."

"He's been practicing."

"Practicing?"

"He tells you no sometimes, doesn't he?"

I thought about it. "Sometimes he won't repeat conversations to me, or tell me things. He says I'll get mad at him, and so I should ask the other person."

"You wanted, no, demanded, that Nathaniel be more responsible for himself. You made him get his driver's license. You've forced him to be less dependent, right?"

"Yeah."

"But you didn't think what it would mean, did you?"

"What do you mean?"

"You wanted him to be independent, to think for himself, to decide what he wanted out of life, right?"

"Yeah, in fact, I said almost exactly that to him. I wanted him to decide what he wanted to do with his life. I mean he's only twenty for God's sake."

"And what he's decided he wants to do is be with you," Jason said, and his voice was softer, gentle.

"That is not a life decision. I meant like a career choice, maybe go back to college."

"He's got a job, Anita, and he makes better money as a stripper than most college graduates do."

"You can't strip forever," I said.

"And most marriages don't last forever either."

My eyes must have gotten too wide, because he hurried with his next words. "What I mean is, that you treat everything like it's a forever question. Like you can't change your mind later. I don't mean to imply that Nathaniel wants you to make a honest man of him. That never came up, honest."

"Well, that's a relief, at least."

"You'll need a *pomme de sang* for years, Anita. Years."

"Jean-Claude said maybe in a few months I'd be able to feed from a distance, and not need the up close and personal stuff."

"You've made progress on going longer between feedings, Anita. But you haven't made much progress on truly controlling the ardeur."

"I controlled it on the dance floor," I said.

He sighed. "You shut it down on the dance floor. That's not control, not really. It's like you have a gun, and you can lock it in the gun safe, but that doesn't teach you how to shoot it."

"A gun analogy? You've been thinking on this for awhile, haven't you?"

"Ever since Nathaniel told me that you hadn't been allowing him release during the feedings."

"Allow? He didn't ask, and how was I supposed to know he wasn't even doing himself in private? I mean, I didn't tell him not to."

"You can play with yourself, and it feels good, but it doesn't meet the real need."

I pushed my back tight into the tree, as if the solid wood could catch me, because I felt like I was falling. Falling into a chasm so deep that I'd never get out. "I don't know if I can do Nathaniel, and still look myself in the mirror in the morning."

"Why does doing Nathaniel bother you that much?"

"Because he confuses my radar. I have friends, I have boyfriends, I have people who are dependent on me, people I take care of. I do not fuck the people I take care of. It would be like taking advantage of your position."

"And Nathaniel falls into the taking care of category?" he asked.

"Yes."

"You think by having sex that you're taking advantage?"

"Yes."

"That's not how Nathaniel sees it."

"I know that, Jason, now." I closed my eyes and leaned my head back against the roughness of the bark. "Damnit, I want the ardeur under control so I don't have to keep making these kinds of decisions."

"And if I could wave a magic wand over you and you instantly could control the ardeur, what then? What would you do with Nathaniel?"

"I'd help him find a place of his own."

"He does most of the housework around your place. He buys your groceries. He and Micah do most of the cooking. Nathaniel taking care of the domestic stuff is what allows

Micah and you both to work all those hours. Without Nathaniel, how would you organize it?"

"I don't want to keep Nathaniel just to make my life easier. That's like evil."

Jason let out a big sigh. "Are you really this slow, or just driving me crazy on purpose?"

"What?" I said.

He shook his head. "Anita, what I'm trying to say is that Nathaniel doesn't feel used. He feels useful. He doesn't need a girlfriend, because he thinks he already has one. He doesn't want to date because he's already living with someone. He doesn't need to look for a place of his own, because he already has one. Micah knows that, Nathaniel knows that, the only person who doesn't know that seems to be you."

"Jason . . ."

He stopped me with a raised hand. "Anita, you have two men who live with you. They both love you. They both want you. They both support your career. Between the two of them, they're like your wife. There are people in this world who would kill to have what you have. And you'd just throw it away."

I just looked at him, because I didn't know what to say.

"The only thing that keeps this little domestic arrangement from being perfect for all concerned is that Nathaniel is not getting his needs met." He stepped in close to me, but the look on his face was so serious, that it never occurred to me that kissing was coming, because it wasn't. "You've set up the dynamics so that you wear the pants in this trio, and that's fine, it works for Micah and Nathaniel. But here's the hard part about wearing the pants, Anita, it means you get to make the tough decisions. Your life is working better than it's worked since I met you. You've been happier, longer, than I've ever seen you. Micah, I don't know that well, but Nathaniel has never been this happy in all the years I've known him. Everything is working, Anita. Everybody is making it work. Everybody but . . ."

"Me," I said.

"You," he said.

"You know, Jason, I can't say you're wrong about any of it, but I hate you right this second."

"Hate me, if you want to, but I'm tired of watching people have everything their heart's desire and throw it away."

"This isn't what my heart desired," I said.

"Maybe not, but it's what you needed. You needed a wife in that old 1950s sort of way."

"Doesn't everybody," I said.

He grinned at me. "No, some people would like to be the wife, but I just can't find a woman who's man enough to keep me in the style to which I have not yet become accustomed."

It made me smile. Damnit. "You are the only one who can say shit like this to me, and not have me pissed at them for days, or longer. How do you get away with it?"

He planted a quick kiss on my my lips, more brotherly than anything. "I don't know how I get away with it, but if I could bottle it, Jean-Claude would pay a fortune for it."

"Maybe not just Jean-Claude."

"Maybe not." He stepped back, smiling, but his eyes had that serious look again. "Please, Anita, go home, and don't freak. Just go home, and be happy. Be happy, and let everyone around you be happy. Is that so hard?"

When Jason said it like that, it didn't seem hard. In fact, it seemed to make a lot of sense, but inside, it felt hard. Inside it felt like the hardest thing in the world. To just let go, and not pick everything to death. To just let go and enjoy what you had. To just let go and not make everybody around you miserable with your own internal dialogue. To just let go and be happy. So simple. So difficult. So terrifying.

I turned away from him then, and walked back to the car.

NATHANIEL was leaning against the side of the Jeep watching us walk towards him. He was leaning with his hands behind him so that his weight trapped his hands behind him, pinned between his hips and the Jeep. It wasn't just intercourse that Nathaniel hadn't been getting with me. Nathaniel had other "needs" that I was, if possible, even less comfortable with. It made him feel peaceful to be tied up. Peaceful to be abused. Peaceful. I'd asked him why he enjoyed it once, and he'd told me that it made him feel peaceful. It made him feel safe.

How could being tied up make you feel safe? How could letting someone hurt you, even a little, make you feel good? I didn't get it. I just didn't get it. Maybe if I'd understood it better, I'd have been less afraid to go that last mile with him. What if we had intercourse and it wasn't enough? What if he just kept pushing, pushing me to do things that I found . . . frightening? He was supposed to be the submissive, and I was his dominant. Didn't that mean that I was in charge? Didn't that mean he did what I said? No. I'd had to learn enough to understand Nathaniel and some of the other wereleopards, because he wasn't the only one with interesting hobbies. The submissive had a safe word, and once they said that word, all the play stopped. So in the end, the dominant had an illusion of power, but really the submissive got to say how far things went, and when they stopped. I'd thought I could control Nathaniel because he was so submissive, but it was tonight that I realized the truth. I wasn't in control anymore. I didn't know what was going to happen with Nathaniel, or me, or Micah. The thought terrified me, so I thought about it, really thought about it. What if I found Nathaniel a new place to live? What if I found him a new place to be? A new life?

I rolled it over in my mind as we walked across the pavement. I thought about sending him home with someone else, letting him weep on someone else's shoulder. But more than that, I thought about getting under the covers with only Micah on one side, and no one on the other side. Nathaniel had his side of the bed now. I hadn't realized it until that second, hadn't let myself realize it. The three of us enjoyed reading to each other. For Micah and me it was a revisiting of childhood favorites, for the most part, but for Nathaniel most of the books were new to him. He'd never had anyone read to him before bedtime. Never had anyone share their books with him. What kind of childhood is it without books, stories to share? I knew that he'd had an older brother, who died, and a father who died, and a mother who died. That they'd died, I knew, but not how, or when, except that he'd been young when it happened. He didn't like talking about it, and I didn't like seeing the look in his eyes when he did, so I didn't push. I didn't have a right to push if I wasn't his girlfriend. I didn't have a right to push if I wasn't his lover. As his Nimir-Ra, he didn't owe me his life story.

I thought about not having Nathaniel in the bed, not for feeding, but not having him there to hear the rest of the book we were reading. The thought of him not being there was painful, a wrenching kind of pain, as if my stomach and my heart both hurt at the same time.

He opened the door and held it for me, because this close to the ardeur, it wasn't always good that I was driving. He held the door and was as neutral as he could be, as I moved past him. I didn't know what to do, so I let him be neutral and I was neutral, too. But as I buckled my seat belt in place and he closed the door, I realized that I would miss him. Not miss him because my life ran smoother with him than without him, but I would simply miss him. Miss the vanilla scent of him on my pillow; the warmth of his body on his side of the bed; the spill of his hair like some tangled, living blanket. If I could have stopped my list there, I'd have sent Nathaniel to his room for the night; he did still have a room where all his stuff stayed, all his stuff but him. But I couldn't stop the list there, not and be honest.

He'd cried when Charlotte died in *Charlotte's Web*. I wouldn't have missed seeing him cry over that for anything. It had been Nathaniel's idea that we could have a movie marathon of old monster movies. You have not lived until you've sat through *The Wolfman, Frankenstein Meets the Wolfman, Curse of the Werewolf,* and *Face of the Screaming Werewolf* with a bunch of shapeshifters. They had heckled the screen and thrown popcorn, and howled, sometimes literally, at the movie version of what they knew all too well. The wereleopards had all complained that at least werewolves had some movies, that once you'd named *Cat People*, the leopards didn't have any movies. Most of the werewolves had known about the 1980 version, but almost no one had known about the oringial in 1950. We had another movie night planned where we were going to watch both versions. I was sure we'd spend the night complaining, cheerfully, at how far off both films were, and get eerily silent when it hit close to home. Alright, they'd be eerily silent and I'd watch them watching the screen.

I was looking forward to it. I tried picturing the night without Nathaniel. No Nathaniel coming and going out of the kitchen with popcorn and soda making people use coasters. No Nathaniel sitting on the floor, next to my legs, half the night spent with his head on my knee, and the other half playing his hand up and down my calf. It wasn't sexual, he just felt better touching me. The entire pard, and pack, felt better touching each other. It was possible to be up close and personal without it being sexual. It really was, just not usually for me.

Which brought me back to the problem at hand. Funny how the thinking led back to it. Tonight when the ardeur finally surfaced, what was I going to do? I could exile Nathaniel to his room, legitimately, because I'd need to feed tomorrow, too. I could save him like for dessert. But we'd both know that that wasn't it. I wasn't saving him, I was saving myself. Saving myself from what, I wasn't sure, but it was definitely about saving me, and had nothing to do with saving Nathaniel.

He didn't want to be saved. No, that wasn't true. Nathaniel already thought he had been saved. I'd saved him. I'd been treating him like a prince who needed to find his princess, but that was all wrong. Nathaniel was the princess and he had been rescued, by me. As far as Nathaniel was concerned, I was the prince in shining armor, I just needed to come across, and then we could all live happily ever after.

Trouble was, I was no one's prince, and no one's princess. I was just me, and I was all out of armor, shiny or otherwise. I just wasn't the fairy-tale type. And I didn't believe in happily ever after. The question was, did I believe in happily for now? If I could have answered that question, then all the worry would have been ended, but I couldn't answer it. So as Micah drove us towards home in the October dark, I still didn't know what I'd do when the ardeur finally rose for the night. I didn't even know what the right thing to do was anymore. Wasn't right supposed to help people, and wrong supposed to hurt people? Didn't you make the right choice because it was the right thing to do?

I always felt squeamish about praying to God about sex, in any context, but I prayed as we drove, because I was out of options. I asked for guidance. I asked for a clue as to what was the best for everyone. I didn't get an answer, and I hadn't expected one. I have a lot psychic gifts but talking directly to God is not one of them, thank goodness. Read the Old Testament if you don't think it's a scary idea. But worse than no answer, I didn't feel that peace that I usually get when I pray.

WHEN we reached our house, Micah and Nathaniel got out of the Jeep first. I followed behind, slowly, still not sure what I was going to do.

The living room was dark as I entered the house. The only light was from the kitchen. One or both of them had walked through the pitch-dark living room and only hit a light switch when they went to the kitchen to check messages on the machine, which was on the kitchen counter. Leopards' eyes are better in the dark than a human's, and Micah's eyes were permanently stuck in kitty-cat mode. He often walked through the entire house with no lights, just drifting from room to room, avoiding every obstacle, gliding through the dark with the same confidence I used in bright light.

There was enough light from the kitchen, so I, too, left the living room dark. The white couch seemed to give off its own glow, though I knew that was illusion, made up of the reflective quality of the white, white cloth. I was pretty sure the men had both gone to change for the night. Most lycanthropes, whatever the flavor, preferred fewer clothes, and Micah didn't like dressing up, not if it included a tie. I walked into the empty kitchen not because I needed to, but because I wasn't ready to go to the bedroom. I still didn't know what I was going to do.

The kitchen held a large dining room table now. The breakfast nook on its little raised platform with its bay window looking out over the woods still held a smaller four-seater table. Four had been more chairs than I needed when I moved into this house. Now, because we usually had at least some of the other wereleopards bunking over due to an emergency, or, often, just the need to be close to more of their group, their pard, we needed a six-seater table. Actually we needed a bigger one than that, but it was all my kitchen would hold.

There was a vase in the middle of the table. Jean-Claude had sent me a dozen white roses a week, after we started dating. Once we had sex, he'd added one red rose so it was actually thirteen. One red rose like a spot of blood in a sea of white roses and white baby's breath. It certainly made a statement.

I smelled the roses, and the red one had the strongest scent. Hard to find white roses that smelled good. All I had to do was call Jean-Claude. He was fast enough to fly here before dawn. I'd fed off of him before, I could do it again. Of course, that would simply be putting off the decision. No, it would be hiding. I hated cowardice almost worse than anything else, and calling on my vampire lover in this instance was cowardice.

The phone rang. I jumped back so hard that the roses rocked in their vase. You'd think I was nervous, or guilty of something. I got the phone on the second ring. It was for Micah, a Furry Coalition emergency.

One of the shifters had had an accident. He was in the hospital emergency room right now. But the cops were making noises about taking him to a so-called safe house.

They were actually prisons for lycanthropes. Once you went in, they never let you out.

Someone had to go and get him before that could happen.

Micah got on the phone long enough to take the address and name of the hospital down, then hung up. He looked at me, face careful, neutral with an edge of concern. "I'm okay with you and Nathaniel being here alone for the ardeur. The question is, are you okay with it?"

I shrugged.

He shook his head. "No, Anita, I need an answer before I leave."

I sighed. "You need to get there before the wolf loses it. Go, we'll be all right."

He looked like he didn't believe me.

"Go," I said.

"It's not just you I'm worried about, Anita."

"I will do my best for Nathaniel, Micah."

He frowned. "What does that mean?"

"It means what it says."

He didn't look happy with the answer.

"If you wait around for me to say, Oh, yes, it's fine that I'm going to feed the ardeur and fuck Nathaniel; the wolf in question will have shapeshifted, been shot by the cops, and maybe taken some civilians with him before you even leave the house."

"You're both important to me, Anita. Our pard is important to me. What happens here tonight, could change . . . everything."

I swallowed hard, because I suddenly didn't want to meet his eyes.

He touched my chin, raised my face up to meet his gaze. "Anita."

"I'll be good," I said.

"What does that mean?"

"I'm not sure, but I'll do my best, and that is the best I can offer. I won't really know what I'm going to do until the ardeur rises. Sorry, but that's the truth. To say anything else would be a lie."

He took a deep breath that made his chest rise and fall nicely. "I guess I'll have to settle for that."

"What exactly do you want me to say?" I asked.

He leaned in, and laid a gentle kiss against my lips. We rarely kissed so chaste, but this close to the ardeur, he was being careful. "I want you to say you'll take care of this."

"Define take care of it?"

He sighed again, shook his head, and stepped back. "I've got to get dressed."

"Are you taking your car or the Jeep?"

"I'll take my car." He smiled at me, almost sadly, and left to go get dressed. He made a soft exclamation as he went around the corner. He spoke in low voices with another man. The cadence was wrong for Nathaniel.

Damian glided around the corner. "You must be very distracted not to have sensed me sooner." He was right, I was good at sensing the undead. No vamp should have been able to get this close without me knowing, especially not Damian.

Damian was my vampire servant, as I was Jean-Claude's human servant. The ardeur was Jean-Claude and Belle Morte's fault, something about their line had contaminated me. But Damian as my servant, that was my fault. I was a necromancer, and apparently mixing necromancy with being a human servant had some unforseen side effects. One of them was standing across the kitchen staring at me with eyes the color of green grass. Humans didn't have eyes like that, but apparently Damian had, because becoming a vamp doesn't change your original physical description. It may pale you out, lengthen some of the teeth, but your hair and eye and skin color remain the same. The only thing that was probably more vibrant was his hair. Red hair that hadn't seen the sun for hundreds of years, so that it was almost the color of fresh blood, a bright, fresh scarlet, so that he moved in a swirl of crimson hair. All vamps are pale, but Damian started life with that milk and honey complexion that some redheads have, so he was even paler. Or maybe it was the quality of his paleness, like his skin had been formed of white marble, and some demon or god had breathed life into that paleness. Oh, wait, I was that demon.

Technically, my power, my necromancy, made Damian's heart beat. He was over a thousand years old, and he would never be a master vampire. If you aren't a master, then you need a master to give you enough power to rise from the grave, not just the first night, but every night.

Damian must have come straight from work, because though he, like most of the vamps fresh over from Europe, almost never wore jeans and tennis shoes, he also didn't like dressing up as much as Jean-Claude insisted on.

He was wearing a coat I'd seen before. It was a deep pine green, a frock coat like something out of the 1700s, but it was new, designed to gape open to expose the pale gleam of his chest and stomach. Embroidery nearly covered the sleeves and lapels, putting a little glitter of color near all that white skin. His pants were black satin, poofy, like there was way more cloth there than was needed for Damian's slender legs. He wore a wide green sash for a belt, and a pair of black leather boots that folded over just above the knee. The outfit was very pirate-y.

"How was work?" I asked.

"Danse Macabre is the hottest dance club in St. Louis." He kept walking towards me, gliding rather. There was something about the way he looked at me that I didn't care for.

"It's the only place where people can go and dance with vampires. Of course it's hot." I looked at him, and I knew he had fed tonight, on some willing woman. Willing blood feeding was considered the same as willing sex. Just be of age, and you could feed the undead, and have bite marks to show your friends. I'd ordered Damian to only feed from willing victims, and because of our bond together, he could not disobey me. Necromancers of legend could boss around all types of undead, and they had to do your bidding. The only undead I could boss around was Damian, and frankly, I found even that unsettling. I didn't like to have that kind of control over anyone.

But then, Damian had a kind of control over me. I wanted to touch him. When he entered a room, I had an almost overwhelming urge to touch his skin. It was part of what it meant to be master and servant. This attraction to your servants, this need to touch and tend them was one of the reasons that most servants were treasured possessions. I think it also kept even the craziest, most evil of vamps from killing their servants out of hand. For often a vamp didn't survive the death of his servant, the bond was that close.

He walked around the table, fingers trailing on the backs of the chairs. "And I am one of the vampires that they have been pressing their bodies up against all night."

"Hannah is still managing the club, right?"

"Oh, yes, I am merely a cold body to send into the crowd." He was around the table now, to the island that separated the working area of the kitchen from the rest of the room. "I am merely color, like a statue, or a drape."

"That's not fair. I've seen you work the crowd, Damian. You enjoy the flirting."

He nodded, as he came around the end of the island. Nothing separated us now but the fact that I was still leaning against the far cabinets, and he had stopped at the end of the island. The urge to close that distance, to wrap my hands around his body, was almost overwhelming. It made my hands ache with the need, and I ended with them pressed behind me, pinned by my body the way Nathaniel had leaned against the Jeep earlier.

"I enjoy the flirting very much." He traced pale fingers along the edge of the island, slowly, tenderly, as if he were touching something else. "But we are not allowed to have sex while we work, though some of them beg for it." The emerald of his eyes spread and swallowed his pupils, so that he looked at me with eyes like green fire. His power danced along my skin, caught my breath in my throat.

My voice started out a little shaky, but I gained firmness as I talked, until the last was said in an almost normal voice. "You've got my permission to date, or fuck, or whatever. You can have lovers, Damian."

"And where would I take them?" He leaned against the island, arms crossing over that expanse of pale chest.

"What do you mean?"

"I have a coffin in your basement. It is adequate but hardly romantic."

He could have said a lot of things that I'd expected, but that wasn't one of them. "I'm sorry, Damian, it never ocurred to me. You need a room, don't you?"

He gave a small smile. "A room to use for my lovers, yes."

Then I realized something. "You mean like bring strangers here. People you've just picked up, and have them like sleep over, be at the breakfast table in the morning?"

"Yes," he said, and I understood the look on his face

now; it was a challenge. He knew I wouldn't like the thought of strangers coming into the house, much less facing a strange woman that he'd simply brought home to fuck, first thing in the morning.

I had a tiny spurt of anger, and that helped me think. Helped push back that need to touch him, that had nothing to do with the ardeur, and everything to do with power. "I know you had a room at the Circus. Maybe we could arrange something with Jean-Claude, so you could take lovers back there."

"My home is here, with you. You are my master now."

I cringed a little at the master part. "I know that, Damian."

"Do you?" He pushed away from the island, and came to stand just in front of me. This close the power shivered between us. It made him close his eyes, and when he opened them they were still drowning emerald pools. "If you are my master, then touch me."

My pulse was jumping in my throat like a trapped thing. I didn't want to touch him, because I wanted to touch him so badly. In a way, this was part of the attraction between Jean-Claude and me, as well. What I'd taken for lust and new love was also partly vampire trickery. A trick to bind the servant to the master, and the master to the servant, so that both served the other willingly, joyfully. It had bothered me when I first realized that part of what I felt for Jean-Claude was somehow tainted with vampire mind games, though it wasn't on purpose from Jean-Claude's point of view. He couldn't help how it worked on me any more than I could help how it worked on Damian.

He was standing so close I had to crane my neck backward to see his face clearly. "I want to touch you, Damian, but you're acting awfully funny tonight."

"Funny," he said. He moved in so close that the edges of

his coat, the poofy satin of his pants brushed the thick cloth of my tuxedo pants. "Funny, I don't feel funny, Anita." He leaned his face close to mine, and whispered his next words, "I feel half-crazed. All those women touching me, rubbing themselves against me, pressing their warm," he leaned in so that his hair brushed my cheek, "soft," his breath felt hot against my skin, "wet," his lips touched my cheek, and I shuddered, "bodies, against me."

My breath shook on its way out, and my pulse was suddenly loud in my ears. It was hard to concentrate on anything but the feel of his lips against my cheek, though all his lips were doing were resting lightly against my skin. I swallowed hard enough that it hurt, and said, "You could have gone with any one of them."

He laid his cheek against mine, but it meant he had to bend over more, which moved his body farther from mine. Compromise. "And could I trust that their windows were proof against sunlight?" He stood up, and put a hand on either side of the cabinet behind me, so that I was trapped between his arms. "Could I trust that they would not harm me, once the sun rose and I lay helpless?"

I tried to think of something to say, something helpful, something that would help me to think about something other than how much I wanted to touch him. When in doubt be bitchy. "I'm getting a crick in my neck with you standing this close." My voice was only a little breathy when I said it. Good.

Damian put his hands around my waist, and just the solid feel of his hands around me stopped whatever else I meant to say. It stopped him for a moment, too. Made him bend his head down, eyes closed, as if he were trying to concentrate, or clear his mind. Then he lifted me, suddenly, and sat me on the edge of the counter. It caught me off guard, and he had put his hips between my knees before

I could react. We weren't pressed together, except for his hands on my waist, but we were one step away from it.

"There," he said, voice hoarse, "now you can see me better."

He was right, but it hadn't been what I meant him to do. I wanted breathing space, and instead my hands were free, and he was a hard thought away. My hands came to rest on his arms, and even through the heavy material of his coat I could feel the solidness of him. It was as if my hands had a mind of their own. I traced up the line of his arms, found his shoulders, and ended with my hands on the broadness of those shoulders, with his hair tickling along the back of my hands. There was something about my hands on his shoulders, or the silk of his hair on my skin that made me bend towards him. I wanted a kiss. Simple as that. It seemed wrong to be this near and not touch him.

He bowed his head towards mine. His eyes were like deep green pools, deep enough to drown in. He whispered, "You have but to tell me stop, and I will stop."

I didn't say stop. I slid my hands to the smooth pale line of his neck, and the moment I touched his bare skin with mine, I was calmer. I could think again. That was his gift to me, as my servant. He helped me be calmer, more in control. When I was touching him, it was almost impossible for me to lose my temper. He lowered my blood pressure, helped me think.

I cupped his face between my hands, because I wanted to touch him, but what I gained from his centuries of controlling his own emotions was that when he put his lips against mine, I was not lost. Not overwhelmed unless I wanted to be overwhelmed. It wasn't that I felt nothing, because it wasn't possible to be enfolded in Damian's arms, pressed against his chest, have his lips caressing mine, and be unmoved. You'd have had to be made of stone not to melt into that embrace, just a little. But, as I'd gained calmness from him, he had begun to gain back the passion that he'd lost over the centuries. A passion not just for sex, but any strong emotion, because the master that made him tolerated no strong emotion, save fear. She'd beat everything else out of him over more centuries than most vampires ever survived.

He drew back enough to see my face. "You're calm. Why are you calm? I feel crazed, and you give me peaceful eyes!" He grabbed my upper arms, and dug his fingers in until it hurt, and I still felt calm. "It is cruel fate that makes you calmer and calmer the more we touch, and drives me more and more wild." He gave me a small shake, his face was raw with emotion. "I am being punished and I have done nothing wrong."

"It's not punishment, Damian," and even my voice was low and calm.

"Jean-Claude says that if you wished, you could gain calm only when you needed it. That you could touch me and enjoy touching me, but not be trapped behind this mask." His fingers were digging in so hard, I was bruising.

"You're hurting me, Damian." My voice was still calm, but there was an edge of heat to it, an edge of anger.

"At least you feel something when I touch you."

"Let go of my arms, Damian." And just like that, he released me, let me go as if my arms had grown hot to the touch, because he could not disobey a direct order from me. Whatever that order might be.

"Take a step back, Damian, give me some room." I was angry now, even with the rest of his body touching me. When he did what I told him, and was no longer touching me at all, the anger filled me up and spilled over my skin like heat. God, it felt good. I was used to being angry. I liked it. Not the most positive thing to say, but still true.

I started to rub my arms where he'd squeezed, then stopped. I didn't like letting anyone know how much they'd hurt me.

"I didn't mean to hurt you," he said, and he was holding his own arms. I thought for a moment he was feeling my pain, then realized he was hugging himself to keep from touching me.

"No, you just want to fuck me."

"That's not fair," he said.

He was right, it wasn't fair, but I didn't care. Without him touching me, I could be as unfair as I wanted to be. I wrapped my anger around myself. I fed it with every petty impulse I'd fought for days. I should have remembered that one control is much like another. That if you throw away one kind of control, it makes other kinds harder to hold onto.

I unleashed my anger like you'd unleash a rabid dog. It roared through me, and I remembered a time when my rage had been the only warmth I allowed in my life. When my anger had been my solace and my shield. "Get out, Damian, just go to bed."

"Don't do this, Anita, please." He held his hand out to me, would have touched me, but I moved back, just out of reach.

"Go, now."

And with that he couldn't help himself. I'd given him a direct order. He had to obey.

He walked out, tears glittering in his green eyes. He passed Nathaniel in the doorway.

I hadn't let myself get this angry in so long. It had felt good for a few moments, but I was already beginning to regret how I'd treated Damian. He hadn't asked to be my servant. The fact that I'd done it accidentally didn't make it any more right. He was an adult person, and I'd just or-

dered him to bed like he was a naughty child. He deserved
better than that. Anyone did.

The anger pulled back, and even my skin felt cooler.
The term hot with anger was very real. I was ashamed of
what I'd just done. I understood why, in part. I so did not
need another man tied to me by metaphysics that demanded a piece of my bed, or at least my body. I didn't
need that. I especially didn't need a man who might not
even be capable of feeding the ardeur. Because even in the
middle of the worst of the ardeur, Damian's touch could
cool that fire. With him holding my hand, the ardeur could
not rise, or at least it could be put away for hours. So why
didn't I paste Damian to my body? Because of how much
more he wanted from me than I was comfortable with giving. I could not use him to help me fight the ardeur if I
wasn't willing to give in to that skin hunger we both felt for
each other.

Nathaniel padded into the room, wearing nothing but a
pair of silky jogging shorts. He'd taken his braid out, so
that his thick hair spilled around him like some kind of
cape. "Are you alright?"

I started to say, I owe Damian an apology, but I didn't
say it, because in that one breath, the ardeur rose. No, not
rose, engulfed, drowned, suffocated. I suddenly couldn't
breathe past the pulse in my throat. My skin felt thick and
heavy with it. I don't know what showed in my eyes, but
whatever it was, it stopped Nathaniel where he stood, froze
him like a rabbit in the grass that knows the fox is near.

The ardeur spilled outward, like invisible water, hot,
wet, and suffocating. I knew when the power hit Nathaniel,
because he shivered. Goose bumps broke on his body, as
his very skin reacted to the power.

I'd shoved the ardeur down once tonight, and that had a
price. I'd refused the touch of my servant, and that had a

price. I'd embraced my anger, and let it spill out onto someone I cared about. That had a price, too. I didn't want Nathaniel to be the one who paid that price.

I didn't remember crossing the room, but I must have, because I was standing in front of him. His eyes were wide, so wide, his lips half-parted. I was close enough to see the pulse in his throat beating against the skin of his neck like a trapped thing. I leaned in towards him, leaned just my face until I could smell the warm vanilla scent of his neck. Close enough to taste his pulse on my tongue like candy. And I knew this candy would be red and soft and hot. I had to close my eyes so that I didn't lean my mouth down to that point, didn't lick over his skin, didn't bite down and free that quivering piece of him. I had to close my eyes so I wouldn't keep staring at that pulsing, jumping . . . My own pulse was too fast, as if I would choke on it. I'd thought that feeding the ardeur on Nathaniel was the worst I could do, but the thoughts in my head weren't about sex. They were about food. Thanks to my ties with Jean-Claude and Richard, my werewolf ex-fiancé and the other third of our triumverate, I had darker things inside me than the ardeur. Dangerous things. Deadly things.

I stayed perfectly still, trying to master my own pulse, my own heartbeat. But even with my eyes closed, I could still smell Nathaniel's skin. Sweet and warm and . . . close.

I felt his breath on my face, before I opened my eyes.

He had moved in so close that his face filled my vision. My voice came soft, half-strangled with the needs I was fighting, "Nathaniel . . ."

"Please," he whispered it as he leaned in, whispered it again as his mouth hovered above mine, he sighed, "Please," against my lips. His breath felt hot against my mouth, as if when we kissed it would burn.

His lips this close to mine had done one thing. I wasn't

thinking about ripping his throat out anymore. I understood then we could feed on sex, or we could feed on meat and blood. I knew that one hunger could be turned into another, but until that moment, where I could almost taste his lips on mine, I hadn't realized that there would come a point where *something* must be fed. I did not feed Jean-Claude's blood lust, though there was a shadow of it in me. I did not feed Richard's beast, with its hunger for meat, but that lived in me, too. I held so many hungers in me, and fed none of them, except the ardeur. That I could feed. That I did feed. But it was in that heartbeat, as Nathaniel kissed me, that I understood why I hadn't been able to control the ardeur better. All the hungers channeled into that one hunger. Jean-Claude's fascination with the blood that ran just under the skin. Richard's desire for fresh, bloody meat. I had pretended I didn't carry their hungers inside me, not really. But I did. The ardeur had risen to give me a way to feed, a way that didn't tear people's throats out, a way that didn't fill my mouth with fresh blood.

Nathaniel kissed me. He kissed me, and I let him, because if I drew back from it, fought it; there were other ways to feed, other ways that would leave him bleeding and dying on the floor. His lips were like heat against my skin, but part of me wanted something hotter. Part of me knew that blood would be like a scalding wave in my mouth.

I had a sudden image so strong that it made me stumble back from him. Made me push away from that warm, firm flesh.

I felt my teeth sinking into flesh, through hair that was rough and choking on my tongue. But I could feel the pulse underneath that skin, feel it like a frantic thing, the pulse running from me, like the deer had run through the forest. The deer was caught, but that sweet, beating thing lay just out of reach. I bit harder, shearing through the skin with teeth that were made for tearing. Blood gushed into my mouth, hot, scalding, because the deer's blood ran hotter than mine. Their warmth helped lead me to them. Helped me hunt them. The heat of their blood called me to them, made their scent run rich on every leaf they passed, every blade of grass that brushed them, carried that warmth away, betrayed them to me. My teeth closed around the throat, tore the front of it free. Blood sprayed out, over me and the leaves, a sound like rain. I swallowed the blood first, scalding from the chase, and then the meat that still held the last flickering of pulse, a last beat of life. The meat moved in my mouth as it went down, as if it were struggling, even now, to live.

I came back to the kitchen, on my knees, screaming.

Nathaniel reached out towards me, and I slapped at his hands, because I didn't trust myself to touch him. I could still taste the meat, the blood, feel it going down Richard's throat. It wasn't horror that made me slap at Nathaniel. It was that I had liked it. Gloried in the feel of blood raining down on me. The struggles of the animal had excited me, made the kill all the sweeter. Always when I touched Richard, there had been hesitation, regret, revulsion about what he was, but there had been no hesitation in that shared vision. He had been the wolf, and he had brought the deer down, taken its life, and there had been no regret. His beast had fed, and for this one moment, the man in him had not cared.

I shut down every shield I had between him and me, and it was only then that I felt him look up, felt him raise his bloody muzzle, and look as if he could see me watching him. He licked his bloody lips, and the only thought I had from him was good. It was good, and there was more, and he would feed.

I couldn't seem to cut myself off from him. Couldn't shut it down. I did not want to feel him sink teeth into the deer again. I did not want to be in his head for the next bite. I reached out to Jean-Claude. Reached out for help, and found . . . blood.

His mouth was locked on a throat, fangs buried into that flesh. I smelled that flesh, knew that scent, knew it was Jason, his *pomme de sang*, that he held clasped in his arms, clasped tighter than you hold a lover, because a lover does not struggle, a lover does not feel their death in your kiss.

The blood was so sweet, sweeter than the deer's had been. Sweeter, cleaner, better. And part of that better was the feel of his arms locked around us, holding us as tight as we held him. Part of what made this more was the embrace. The feel of Jason's heart beating inside his chest, beating against the front of our bodies, so that we could feel the franticness of it, as the heart began to realize something was wrong, and the more frightened it got, the more blood it pumped, the more of that sweet warmth poured down our throats.

All I could taste was blood. All I could smell was blood. It spilled down my throat, and I couldn't breathe. I was drowning. Drowning in Jason's blood. The world had run red, and I was lost. A pulse, a pulse in that red darkness. A pulse, a heartbeat, that found me, that brought me out.

Two things came to me at once. I was lying on cool tile, and someone had me by the wrist. Their hand on my wrist. I opened my eyes, and found Nathaniel kneeling beside me. His hand on my wrist. The pulse in the palm of his hand beat against the pulse in my wrist. It was as if I could feel the blood running up his arm, smell it, almost taste it.

I rolled closer to him, curled my body around his legs, laid my head upon his thigh. He smelled so warm. I kissed the edge of his thigh, and he opened his legs for me, let my face slip between them, so that the next kiss was against the smooth warmth of his inner thigh. I licked along that warm, warm skin. He shuddered, and his pulse sped against mine. The pulse in the palm of his hand pushing against the pulse in my wrist, as if his heartbeat wanted inside me. But it wasn't his heartbeat that he wanted inside me.

A roll of my eyes, and I could see him swollen and tight against the front of his shorts. I licked up the line of his thigh, licked closer and closer to that thin line of satin that stretched over the front of his body.

I tasted his pulse against my lips, but it wasn't an echo from his hand. My mouth was over the pulse in his inner thigh. He let go of my wrist, as if now we didn't need it, we had another pulse, another, sweeter place to explore. I could smell the blood just under his skin, like some exotic perfume. I pressed my mouth over that quivering heat, kissed the blood just under his skin. Licked the jumping thud of his pulse, just a quick flick of my tongue. It tasted like his skin, sweet and clean, but it also tasted of blood, sweet copper pennies on my tongue.

I bit him, lightly, and he cried out above me. I slid hands over his thigh, held it tight, so that the next bite was harder, deeper. His meat filled my mouth for a second, and I could taste the pulse under his skin. Knew that if I bit down, that blood would pour into my mouth, that his heart would spill itself down my throat as if it wanted to die.

I stayed with my teeth around his pulse, fought with myself not to bite down, not to bring that hot, red rush. I could not let go, and it was taking everything I had not to finish it. I reached down those metaphysical cords that bound me to Jean-Claude and Richard. I had a confusing image of meat and viscera, and other bodies crowding close. The pack was feeding. I shoved that image away, because it wanted me to bite down. Richard's muzzle was buried deep into the warmth of the body, buried in the sweet things inside. I had to run from those feelings, before I fed on Nathaniel the way they were feeding on the deer.

I found Jason lying pale on Jean-Claude's bed, bleeding on the sheets. Jean-Claude's blood thirst was quenched but there were other hungers. He looked up at me, as if he could see me. His eyes were drowning blue, and I felt it, the ardeur had risen in him. Risen in a wave of heat that left him staring down at Jason's still form with thoughts that had nothing to do with blood.

He spoke, his voice echoing through me. "I must shut you out, *ma petite*, something is wrong tonight. You will force me to do things I do not wish to do. Feed the ardeur, *ma petite*, choose its flame, before another hunger comes and carries you away." With that, he was gone. Gone as if a door had slammed shut between us. I had a moment to realize that he'd slammed a door between not just himself, but Richard and me, as well. So that I was suddenly cut adrift.

I was alone with the feel of Nathaniel's pulse in my mouth. His flesh was so warm, so warm, and his pulse beat like something alive inside his skin. I wanted to free that struggling, quivering thing. I wanted to break it free of its cage. To free Nathaniel of this cage of flesh. To set him free.

I fought not to bite down, because some part of me knew that if I once tasted blood that I would feed. I would feed, and Nathaniel might not survive it.

A hand grabbed mine, grabbed mine and held on. I knew who it was before I raised my face from Nathaniel's thigh. Damian knelt beside us. His touch helped me get to my knees, helped me think, at least a little. But the ardeur didn't go away. It pulled back like the ocean drawing back from the shore, but it didn't leave, and I knew it would come back. Another wave was building, and when it crashed over us, we needed a plan.

"Something's wrong," I said, and my voice shook. I held on to Damian's hand like it was the last solid thing in the world.

"I felt the ardeur rise, and I thought, great, just great, left out again. Then it changed."

"It felt wonderful," Nathaniel's voice came distant and dreamy, as if all he'd been having was good foreplay.

"Didn't you feel it change?" I asked.

"Yes," he said.

"Weren't you afraid?"

"No," he said, "I knew you wouldn't hurt me."

"I'm glad one of us was so sure."

He raised up onto his knees, from where he'd half swooned. "Trust yourself. Trust what you feel. It changed when you tried to fight it. Stop fighting it." He leaned in towards me. "Let me be your food."

I shook my head, and clung to Damian's hand, but it was as if I could feel the tide rushing back towards the shore. Feel the wave building, building, and when it came, it would sweep us away. I didn't want to be swept away.

"If Jean-Claude told you to feed the ardeur, then feed it," Damian said. "What I felt from you just now was closer to blood lust." His face was very serious, sorrowful even. "You don't want to know what blood lust can make you do, Anita. You don't want that."

"Why is it different tonight?" It was a child asking someone to explain why the monster under the bed has grown a new and scarier head.

"I don't know, but I do know that for the first time when you touch me, I feel it. A dim echo, but I feel it. Always before, Anita, when you touched me, it went away." He made a movement with his fingers like putting out a candle, "snuffed out. Tonight . . ." He leaned over my hand, and I knew he was going to lay his lips across my knuckles. One of the gifts of the ardeur is that it lets you look inside someone's heart. It lets you see what they truly feel. When his lips touched my skin, I felt what Damian was feeling. Satisfaction. Eagerness. Worry, but that was fast fading under the feel of his lips on my skin. He wanted. He wanted me. He wanted to feed the hunger of his skin. The hunger of his body, not so much for orgasm but for that need to be held close and tight, that need we all have to press our nakedness against someone else's. I felt his loneliness, and his need, even if it was only for one night, not to be lonely, not to be exiled down in the dark, alone. I saw how he felt about his coffin down in the basement. It was not his room. It was not his in any way. It was just the place he went to die every dawn. The place where he went to die, alone, knowing that he would rise as he had died, alone. I saw the endless stream of women that he had fed on, like pages in a book, a blonde, a brunette, the one with a tattoo on her neck, dark skin, pale skin, the one with blue hair, an endless stream of necks and wrists, and their eager eyes, and grasping hands, and nearly every night, it was in public view, as part of the floor show at Danse Macabre. So that even his feedings were not private. Even that was not special. It was eating so you wouldn't die, with no meaning to it.

In the center of his being was a great emptiness.

I was supposed to be his master. I was supposed to take care of him, and I hadn't known. I hadn't asked and I'd been so busy trying not to be tied to another man through some weird metaphysical shit that I hadn't noticed that Damian's life sucked.

"I'm sorry, Damian, I . . ." I don't know what I would

have said, because his fingers touched my lips, and I couldn't think. His fingers held heat and weight that they'd never had before.

His eyes widened, surprised, I think, as surprised as I was at the sensation. Or did my lips give heat to his skin, too? Did my lips suddenly feel swollen and eager as his fingertips did to me, as if both mouth and fingers were suddenly more?

I moved my lips against his touch, a bare movement, just enough to press my mouth against the ripeness of his fingers; barely enough to call it a kiss, but it wasn't his skin I tasted, or not the skin I was touching. It was as if I laid my mouth against the most intimate parts of him. There was the hard, solid press of his fingers, but the taste, the smell of him, was the perfume of lower things, as if I were a dog on the scent of where I wanted to be.

His breath drew in a shaking gasp, and when I rolled my eyes up to see his face, the look in his eyes was one of drowning, as if I already touched what I could taste. His eyes filled with emerald fire, and just like that there was a line of desire carved from my mouth down his fingers, his hand, his arm, his chest, his hips, to the center of his body. I could feel him thick and rich and full of blood. Could taste the warmth of him as if my mouth were nestled against his groin. I could taste him, feel him, and when I slipped my mouth over the tips of his fingers, slid something so much smaller, harder into my mouth; his green eyes rolled back into his head, ginger lashes fluttering downward. His breath sighed out in one word, "Master."

I knew he was right, in that one moment, I knew, because I remembered being on the other side of such a kiss. Jean-Claude could push desire through me as if his kiss were a finger drawn across my body, down my very nerves so that he touched things that no hand or finger could ever caress. For the first time I felt the other side of such a touch; felt what Jean-Claude had felt for years. He'd tasted my most intimate parts, long before he'd ever been allowed to touch them, or even see them. I felt what he'd felt, and it was wondrous.

Nathaniel touched my hand. I think I'd actually forgotten about him, forgotten about anything but the sensation of Damian's flesh against mine. Then Nathaniel touched me and I could feel his body through the palm of my hand as if a line ran from the pulse in my palm down his body in a long line of heat and desire and . . . power.

I felt that power flare outward from my mouth and hand to their bodies. It was my power, the power Jean-Claude had woken in me by his marks, but it was also my power, my necromancy that burned like some cold fire through Damian's body, but when it hit Nathnaiel's body, the power changed, shifted, became something warm and alive. In the blink of an eye, the power flared through me, through all of us, but it wasn't sex that I felt anymore, it was pain. I was trapped between ice and fire; a cold so intense that it burned, and the fire burned because that was what it was. It was as if half the blood in my body had turned to ice, so that nothing flowed, and I was dying; and the other half of my body held blood that was molten like melted gold, and my skin could not hold it. I was melting, dying. I screamed, and the men screamed with me. It was the sound of Nathaniel and Damian, their screams, not my own, that dragged some part of me above the pain.

That one blinded, aching part knew that if I let this consume me, we would all die, and that was not acceptable. I had to find a way to ride this, to control this, or we would be destroyed. But how do you control something that you don't understand? How do you ride something you can't see, or even touch? I realized in that moment that I touched nothing. That somewhere in the pain I'd let go of both of them. My skin was empty of their touch, but the link between us was still there. One of us, or all of us, had tried to save ourselves by letting go, but this was not a magic so easily defeated. I knelt alone on the floor, touching no one and nothing, but I could feel them. Feel their hearts in their chests as if I could have reached out my hand and carved those warm, beating organs from their bodies; as if their flesh was water to me. The image was so strong, so real, that it made me open my eyes, helped me ride down the pain.

Nathaniel was half crouched, his hand reaching out to me, as if I'd been the one who pulled away. His eyes were closed, his face screwed tight with pain. Damian knelt, pale face empty; if I hadn't been able to feel his pain I wouldn't have known that his blood was turning to ice.

Nathaniel's hand touched mine, like a child groping in the dark, but the moment his fingers brushed me, the burning began to fade. I gripped his hand, and it didn't hurt anymore. It was still hot, but it was the beating pulse of life, as if the heat of a summer's day filled us.

The other half of my body was still so cold it burned. I took Damian's hand, and the moment we touched that, too, ceased to hurt. The magic, for lack of a better term, flowed through me; the chill of the grave, and the heat of the living, and I knelt in the middle like something caught between life and death. I was a necromancer; I was caught between life and death, always.

I remembered death. The smell of my mother's perfume, Hypnotique, the taste of her lipstick as she kissed me good-bye, the sweet powdery scent of her skin. I remembered the feel of smooth wood under small hands, my mother's coffin; the clove scent of carnations from the grave blanket. There was a bloodstain on the car seat, and an oval of cracks in the windshield. I laid a tiny hand on that dried blood, and remembered the nightmares afterward, where the blood was always wet, and the car was dark, and I could hear my mother screaming. The blood had been dry by the time I saw it. She had died without me ever saying good-bye, and I had not heard her screams. She'd died almost instantly, and probably hadn't screamed at all.

I remembered the feel of the couch, rough and nobbly, and it smelled musty, because after Mommy went away nothing got cleaned. In that moment I knew it wasn't my memory. My father's German mother had moved in and kept everything spotless. But I was still small and hugging the side of that musty couch, in a room I'd never known, where the only light was the flicking of the television screen. There was a man, a huge dark shadow of a man, and he was beating a boy, beating him with the buckle end of a belt. He kept saying, "Scream for me, you little bastard. Scream for me."

Blood spurted from the boy's back, and I screamed. I screamed for him, because Nicholas would never scream. I screamed for him and the beating stopped.

I remembered the feel of Nicholas spooning the back of my body, stroking my hair. "If anything happens to me. Promise me, you'll run away."

"Nicholas . . ."

"Promise me, Nathaniel, promise me."

"I promise, Nicky."

Sleep, and the only safety I ever knew, because if Nicholas watched over me, the man couldn't hurt me. Nicholas wouldn't let him.

The images broke then, shattering like a mirror that had been hit; glimpses. The man looming up and up; the first blow, falling to the carpet, blood on the carpet, my blood.

Nicholas in the doorway with a baseball bat. The bat hitting the man. The man silhouetted against the light from that damned television, the bat in his hands. Blood spraying the screen. Nicholas screaming, "Run, Nathaniel, run!" Running. Running through the yards. A dog on a chain, barking, snarling. Running. Running. Falling down beside a stream, coughing blood. Darkness

I remembered. And try as I might, chaos was all I could see. A man's throat exploding in a bright gush of blood; the feel of my blade hacking so deep that it numbed my arm; the force of running headlong into someone else's shield with my own; being forced back down narrow stone steps; and over all that was a fierce joy, an utter contentment; battle was what we lived for, everything else was just biding time. Familiar faces swam into view, blue eyes, green, blond and red-haired, all like me. The feel of a ship under me, and a gray sea, running white with the wind. A dark castle on a lonely shore. There had been fighting there, I knew that, but that was not the memory I got. What I saw was a narrow, stone stairway, that wound up and up into a dark tower. Torchlight flickered on those stairs, and there was a shadow. We ran from that shadow, because terror rode before it. The gate crashed down, trapped against it, we turned and made our stand. The crushing fear, until you could not breathe. Many dropped their weapons and simply went mad, at the touch of it.

The shadow stepped out into the starlight, and it was a woman. A woman with skin white as bone, lips red as blood, and hair like golden spiderwebs. Terrible she was, and beautiful, though it was a beauty that would make men weep, rather than smile.

But she smiled, that first curve of those red, red lips, that first glimpse of teeth that no mortal mouth would hold. Confusion, then the feel of small white hands like white steel, and her eyes, her eyes like gray flames, as if ashes could burn. The images jumped, and Damian was lying in a bed, with that terrible beauty riding him. His body was filling up, about to spill over and into her; riding the edge of pleasure, when she changed it, with a flex of her will, as a flex of her thighs could give pleasure; a thought and he was drowning in fear. A fear so great and so awful that it shriveled him, tore him back from pleasure, threw him close to madness. Then it would pull back like the ocean pulling away from the shore, and she would begin again. Over and over, over and over; pleasure, terror, pleasure and terror, until he begged her to kill him. When he begged she would let him finish, let him ride pleasure to its conclusion, but only if he begged.

A voice broke thorough the memories, shattered it. "Anita, Anita!"

I blinked and I was still kneeling between Nathaniel and Damian. It was Damian who had called my name. "No more," he said.

Nathaniel was crying, and shaking his head. "Please, Anita, no more."

"Why are you blaming me for the tour down bad memory lane?"

"Because you're the master," Damian said.

"So it's my fault we're reliving the worst events of our lives?" I searched his face, while I kept a tight grip on his hand. It wasn't erotic anymore, it was more like their hands were safety lines.

"You are the master," Damian repeated.

"Maybe it's over, whatever it was, maybe it's finished." He gave me a look that was so like one of Jean-Claude's that it was unnerving. "What's with the look?" I asked.

"I can still feel it," Nathaniel said, and his voice was hushed, thick with fear.

"If you would stop arguing, and start paying attention to what's happening, you'd feel it, too," Damian said, and he wasn't talking to Nathaniel.

I shut my mouth, it was the best I could do for not arguing, but even silence was enough. Into that brief silence I felt power like something large had pushed against a door in my head. A door that would not hold for long.

"How did you break us free of it this much?"

"I'm not a master, but I am over a thousand years old. I've learned some skills over the years, just to stay sane."

"Alright, Mr. Smartie-Vampire, what's happening to us?"

He squeezed my hand, and something in his eyes said plainly that he didn't want to say it out loud. I realized that I couldn't feel his emotions.

"You're shielding us all, aren't you?"

He nodded. "But it won't hold."

"What is it? What's happening to us? Why are we sharing memories?"

"It's a mark."

I frowned at him. "What?" Marks were metaphysical connections. I shared them with both Jean-Claude and Richard.

"I don't know what number, but it's a mark. It's not the first, maybe not even the second. Maybe the third? I've never had a human servant, or an animal to call. I've never been part of a triumverate. You have, so you tell me."

"Us," Nathaniel said, in that breathy, scared voice.

I looked into those wide lavender eyes. He was waiting for me to make this better. The problem was, I didn't know how. I didn't know how it had begun, so how could I end it? I turned away from the utter trust in his face, because I couldn't think looking into his eyes. I tried to think back to the third mark. There had been a sharing of memories, but it had been benign. Glimpses of Jean-Claude feeding on perfumed wrists, sex with women wearing way too many undergarments; Richard running in wolf form in the forest, the rich world of scent that he had in that form. They had all been sensual, but safe memories. It had never occurred to me to ask either of them what memories they'd gotten from me. I probably didn't want to know.

"Third mark, I think. Though with Jean-Claude in charge it was just flashes of memory; mostly sensual, nothing too serious. Why are we trapped in therapy hell?"

"What did you think of just before the memories began?" Damian asked.

"Death," I said, "I was thinking about death, I don't know why."

"Then think of something else, quickly." His voice held a hint of panic, and I could feel why. I could feel that door in my head beginning to bow outward as if it were melting. I knew when it went, that we better have a plan.

"I didn't try to mark anybody," I said.

"Do you know how to stop it?" he asked.

"No," I said.

"Then think of something else, something better."

"Think happy thoughts," Nathaniel said.

I gave him a look. "Who do I look like—Peter Pan?"

"What?" Damian asked.

"Yes, I mean no, but think," Nathaniel said. "Think happy thoughts. Think like you need to fly. I survived what happened after . . . after Nicholas died. But I do not want to live through it twice. Please, Anita, think happy thoughts."

"Why don't one of you think happy thoughts?" I asked.

"Because you're the master, not us," Damian said. "Your mind, your attitudes, your desires, are what will rule how this goes, not ours. But for God's sake, stop thinking about the worst things that ever happened to you, because I don't want to see the worst that I remember. Nathaniel's right, think happy thoughts."

"Happy thoughts," Nathaniel said, and he wrapped both his hands around one of mine. "Please, Anita, happy thoughts."

"I am fresh out of pixie dust," I said.

"Pixie dust?" Damian said, but he shook his head. "I don't know what you are talking about. Just think of something pleasant, happy, anything, anything at all."

I tried to think happy. I thought about my dog, Jenny, who had died when I was fourteen, and crawled out of the grave a week after she died. Crawled out of the grave and into bed with me. I remembered the weight of her, the smell of fresh turned earth, and ripe flesh.

"No!" Damian screamed. He jerked me to face him, his eyes wild. "No, I will not see what comes next in my story. I will not!" He grabbed my upper arms and turned me to face him, shaking me. Nathaniel wrapped himself around my waist, huddling around my body. Damian said, "Don't you have any good memories?"

It was like one of those games where they tell you not to think of something or to think of something. I was supposed to think of good things, and for the life of me, everything ended badly. My mother had been wonderful, but she'd died. I'd loved my dog, but she'd died. I'd loved Richard, but he'd dumped me. I thought I'd loved someone once in college, but he'd dumped me. I thought about the feel of Micah's body, but I was waiting for him to dump me, too. Nathaniel hugged me tighter, his face buried against my back. "Please, Anita, please, happy thoughts, fly for me, Anita, please, God, fly for me."

I touched his arm, his hand, and thought of the vanilla scent of his hair. Thought of his face alive and listening as Micah read to us. I still thought Micah would go from

Prince Charming to the Big Bad Wolf (no anthropomorphic bias intended), but Nathaniel would never dump me. There were moments when the thought of having Nathaniel with me forever panicked the hell out of me, but I forced that worry down. Pushed it away. I concentrated on the feel of him, and as if he felt my thoughts, he began to relax against me. He came to his knees behind me, his arms still around my waist, spooning our bodies together. He leaned his face over my shoulder, and I caught the sweet scent of his skin. I had my happy thought. I wouldn't fly because Nathaniel had asked me to, I would fly because of Nathaniel.

I laid a kiss against his cheek, and he wound himself around the back of my body, rubbing his cheek against the side of my face, my neck.

Damian still held my arms in his hands, but loosely now. He stared down at both of us. "I take it you found a happy thought?"

I breathed in that clean vanilla scent and gazed up at Damian. "Yes." My voice was already thick with the scent of skin and the sensation of Nathaniel's body against mine. I thought, it's like he's a living comfort object, like a teddy bear or a penguin, but even as I thought that, I knew it was only partial truth. My stuffed toy penguin, Sigmund, had never kissed my neck, and never would. It was one of Sigmund's charms. He didn't make many demands on me.

That door in my mind was melting, like a block of ice left in the sun. Panic fluttered in my chest, and I knew that panic would be a bad emotion to take behind that melting door. I pulled Damian down to us, and whispered, "Kiss me."

His lips touched mine, and the door vanished. But we didn't get memories this time, we got the ardeur. For the first time, I embraced it, called it pet names, and did the metaphysical equivlent of saying, Come and get me. Come and get us.

I'd never embraced the ardeur before. I'd been over-whelmed by it, conquered by it, given in to it, but never low-ered my flag and surrendered to it, not without at least a fight. Jean-Claude had told me that if I could only stop fighting it wouldn't be so terrible. That once a little control was gained, you needed to "make friends" with the power. I'd given him a look, and he'd dropped the subject, but he was right, and he was wrong. For him I think it would have been a seduction, but it was me, and the fact that I could still think while it was happening was a problem more than a blessing.

I was okay with my tuxedo jacket going bye-bye. I was okay with Damian's green coat sliding to the floor, even if it did leave his upper body pale and naked, with the fine muscles gliding under skin the color of fresh, white sheets. Nathaniel was the problem, or rather my confusion about him. I ran my hands up the unbelievable warmth of his skin, but the look in his lavender eyes was too much. I did not love Nathaniel, not the way I needed to, but the look in his eyes left no doubt how he felt about me. This was wrong. I could not take this from him, if he were in love with me, and I was not in love with him. I could not do it.

I pulled my hands away, shaking my head. Damian was molded against my back, but the moment I pulled away from Nathaniel, his eager hands slowed. "Shit," he whis-pered, and leaned his face against the top of my head.

Nathaniel's eyes went from shining with love, to some-thing darker, older. He put his hands on either side of my face, cradling me. "Don't pull away," he said.

"I have to."

"If it's not sex, it will be blood, Anita, can't you feel it?" Damian asked.

I could feel something. It was as if this time it was I who

put up the shields. But there was still something large and frightening on the other side. Something that I had put in process, but not on purpose, something that was hungry. It didn't care what it fed on, but it would, eventually, feed on something.

Damian's hands were still on my shoulders, but he'd leaned his body back enough so we no longer touched anywhere else. "Anita, please . . ."

I turned in Nathaniel's hands, so that I could glimpse Damian's face. "It's wrong, Damian."

"The sex, or who the sex is with?" he asked.

I took a breath to answer him, but Nathaniel's hands closed round my face. He turned me back to look at him, and I was suddenly almost painfully aware of the strength in his hands. A strength that could have crushed my face rather than cradled it. He was so submissive that he rarely reminded me of how very strong he was, how dangerous he could have been, if he'd been a different person.

I started to say, Let go of me, Nathaniel, but only got as far as, "Let go," before he kissed me. The feel of his lips on mine stopped my words, froze my mind. I couldn't think, couldn't think about anything but the velvet feel of his mouth on mine. Then something seemed to break inside of him, some barrier, and his tongue thrust into my mouth as deep and far as it could go. The sensation of him thrusting that much of himself that deeply into me tore my shields away, and since no one else was fighting, the ardeur roared back to life. It roared back to life on the edge of Nathaniel's lips, his hands, his need.

There was a confusion of ripping cloth, buttons snapping and raining down on us. Hands, hands everywhere, and the sound of clothing ripping. My body jerked with the force of my clothes being ripped away, and my hands were ripping at their clothes. It was as if every inch of my skin craved every inch of their skin. I needed to feel their nakedness glide over mine. My skin felt like a starved thing, as if I hadn't touched anyone in ages.

I knew whose skin hunger I was channeling. It wasn't just sex that Damian had missed. There are needs of the body that can be mistaken for sex, or lead to sex, but it isn't sex that they are about.

There was one leg left of my pants, pooled around my ankle. My vest flapped open, and the shirt was in shreds. It was Damian's hand from behind that grabbed a handful of my panties and pulled, ripping them off my body, leaving me nude from the waist down. I might have turned around to see how much clothing he still had on, but Nathaniel was in front of me. His shorts had been shredded. By me I think. He knelt on the floor in front of me, naked. I almost never let Nathaniel be nude around me. It had been one of the reasons I'd been able to resist taking those last steps with him. Just keep your clothes on and nothing too bad will happen.

Now, he knelt in front of me, and all I could do was gaze up the line of his body. His face with those amazing eyes, that mouth, the line of his neck spilling into the wide, hard flesh of his shoulders, the chest that showed the weight lifting he'd been doing, the curve of his ribs under muscle leading my gaze to the flat plains of his stomach, the slight dimple of flesh that was his belly button, the rich swell of his hips, and finally the ripeness of him. I'd seen him totally nude and excited only once before. I didn't remember him being this wide, not quite this long, of course he hadn't been pressed this tight to his own stomach, as if the very ripeness of his flesh was almost too much to contain. He seemed thick and heavy with need, as if the lightest touch might make him spill that ripeness out and over me.

I started to reach for him, but Damian chose that moment to brush the head of his own ripeness against the back of my body. The movement made me writhe, and lower the front of my body, raising myself upward to him like an offering, like something in heat. The thought helped me swim back up into control, at least a little. I'd never even seen Damian nude, and now he was about to plunge that nudeness into my body. It seemed wrong. I should see him first, shouldn't I? There was no logic to the argument. No logic left to anything, but it made me turn my head, made me look at him.

The blood red of his hair spilled over his shoulders so that it framed the unbelievable whiteness of his body. He was narrower of shoulder, of chest, and his waist seemed to go on forever, smooth and creamy, like something you should lick down, until you found the center of his belly button, and just under that, the length of him. He rode out from his body, so it was harder to judge length. He seemed carved of ivory and pearl, and where the blood ran close to the surface he blushed pink like the shine inside a seashell, delicate and shining. I realized in that moment that he had been paler in life than any vampire I'd ever seen nude, and his body was almost ghostlike in its coloring, as if somehow he wouldn't be real.

Nathaniel's face brushed mine, brought my attention back to him. He had knelt down so low that his face, like mine, was almost touching the floor. He pressed his cheek against mine and whispered, "Please, please, please," over and over, and between each please, he kissed me, a light touch of lips; please, kiss, please, kiss. With his kisses and his voice warm against my face, he brought us both up to our knees again. I'd been so aware of his face, his mouth, his eyes, that I hadn't thought what kneeling this close would do until his nude body pressed against the front of mine. Until the thick, solid length of him pressed between

us, pinned against my stomach by the push of our bodies.
He was so warm, so unbelievably warm, so warm, almost
hot, and the push of him against my body was so solid, as
if he were fighting not to push himself through the front of
me. To make a new opening, anything, anything, just to be
in the warm depths of my body. It took me a second to understand it was Nathaniel's need I was feeling. That he did
want that badly, but it was my wanting, too. My wanting
and denying that want, that helped make this moment what
it was. Over all that was Damian at my back, his body one
huge piece of need. Nathanial and I were being drowned in
Damian's skin-hunger. So lonely, so terribly lonely. And
under that was Damian's fear. Fear that this would not happen, that he would be exiled back to his coffin, with all this
undone. His loneliness was like a theme underneath his
lust, and I had a glimpse of a room high in the castle. A
room that overlooked the sea. Silver bars upon the windows, heavy with runes, and the sound of the surf always
through the windows, so that even if he turned away, he
could still hear it. She'd given him one of the best rooms in
the castle as his prison, because she had a way of knowing
what things meant to you. A way of knowing what would
hurt the most. It was her gift.

Someone kissed me, hard and fast, forcing my mouth
open, pushing his tongue so far in I almost choked, but it
brought me back, brought us all back from that lonely
room and the sound of the sea on the rocks below.

Nathanial drew back enough to say in a harsh whisper,
"Happy thoughts, Anita, happy thoughts." Then his mouth
was on mine, tongue, lips, even teeth light against my own
lips, so that it was more eating than kissing, but it brought
a whimper from my throat, a small helpless sound of
pleasure.

My hands were on his body, following the flow of his

shoulders, his back, and the smooth silken curve of his ass. The back of his body filled my hands, and the front of him was like heat wrapped in flesh, as if we'd burst into flame.

Damian's hands were on the back of my bra; somehow it had survived that first rush. He snapped it open, and the front of it fell against Nathanial's chest. Hands spilled over my breasts; one from behind, and one from the man pressed against the front of my body. Damian's touch was delicate, stroking. Nathanial wrapped his hand around my breast and dug his nails into my flesh. It was Nathaniel's hand that bowed my back, tore my mouth away from his, and forced a scream from my mouth.

Damian hesitated, pulled back from that scream, though he had to feel that it was pleasure and not pain. He didn't like to hear women scream. And just like that we were back in his memory. There was a room underneath the castle, torches, darkness, and women, any woman that she thought was prettier than she. No one was allowed hair more yellow than hers, eyes more blue, or breasts larger. These were all sins, and sins were punished. A rush of images; piles of yellow hair, wide blue eyes like cornflowers, and the spear that put them out, a chest as pale and fair as any he'd seen, and the sword . . .

Nathaniel screamed, "Noooo!" He reached past me, and grabbed a handful of red hair. He jerked Damian so hard against me, that just feeling the hard length of him made me writhe between them. "Happy thoughts, Damian, happy thoughts."

"I don't have any happy thoughts," and on the heels of that statement were other dark rooms, and the smell of burning flesh.

I was the one who screamed this time, "God, Damian, no more. Keep your nightmares to yourself." The memory that had gone with that smell had dampened the ardeur. I could think again, even pressed between both their bodies.

"Tell him to fuck you," Nathaniel said.

I stared at him. "What?"

"Order him to do it; then he won't be conflicted."

It seemed almost ridiculous to be huffy, kneeling pretty much nude between two nude men, but it was still how I felt. "Maybe *I'm* conflicted."

"Almost always," he said, and smiled to soften the words.

Damian's voice came, low and heavy with something like sorrow. "She doesn't want to do this. She wants me to help her stop the ardeur, not to feed it. That's what she really wants, I can feel it, and that's what I have to do."

"Anita, please, tell him."

But Damian was right. He was the only port in a storm of sexual temptation. I valued his ability to make me not feel the ardeur. I valued that more than anything his body could do for me. And because I truly was his master, and that was my true wish, he had to help me do it. The coolness of the grave rose between us, and it wasn't frightening this time. It was soothing, comforting.

"Anita, no," Nathaniel said, "no." He put his face against my shoulder. The movement put his body further away from mine, and that helped me think, too.

I turned to look at Damian, though I didn't need to see his face to feel the overwhelming sadness. The sense of aching loss that seemed to fill him, like some bitter medicine. But the look on his face drove the sorrow home like a blade thrust through my heart. It hurt to see anyone's eyes full of such pain.

I turned to face him still held lightly in both their arms. Nathaniel put the top of his head against my naked back, shaking his head. "Anita, can't you feel how sad he is? Can't you feel it?"

I looked into Damian's cat-green eyes and said, "Yes."

He turned his face away, as if he'd shown me more than he was comfortable with. I touched his chin and brought his face back to me. "You don't want me," and there was a world of loss in those words. A loss that tightened my throat, made my chest hurt. I wanted to deny it, but he could feel what I was feeling. He was right, I didn't want him, not the way I wanted Nathaniel, let alone the way I wanted Jean-Claude or Micah. What do you say when someone can read your emotions, so that you can't hide behind polite lies? What do you say when the truth is awful, and you can't lie?

Nothing. No words would heal this. But I'd learned there were other ways to say you're sorry. Other ways to say, I'd change it, if I could. Of course, even that was a lie. I wouldn't lose the cool reserve that Damian could give me, not for anything.

I kissed him, and meant for it to be light, gentle, an apology that words could not make, but Damian thought he'd never get this close to me again. I felt a fierceness rise up through him, a desperation, that made him tighten his grip on my arms, made him thrust his tongue into my mouth, and kiss me hard and eager, and angry.

I tasted blood, and assumed he'd nicked me with his fangs. I swallowed the sweetish taste of the blood without thinking. Then I could smell the ocean, smell it like salt on my tongue. We drew back enough to look into each other's faces, and I saw the trickle of blood trailing over his lower lip. Nathaniel had time to say, "I smell seawater." Then the power flooded up and up, and smashed us against each other. It ground us against the floor like a wave cracking a boat against the rocks. We screamed, and writhed, and I

could not control it. If I'd been a true master, then I could
have ridden it, helped us all, but I'd never meant to mark
anyone. Never meant to be anyone's master. We were being swept away and I didn't know what to do. The inside of
my head exploded in white star bursts and gray miasma.
Darkness ate at the inside of my head. If I'd been sure we'd
wake up again, I'd have welcomed passing out, but I wasn't
sure. I didn't know. But it didn't matter; darkness filled up
the inside of my head, and we all fell into it. No more
screaming, no more pain, no more panic, no more anything.

My last clear thought was the realization that I'd accidentally drunk the blood of a vampire I was tied to by three
marks. His blood had been the fourth mark. The one step
Jean-Claude, Richard, and I had denied ourselves—now
I'd done it by accident, God help us all.

DEAD GIRLS DON'T DANCE

MaryJanice Davidson

For my children,
Christina and William,
who share me without complaint.

ACKNOWLEDGMENTS

Thanks to Cindy Hwang and Ethan Ellenberg, who help make my dreams come true. Thanks also to all the Betsy fans out there who have written me, wondering what the queen has been up to . . . this one's for you.

AUTHOR'S NOTE

This novella takes place just after the events of *Undead and Unwed* (Berkley, March 2004), and just before the events of *Undead and Unemployed* (Berkely, August 2004).

Also, there's no such thing as vampires. Or so the United Shoe Cooperative would have you believe.

Death cannot stop true love. It can only delay it for a while.

Westley, *The Princess Bride*

Nor bird nor beast
Could make me wish for anything this day,
Being old, but that the old alone might die,
And that would be against God's Providence.
Let the young wish.

W. B. Yeats

Prologue

⁂

SHE stood on the shore of Lake Michigan and looked out at the black water. At her back, Chicago rocked and reeled; it was Saturday night, and all the colleges were back in session.

It wasn't the first shore she'd stood on, nor the first body of water she'd stared at. It certainly wasn't the first evening she'd spent pacing the beach after a meal, nor the first big city she'd visited. Always a visitor, never a resident.

One thing remained the same, of course: it was dark. Dawn was coming—she could feel the sun, her enemy, slipping up over the horizon. She would have to leave soon.

She hadn't felt anything but artificial light on her face in a long, long time. And now, of course, if she ever did feel the sun, it would be the last thing she felt.

Like that was a bad thing.

There were nights when it was tempting to stay on the beach, watch the sun come up, die in fire and light and blazing agony, be done, be over, be still.

Be dead . . . for real.

At her feet, her supper gasped and thrashed and finally passed out. He was big and dark and strong—*had* been strong—but she'd had no trouble taking him. His kind went easy. They never thought the rabbit would turn into a fox; certainly not before their very eyes. And even a fox didn't have teeth as long and as sharp as hers.

She preferred to take men. She especially preferred men who bullied women. Cut him from the herd, take him, and quiet that thirst inside her, that constant, never-ending, hellish, unbeatable *thirst*.

Still, it was time to go. Her supper would recover and go home and not remember a thing. She would find another meal tomorrow. At least she wasn't such a mindless, insatiable newborn anymore. At least she could remember something beyond the thirst.

Yes, time to go.

But still she lingered, and wept dry tears, and stared out at the water, and wished she were dead. For real, this time.

Chapter 1

ANDREA sat up and coughed out a lungful of sand. The man crouched beside her scrambled up and away, as if she had—imagine it!—come to life.

"Holy shit!" he cried. "I thought you were a corpse!"

She coughed out more sand, cursing herself. She'd been so moody last night, instead of finding a decent alley to skulk in or a flophouse to cower in, she'd just burrowed into the beach sand like a big old worm, and waited for sunset.

Except this idiot found her before she could rise.

"Did—" Cough, hack. "—you call—" Hack-hack. "—anybody?"

"Well, yeah," he said, sounding weirdly apologetic. "I mean, I was running down the beach here—I've just gotta get down to two-twenty-five, y'know, and lay off the Cheez E Brats—anyway, I was running and tripped over something, and I thought it was a piece of driftwood but it was your foot, so I started to unbury you and then I couldn't find a pulse so I called the cops on my cell phone. You didn't look, y'know, grody or anything. In fact, for a corpse, you looked pretty good."

He's an idiot. Perfect. She finished coughing. It was amazing—even if you didn't have to breathe, sand got *everywhere*. Every time she moved, more of it trickled into her underpants. "How long ago did you call?"

"Uh . . . coupla minutes . . . look, are you sure you're all right? The sun's just about down, and it's getting kinda chilly, even for June—"

"The sun set," she said, wiping her mouth with her forearm, then grimacing at the way the sand stuck to her lips—worse than ChapStick!—"at seven fifty-six P.M. It's technically dark."

"Well, uh, okay, but—"

"So I have time for a snack before the authorities arrive."

"Okay. Like, um, you want an Orange Julius or something? My treat."

"I know." She leaned toward him—easy enough, he was hovering over her like a—heh, heh—grave robber—and grabbed him. He was wearing a tan t-shirt and green swimming trunks and beach shoes; the t-shirt shredded under her preternatural strength, the beach shoes went flying, and then she sank her fangs into his jugular.

"Ow! Hey!" Outraged, his big hands came up to push her away. "That's—are you fucking *biting* me? That's so weird! And kinky! Now cut it out! Ahhhh. No, I mean it . . . stop. Don't! Don't stop!" He grabbed her head, she hung on like a leech, and they grappled in the sand for a few seconds. She could feel his throat working beneath her lips as he babbled. "Seriously, this is so bogus! I save a dead chick—sort of—and she *chews* on me? You just wait 'til the cops get here, chickie, they'll, like, commit you or something. Ha!"

She broke away—something she had *never* done before; in fact, as early as a year ago, she wouldn't have been able to break off until her thirst had been satisfied—and said, trying not to whine, "Are you going to talk through this whole thing?"

"What, I'm supposed to sit here and think about England?"

"They usually start screaming about now, and then they faint."

"Well, forget it." He jerked a thumb at himself. "Daniel Harris don't faint, baby. No matter how much you chew on him!"

She stared at him. "Daniel Harris?"

"Yup. And I don't scream, either, except for that one time I saw a really grody spider fall into the toilet when I was taking a whiz, talk about a shocker! I didn't know pee could—y'know—crawl back *up* if you were surprised, but I'm here to tell you—"

"Daniel Harris, St. Olaf college?"

"Uh . . . yeah." He peered at her. "Do I know you, Weird Babe?"

She sighed. "I'm Andrea Mercer."

"Andrea . . . Andrea . . ."

"From Carleton College. Right across the river from St. Olaf. I transferred to Olaf my sophomore year. We were in Calc II, Psychology, and Sociology I together."

"Andrea . . ."

"You copied off my notes most of our senior year in college."

"Ohhhh! Andrea!"

"And," she continued, "you told me if I shaved my armpits I'd be, like, almost pretty 'n' stuff."

He snapped his fingers. "Right! Andrea! Got it!"

"Swell," she said dully. Unburied by Daniel "Big Cock" Harris, who of course didn't remember Andrea-the-Mouse. She'd chomped on him, drank his blood, and she was still only a minor annoyance in his life.

She was surprised she hadn't recognized him earlier—it had only been seven years, and he still looked much the same. Same surfer-boy, tanned, blond good looks. A little broader through the shoulders, a little longer through the legs. His faded blue eyes—the color of old denim—were still friendly, the expression still low-key. He looked exactly like what he was: a handsome, mild, life of the party fella who never ever had trouble getting a date.

She'd even asked him out once, their junior year, but . . .

He cleared his throat. "Uh, Andrea . . . the reason I didn't recognize you right away—"

"I know why," she said thinly, climbing to her feet and brushing sand off her jeans.

"—um—aren't you supposed to be dead?"

"Of course I'm dead, you idiot. But that's not why you didn't recognize me."

She walked away, hearing faint sirens in the distance.

Chapter 2

·‡·

"ANDREA? Andrea! Hey! Wait up!"

"What?" she growled, not turning around. A chill breeze was picking up off the lake, making her hurry. Of course, she was always cold, so what did a breeze matter? "Go away." *I'm still hungry.*

"So, you're dead and hanging around beaches and biting guys now? I thought you were an Economics major."

She almost laughed. Ah, the days when her biggest problem was figuring out the effect of interest rates on capital investment flows . . . or was it the other way around? "I was. Then I had an accident. Now I'm here."

He jogged up beside her. "Hey, listen. About before. I didn't mean to hurt your feelings. Sure I remember you. You were—you were really cute."

"You're an idiot," she replied. "It's all right, I'm leaving. You don't have to talk to me anymore."

"Hey, it's okay," he said, completely ignoring her broad hint. "I *want* to. So, like, what happened to you?"

She nearly tripped over her own feet. "Why in the world do you care?"

"Well . . . doesn't look to me like you're having much fun these days."

"What a tragedy," she mocked.

"Well . . . yeah."

To Daniel Harris, she realized, it probably *was*. The man had always been waiting for a party to happen. At college he'd been infamous for the fact that the lights were never out in his room.

"You wouldn't believe me anyway," she said, weakening.

"Uh . . . you bit me, remember? And I was a lifeguard back home. You really didn't—don't—have a pulse. I mean, when you sat up I tried to fool myself like maybe I'd made a mistake, but how hard is it to check a pulse? So are you—okay, this is gonna sound really dumb—like something out of the movies—but are you—don't laugh, now—"

"Yes. I'm a vampire."

He digested that in silence. They had reached the parking lot, and she shook more sand out of her hair.

"Well, how come?"

"How *come*? It's not like being a Republican, moron. I didn't exactly have a choice."

"You want to go get a drink? Talk about it?"

"Is that supposed to be a joke?"

"Well . . . not like *that*," he said uneasily, fingering his already-fading bite mark. "Like at a bar."

"No." But that was a lie. She was sorely tempted. And never mind her long-dead crush on Daniel Harris . . . the cold fact was, she was lonely. At times, almost unbearably so. It was nice—if weird—to run into a familiar face.

And he *was* pleasant. Even when he turned girls down for dates, he'd always been nice about it. One of those guys who honestly had no idea how popular and sought-after they really were.

"Aw, c'mon," he was coaxing. "Look, my car's right over there. We can head over to Joe's, grab a drink. Catch up."

"Catch up," she repeated. It was absurd and sad at the same side.

"Come on, Alison."

"Andrea."

"Right, Andrea."

"For crying out loud." But when he unlocked the passenger side of the silver Intrepid and held the door for her, she climbed in.

Chapter 3

❖

"I'LL have a Bud," Daniel said. *Huge* surprise. He turned to her. "Can you—uh—"

"White wine." She sighed. "Anything from 1985."

"So you can drink stuff that isn't blood?" he asked after the waitress swivel-hipped away.

"Yes. I can drink anything, it just doesn't—ah—satisfy me."

"Oh. So, how'd you become a vampire?"

She shrugged.

"Oh, come on. I really want to know! I mean, this is just so cool!"

"Yes, being undead is a laugh a minute. I can't think why I didn't do it before."

"Come on, it can't be all bad. I bet you're really super-strong, right? And fast?"

She shrugged.

"And you can prob'ly see in the dark like a cat. And you've got that whole sex appeal thing going."

She stared at him. "I'm not sexy."

"No, you *weren't* sexy. Now you are. I mean, come on, you think any girl dug up on the beach is gonna be cute? But you were seriously cute. I was scared when you sat up but I was, y'know, kinda glad, too."

"Oh." That was . . . that was actually kind of sweet. Gross, but sweet. "Well, thank you."

"So how'd you do it?" He leaned forward eagerly. "Was it hard? Did it hurt? Did it take a long time?"

"It was very hard, it hurt tremendously, and it took no time at all."

"Oh." Slightly crestfallen, he didn't say anything until the waitress put down their drinks and left. "Really bad, huh?"

"Really very unbelievably bad." She stared moodily into her white wine. A nineteen eighty-*four* Riesling, dammit.

"You want to talk about it? Sometimes it helps to talk about it. Also, you've got sand in your eyebrows."

She shook her head impatiently and watched as a tiny grain of sand flew away from her table, arched a few feet over, and landed in the precisely parted hair of the woman sitting at the table beside them. *Why, he's right*, she thought, uncharacteristically amused. *I do see in the dark like a cat.*

"It's kind of a long story," she warned him.

"Hey, I got time. I wasn't leaving for home until tomorrow morning."

"Home? Minnesota, you mean?"

"Sure, I still live in St. Paul."

"What do you do?"

"Oh . . ." He shrugged sheepishly. "Nothin'. I came into my trust fund a couple of years ago, so mostly I play golf n' stuff. I'm only in town for a wedding. You remember Mike Freeborg? Played shortstop? He got married yesterday."

"Fascinating. So . . . you're driving back? Flying?"

"Driving. It's not far . . . six, maybe seven hours."

"Hmmm."

"Why?"

Why? Oh, no big deal . . . I just need to be in Minneapolis soon to pay homage to the new vampire queen. And you just might be my means, Daniel Harris.

She supposed she could play Scheherazade for him. Keep him hooked on her grisly, yet interesting (for a non-vampire, that was) story, all the way to the Twin Cities. Then she could pay homage to the new queen, and see what happened from there.

The new queen might press her into service.

Or destroy her.

Andrea was fine with either one.

Chapter 4

❖

"LOOK, I'm happy to play driver-guy and all—"

"The word is chauffer, Daniel."

"—but aren't you gonna explode or something when the sun comes up?"

"No, but I *will* burst into flames and make a terrible mess in your car. I'll probably scream a bit, too."

"Well, we'll just stop and stay at a motel before sunrise."

She shrugged. "Or you could just put me in the trunk and keep going."

"I couldn't do that!" he said, shocked, big dumb blue eyes wide with distress.

"We'd make better time."

"You know, you're still a cool one. I remember that about you in school. Just cool as a—a—"

"Cucumber?"

"Yech, I hate cucumbers. You're as cool as a chilly

tomato. Anyway, I'm happy to take you back to the Cities, but you were gonna tell me about how you got vampired, don't forget now."

"Telling you how I got turned won't even get us out of the city."

"Well, then I'll tell you everything I've been up to."

"Swell," she mumbled. Then, louder, "All right. A deal is a deal. I was working late—this was my internship at KPMG. And I got grabbed while I was in the parking ramp—the big one on Marquette?"

"Sure, I know it. I park there when there's no parking at the Target Center, you know, if there's a game or something."

"Terrific. We have more and more in common all the time. Anyway, it turns out it was the three hundred fiftieth year of Nostro—he was like the vampire king—anyway, it was the anniversary of his reign. Very big deal. And because he was a dramatic fuck, he had his underlings kidnap a bunch of women and made us part of his ceremony. And—and a bunch of vampires sort of—sort of pounced on us all at once. He—they—kept us for days. Then they threw us away when they were done with us. The other girls died. But I caught the infection, and rose."

Nobody around; the moon high. Smells . . . rotting meat, fresh earth. The moon, so bright. So thirsty. Climbing over dead girls, so thirsty. It didn't matter what happened; didn't matter where she was, who she was; only the thirst mattered. So thirsty. So—

"That fucking sucks! Those pieces of shit!"

"It was . . . it was extremely awful." And, oddly, she felt better for telling it. For finally telling it.

"What a fucking awful way to die!"

"Yes. Anyway, I rose from the dead and started feeding

and eventually ended up passing through Chicago and that's what I've been up to for the past six years, how about you?" she asked with faux brightness.

"Jesus, Andrea," he said, not noticing her flinch, "I'm really sorry. That sucks the root."

"Thank you. You're about to miss our exit."

Cursing, he wrenched the wheel to the right and, ignoring the hail of horns, careened over into the proper lane. "You said—you said you caught an infection. Is that like how you become a vampire? I thought you had to drink a vampire's blood and he had to drink yours, or something."

She shook her head. "Old wives' tale. Most people die of extended . . . attention. If you catch it, you rise from the dead. It's not a big mystery."

"So you've been roaming the streets of Chicago for the last six years?"

"I— I think so."

"Huh?"

"Which word didn't you understand?" she snapped, then instantly softened. She should be flattered that he was so curious. He certainly hadn't shown this kind of interest in her in college. Not Andrea Mercer, she of the mousy hair, mousy eyes, mousy life.

And had anybody cared enough in the last few years to ask her anything? Anything at all? She would do well, she reminded herself, to not be such a damned snob and remember Daniel was only asking questions because he cared. Or was morbidly interested. Same thing, in her world. "I don't remember much of the early years. You have to—you think about feeding all the time. *All* the time. And once you've fed you start thinking about when you can feed again."

"Jeez," he said, respectfully, if not very originally.

"It's like the worst thirst you've ever had, times a million, every minute you're awake. I might have made some vampires myself; I just don't know. I—I hope not."

In fact, this mindless frenzy, this constant hunger, and the complete inability to remember anything beyond the hunger, was a source of deep shame for her. She, always the top of her class, a precocious child. She'd memorized the periodic table in half an hour. But all of last year was a blank. Likewise the year before. And the year before. And the—

"Well, you seem a lot better now. You seem just like you were in school. You know, standoffish, smart, bitch—uh, temperamental."

"Thanks," she said dryly. "The reason I seem 'better' is because I'm a little older. Don't get me wrong, I'm still a positive infant by vampire standards, but I'm not a newborn anymore, either."

"So you're not thirsty all the time?"

"Oh, sure I am." She glanced at his neck and grinned. "I can just control it a little better. Lucky for you."

"You didn't look like you were controlling yourself too good when you started chewing on me," he grumbled.

"I didn't know you then," she explained. "I thought you were just some guy."

"Oh, that makes me feel *much* better."

"It should," she said truthfully.

Chapter 5

✦

"I still say I should just get in the trunk. We could be in the Cities in another four hours."

"Look, I'm not driving around with a vampire in my fucking car trunk, okay? I can afford the hundred bucks for a hotel room."

"Waste of money," she grumbled, crossing her arms over her chest and waiting while he fiddled with the key card.

"Says you. I'm driving, I get to say when we stop."

"What exactly do I get to say?"

"Tell me more about being a vampire."

"Bo-ring."

"That's because you don't have any . . . uh . . . what's the word?"

"Perspective."

"Right. You don't have that. But I have tons of it."

He opened the door and gestured for her to move ahead of him. She stopped short and stared at the single king-sized bed.

"Oh," he said.

"Right," she said.

"I asked for a double."

"It's no big deal. I'll sleep under the bed."

"Oh, good, because that's not incredibly creepy or anything. Look, you can trust me. I won't lay a finger on you while you're . . . er . . . slumbering or whatever."

"I wouldn't notice if you did." She marched across the room, turned the air conditioner off—

"Aw, you're killin' me!"

—and pulled the drapes. The room, a perfectly adequate Holiday Inn, became nicely gloomy.

"I'm sure you don't mean anything by it," he began, "but this is seriously fucking creepy."

"Your bright idea, Daniel. Okay, well, good night."

"Night," he said, a bit nervously. He watched her kick off her tennis shoes and stretch out on the bed. Straight-faced, she folded her hands over her breasts.

"Did I mention you're killin' me?"

"Quit your whining," she said, and was insensible for the next thirteen hours.

"TIME to get up," she said, poking him. As always, there was no sense of time passing. One minute she'd closed her eyes, and now it was sunset again. "Rise and shine."

"Aaaggghhhhh!" he cried, and nearly fell off the bed, unintentionally smacking her as he did so. "Don't *do* that!"

"Don't do *that*," she snapped back, feeling her cheek. "What's the problem?"

He sat up, rubbing his face. His shirt, she suddenly noticed, was draped over the far chair. She assumed he was still swimming to keep in shape. The broad shoulders, sweetly defined pecs, and flat stomach meant he was doing something, that was for damned sure. His blond hair was standing up in all directions, as if showcasing his startlement. "Look," he was saying, "I'm sorry to yell, but it's not every night I wake up with a vampire bending over me. Even one I know."

You never knew me. She didn't say it out loud. *Be nice, he's giving you a ride. Plus, he knows what you are and he didn't pull the curtains open at two o'clock in the afternoon.*

"We can get going now," she said helpfully.

"Forget it. I need to shower and change." He rubbed his cheek, which rasped. "And shave. Well, maybe not shave. D'you want to shower first?"

"I don't need to."

He stopped in mid-yawn. "How come?"

"I don't sweat, pee, or even shed hair. Why would I shower?"

"Um . . . so you're not skanky and nasty?"

"Takes one to know one," she said, stung. Great. Half a day with him and she was regenerating to grade school. "Look, just go take your shower, all right?"

"All right, all right. You're definitely not an early morning vampire. Early evening, I mean." He stood and began unbuckling his belt, then stopped and stared at her. "Oh. I s'pose I should do this in the bathroom. I mean . . . I didn't think you'd care, but—"

"I'm dead, not asexual," she said dryly.

"Ah-ha!" he cried, startling her. He bounded (awkwardly; his pants were falling down) across the room and fumbled for the Barnes and Noble bag on the small table. He pulled out a small, red-bound book. *American Heritage*

Dictionary, it read. "Now I can understand you and we can actually talk and stuff."

She burst out laughing; she couldn't help it. The effect on him was startling; his grin lit up his whole face, made his blue eyes twinkle. "There! I knew you'd do that sooner or later."

"Oh, come on. I'm not that much of a grump."

"Sweetie, you were grumpy *before* you died. Now . . . well, never mind. Asexual . . ." He started flipping pages. "Asbestos . . . ascend . . . ascetic . . ."

"You don't need that," she said, exasperated. "I can tell you what it means."

"And have you lording it over me all night? Forget it. Ah-ha! Asexual. According to this, it's an adjective and it means—"

"I *know* what it means."

"So if you're *not* asexual it means the opposite, which is sexual."

"This is an enthralling topic," she said, suddenly nervous, "but we have places to go."

He looked up from the dictionary and squinted at her. "So, do vampires have sex, or what?"

"Uh . . ."

"Holy cow, you're blushing! As much as you can."

"I am not."

"Oh, you absolutely are! Jeez, you're acting like you've never had sex as a vam—oh."

"Can you please," she asked desperately, "go take your shower?"

"Uh, sure. Won't be a minute." He was looking at her in a very curious way.

And he was right; she *was* blushing. Her face actually felt warm.

"Huh. That's kind of interesting."

"Interesting," she said thinly. "Exactly the word I was thinking."

"Well, you don't have to get all weird about it. It's just sex."

"And you're just an idiot," she snapped. "Go shower."

"Okay, okay."

He kicked the rest of the way out of his jeans and went into the bathroom without another word. She struggled not to stare at his ass, and almost succeeded.

Chapter 6

—•◦•—

"WELL!" he said cheerfully, toweling his hair ten minutes later.

Annoyingly, he hadn't put his shirt back on. At least he was wearing jeans. Tight, faded jeans that clung to his—

"That was super awkward. Oh, well. Saddle up, Andy, let's hit the trail."

"It's Andrea, and we have to . . . um . . . stop first."

"Huh? How come?"

"I have to eat."

"What?"

"I said, I have to eat." She was, in fact, starting to feel a little desperate. Not to mention horribly embarrassed. "And soon."

"Oh. Oh! Right. Eat. Except you don't mean eat, do you?"

"Soon," she repeated.

"What's the rush?"

"Haven't you been listening?" she cried. "I'm thirsty *all the time.* And the longer I go without, the more . . . desperate . . . I become. It's—"

"You get stupid," he said bluntly. "That's what you don't like. You get totally obsessed with chomping and you can't think about anything else. And you fucking hate it, don't you?"

"How analytic of you," she said, calming . . . the worst was over. She had dreaded the telling of it more than anything else. And he was finding out all her secrets. It was alarming . . . but kind of comforting, too. "And you're right. I fucking hate it. And . . . it's been a while since my last . . . I mean, there was *you,* but I managed to stop myself, and . . ."

"Well, how much do you need?"

"I never measured," she snapped.

"Like, a pint? A half-pint? A gallon? What?"

"Daniel, what difference does it make?"

"Well." He cleared his throat. "The reason I was asking was, you could chomp on me again."

"Oh, no!" She couldn't recall ever being so shocked. And gratified. He was so kind. He had always been kind. "No, I couldn't do that to you."

"Don't get me wrong, I'm not volunteering to be the horse led to slaughter—"

"Sheep."

"Not that, either. And I don't want you to, like, *drain* me. But you could have a little. Holy shit, what the hell happened to your mouth?"

She clapped her hands over her lips. His words had brought out her fangs; she was very much afraid she had started to drool. "Nothing," she mumbled. "Let's talk about something else."

He came closer, trying to get a better look; she backed

away. "That is so cool! And scary. It's like all of a sudden you sprouted about twenty more teeth."

"Let's change the subject."

"Okay, but don't say I never gave you anything." But he sounded relieved, and she knew at once he had been secretly hoping she wouldn't take him up on it.

He wasn't afraid of her, exactly, but he was cautious. She thought it was a very healthy reaction.

"Let's get out of here," she said, still muttering around her fingers, "before I change my mind. Don't forget your dictionary."

"YOU know, if you'd told me last week that I'd be in a bar trying to help a vampire suck some poor guy's blood, I'd have said you were on drugs."

"The night is young," she said, staring into her wine.

"So, uh, how do you usually do this?"

"*I* usually skulk in a dark alley until someone tries to rob or rape me. Then I assault them. Then I sulk. Then—"

"I think I get it," he said.

"But with you hovering over me like an overprotective linebacker, I'm not sure at all how this is going to work. Can't you just . . . wait for me in the car, or something?"

"And leave you alone? In *here?*" He looked around, clearly appalled. It really was a dive, with dirty floors and the pervasive odors of beer, sweat, and urine.

But she could also smell blood under the rest of it, which told her this was the right place to go trolling. Violence was no stranger here.

"It's perfect."

"No way, Andy."

"*Andrea,*" she growled, and drained the rest of her wine. "Well, then, I don't know how we—oof!"

"Shorry, little lady," the hulk behind her slurred. She craned her neck, and craned it some more . . . he was *big*. Easily six foot four, possibly a hair over. And broad. And smelly. He was wearing a filthy t-shirt, filthier jeans that might have once been blue, and Doc Martens. "Gut stompers," her dad used to call them. "Buy m'drink?"

"I think you're supposed to buy *her* a drink," Daniel said.

"You lookin' f'r a fight?"

"You lookin' for a shower?"

"I would *love* to buy you a drink," Andrea said, glaring at Daniel. "Possibly five. Have a seat."

"Oh, Andrea, come on!"

"Andeuh? S'pretty name."

"Daniel, will you stay out of this?"

"Bet y'got a pretty l'il pussy, too."

Daniel stood so quickly his chair tipped. "Okay, that's *it*."

"He's perfect!" she cried rapturously. The perfect bar, and now the perfect entrée. Drunk, obnoxious, and all the knuckles on his left hand were scraped—he'd already been in a bar fight. It was doubtful he'd picked on someone his own size. A glance around the bar confirmed there *was* no one his own size.

She stood also, fumbled in her jeans, remembered she had no money, then fumbled in Daniel's jeans.

"Hey, quit! That tickles!" She pulled a couple of fives out, dropped them on the bar, then turned to her O-negative in shining armor.

"Why don't we go for a walk? Get some fresh air?"

His brow wrinkled as he tried to decipher her request. "Nnnnn . . . walk? Don' wanna walk . . . wanna stay here n' talk t'you."

"You can bring your beer," she suggested, and that was good enough.

Annoyingly, Daniel stomped behind them as they left the bar. Smelly slung an arm over her shoulders as she half-led, half-carried him around the back of the building.

"Daniel . . . if you could just wait in the car, I'll be right with—"

"No way. I'm not leaving you alone with this—this—ugh!"

"Don't get too cocky," she muttered. She was glad Daniel couldn't see Smelly was using the opportunity to grab and paw at her left breast, the only one he could reach. "You're about as articulate as he is."

"I can't believe this is how you spend your nights," he whined, trudging after them. "It's so bogus."

"As opposed to the fun-filled nights I could spend with Dictionary Boy," she snapped. "Don't judge *me*. I'm doing the whole neighborhood a community service. Instead of picking another fight or indulging in a little felony rape, he'll sleep the rest of the night and stagger home in the morning, hungover, violently ill, and remembering nothing."

"So, getting bitten by a vampire is the same as having six tequila shots?"

"Hilarious. I have laughed. My point—ow!"

"What?"

"Nothing." She glared at her boozy meal, who was leering at her with bleary satisfaction. What he doubtless considered "being playful" was painful as hell. Did he not understand nipples were *attached?* "My point is, he won't be picking any more fights tonight, bullying women, committing date rape . . . none of it."

"Can't we just hit him over the head? We'll get the same result. Right down to the headache!"

"Daniel, I have to eat." She said it as simply as she could, because to her, it *was* simple. She was too much a coward to end herself, and too hungry to starve herself. She had chosen to live . . . after a fashion. This was her means.

She seized her knight in shining platelets, bent him back . . .

"Whu?"

. . . and sank her teeth into his jugular. Took her a second to find it; he had an extremely thick neck.

"Jesus! You're doing it now? Right this second?" Daniel jumped in front of her—them—arms spread wide, shielding her from passersby. Not that there were any at this hour, this location. "Andy, we're not even all the way out of the ally yet!"

"Grgle," she said, or something like it.

"Purrrrrrteeeeeeeeee . . ." her knight in shining plasma slurred, slipping into unconsciousness as easily as a child slid down a slide. "Mmmmm . . . purrrrrrrr . . . gaaaaahhh."

Daniel had a hand over his eyes. "They're never going to believe this at the reunion."

Chapter 7

❧

"HEE! That was a piece of cake." She stumbled and Daniel steadied her. "Course, it usually is . . . piece of cake I mean . . . hee . . . I miss cake. . . ."

"Are you all right? You look kind of . . . uh . . . flushed, actually."

"Rush of blood," she said giddily. "Straight to the head! Zoom! Do not pass go, do not collect any wooden stakes."

Daniel was peering worriedly down at her. He was so big, he was so strong. She snuggled into his manlike—manful? manly?—arms, so gorilla-like in their soothing strength. Ahhhh.

"Are you sure you're okay?" he asked again. "You really don't seem like yourself. At *all.*"

"You wanta see something super supercool? Like comic-book cool? I used to watch Wonder Woman alla time when I was a kid."

"Uh . . ."

"Watch this!" She straightened out of his embrace and lurched toward the streetlight. It was one of the old-fashioned wooden ones, with a halo of moths and mosquitoes circling the globe at the top. She threw her fist and hit the wooden pole dead-on (a good trick, since at the moment, the pole was revolving lazily, as was the street, and Daniel's head). It shuddered and splinters jumped away from it, pattering to the street. She, of course, didn't feel a thing.

She hit it again, and it slooooooowly tipped over with a groan, hitting the street and bouncing up about a foot, then settling back and rolling over the curb.

"Holy shit!" Daniel just about screamed.

"I told you it was cool," she said. "Could you stop spinning around like that? It's annoying."

"I'm standing still. Uh, don't knock over any more light poles, okay? Are you *sure*—wait a minute!"

"Okay, but only a minute."

"That guy was three sheets to the wind, and you drank his blood—you're drunk!"

"I know you are," she said cleverly, "but what am I?"

"Great. A drunk, insanely strong vampire wandering the streets of—of whatever town we're in. With me."

"Drunk*en*," she corrected muzzily. "And I am not."

"You totally are! Does this happen a lot?"

"I thought I was high on life," she said, and giggled. "Guess I was high on O-neg and Jack Daniel's." She laughed again, harder. It was all so stupid! And funny! And stupid! "He was so silly! And smelly! He thought he was gonna get a little, but instead *I* got a little. Ha!"

"Look, let's just—go back to the car, okay? This giddy, happy side of you is kind of freaking me out. We'll get to the car and we can make it all the way to the Cities before the sun comes up."

"No," she said.

"Uh . . . what?"

"No. You shouldn't be with me. You should leave me here and drive away as fast as you can. Put that big smelly foot to the metal."

"It's not smelly," he said, "and you're talking crazy." He reached for her arm but she shook him off like a fly.

"Go *away!*" she shouted.

He didn't go away. Instead, he hurried after her. "What the hell's gotten into you *now?* What's the problem?"

"Just . . . leave me alone." She weaved unsteadily down the street. The mood she was in, if those damned street-lights didn't stop wobbling, she was knocking them all over. So there!

"C'mon, Andy, will you come to the car already? You're totally screwing up our plan." She felt his fingers brush her elbow and whirled on him like a cat. She could tell from the way the color fell out of his face that all her teeth were showing.

"Leave. Me. *Alone.*"

He rallied quickly, she noticed grudgingly; she'd give him that much. Too dumb to stay scared. It was endearing, yet irritating. "What's the matter with you?" he demanded. "Well . . . I mean . . . what *else* is bothering you?"

"I'm no good, Daniel," she said, her anger abruptly shifting to racking sobs. "I have to drink blood to survive, *get it?*" He reached for her again and this time she let him. "I'm the worst thing there is to be . . . a vampire! Pull over at lunchtime," she begged, "and open the trunk."

He winced away from her, horrified. "I couldn't do that, Andy—"

"And! Ree! Uh!" she screamed into his face.

"Okay," he said, rubbing his ear. "Now, come on. You're not bad, Andy, you're just—in a bad situation. Yeah. And it's so totally not your fault, it should be a crime. In fact," he said, warming to his subject, "it *was* a crime! Like, murder, anyone? You're just doing the best you can. And you said yourself you only go after scumballs. You're—you're doing a community service! Yeah, that's it, they oughta give you a friggin' medal. Now—now quit crying, all right?"

"Sorry," she muttered.

"Come on. Let's get to the car. You'll feel better when we get closer to St. Paul."

"I doubt it." Did vampires get hangovers? She was afraid she was about to find out. "Thanks for listening to my hysterical ravings."

"Aw, that's okay. It's kind of nice to hear you raise your voice once in a while. You're a pretty cool customer, y'know?"

"I used to think so." She sighed, fell into step beside him, and made a conscious effort not to rest her head on his shoulder.

They found his Intrepid and climbed into it. When she refused to buckle her seat belt ("Honestly, Daniel, what could possibly happen to me?") he leaned across her and belted her in. His chest pressed briefly against her shoulder, and his breath, redolent of spearmint gum, tickled her ear.

"So!" he said cheerfully, starting the car and playfully racing the engine. "We're off to see the Wizard! I figure we got about seven hours of darkness left. Plenty of time."

"That's true," she said, cheering up. "I'll see the new vampire queen soon, so I probably won't have to worry about anything much longer."

"What are you talking about?" He pulled into traffic after checking blind spots she didn't know existed. For a happy-go-lucky laid-back type, he was fanatically careful behind the wheel. "Won't worry about what?"

"Well, the new queen probably won't want any baby vampires around."

"Baby vam—what does *that* mean?"

She was momentarily surprised, then remembered he really didn't know anything at all. "Sorry, I thought you knew. She'll kill me, of course. All the young ones. I mean, we're not much use to her, and it's a great way to get her point across. So I'm dead meat. Again," she added cheerfully.

He nearly drove into the stoplight. *"What?"*

"It's not like killing a real person," she said, trying to soothe him. She should have guessed he'd take power-killing entirely the wrong way. "I've already got a death certificate, remember." She rubbed her hands together in anticipation. "Yep, she'll take one look at me and know I'm useless to her and—*gllllkkkkkk!*" She drew her finger across her throat. "Sayonara, sweetheart."

"Jesus Christ!" Daniel yelled, which nearly made her throw up. "Are you insane? You're taking a trip to see a vampire who you're pretty sure is gonna kill you?" He slammed on the brakes. In fact, he stood on them. The car shrieked like a cat and the cords stood out on his neck as he wrestled with the wheel. Her breath was cut off (big deal) as the seat belt locked. Hmm. Maybe it was a good thing he'd belted her in . . . otherwise she'd probably be skimming the road like a tiddledywink about now.

"For crying out loud," she said when the car had shuddered to a smoking stop. "What is your problem?"

"My problem? My—well, forget that shit! No way am I driving you to your own murder! I'm turning this car around *right now* and we're going back to Chicago."

"Oh, for the love . . ." She put a hand over her eyes.

"Yeah, you heard me." He twisted in his seat, glared through the rear window, then slammed the car in reverse.

"Look, Andy, I'm real sorry you hate your life right now, but *I* think you're a super chick, and I'm not driving you to be some damn vampire queen's hors doover!"

"It's pronounced," she said gently, "hors d'oeuvre."

"I give a shit!"

"That's fine," she said, "but I guess I'll just have to steal a car—it's not difficult, I assure you—and go myself. Alone."

He glared at her. "No you won't!"

"Sure I will."

"Won't!"

"Ah . . . will."

"Dammit!"

He put the car in neutral and fumed while it idled. She hummed and studied her nails. Eck. She had some of Big 'n' Smelly's blood under her index nail. Could she lick it off without Daniel noticing? Maybe he—

"Okay," he said abruptly. "Here's the new plan."

"I'm breathless with anticipation."

"I still drive you to Minneapolis—"

"So, the new plan is the old plan."

"—*but,* I'm going with you to meet the vampire queen."

"I beg your pardon," she said politely, "but you certainly are not."

"No escort, no ride! That's the way it is."

She studied him and briefly considered knocking him out and stealing the Intrepid. But she had the odd feeling it might not be quite as easy as she thought.

Well, she had a ride (again), and she could always ditch him at an opportune moment.

And his concern was really . . . well . . . really . . .

"Let's go," she said, "before I start to cry again."

Chapter 8

⁕

"Hey, I have a present in the trunk," he said, returning to the car with their room key.

"A pillow?" she asked brightly. "Your trunk's certainly long enough to stretch out in."

"Yuck, no." He opened her door, waited impatiently while she slowly climbed out, then slammed it and popped the trunk. He withdrew a bag with the Target logo, and tossed it to her.

"Awww," she said. "Plastic. Gee, I didn't get you anything."

"Open it, wiseass. Sheesh. If I hadn't known you before you were a blood-sucking fiend of the night, I'd think all vampires were this weird."

"Oh, we are." She opened the bag and saw several t-shirts, a few pairs of shorts, two cardigans: one in white, one in black. "Oh. Clothes."

"Well, you sort of joined me with, like, just the stuff on your back, and I know you don't need to shower or anything, but new clothes are kind of nice, doncha think?"

He was watching her so anxiously, her dead heart almost skipped a beat. "They're very nice," she assured him. "Very thoughtful. Thank you."

"Sure."

"I don't have any money to pay you b—"

"Forget it. We're on the end, here, second floor." He led her through the lobby and into the elevator. "Listen," he continued when the doors closed, "what *have* you been doing for money?"

She blinked at him. She didn't have to blink much anymore, but she liked to do it for effect. "Nothing, of course. What do I need money for? Food? Shelter? Warm clothes? Bikinis? Sunscreen? A family to feed?" She tried—and failed—to keep the bitterness out of her voice. "Let's not forget, for the last few years I've been little more than an animal. This is probably the first time I've even *thought* about money in six years."

"Huh."

That was all he said as they exited the elevator, walked down the hall, and entered their room like robots who didn't know each other. The room faced west, and she was gratified to see the curtains were thick.

"So what about your folks?" he asked, just when she thought he was going to shut up for a while.

She'd been pretending to read the "Welcome to the Super 8" brochure. "What about them?"

"Well . . . aren't you going to tell them you aren't dead?"

She stood, crossed to him, took his hand, and placed it in the middle of her chest. Then waited patiently. Then said, "I am dead, Daniel. Please note the absence of a pulse."

He didn't move his hand, but made an impatient expression with his eyebrows. "You know what I mean."

"Well, let's see . . . my mom left my dad when I was twelve, and I haven't seen her since, and last I heard Dad was off somewhere in New Jersey with Stepmother Number Three. I doubt they noticed I was dead."

"Oh," he said. Then, "Sorry."

"It's nothing."

"How come I didn't get invited to your funeral?"

"I'm sorry," she said politely. "Your invitation must have gotten lost in the garbage disposal."

"Now, cut that out! You know what I mean."

"Look, I wasn't exactly around to plan the fucking thing, okay? Ask the funeral director why you weren't invited. *I* was busy clawing my way out of my own grave."

"O-*kay.* Y'don't have to be so touchy."

"And you don't have to be such a dumbass," she snapped, "and yet, you seem unable to stop."

"Well, it's better than being a bitch!"

"No, it is *not!*"

"Yeah, it *is!*"

"You know, *most* people would have the sense to be afraid of me, but *you,* you're too dumb!"

"Afraid of what? A bloodsucking shrew?"

"Do you even know," she asked with deadly venom, "what a shrew is?"

"A shrew," he said, his index finger stabbing her nose, "is a woman of violent temper. It's also a small mouselike animal with a sharp nose."

She paused. "I'm going to make you *eat* that dictionary."

"Try it, cutie. I'll bounce you across this room like a Super Ball."

"I don't want to be bounced like a Super Ball," she admitted, and he cracked up.

"Awwwww," he said when he had finished hee-hawing like a donkey. "Our first fight."

"I could snap your neck," she commented, "like a toothpick."

"You'd never hurt your driver, sugar buns!"

She concealed a shudder. "Please don't ever call me that again."

"What were we fighting about again? Because we shouldn't go to bed angry at each other."

"You're confusing us with newlyweds." The thought would have made her blush, if she still could have. Sadly, Smelly's blood had been long metabolized and she was back to being corpse white until she fed again. "Never mind. Chalk it up to a long day."

He patted the bed. "Well, you can sleep . . . or whatever you do . . . right now." He flopped onto the bed and groped for the remote. "The nice thing about having you for a roommate, absolutely nothing wakes you up."

"I'm so happy for you." She gingerly climbed on the bed and stretched out beside him. "Honestly? It doesn't . . . creep you out or anything?"

"Heck no!" he said, a little too heartily. At her piercing stare, he added, "Well . . . a little. I held my finger under your nose for, like, an hour—nothing. Not a single tickle of breath."

"I hope you washed it first."

"My finger?" he teased. "Or your nose?"

"Very funny."

"But anyway, once I got used to it . . . no biggie. I mean—no offense—but you were always different."

"Yes," she said, staring at the ceiling. "I suppose I was."

"I should have gone out with you in college."

"It doesn't matter now."

"I was an idiot."

"Yes."

"But sometimes," he said, reaching for her hand, "things can be fixed."

"And sometimes," she said, gently extricating her fingers from his, "they can't. It's too late now, Daniel. Years too late. We were just different people *then*. Now we're different creatures entirely."

"That doesn't mean you can't have a fresh start."

She sighed and put a hand over her eyes. "Daniel, dear, you're so dumb you make me tired. Because that's exactly what it means. I'm sorry to be blunt."

"I'm not as dumb as you think, you know," he said with mild heat, but half his attention was already captured by ESPN.

"Of course not," she agreed. "You're just dumb compared to *me*."

"Go to sleep," he said sourly.

"I can't. The sun isn't up y—"

Chapter 9

❧

THE first thing she heard, hours later, was Daniel yawning like a bear at the end of winter. "Finally," he said by way of greeting. "I didn't think you were ever gonna wake up. And did you know it's one, two, three, you're zonked? I thought you'd had a stroke or something."

"Fine, thanks, how are you?"

"Very funny." He yawned again. "Would you check in that bedside drawer for the HBO guide? I can't find it anywhere."

"Why?" she asked, rolling over and groping for the knob. "We're staying in to watch *The Sopranos* instead of driving the last half hour to St. Paul?"

"I just like to know what's on," he said. "Hey, you should be glad I'm reading."

"Oh, I'm thrilled," she assured him. Her lips wanted to smile but she sternly repressed them. "I'm—" Her hand dropped into the drawer and instantly she was on fire; her mind was equal parts agony and surprise and fury: surprise at the pain, agony at the pain, fury that she could be so stupid.

Her shriek brought Daniel off the bed and at her side in less than a heartbeat; she didn't think a mortal could move so fast. She was holding her wrist with her left hand. Her right hand was smoking. The drawer had pulled all the way out of the table, and the Gideon Bible had tumbled to the floor.

"Oh my *God,*" Daniel gasped, which made her shriek louder. "Your hand, Andy, your poor—" He hauled her off the bed, kicked the Bible under the bed, and then he was running the tap in the bathroom, taking her poor crisped paw and running it carefully under the cool water. "Andy, I'm so sorry, I didn't—I should have—"

She took a deep shuddering breath, which made her dizzy, but calmed her a bit, too. "It's my own fault. I should have known it was in there. It's in every bedside drawer in every motel in the country." She shivered against him. "It hurts," she added dully.

"Of course it does, poor baby. If you were anyone but . . . well, *you,* we'd be calling 911 this minute and taking you to the ER. But . . ." He looked at her doubtfully, doubtless picturing a frantic intern trying to find her pulse, her blood pressure, anything.

"It will heal," she said. She dared a peek at her hand. At least it wasn't boiling smoke anymore. Her thumb was blackened, but the rest of her fingers merely had the dark red look of boiled lobster. "Eventually."

"This is bogus," Daniel said angrily. "I get that you're a vampire and all, but you were forced into it, and it's not like you're munching on first-graders. What's God got against you?"

"I don't know," she replied, "but He appears to be plenty pissed."

"Well, shit. That's not fair."

"This is—is the Creator, remember? Not known for his scrupulous sense of fair play. He asked Jacob to kill his own son, if memory serves, set Eve up, screwed over the Jews . . . oh, all sorts of things. He never plays fair. He doesn't have to—it's his board game."

"For a vampire, you know a lot about it."

"Theology minor," she reminded him.

He turned the water off, took a snow-white hand towel from the shelf, and gently patted her hand dry. It stung like mad, but it wasn't the burning agony it had been before.

"Poor Andy," he said again, and kissed the tip of her middle finger, which was dark pink. "I'm really sorry. Should have got the damned HBO guide myself."

"You read my mind."

He laughed and hugged her to him. "Cripes, woman, you scared the shit out of me. You got some lungs on you, didja know?"

"It's not every day I feel the agony of myself bursting into flames. To think I used to fantasize about walking on the beach during sunrise! Well, forget that."

His grip tightened. He was so tall, his chin rested on her head. "Don't talk about that," he said into her part. "Not anymore, okay?"

"I think it's safe to say my self-destructive streak is at an end for now," she said truthfully into his neck. His lovely, taut neck. She could actually see the blood pressure pumping up his jugular, and jerked back.

"Oh, come on, don't do that," he said coaxingly, grabbing her elbow and pulling her back into his embrace. Her burned hand stuck out behind him like a crosswalk sign. "We were kind of having a moment and everything."

"Uh . . . Daniel . . . it's not that I'm not finding this pleasant, because I truly am . . ."

"Good. Now stop talking and enjoy it."

She growled at him.

"Oh, go ahead and bite, then," he murmured. "I don't care. And I bet it'll make your hand feel better, huh? The only thing is, if I pass out, you've got to get me to the car and drive the rest of the way."

"Daniel, you have no fucking idea what you're saying."

"Sure I do. I think you're pretty cool. It's not that I didn't like you in school; I just didn't bother to get to know you. But now . . . I think you're a tough chick handling herself in an unbelievably sucky situation. Also, you've got a great rack for a dead girl."

"For crying out loud," she said, resting her forehead on his shoulder. "I suppose you think you're being sweet."

"Awww, you can't resist me, gorgeous."

"Dammit!"

"I couldn't help but notice," he said, running his hands up and down her back as she snuggled more firmly into his embrace, "that you didn't exactly deny it. You just swore again. It totally proves me ri—mmph!"

She was kissing him. She couldn't believe she was doing it . . . had gotten up just the right amount on her tiptoes and mashed her lips to his. Oh, sweet relief. She'd wanted to do it for eight years. Of course, she'd only remembered wanting to do it for the last seventy-two hours, but forgetting hadn't made him less of the boy she'd pined after in college, the boy she'd followed to St. Olaf from Carleton College, the man she pined for now. She'd left a school to follow a football player, and had despised herself for it at the time, and ever since.

There was nothing to despise, now. He was good, he

was kind, he liked her, he didn't wince away in horror at what she was. So what if she had a few IQ points on him? What had that gotten her, exactly? An early grave, that's what.

His tongue eased past her lips and her good hand slid through his short hair, caressing the fine hairs at the back of his neck. His hand was under her shirt, stroking her bare back, and then she bit him.

Now he was the one up on his toes, trembling, and as his hot salty essence flooded her mouth the burning agony in her hand faded, faded, was a slight pain, was a negligible itch, was gone. She could hear him groaning, could feel him groping at her, and then her shirt was in shreds, and his was split down the middle, and they were dancing/ staggering out of the bathroom, toward the bed, pulling and tugging and biting and drinking and kissing.

Her back hit the bed and she disengaged, threw her head back and groaned at the ceiling. He leaned down and kissed the blood from her fangs and she nipped him again, gently, and sucked on his upper lip, and then he was tearing her cotton shorts down the middle, ripping her panties away, and she got the fly of his jeans open, got them partway down his hips, burrowed past his Jockeys and got hold of his cock—oh, warmth, warmth, hot stiff warmth and he wanted her so badly he was shaking with it and she could have wept with sheer gratitude, but instead she arched toward him, locked her ankles around his back, and when he came in for the stroke she bit him again, on the other side of his neck.

He hissed, but not in pain.

He was so warm, it was like being fucked by an electric blanket, except infinitely sexier, and she came at once, with fresh blood in her mouth and that hot hard part of him digging into her, pushing, stroking, shoving.

She shoved back and he groaned and gently slid his palm over her nipple, then gripped her breast, hard, and bent, and pulled the stiff peak into his mouth, and bit her. She was swallowing and licking the blood from her fangs and came again when his warm mouth closed over her, when his teeth nipped her tender flesh. She grabbed the bedspread and heard it rip beneath her groping fingers.

"Daniel," she called, wild with wanting and fear that she was hurting him, he was mortal, he was fragile, he—he was coming inside her, she could feel her temperature change as he filled her up.

"Andy," he managed.

"Don't—call me—that—"

"Andy," he said again, and dropped his head to her shoulder, and was insensible for half an hour.

"DAMN!" he said when he regained consciousness. "You are a *demon* in the sack! You've, like, ruined me for live girls forever."

"Eww, don't say it like that," she said. "And get off me, will you?"

"Oh, right. Sorry." He rolled to his side. "Cripes, you're squashed right into the mattress. I must have been crushing you—how long was I out?"

"It's no big deal. It's not like I had to breathe." Actually, she had spent that half an hour stroking his hair and listening to his long and even breaths, listening to his pulse, wondering at the thud-thud-thud thundering in her ears, and thinking maybe, just maybe her life hadn't gone into the shitter after all.

She had no idea vampires could have sex—well, she'd imagined they *could,* they had all the right equipment, but she hadn't thought it would be like flying, like soaring above the clouds, like—like being alive. It was—traitorous thought!—better than drinking blood.

"Are you all right? Not too shaky or anything? I'm afraid I might have gotten carried away."

"No chance, sugar, check this." He bounded up, then did half a dozen jumping jacks. She watched his penis bob around energetically and fought a grin. "I feel like a million bucks! I feel like I could go clubbing all night long! Want to?"

"Dead girls don't dance," she laughed.

He pounced on her and nuzzled her cleavage. "Fine, be a grump . . . how about you? How's the hand?"

She flexed it for him.

"Niiiiice," he said, gently stroking the unblemished skin. "I'll be taking full credit for that, by the way. My kick-ass blood and mighty dick were just the curative powers you needed."

"I'm about three seconds from putting you through the window," she said, smiling. "I don't think there's enough room on this bed for you, me, and your overly satisfied male ego."

"We'll *make* room, bay-bee!" He gave her a hearty smack on the mouth. "Ummm . . ." He busied himself with her mouth for a minute and she kissed him back, thinking about flying, thinking about being alive, when he pulled back and said, "How about you? Did you like it? I know it's been a while and you were kind of freaking out about it . . . Jeez, like—sorry," he added, seeing her flinch. "I keep forgetting."

"It's not your fault. And it was wonderful. Really very wonderful. Thanks for letting me feed."

"Oh, baby, if I get laid when you feed, then slap a sign on my ass and call me a buffet."

She started giggling and couldn't stop. He bounded into

the bathroom and she heard him yell, "Check this! All my bite marks have totally healed!"

"I think there's an enzyme or something in a vampire bite," she called after him. "It promotes fast healing."

"Well, Jeez, that's the coolest—sorry." He came out, looking at her curiously. "What's it like?"

"What? Watching you preen? Stupefying."

"No, when I say something about G—uh, the Big Guy. I mean, I know what it's like when something from that neighborhood touches you—" He shuddered. "And I never want to see it again. Or hear it! You screamed like you were—"

"On fire?" she suggested dryly.

"But what's it like for you, just hearing the name or whatever?"

"It makes me feel like throwing up," she said simply. "Like my stomach has turned inside out and I'm going to vomit or die or both. It's—it's awful."

"Oh. Well, I'll try really really hard to curb the taking of the Big Guy's name in vain."

"You won't have to worry about it much longer," she pointed out, though her stomach turned inside out—and he hadn't even cursed!—at the thought. "We're almost there. Drop me off and away you go."

"No," he said stubbornly. "That wasn't the deal. I'm taking you to see this badass vampire queen, *that* was the deal."

"Mmmmm."

"Don't grunt at me, missy. And don't be thinking about ditching me, either."

"Wouldn't dream of it. But Daniel, have you really considered this? Not all vampires are like me, you know."

"Cripes, I hope not." He was examining his shredded clothing and scowling at her.

"No, I mean it. Comparably speaking, I'm a pussycat.

Most vampires are much, much worse." She shivered. "The ones that killed me, for example. Minnesota nice, my ass."

"For crying out loud, Andy, did you, like, *eat* my jeans?" He tossed the ruined clothes toward the garbage can. "Have you ever met any? Bad vampires, I mean? Since you've been one?"

"I ran into one or two while I was passing through, but they didn't have anything to do with me. I wasn't really fit for adult conversation at the time," she admitted. "Too young. One of them tried to help me but I ran away from him. He was . . ." Terrifying. All height and dark flashing eyes and power, such a sense of power! He wore it like he wore the expensive clothes. And his eyes . . . she knew if she stayed a second longer she wouldn't be able to refuse him, so she'd fled. He'd been kind ("What is your name?") and concerned ("How old are you?") but he'd been too strong ("Stay a minute.") and she couldn't abide being near him, not for another minute, another second. And he'd let her go. She'd been as relieved as she'd been disappointed. "Anyway. Most of them are bad. And the queen . . . the new queen . . . she'll be the worst of us all."

"How come?"

"Because the vampire she defeated—Nostro—was really *really* bad."

"Really really bad?" he teased.

She shook her head at him, unsmiling. "I don't have words to explain it to you, to make you understand how bad. And he was in power for hundreds of years, and with vampires, the older you are, the more power you gain. He was considered completely unstoppable, for centuries.

"And she killed him, Daniel. She just—just woke up one night and killed him and took his seat of power and there was nothing more to be done. No warning, no formal declaration of challenges, nothing. It was like she rose one day and said, 'I think I'll kill the old vampire king,' and then it was done.

"And to do that, she had to be more powerful and more wicked and—and—" She paused, remembering something she'd heard, a scrap on the wind, a whisper. "They call her Elizabeth, the One. The most powerful vampire in two thousand years. And she's fated to rule at least two thousand more."

"Wow," he said respectfully.

"So I *strongly* urge you to reconsider this notion you've gotten about—"

"No."

"Idiot," she muttered.

"Ah, but I'm *your* idiot, bay-bee. And howcum you don't reconsider?"

"What do you mean?"

"Why go see this Liz the One at all? Let's hang out, have some more fun."

She blinked, caught completely flat-footed by his offer. "That's a nice . . . a wonderful offer . . . but this is something I have to do. It's like her name is in my head, all the time. Like she's calling me to her." She shuddered. "I imagine there's thousands of us on the way to Minnesota these days."

"Talk about a creep-out. Come take a shower with me."

"Why?"

He made an exasperated sound. "Because."

"We're wasting valuable driving time."

"We've got the whole damn night, and just half an hour to go."

"Fine," she grumbled, and rose from the bed, but secretly she was glad; glad to keep half an hour between her and the queen.

Chapter 10

❧

THE shower was delightful. She'd forgotten. Daniel was all slippery hands and long limbs and broad pecs and the water beat down on them and then he kissed her and one thing led to another and he was bleeding again—

"S-sorry."

"Shut up," he groaned, "and move a bit to your left."

—and then they were writhing together beneath the spray, and at the height of her pleasure she grabbed the shower curtain, which let go with a *pok-pok-pokking* sound and tumbled her onto the bath mat.

"Wow," Daniel panted, peering down at her. "Just like the shower scene from *Psycho*. Except a lot sexier."

"Help me up, you idiot," she said, hardly able to speak, she was laughing so hard.

"As soon as I can take a step without falling on my ass,

I'm all yours." Moving like an old man, he turned and shut the water off, then settled into the tub with a sigh. "Damn!"

"I have to say, if I was going to break the no-shower barrier, that was the way to do it."

"Anybody ever tell you you're really . . . uh . . . flexible? Like, Olympic gymnast flexible?"

"Not in the last few hours. You should see what I could do if we filled that tub."

"Eh? What could you do?"

She sat up and tweaked his ear—playfully, she thought, but he yelped and jerked away. "Oh, sorry, forgot my own strength. Anyway, I don't have to breathe, remember? One time I was in a mood—"

"You? Naw!"

"—and instead of hiding underground I spent the day in the middle of Lake Michigan, just walking around on the bottom. Did you know there are muskies bigger than me down there?"

"That's the saddest, and creepiest, thing I've ever heard."

"Oh, it's not so bad. Anyway, my point is, think of the fun we could have in a hot tub!"

He didn't say anything, so she stood, shook herself, grabbed a towel, and started blotting herself dry. "Well, I suppose we should check out and hit the road. No time like the present, let's get the show on the road, pick your cliché—Daniel?"

"I sort of locked up when you said hot tub," he admitted, shaking his head like a dog. "Damn! Okay, we have to find one right now."

"Forget it," she giggled. "We have to get going. We've pissed away enough time tonight already."

"Rain check," he said grimly.

"Fine, fine." *If we live through the night, I'll do you in a public fountain if that's your pleasure.* "Now let's get dressed and get out of here."

"Sure thing, Nancy Drew!" he said enthusiastically, climbing out of the tub on rubbery knees. "Lucky for you I've got more clean clothes. Try to resist your unholy urge to shred them or eat them or whatever you've been doing to my jeans."

"I'll try," she said solemnly, and shrieked as he smacked her bare ass on the way past.

MINNEAPOLIS, MINNESOTA
WAREHOUSE DISTRICT

"STAAAWWWWWPPPPPP!" Andrea screamed, and Daniel stood on the brakes again.

"This—is—very—bad—for—my—car—" he managed through gritted teeth as his Intrepid narrowly avoided crashing through a wooden fence.

"I'm sorry, I just saw it out of the corner of my eye . . ." She was out of her Daniel-mandated seat belt in a flash and standing beside the car, staring at the building. "Will you look at that?"

Daniel climbed out, panting from the adrenaline surge, and leaned against the car. "Look at what? It's an old building. News flash, dead girl, we're in the warehouse district."

"You can't see that?" She knew he couldn't smell it, but how could he not see it? The letters were a foot high.

"See what?"

She pointed. "It says 'Private Library; Patrons Welcome.' "

"Uh . . . says it where, exactly?"

"There. Right *there*. The letters are a foot high and they're written in dried blood. In fact, that's interesting in and of itself . . . how do they keep it from wearing off? Washing off in the rain? Crawling with bugs?"

"Who the hell cares? It doesn't have anything to do with—oh, shit," he added, falling into step beside her. "You really are Nancy Drew. Why check this out?"

"I've never seen a welcoming sign in blood before. Maybe—" She looked at him doubtfully. "Maybe you—"

"No *way*."

"Okay, okay, it was just a suggestion. A logical suggestion from a vastly superior intellect, but ignore me, see if I care."

"Well, I will."

"And stay behind me."

"Pass!" His hand clamped firmly over her elbow. "Man oh man, like this area of town wasn't creepy enough without vampire buildings."

She paused outside the door, which looked like it was hanging on only one set of hinges, tapped, then watched in amazement as the door straightened, settled, and slowly swung open.

"Eeeeeeeeennnnnnnnnnnnnhhhhhhh," Daniel creaked.

"Hush up!" she hissed. "This is creepy enough without your sound track."

They both stepped inside, expecting a dusty warehouse. Instead, they saw shelves and shelves of books, low lighting, a hardwood floor gleaming mellowly from countless applications of wax. The place smelled like old paper, wax, and coffee.

Daniel whistled. "This place is bigger than the libe at the U of M."

"Of course it is," someone said from their left, and they both jumped.

"Sorry," the woman said. "I thought at least one of you could hear me coming."

Daniel and Andrea stared at her in frank wonder. She looked like someone's mother . . . her chocolate-brown hair was streaked with gray, and her brown eyes were bracketed with laugh lines. She stood straight and erect in her dark blue suit, frothy white blouse, tan panty hose, and sensible shoes. She was very pale, but the lightest touches of makeup on her face served only to play up her features, not make her unusual coloring stand out.

"Welcome to the library," she was saying. "I'm Marjorie, the head librarian. How can I help you, Andrea?"

Daniel gasped and his fingers sank into her elbow like claws.

"Ouch!"

"Andy, she knows your name!" he hissed in her ear. "Let's get the hell out of here!"

"I'm standing right here, dear," Marjorie said dryly.

Andrea plucked Daniel's hand off her elbow. "I'm sorry, I've never been here before, how do you know my name?"

"You have been here, dear," Marjorie said, looking at her with something like compassion. "You just don't remember. When Nostro's followers finished with you, you and the other girls were brought here for cataloging."

"Say *what?*" Daniel growled.

"We took fingerprints, DNA samples, everything. In case you survived your first decade and found your way back here, we could tell you who you were. Had been," she corrected herself. "Of course, the other girls never rose, poor things, and you wasted no time leaving town. We tried to talk to you, but . . ." Marjorie shook her head.

"But . . . I don't remember any of that! I thought I'd been buried, or—"

"You assumed you had been. But those who die at the hands of a vampire are brought here when it's at all possible. Of course, in the first place very few of them come back, and in the second, there's little we can do to help them, but when they *do* return we have their credit cards, their check-books—we keep all those accounts open, we help you hang on to your house—or sell it, if that's your wish—in fact, ku-dos, Ms. Mercer! You're about three and a half years ahead of schedule. And showing up with a sheep, of all things!"

"A what?" they said in unison.

"Oh. Ah. Pardon me." Marjorie coughed into her fist, a dry sound like a bullet. "I assumed . . . I assumed you were keeping this nice young man for feeding."

"Well, she isn't. I'm her driver, so there," Daniel snapped. "Anything else going on is between two consent-ing adults."

"Yes, of course."

Andrea was rolling her eyes. "Daniel, could you not pick a fight with the first vampire we meet?"

He ignored her. "*And* I want to know about the fucks who killed her. What happened to them?"

"Well . . . nothing, at the time. Nostro was still in power. But now that Elizabeth, the One, has taken the throne, things will change. Three of them, in fact, died defending Nostro's throne." Marjorie smiled. It was kind of terrify-ing, like watching winter grin. "Too bad, so sad."

"Awwwwwww," Andrea said, feeling for the first time in a long while like it was her birthday.

"As to the others, you could certainly take your griev-ance to Her Majesty. You have considerable cause. What they did to you . . ." She shook her head. "Shameful. *No* excuse. We're not animals."

"Well, thanks, but I'm a little new around here to ask the queen to solve my problems. I'm—"

"*We're.*"

"—just here to pay tribute. We stopped when we saw your sign."

"I'm flattered!" Marjorie actually clapped her hands. "And you have no idea how much good it does this old lady to see you in such control of your faculties. Why, you could be fifty years old!"

"Really?" she said, thrilled. "That's so nice of you."

"And to think you came to see the library when you have pressing business with the queen."

"What's—uh—what's she like?"

Marjorie fixed her with a paralyzing stare. "She is unlike any vampire sovereign I have ever seen, and I have lived through three."

Out of the corner of her eye, Andrea could see Daniel mouthing numbers and counting on his fingers.

"I'm eight hundred sixty-eight years old, dear," Marjorie said. "If you were wondering."

"Are you *shitting?*"

Andrea elbowed him sharply in the side. "But—Marjorie—why aren't *you* the queen?" She could get behind a queen—a scholar—like Marjorie.

Marjorie made a face like she smelled something bad. "Ech! Not hardly. This," she said, her hand indicating the huge library, "is my passion. I'd rather eat a garlic sandwich than run the world. Can you imagine the headaches? The paperwork? The hostess duties?" The ancient scholar actually shivered.

"Oh. Um, do you know where we can find the new queen?"

"Certainly. Nostro's holdings now belong to her—that law is a thousand years old—and his old properties are out on the edge of Lake Minnetonka. I'll get you a map."

She clacked away in her sensible shoes and Daniel let out a breath. "That nice middle-aged lady is older than America? Shit!"

"Much older, and be nice. She could have ripped both our heads off and used them for bookends."

"Yeah, well, she might be super decrepit, but I'm still—aagggghhh!"

"Here you are, dear," Marjorie said, coming around—somehow—from behind them. "I've marked the queen's territories in red. You should have no—well," she added, fixing her gaze on Andrea, "*you* should have no trouble."

"Thank you very much, ma'am."

"Feel free to poke about in the stacks before you leave—hardly anybody ever comes here to *read*," she said with a disapproving sniff.

"Wh-what do they come for?" Daniel managed.

"Maps."

"Oh. That's a toughie, Marjie."

She fixed him with a forbidding look. "Marjorie. And thank you for your sympathy, shee—Daniel."

"Thanks again," Andrea said. "I'll be back, if the queen doesn't kill me. I love libraries."

"You're welcome here any time. As to the other matter . . ." Marjorie made a vague gesture and clacked off.

"What's that supposed to mean?" Daniel whispered in her ear.

"Don't do that, it tickles. And I guess it means I'm supposed to find out for myself. Come on, let's look me up in here."

They found the *M*s after a few minutes. The library was a peculiar combination of the old card catalog system, and up-to-date computer files. They found a card which simply read, Mercer, Andrea. DOB 07/29/76; DOD 07/29/97.

"Oh, that sucks!" Daniel cried. "They killed you on your birthday?"

"My twenty-first birthday," she added thoughtfully. "Must have needed people that exact age for his dumb ceremony. Barely drinking age forever . . . oh, the humanity!"

"You're in a weirdly good mood," he muttered, jumping at small noises—who knew when Marjorie would appear out of nowhere again?

"I like libraries." She took the card with her name on it and inserted it into the slot in the computer. Instantly information about her began to scroll down the screen . . . there was her old house, there was her high school, her parents' names and occupations, her grandparents . . . there were her college transcripts, including her transfer paperwork to St. Olaf . . . there was her credit report, there was her bank account . . . "Huh. Would you look at that?"

"It's creepy, is what it is. Creepy dead librarians keeping track of your whole life, lurking here waiting for you to come back . . . yech!"

"It's a pretty logical system, actually—what the hell?"

"What, what?"

She froze the screen. Under Affiliations, there was a single name: Sinclair.

"What's a Sinclair?"

"I have no idea. I don't affiliate with any vampires."

"Shit, you barely affiliate with me."

"I wish we could cross-reference my file with Sinclair's to find the—whoa." The computer unfroze and started to do exactly that. In a few seconds, they were staring at the screen, which read:

04/06/00. His Majesty King Sinclair, passing through Des Moines on business. See transcript.

"Let's see it," she ordered.

Instantly a dark, slightly amused voice came out of the

computer. "I was passing through town—this was a couple of years before I became Elizabeth's consort—and back-trailed a young vampire. It was a chilly night; I thought she might need a hand. She was *very* young; I doubt she knew her own name at the time. She was afraid and wouldn't come with me. I made a few attempts and left her to her own devices. See if her description matches anyone in your files: about five foot six, shoulder-length brown hair, brown eyes, pale coloring—hereditary, not as a condition of being dead—slender, no tattoos or birthmarks that I could see, but she had a beauty mark high on her left cheek. Transmission ends."

"Holy shit," Daniel said, poking her beauty mark. "You met up with the king of the dead guys!"

"I remember him, too," she said faintly. "I was too scared to talk to him. I'm not surprised he's Elizabeth's consort. Still, it was nice of him to try to help me."

Daniel snorted. "He barely tried and gave you up as a bad job quick enough."

"It's not really in a vampire's nature to help another vampire," she explained. "For him, for what he was, he went above and beyond, believe me."

"Well, d'you want to look up more toothy dead guys, or finish what we came to do?"

She was tempted to remain in the library—to sleep in the library!—but Daniel was right, they were just postponing the inevitable. She had no desire to look up Elizabeth's file—for one thing, it was probably forbidden, and for another, why find out more information that was just going to scare her? And she had no wish to look up Nostro's file, since he was dead and gone.

"Elizabeth must be a thousand years old," Andrea muttered. "Maybe more."

Daniel puffed out his chest. "Well, she's no match for the baby and the sheep, tell you that right now."

Andrea had to smile. "Still got that map?"

"No, in the three minutes since Marjie gave it to me, I've managed to lose it. Yes, I've got the damned map."

"All right, then. Let's go find the queen."

Chapter 11

⁘

"THIS place is so totally creepy," Daniel commented, his hand firmly in the center of her back as they moved through the ankle-high grass of the lawn. "I feel like Shaggy on *Scooby-Doo*."

"The resemblance," she agreed, "is remarkable."

"Man, if you hadn't told me a ton of badass vampires lived here, I'd have totally figured it out on my own."

"Sure you would have. Stay close."

"Don't worry, Andy. Anything comes shooting out of the dark, I'll kick their ass."

"Don't call me that. And if anything comes out of the dark, you get down and you stay down and you let me handle it, do you understand?"

"Sure. Not too lame," he muttered.

She could hear a chain-link fence rattling and, after a

moment's effort, could see it, barely illuminated by the cold sliver of the moon. "There. That way."

"*What* way?" he complained, stumbling beside her. "It's darker than a woodchuck's asshole out here."

"Never mind. I can see."

"What, you've got flashlights for eyes now? Is that, like, a vampire power?"

"Daniel, *hush up.*" To her left, she heard a low, feral growl, and stopped suddenly. Another to her right.

"What?" His voice seemed very loud in the night air; booming. "What's the matter? Change your mind? Because we could be back in Chicago in—"

"*Shhhhh.*"

Another, flanking them . . . no, two of them. No, three. Shit. She didn't worry for herself—what did she care if she was ripped to pieces? But Daniel was easy meat. She wasn't about to stand and watch one of these things eat his dear face.

She heard them coil to charge and jerked him behind her ("Hey!") and got ready. She felt her fangs come out; part of her was always ready for a fight, *welcomed* a fight, and that was the true tragedy of her condition.

She could see their attackers now, scrambling toward them on all fours, but they weren't wild dogs, as she had first thought. Or even wolves. They were too big, too long-limbed, too . . . pale?

They were . . . they were *people.*

She could smell their breath; old blood, and death. She could see their eyes; devil's eyes, all black, like pits, but far down, sullen red light . . . their pupils? Their pupils were red? She could see their fur—hair, rather—long and falling to their shoulders in greasy clots. She could—

"Hey! Stop! Quit it, you guys! *Bad* fiends. Baaaaaad fiends!"

Blinking, she saw a tall blond woman stumbling after the—the whatever-they-were. The woman's progress was impeded by her footgear . . . ridiculously high heels in electric blue, with white toes. She was wearing a black skirt and a black double-breasted jacket, sleeveless. Her arms were slender; the wrists tiny, barely two inches across. Odd, on such a tall woman. Her hair was light blond and curled under at the ends, framing an attractive face with high cheekbones. Her eyes were bright green. Andrea had never seen such green eyes before.

There was a gold cross nestled in the hollow of the woman's throat; it made her slightly sick to look at it.

Perhaps oddest of all: the things were listening to the woman.

"Bad, bad, bad!" she was saying as she neared them. The things cowered and whimpered but kept their distance. "You guys! Gross! I mean, just stop it now! You just had, like, ten buckets of blood apiece, how could you possibly be hungry? Bad!" She turned to Andrea and Daniel, and covered her eyes with her hands. Her nails were beautifully French manicured, Andrea saw, and the fingers were long and slender. No rings. "This is, like, *so* embarrassing. I'm not with these fiends, you know. I mean, I'm *with* them, but I'm not *with* them with them, y'know?"

"Sure," Daniel said, which was a relief, because Andrea was completely mystified. It's like the woman was speaking another language. One Daniel could understand! Thank goodness she'd brought her own interpreter.

"Like, just really gross-out, you know?"

"Totally," Daniel said.

"*Thank* you! Usually people don't get it, but it's just . . . yech!"

"Not to mention massively bogus 'n' stuff."

"I *know!*" The blonde shook her head and rested her

hands on her hips. "So, what brings you guys to Hell's Acre? In case you missed the memo, it's so *totally* dangerous out here. Probably looking for a nice place to make out but this is so *not* it. I hate to be a hardass, but I'm really gonna have to ask you to leave."

"Hel*lo*," Daniel muttered. It was obvious his eyes had finally adjusted to the dark . . . while remaining oblivious of the danger. "Babe alert."

"Down boy," Andrea muttered. Louder, she said, "We'll be glad to go, miss, but we can't just yet. We're in town for— never mind. Thanks for helping us. Are these your . . . ah . . ."

"They're mine, all right," the woman said grimly. "Unfortunately. Don't get me started. I mean, yech! We try to keep them clean, but they're like puppies . . . they roll in *everything*."

"Sure," Andrea said, humoring the woman. Puppies. Undeniably evil puppies with foul dispositions and the appetites of rabid, starving tigers. All righty. "Well, thanks for calling them off. Listen, this might sound kind of weird, and I promise we're not crazy, but we're looking for a vampire."

"Oh, yeah?" she said, totally unfazed. "Which one?"

"Well, the, uh, the queen. Of the vampires."

"Whyyyyyyyy?" the blonde whined. "I mean, you've got nothing better to do with your time? What do you want?"

The blonde was weirdly unfazed by this . . . maybe she was a what-do-you-call-it, a sheep. Before Andrea could answer, Daniel was bulling in.

"Well, *she's* here to pay her respects n' all, and I'm here to kick the queen's ass if she tries to do anything to my girl."

"Oh."

"Daniel!"

The blonde snickered. "Well, the queen is me, and I don't want to kick anybody's ass."

"Don't be ridiculous," Andrea snapped, her nerves almost at the breaking point. "You're not a vampire."

"Am, too!"

"You certainly are not."

"I am, too!"

"Oh, now just stop it! You can't be a vampire, and you certainly aren't an all-powerful queen. For one thing—" Andrea pointed triumphantly. "You're wearing a cross."

"Oh, that." She shrugged. "It was a present from El Jerko, aka Eric Sinclair."

"Eric Sinclair? As in *the* Sinclair?"

"Guy gets around," Daniel muttered, then gasped as a fiend licked his hand with her cold tongue. "Uh . . . nice kitty. Go away."

Andrea, puzzled, said, "But Eric's the consort of—"

"Let's not talk about it," the blonde said thinly. "Look, you're just going to have to take my word for it: I'm a vampire. The—uh—the queen." She choked back a giggle. "Believe me, I know how it sounds."

"This isn't fair!" Andrea wailed. "I come all this way—I was scared, but I came anyway—and you won't take me to the queen! You're just playing games!"

"Look, babe, do I have to write it on my forehead? *I'm the queen.* I sicced these guys . . ." Indicating the fiends. ". . . on Nostro. They had him for lunch. I didn't *know* that by doing that I'd end up the queen; I thought I was just saving my friends. Now I'm stuck with this fucking crown and that sneak, Sinclair, and frankly, I'm pretty pissed off about it!" She was shaking her perfectly manicured finger in Andrea's face, while Andrea was trying not to vomit from being so close to the woman's cross. "So believe me or don't, but either way, get lost!"

"Perhaps I can be of some assistance?"

"Aaaaagggghhhhhh!" all three of them howled in unison.

Andrea literally couldn't speak, and Daniel was busy sucking gasps of oxygen into his lungs. So only the woman whirled on the darkness that had approached them. "God *damn* it, Sinclair! Stop doing that! And stop following me, it's so fucking creepy and you *know* I can't stand it!"

"Good evening to you, too, Elizabeth. Away, fiends," he said, snapping his fingers, and the poor things scattered.

"My heart," Daniel muttered, "is not having a good day."

"I do apologize," Sinclair said smoothly. "I didn't mean to startle you. Elizabeth, aren't you going to introduce me to your—" He saw Andrea and his black eyes narrowed. "You. Iowa?"

"Yes, we ran across each other there, sir," she said faintly. It made her extremely nervous to be chitchatting with the king. He was just as terrifying, just as powerful, just as frighteningly polite as he had been that long-ago snowy night. He was, in fact, everything Elizabeth, the One, was not.

"You seem better now. In fact, you're a couple of years ahead of schedule." He carelessly turned his back on her. "Why are you here, Elizabeth? We have staff to take care of the grounds. If you won't live here, why can't you stay away?"

"If you won't fuck off and die, why do you keep bugging me?" she snapped back. Andrea was filled with admiration: the woman seemed more irritated than terrified. "These guys are here to pay homage to the—" She gnashed her teeth and finally spat it out. "The *queen,* but they didn't believe me when I told 'em—"

"We believe you now," Daniel and Andrea chorused.

"Oh. What gave it away? My innate royalness? My fabulous highlights? My shoes, did you see my shoes?" She propped one of her feet up on its heel, showing off her slender ankle. "Aren't they cute? I knew if Kate Spade put her mind to it she could do decent pumps."

"Actually," Daniel said, jerking a thumb toward Sinclair, who looked gratified, "it was him."

"Welllllll, isn't that *great.*" Elizabeth, the One, scowled at them, then whirled on Sinclair. "Dammit! You told me this was going to stop eventually! It's like some sort of twisted *The Incredible Journey*, except with dead people instead of animals." She turned back to Andrea and Daniel. "Why, why, *why* do you all have to be so dumb and dependent? Can't you just migrate somewhere else? Like to North Dakota, or the Antarctic Ocean?"

Daniel snickered and poked Andrea. "Queen says you're dumb."

"Shut up, sheep," she muttered. Then, louder, "But you—you've been calling me!"

"Nuh-uh!"

Sinclair ahem'ed. "It's a function of your power as sovereign," he explained. "You probably *have* been calling them. Her. And the others who have been—"

"Well, shit!"

"Yup," Daniel said.

The queen frowned. "What do you want, anyway?"

"N-nothing," Andrea managed. "Just to see you. To make myself—"

"Us," Daniel corrected firmly.

"—known to you."

"Well, that's nice and all, but you sure didn't have to come all this way just to see me. Ever heard of e-mail?"

Daniel laughed, and the queen smirked as he exclaimed, "Don't even tell me we could have avoided this whole trip!"

"Okay, I won't tell you, but you could have. What's your name?"

"Baaaaaaaaa," Daniel said.

Andrea smacked his arm. "Very funny. I'm Andrea Mercer, and this is my friend, Daniel Harris." She shook the queen's—the queen's!—hand. "It's very nice to meet Your Majesty."

"Betsy, for the love of God. Sorry," she added, seeing Andrea flinch and Sinclair wince. "I keep forgetting."

"Hey, I do that all the time, too! Whoa." Daniel made the time-out sign. "You can swear? And wear crosses?"

"Uh-huh. Don't ask me why."

"Okay, I won't, but then you can't get mad at people when they don't think you're a vampire."

"Can, too! If I'm the queen I figure I can do whatever the heck I want, so there. Although I have to say it's nice to meet a vampire who has a sense of humor—"

"He's not a vampire," Sinclair and Andrea said in unison.

"Oh. My bad. I usually can't tell until they jump on me and start chewing, anyway."

"You mean vampires attack the queen of the vampires because they don't know you're a vampire?"

"My life," she sighed, "in a nutshell."

"And he's not my sheep, either," Andrea blurted out, glaring at Sinclair, who was looking entirely too smug. "He's—he's my—"

"Hot love monkey," Daniel supplied helpfully.

Andrea buried her face in her hands. "Anyway," she said to her fingers, "if Your Majesty doesn't require anything of me at this time—"

"Go hit a Dairy Queen, have a shake, go crazy," Betsy said carelessly. "Have fun with your love monkey."

"As long as we're on the subject of hot monkey love," Sinclair began.

"Forget it, pal! The last time I got naked with *you,* I got stuck with a crown. And *you.* I'd rather have gotten a hemorrhoid!"

Andrea grabbed Daniel's elbow and began to slowly lead him away. "Well . . . we'll be going, then . . ."

"Ah, Elizabeth, you really should succumb to the inevitable."

"How about if instead I set your shoes on fire!"

"You wouldn't: they're Kenneth Coles."

"Nice meeting you!" Daniel called.

Faintly, the queen: "I didn't ask you to come out here, FYI."

"Ah, my queen, you know I can't stay away."

Louder, the queen: "Well, you better!"

"Good-bye!" Andrea yelled and, holding hands, they ran to the car.

"What's the rush?" Daniel gasped, keeping stride.

"Do you want to be around if they start throwing punches?"

He picked her up and ran the rest of the way.

Chapter 12

⁂

"So now what?" Daniel asked. They were in yet another anonymous hotel room, this one the downtown Minneapolis Marriott. Andrea had to admit it was much nicer than the others. "Do we stay? Do we go back to Chicago? Do we keep driving west, running from the rising sun? What?"

"I don't know. I—I didn't expect to still be alive. Or in charge of my own destiny. I thought she'd kill me or enslave me."

Daniel snorted. "Her? The only thing she'd enslave is a pair of high heels. She was cute, though. Really cute. If you like 'em annoying, flighty, and fashion-obsessed."

"Which you do," she said thinly.

He tackled her, bringing her to the bed. "Nope. Used to like 'em that way." He nuzzled her nose. "Now I like them stuck-up and brainy and on a liquid diet."

"Daniel, that's so—"

"And the dude with her! Cripes! It was like the devil showed up in her backyard!"

"Tell me."

"No wonder you got the hell away from him when you were still a drooling baby vamp."

"Yes, rushing off while fueled by cowardice was one of my finest moments."

"Don't knock yourself, Andy. He was scary. I don't know how she's gonna keep him in line."

"Oh, that's obvious enough." For some delightful reason, Daniel was nuzzling her earlobe. She'd thought, once his obligation had been discharged, he'd be long gone. It was odd that he was lingering, but nice. "Did you see how he looked at her? He loves her. And not like a subject loves a queen, I think."

"Mmmph."

"Stop it, that tickles."

"Nuh-uh. I've got something else to tickle you with, by the way."

She laughed. "That's terrible!"

"So, look." He straightened up and propped his chin on his elbow. "You gonna ditch me?"

"I was sort of waiting for you to ditch me," she admitted.

"Because the way I see it, you can go to that weird library and reactivate all your accounts, your credit cards and stuff. And get a vampire-type job. So you don't really need me anymore."

"Such a lie."

"Right, but—what?"

"Daniel, you moron, I was never hanging around with you for the clothes from Target. You were the first person in six years to take an interest in me. Even when I was at my worst, you took everything I could dish out and you were always waiting for me the next night. You could have killed me anytime but you didn't. That's . . ." She started to sniffle, and sternly ordered herself to cut it out. "That's priceless to me."

He was frowning at her. "Let me get this straight. You're all goo-gooey about me because I didn't ditch you? Or kill you? Andy, you are *such* a weirdo."

"Yes, so they tell me."

"Well, I don't care if you don't need my money or if you want a big ring or whatever. I'm staying. I—I kind of love you."

"Kind of?" she teased.

"I told you, you ruined me for live girls."

"That's very . . . romantic."

"Of course, I'll get old and smelly and you'll always be young and cute, but we can fix that," he said cheerfully.

"Daniel, I'm not turning you into a vampire."

"Oh, sure you will. Not now . . . I'm still in my prime! Maybe in ten years."

"Daniel!"

"It'll be the coolest!"

"Daniel . . ."

"But first . . ." His hand was sliding up her shirt. "Aren't you just the tiniest bit thirsty . . . ?"

"Daniel, I'm *not—*"

"Okay, well, look, let's talk about it in ten years, okay?"

"It's more complicated than that," she said, pretending she wasn't overjoyed. It was amazing . . . she was getting everything she ever wanted, but she had to die first, and see a queen by way of a library. The world was strange. "You can't just decide to shack up with a vampire—"

"I was thinking more like marrying a vampire."

If she could have gasped, she would have. "Well, there are things you haven't considered—"

"Andy, will you please shut up and kiss me?"

"Okay," she warned, "but we're talking about this later. *In depth.*"

"You're so sexy when you're stern and lecturey."

LATER, after making love, she said, "I kind of love you, too."

"Yeah," he yawned. "I know."

"What, you know?" She kissed the bite mark on his neck. "How could you know?"

"Sweetie, you're smart and all, but some things, I just know." And he picked up their entwined hands, and kissed them.

ORIGINALLY HUMAN

Eileen Wilks

Chapter 1

❖

HELEN?

Too dignified. I've never been terribly dignified.

Rachel?

A pretty name . . . it didn't feel right, though. I wasn't in the mood for Rachel. I paused, digging my toes into the sand. Overhead the sky was clear, its black dome fuzzed by the lights ahead. Galveston isn't large, but tourists like a place that's lively at night. I do, too, but prefer to live outside the city proper.

Beside me the great, briny mother was in a quiet mood, her waves lapping at the sand like curled cats' tongues. That made me think of my neighbor, Mrs. Jenks—a nice woman, but with no talent for naming cats. She had three. The one she called Mona was a particular favorite of mine, sleek and black, who referred to herself as Wind-Who-

Leaves-the-Grasses-Silent. Quite a mouthful in English, I'll admit.

Well, what about Mona? A better name for a woman than a cat.

No, it was too close to Molly, which was my current name. I'd be forever signing checks wrong.

I sighed and started walking again. Walking in sand is good for the calf muscles. Doing it at night with the ocean whispering beside you is good for the soul.

I'll admit to being vain about my legs. Otherwise I'm on the nice side of average, with my weight holding steady at fashionable-plus-fifteen and a thoroughly Irish face, complete with freckles and a pug nose. More motherly than cute these days, I suppose; I let my hair go white several years ago. But my legs are still excellent.

Not that I was out walking for the sake of my muscle tone tonight. My calves were in better shape than my soul.

Self-pity is so wearing. Unattractive, too. Really, I needed to settle on a name. It was time to move on. Just last night Sam had commented again on how I never seemed to change.

Dear Sam. I sighed again. I would miss him. And several of the others, too, and Galveston itself. I loved the historic section and the view, breakfast at The Phoenix and seafood at Gaido's. I lived so close to the ocean that the salt-and-sea scent drifted in my window, and I could indulge in the private splendor of walking the beach at night. . . .

I was lucky, I reminded myself. Most women wouldn't feel safe alone on the beach at three in the morning. There have always been predators. But some would say that's what I am, too. I'm not easy to harm.

I'd reached the narrow road that divided the public beach from the RV park where I live. Not that the owners

call it an RV park, mind. It's a mobile-living village. That's
the name, in fact: Beachside Village. I suppose a touch of
pretension is inevitable if you want to charge such outland-
ish prices to rent a spot, and the location is wonderful—
outside the city proper, right on the ocean. I stepped onto
the soft asphalt, still warm from the summer sun.

There was a soft sound, sort of a *pop-whoosh!* And a
naked man lay at my feet. A beautiful, unconscious, *bleeding* naked man.

Oh, dear.

The air turned crisp and my hearing sharpened as those
trusty fight-or-flight chemicals did their thing. But there
was no one to fight—thank goodness—and I couldn't simply run away.

I do not need this, I told myself as I knelt on the soft,
tacky asphalt. My heart was galloping. I had no idea where
he had come from or how he'd arrived, but those slashes
across his chest, belly, and legs looked intentional. Someone did not like this man. I should head home immediately
and call 911.

I touched his throat, found a pulse, and exhaled in relief.
The moon was nearly full, and I have excellent night vision. He was a breathtaking man, with skin so pale the sun
might never have touched it. Pale everywhere, too, not just
in the usual places. His hair was short, very dark, and almost as curly as my own. His eyelashes were absurdly
long, giving him the look of a sleeping child . . . a look
quite at odds with one of the loveliest male bodies I've ever
seen. And I am something of a connoisseur of male bodies.

And the slashes on that lovely chest, flat stomach, and
muscular thighs were slowly closing. Blood barely oozed
now.

Whoever he was, he wasn't entirely human. Not as most
people counted such things, anyway. And though I loved

Texas, there was no denying most people here were not very tolerant of those of the Blood. Not that he was lupus or Faerie or anything else I recognized, but who else could heal a wound so quickly?

One of the Old Ones could.

I shivered and shut a mental door before a name could slip into my thoughts. No point in taking any chances of disturbing Their sleep. Besides, one of Them wouldn't be so poky about healing a few cuts. The bleeding had stopped, but the gashes remained, a couple quite deep—though not, thankfully, the one in his stomach.

One of Them could have made those cuts, though. And zapped Their victim here, or anywhere else They pleased. I did not need to be part of this. I'd call 911 and let them deal—

He opened his eyes.

They were silver in the moonlight, silver framed by a dark fringe of lashes. And so blank that I was sure there was no one home. The ache of that realization was sharp enough to surprise a small, sad "Oh" from me.

All at once he was *there,* his gaze focused and intent, latching on to mine as if I'd tossed him a lifeline. *"Ke hu räkken?"* he whispered.

I am so weak, I thought, annoyed. Long eyelashes and a body to die for, and I lose all sense. I wasn't going to call 911. "I do hope you speak English."

"Enn . . . glish." He repeated the word as if he were holding it in his mouth, testing it for familiarity. "Yes. I can speak . . . English. This is England?"

"No, this is Galveston Island. It's in Texas," I added when he looked blank. His accent was decidedly British—upper crust. "U.S.A.? Never mind. I'm going to help you, but I need to know who hurt you. And if they're likely to be close behind."

"Who . . ." A frown snapped down. He lifted a hand to his side, touched one of the wounds, winced. He looked at his hand, the gory fingertips. "I'm damaged."

"Yes, but not, I think, fatally. Though heaven knows I'm not a doctor. But a doctor would probably notify the police. You *were* attacked, weren't you?"

He nodded slowly. "Who . . ." he said again, then stopped, looking baffled. "I'm bleeding."

"Not as much as you were. Look, do you want me to call an ambulance?"

"Am . . . bulance. An emergency vehicle."

I nodded encouragingly. "Yes, you know—ambulances, doctors, nurses, the hospital, all that. They could take care of you there."

"No." He was suddenly decisive. "No hospital."

I sighed. "In that case, can you walk?"

He considered that briefly. "I think so."

"My motor home isn't far—you can see it from here, the Winnebago with the palm tree and the purple outbuilding. Oh, never mind. You can't see the color now, can you?" I was blithering, which annoyed me. "We need to get you out of sight. Someone might come along—an ordinary someone who would be startled by a naked, wounded man. Or the someone who attacked you. Will he, she, or it be able to follow you here?"

"I don't know."

Not much help. "Well, let's see if we can make it to my place. Please try to be quiet. Mr. Stanhope—he's my neighbor on the west—wakes up if anyone sneezes, and I'd just as soon not have to explain you."

He nodded. Looking as if the motion required every ounce of concentration he could summon, he shifted onto his side, braced himself awkwardly with his hands, and pushed into a sitting position.

He wobbled. I slipped an arm around him. "Dizzy?"

"Not . . . used to this. It hurts."

"I know. I'm sorry. Can you stand?"

"I will try."

Getting him vertical might have been funny if I'd been watching instead of participating. All those lovely muscles worked fine, but he was too woozy to know what to do with them. We did end up on our feet, though, with my arm around his waist where I wouldn't touch any of his wounds, and his feet set wide, like a toddler unsure of his balance.

He didn't feel like a toddler. A decided sexual buzz warmed me, and it wasn't entirely due to the hard male body pressed against my side. He fairly hummed with energy, some breed of magic I'd never encountered before.

He was also only about three inches taller than me, which was a surprise. Not only is everyone taller than I am these days, but he'd looked big lying down. I suppose it was something about the way he was proportioned—perfectly. And packed solid. Very solid. I'm stronger than I look, but if I had to support too much of his weight we might both end up on the ground.

I turned my head and looked into eyes only inches from mine. The skin around those eyes was tight and bleached. "You okay?"

"I'm unsure what okay means in this context. I can proceed. I want me out of sight, too."

"Let's do it."

A short chain-link fence runs all the way around the Village. Three years ago I persuaded management to let me put in a gate at my plot so I didn't have to go the long way around to get to the beach. By the time we reached that gate, neither of us was breathing normally.

He was in pain. I was aroused. "Not far now," I assured him. I was going to have to behave myself, that was all there was to it. I glanced at his face, taut and damp with sweat. He looked to be in his mid-to-late twenties—too young to think of me sexually unless I wanted him to.

Or got careless. I sighed. This was not going to be easy. "I don't have a thing you can wear."

He stared at me, offended. "I am trying . . . to breathe. And not bleed. You are . . . worried about clothing?"

I glanced down. The deep gash in his thigh had started oozing again, which wasn't surprising. I could see bone. "If we can get to the tree, you can lean against it while I get the door open."

He grunted. We lurched forward. Getting through the narrow gate was tricky, but we made it and I more or less propped him against the palm. He looked dreadful. A couple more gashes had started bleeding again, which probably meant he was losing control, perhaps close to passing out. He leaned against the trunk, eyes closed, chest heaving. "I liked . . . lying down better. You have a place . . . I can lie down?"

"You can have my bed. We just have to get you there." I hurried to the nearest door—which, with the way my Winnebago was parked, meant the driver's door. I didn't think he was up to trekking around to the other side.

He was going to make a mess of my leather seat, I thought sadly as I dug in the pocket of my shorts for my keyless remote.

The lock clicked before I punched it. I froze.

"What is it?" His voice was low, hoarse.

I turned slowly, my eyes searching the shadows. "Someone unlocked the door before I could."

"Oh." He sounded apologetic. "That might have been me. I am wishing very much to be inside."

"You aren't sure?" My voice may have been a little shrill.

"I'm not used to this place. The energies are different than . . . they're different." He paused. "Who are you, and why are you helping me?"

Suspicion would be natural, even healthy, under the circumstance. But he sounded more curious than wary. I opened the door, quickly shut off the dome light, and returned to him. "My name is Molly Brown. I'm helping you because you're hurt. Also," I admitted in a flash of honesty, "because I've been rather bored lately."

"You are curious about me." Some fugitive emotion roughened his voice. Disgust? Satisfaction?

"Very. I'll save most of my questions until I get you inside, but—"

"I can't answer your questions."

"You'll have to, if you want my help."

"I cannot," he said hollowly.

The despair in his voice tugged at me. I fought to hold firm against it. "I don't want your life history, but I do need to know who you are, where you came from, who's after you and why."

"I don't know."

"You don't know who tried to kill you?"

"I don't know any of it."

I believed him. I'm a fool sometimes, the same as everyone else, but I believed the crushed bewilderment in his voice. I didn't say anything more, just slid my arm around his waist again.

"You will help anyway?" That was hope I heard now— and oh, how painful hope can be, in all its uncertainty.

"Looks like." I sighed over my folly and and supported him the last few feet to my home.

Chapter 2

⁓

WE got him up the step and into the driver's seat, where he discovered that he liked sitting better than standing, too. But he'd be visible up there, not to mention difficult to work on, so we heaved him onto his feet again and staggered together into my little bedroom, where he fell on the bed and promptly passed out.

I stood there getting my breath back, and not due to unrequited lust this time. He was heavy. Then I tossed a blanket over him, grabbed a smudging stick and the bucket I kept under the sink, and headed back out. He'd left a good deal of blood on the road. He'd probably also left various magical traces. I wouldn't be able to get rid of all the blood or other traces, but I could make them less conspicuous.

Twenty minutes later I'd washed most of the blood off the asphalt and tossed dirt on top of what remained to disguise it. I'd smudged all the way around my little lot, quietly calling up what protections I knew. I'm not Gifted, but there are some things even the magic-blind can do, and the sage I used had been prepared and blessed by a Wiccan High Priestess.

I couldn't help feeling like the little piggy in the straw house, though. I suspected that whoever—whatever?—had clawed up my guest could blow away my puny protections with one big, bad huff.

He was still out cold when I came back in, poor boy. I hated to wake him, but, magic or no magic, those wounds had to be cleaned. He needed fluids, too. But maybe I should call Erin first—my Wiccan friend. I was going to need help. No, better wait until I knew who or what I was dealing with. I needed answers. Or maybe—

Stop it! I told myself sternly. But the body sometimes reveals what we'd rather not know. The hand I lifted to rub my forehead was unsteady, and my insides were gripped by a fine vibration, like a dry leaf aquiver in the wind just before it quits its home on the tree.

Why was I doing this? For all I knew, the unconscious man in my bed was the bad guy, not the victim. Or some complicated mingling of both.

I could do something about that particular uncertainty, at least. I picked up the phone. "Erin?" I said to the sleepy voice on the other end. "This is Molly." For a little while longer, anyway.

"Do you know what time it is?" she muttered. There was a sleepy voice in the background—Erin's husband, Jack, an accountant with a wicked laugh and no trace of a Gift. A good man, though he holds on to trump too long. Erin told him to go back to sleep, then spoke to me. "What is it?"

"I need help."

Now she was crisp, wide awake. "Immediately?"

"No, in the daylight will be fine. Um . . . I've an unexpected guest, mysterious and somewhat damaged. I'd like you to meet him."

Silence, then a sigh. "I suppose you don't want to tell me more over the phone."

"I'd rather not," I said apologetically. It's very difficult to listen in on a call magically—technology is better at that sort of thing. But it is possible. "Oh, and could you bring me some more of that cleansing mixture you made for me? The one with rue, broom, and agrimony." Which, of course, are not cleansing herbs. They were components of a spell granting true vision, used to see through lies. Used by a Wiccan High Priestess, however, the spell could reveal a good deal more.

"Look for me about nine-thirty." She was grim. "I'd be there earlier, but my car's in the shop. I'll have to take Jack to work so I can use his."

"I owe you."

"You know perfectly well it's the other way around. Molly, for heaven's sake, what have you gotten yourself into?"

"I don't know yet," I said, eyeing the man in my bed—who had woken and was eyeing me back. "But it promises to be interesting. I'll see you in a few hours." I disconnected and put the phone down.

In the soft light from my bedside lamp, my guest's eyes were a clear, pale blue. Quite striking. Also filled with suspicion. "To whom were you speaking?"

Wasn't that just like a man? Earlier he'd trusted for no particular reason, now he suspected when there was little cause—and little remedy, if he'd been right. "No one says 'to whom' these days," I told him, heading for my tiny bathroom, where I collected peroxide and gauze and dampened a washcloth. "You'll need to learn more colloquial speech if you stay here long."

"Whom is the object of the preposition." He frowned as I returned, either at having his grammar corrected or at the prospect of having his wounds cleaned. "How else would one say it?"

"Most people would say, 'Who were you talking to?' Which is technically incorrect, but language changes."

"Very well. Who were you talking to?"

"A friend. She'll do you no harm, as long as you mean no harm. This, however, is going to hurt." I poured peroxide into the deep slash on his thigh and started mopping up the dried blood around it.

His breath hissed between his teeth. He grabbed my wrist. "Stop that!"

I have always wanted to be able to raise one eyebrow, but mine only move in tandem. I lifted them. "Are you certain you can prevent infection?"

"Is that what . . ." His eyebrows drew together in a frustrated pleat. "There are other ways to prevent infection."

"You didn't want to see a doctor, remember? You're stuck with me, and this is what I know to do."

Grudgingly he nodded and released my wrist. I sat on the bed beside him.

The next few minutes were harder on him than me. I learned long ago how to move into a mental room where sympathy can't intrude. It's a white, private place, nowhere I'd want to live permanently, but there are times when sympathy is a drawback. Besides, I saw no point in both of us suffering.

There were four slashes in his flesh—one in the lower chest, another on the right side of his belly, and two in his thigh. He was lucky. The upper wounds were shallow, slicing through skin and a bit of muscle but leaving his innards intact. One of the thigh wounds was no more than a deep scratch. The other . . .

I sighed, unhappy with what I saw with the blood cleaned away. "How good are you at healing? The muscle is badly damaged, and I'm not sure my sewing skills are up to putting it back together right."

"Sewing? You wish to sew my muscle?"

"I'll have to, unless you can do something."

He was silent, but with an inward look that suggested he was checking things out in his own way. A moment later, the wound began to close.

It was fascinating to watch. Flesh touched flesh as if hands were gently urging the sides of the wound together, then gradually meshed into unity like dough kneaded back into a single lump. And a delicious energy surged through me, conveyed from him to me through my hand on his leg. My fingers tingled. I licked my lips.

And snatched my hand back. He was a guest, not a meal. Shaken, I let go of my hold on the white, interior space. The slow knitting of his flesh was still fascinating, but my vision was colored by compassion now.

When he finished, the gash was nearly closed and his face was the color of mushrooms. I patted his knee in a motherly way. "Very impressive."

His voice was flat with fatigue. "I cannot do the rest now."

"None of the others are as deep. They'll heal on their own, I imagine." I stood. "Now, if you can stay awake a little longer, you need fluids. Since I can't provide an IV, you'll have to drink as much as you can. Water or orange juice?"

He licked his lips. "Water. Molly?"

I waited.

"What are you?"

I could have pretended I didn't know what he was talking about. That was my first impulse. He was weak, lost, sundered even from his name. He wouldn't be hard to deceive. I could have asked what he meant, then unraveled whatever chain of logic had led him to ask that question. I'm good at that. I have to be. And the thought of how he'd react to the truth ached like a fresh bruise laid down over old wounds.

But those blue eyes held steady on me, and there was something about them . . . "I'm a succubus."

His eyes widened.

"Cursed, not damned," I added firmly. "A long time ago, by someone who knew what She was doing when it came to curses. I'm not a demon. Originally, I was human."

"Ah." The tension went out of his face, and his eyelids drooped. "That explains it. Better hurry . . . with water." His speech was slurring as he let go of whatever force of will had been keeping him awake. He smiled at me. "Thank you, Molly."

Chapter 3

❧

HE liked television. And he loved the remote.

At ten-twenty the next morning he was propped up on my couch, channel surfing madly. He'd woken when Erin arrived and had insisted on moving there, over my objections. But he was doing amazingly well.

Erin was outside, readying herself and the spell. She wouldn't perform it out there—between dogs, children, and nosy neighbors that simply wasn't practical. But she needed earth beneath her feet for the preparation.

I'd shown her the spot where my guest arrived last night. Erin had hmm'd and frowned, nodding now and then like a doctor examining a patient, then sent me away.

I was in my galley—it's too small to be called a kitchen—putting together a *bouquet garni* for the chicken simmering on the stove. The connection between chicken

soup and healing may not have been established scientifi-
cally, but I'm sure it exists.

"Arthur?" I suggested. "Adam? Aillen?"

He looked away from the television, a sudden smile
lighting his face. "You find me handsome?"

"You know Gaelic!" I exclaimed. Another puzzle piece,
but I had no idea what to do with it. He looked Celtic, but
that lovely, upper-crust British accent . . . I shook my head
and plucked a bit of thyme from the pot on the counter by
the window. "Of course I find you handsome. You're gorgeous. You know that. Even if you don't remember, you've
seen yourself in the mirror." Before occupying my couch,
he'd asked where he could relieve himself. I'd had to explain the plumbing.

He touched his jaw as if reminding himself of the face
he hadn't recognized. "It seemed to be a pleasing face, but
standards of beauty vary widely."

"I wonder if you talk that way in your native language.
Have you remembered any more of it?"

"Any more?"

"You said something to me in another language when
you first arrived."

His brows knit. "I don't remember. What way do I talk?"

"Correctly. Formally. Did any of those names ring a
bell?"

"Ring a bell . . . oh. You wonder if they are familiar. No,
not in a personal way."

An interesting distinction. The names were familiar, but
they didn't belong to him. "Well, we have to call you something. Would you object to being Michael for now?"

"Michael . . . Hebrew for 'gift from God.' " He cocked
a single eyebrow at me—which he could do, blast him.
"You consider me a blessing."

The idiot male was *flirting* with me. "What an odd

memory you have. You know the meaning of Irish and Hebrew names, but not your own."

That stole the smile from his face. I tried not to feel
guilty. I tied the ends of the cheesecloth together and lowered the herbs into the simmering pot, catching it in place
with the lid. Keeping my back to him so I wouldn't see the
hurt I caused, I said, "Michael is also the name of a mili-
tant archangel. Evil is capable of masquerading as good,
but generally it prefers not to annoy Michael. One aligned
with evil would not be comfortable borrowing Michael's
name."

"I am not evil."

"I don't think so, but we don't know what you are.
That's what Erin will try to find out." Reluctantly, I abandoned cowardice and turned to face him. "Do you understand what a succubus is?"

"The Latin term for a female demon who draws life
from her victims through sexual intercourse. But you said
you were cursed into your condition, which makes sense."
He smiled suddenly, blindingly. "You aren't evil, either."

"Nor am I good. Michael—"

"You do like that name for me. Very well. I will be
Michael."

I could feel myself softening—inside, where it was dangerous, and outside, my muscles growing lax and warm
with wanting. So I was sharp to him. "Listen to me. I look
like a middle-aged woman, and I am one. A good deal
more than middle-aged, actually. But I'm also a succubus,
and I live off the energy of others. The energy of men, to
be specific, which I acquire through sex."

"Do you not eat?" he asked, curious. "It smells in here
as if you enjoy food."

My breath huffed out. He didn't seem to be getting the
point. "I eat, but I don't have to. Other people need food

and drink to live, and enjoy sex. I need sex to live, and enjoy food and drink."

"I'm glad you didn't lose those pleasures when you were cursed. Do you need to sup in your fashion daily, the same as others need to eat every day?"

"Not every day. Michael, you're either painfully naive or deliberately obtuse. I'm trying to explain why you must not flirt with me. I am not safe."

"You're worried about me!" He was amazed.

I rolled my eyes. The young always think themselves indestructible, but Michael should know better, after what he'd been through. But then, he didn't remember what he'd been through. "Yes," I said. "I'm worried about you."

For an instant his face softened, and I glimpsed in his eyes the ragged edges of adult vulnerability, not the untried trust of youth, as if my simple words had sliced deep into a place that didn't bear touching. "You needn't," he said, and the edges closed up again, hiding whatever memories that deep place held. "You can take nothing from me I don't wish to give."

"What if you wished to give?" My posture shifted as the energy gathered around me, swirling, aching . . . "I could make you want to give, Michael. You'd want to give . . . anything."

The door opened. "Molly!" Erin said sharply.

I snapped back. Then just stood there, disoriented, like a stooping hawk suddenly shoved from its plummet. The breath I drew was ragged. "Well," I said as briskly as I could, "what did you learn?"

"Not much." She came in, eyeing me. Erin is a tall woman, bony by my standards but fashionably slender to her generation. Her face was made for drama, with a wide mouth, sharp cheekbones, and a beak of a nose that she considers unlovely but which I quite envy for its distinction. She's supposed to wear glasses, but often forgets or leaves them somewhere. Her hair is a fabulous red bush that nearly reaches her waist. Today she wore it pulled back from her face with a stretchy headband that matched her apple-green t-shirt.

T-shirts are one of the best things about the current age. And bras. Bras have corsets beat all to pieces. "You must have learned something."

She shrugged. "Node energy isn't my area. You knew he came in at a node?"

I nodded. I'm not so utterly insensitive I'd be unaware of a node so close to where I've lived for twelve years. One of the ley lines from it runs beneath my RV. "What else?"

"He's drawing from it."

I glanced at Michael. "Of course," he said. "I could have told you that, had you asked. How else could I heal?"

"And," Erin added, "he came from a long ways away. I couldn't trace him back—the energies are too foreign—but there's a feeling of a great gulf."

I nodded. "I knew he wasn't from this world."

"Not . . ." She shook her head. "That isn't possible."

Erin is a very good witch and far wiser than I was at her age. But she is young, and thus prone to certainty. "Obviously it's possible, since he's here."

She looked at Michael, eyes wide and suddenly wary.

"Another world," he said thoughtfully, his voice so much deeper than Erin's light soprano. "That makes sense. I don't seem to know much about this one."

"Supposedly you don't remember anything about any others, either," Erin said sharply.

"I don't remember anything, no. But I think perhaps I know a great deal."

"Is that supposed to make sense?" Scowling, she slung

her bag off her shoulder and set it on the table of my little dinette. The bag holds her basic ritual apparatus, and is made of heavy black silk. I'd given it to her for Samhain last year. "The realms haven't been close enough to cross between in over five hundred years. Except for Faerie," she added. "And that's closed to mortals. And you aren't Faerie."

"No," he said agreeably. "I'm fairly sure I'm not."

"What about Dis? The place Christians call hell. It leaks into our world sometimes."

"I'm not demonic, either. No more than Molly is."

She looked startled.

"I told him," I admitted. "Not the details, but it did seem he'd a right to know, if he's to stay with me awhile. Now, let's try applying a little reason. Magic is useful, but logic has its place. Michael said—"

"He's remembered his name?" Her eyebrows made a skeptical comment on that.

"I named him, for now."

Erin's eyes narrowed, for names and naming have power, so I hurried on before whatever lecture was simmering could boil over into speech.

"As I was saying, according to Michael, the energies here aren't what he's used to. And he tastes different, unlike anything I've ever—"

"Molly! He's injured."

"I haven't been nibbling," I said, testy. "But I've touched him. I'm sure I've never encountered his like before—and my experience covers rather a lot of ground."

She nodded reluctantly.

"I don't know what he is, but I know some things he isn't. He's not Gifted, not in the sense we use that term, at least. He's not Lupus. And he's not a sorcerer. Last night he unlocked my door without being aware he'd done it, and sorcery requires focus. So does telekinesis. Poltergeists, though—"

"He is *so* not a poltergeist."

"Will you stop interrupting? Of course he isn't. But he may be from the same place, or a similar realm."

"Or he may be lying."

"No." That came from Michael, who spoke with simple assurance. "I do not lie."

Erin's lip curled. "What, you're from the angelic realm?"

I suspected I knew what lay behind Erin's antagonism, and it wasn't getting us anywhere. I spoke firmly. "That's what you're going to find out, I hope. Are you ready?"

Her brow pleated. "I don't know, Molly. I'm tied to this world—my knowledge, power, and rituals are all of this realm. He uses node magic, not earth magic. If he really is from elsewhere, how much will I be able to learn?"

"Ritual magic is practiced in forty-two realms," Michael said suddenly. "Many are variants of Wicca. Depending on how one defines the parameters, between eight and seventeen religiously oriented magical systems bear strong similarities to it."

"Forty-two realms?" Erin shook her head. "There aren't that many."

"Where did that come from?" I asked.

Frustration was plain in his eyes. "I don't know. It was just there, but when I try to follow it . . . nothing." He spread his hands. "I, too, want very much to know what manner of being I am."

Erin studied him a moment, and I suspected she was using other senses than sight—including, I hoped, the compassionate sense of the heart. Maybe she was finally considering the possibility that he was telling the truth. Erin has a problem with good-looking men. "I'll do what I can," she said at last, and began to unpack her bag.

The tradition Erin follows requires nudity only for major workings, when the god and goddess are called rather than simply included in the rite. This was a spell, not an act of worship—though the two are not entirely distinct with Wicca—so she and I kept our clothes on. Michael sat up on the couch with the blanket providing a modesty drape. Not that he had any, from what I'd seen. Modesty, that is. He was well provided with what the blanket was there to conceal.

Erin took out her athame, a glass vial, a black candle, a little pouch, and two silver bowls, each smaller than a cupped hand. "Stand to the south," she said, nodding at me. "No, a little more to your right. That's good. Michael—you have no objection to that name?"

"I'm content with it."

"I've set wards outside Molly's home for protection, and will cast a circle around the three of us to contain the spell. It's vital that you not break the circle once I've set it. You break the circle by stepping outside."

He looked insulted. "Actually it is a sphere, not a circle, but I understand you are using the accustomed term. What type of spell will you be casting?"

"A basic truth spell. It will urge but not compel the truth from you. If you knowingly speak false, I'll see it. With your permission, after a few questions I'll take the spell deeper. That can feel uncomfortable, intrusive. I'll be trying to bring truth up from wherever it's hiding inside you."

He considered that, then nodded. "A great many things have hurt since I woke and saw Molly. I can abide a little discomfort in order to learn what I am and whether I brought danger here with me."

"Also *who* you are, I hope."

"I am now Michael. As I said, I am content with that."

He looked at me then, and his smile burst over me with the pungent sweetness of summer berries.

I was going to have to be *very* careful.

Erin doesn't use a compass. The direction of the cardinal points is as obvious to her as sunlight is to others. She put her bag on the floor and knelt beside it, then removed her portable altar—a hand-cut, hand-polished square of oak about ten inches on a side and one inch thick. It went on the floor between myself and Michael. On it she set her tools. The two silver bowls were filled with water and salt—salt for the earth, and the north; water for the west. She put a stick of incense in the altar's east quadrant for air, and a candle in the south for fire. Then she waved her hand.

Like a faucet springing a drip, the candle's wick acquired a flame. A thread of smoke drifted up from the incense. She took up her athame and turned in a slow circle, her lips moving, pointing outward.

Michael's eyes followed, not Erin or the athame, but the direction she pointed. I knew he must be looking at the energies she roused, and envied him. I've always wanted to see the colors of magic.

Erin circled three times, then put her athame on the altar with the knife's tip pointing at Michael. She opened the vial, dampened her finger with the contents and touched each of her eyelids. Then she stepped forward and did the same with each of Michael's lips. "As I will, so mote it be."

His eyes widened, though whether he was startled by her touch or some other sensation I couldn't tell.

She nodded, satisfied. "Molly, you ask the questions."

"All right." I licked my own lips, nervous for no good reason. "Michael, do you remember anything of your life from before you arrived here?"

"The first thing I remember is your face. Your skin looked very soft and your eyes were sad. I couldn't see what color they were, and that was strange to me—I think I'm not used to losing colors in the dark. There was a pucker between your eyebrows. I like your eyebrows," he added. "They have a pretty curve."

The eyebrows he'd complimented shot up. Those weren't the curves most men noticed. "You don't know your name from before?"

"No."

"Where do you come from?"

"I don't know. I don't remember it, but it was different from this place. But I do know about this place."

"What do you know?"

"Languages. Facts. Not always the most useful facts," he said ruefully. "And I don't always know that I know until something floats up."

I exchanged a glance with Erin. She nodded, telling me what I was already sure of. He wasn't lying.

She spoke, her voice cool and soothing. "I'm going to take the spell deeper now, Michael. Molly will continue asking questions, but I'll be helping you find the answers."

He nodded fractionally. His eyes never left mine.

"Who gave you those wounds?" I asked.

"I . . ." He licked his lips. "She? Yes, I think . . . I was escaping. That made her angry."

"What is she?"

"I don't . . . that's not coming. But I have the idea she's strong. Very strong."

"Who is she?"

A fine dew of sweat sheened his forehead. "I don't know."

"What do you know about how you got here?"

"They were . . . someone was . . . they want to catch me. Keep me."

"Not to kill you?"

"No, they want to—want to—" His head swiveled towards Erin. "Don't!" And he heaved himself sideways, one arm outstretched like a drowning swimmer reaching desperately for rescue.

The circle broke.

Chapter 4

※

THE *pop!* was like clearing your ears during an airplane's descent with a jaw-cracking yawn, except that it happened under my solar plexus. It should have been similar for Erin, though with more of a sting.

It should *not* have made her eyes roll back in her head as she sank to the floor in a faint.

I jumped and managed to keep her from hitting her head, ending with both of us on the floor with her head in my lap. Michael rolled off the couch so awkwardly I thought something had happened to him, too. But no, he'd simply made an odd dismount, for he fetched up on the other side of Erin's lax body and sat, staring at her in appalled fascination. "I didn't do it," he said. "I didn't mean to do it."

"Breaking the circle shouldn't have harmed her." I checked her pulse. It was strong and steady, thank goodness.

"No, it wasn't that. But it wasn't me, either—at least, it came through me, but I didn't will it. Maybe . . ." He put his hands on either side of her face and focused intently on her.

I looked at him sharply. "What are you doing?"

"Trying to fix her. Be quiet."

Should I let him try to repair whatever he'd inadvertently damaged? Or prevent him from doing more harm? Before I could decide, Erin blinked herself back to us. "What . . . Molly?" She put a hand to her temple. "I have such a headache. What happened?"

"I don't know. Michael broke the circle, and you collapsed."

"Michael? Who's Michael? And what," she demanded, "am I doing lying on the floor with my head in your lap?

"You don't remember?"

She shook her head.

I considered going back to bed.

"The amnesia should be temporary," Michael said. "I think."

"You probably can't remember."

"I believe that's sarcasm."

"Good call."

Erin sat up, pushing her hair out of her face. Her headband had come off. "The last I remember, you'd woken me up at a godawful hour to ask for help. How did—"

Someone knocked on my door. We all jolted.

"Michael, get on the couch and look like an invalid," I said, scrambling to my feet.

"What does an invalid look like?"

"Pale. You've got that part down, so just lie still and pull the blanket up over you. Make sure your wounds and genitals are hidden. Erin—"

"Not wearing a stitch, is he?" She watched Michael's beautiful backside as he moved to the couch. I couldn't blame her for finding the sight distracting. "But I'm clothed, so we weren't performing a ceremony."

"No, we—" The knocking came again, louder. "Be right there!" I called. "Erin, I know you need answers, but for now pretend you're here to help me with my nephew Michael, who's recovering from a mysterious fever. I thought he'd been cursed, which is why I called you." I headed for the door.

"You don't have a nephew," she informed me.

"That's a fiction," Michael said. "We are supposed to fool whoever is at the door." He pulled the blanket over himself and lay down as stiff and straight if he'd been en-coffined. "Do I look ill?"

Erin was staring at him. "If you had a fever, there wouldn't be anything mysterious about it. Not with those wounds. What—"

"Shh! Michael, until our visitor leaves, speak Gaelic." I jerked the door open and sang out a cheery, "Good morning!" to the stranger on my stoop.

He was alone, so he wasn't from the Mormons. Probably not a salesman, either, not in that suit—gray wool, not top-of-the-line but not shabby, either. Either a Baptist or a business clone, I concluded. Probably the latter. Houston was only forty-five minutes away, and the dress-for-successers there wore suits in spite of our subtropical weather. This was not a testament to endurance; they simply never experienced more than a nibble of it, moving as they did between air-conditioned house, air-conditioned car, and tall, chilly office building.

Or maybe they were icing down the parking garages now, too. "Such nice weather we're having," I told him.

"Lovely," he agreed politely. He was about thirty, with seriously thick lenses on his gold-rimmed glasses. "I need to speak with you a few minutes, ma'am."

"This isn't a good time. Have they started air-conditioning the parking garages yet?"

"Uh . . . not to my knowledge. Perhaps I should introduce myself." He reached into a breast pocket, then held out a leather case. "Agent Rawlins. FBI."

Going back to bed was sounding better all the time. "A real FBI agent," I said weakly. "How exciting. Are you looking for kidnappers? Terrorists? The Mob?"

"Not today. May I come in?"

"Oh, dear. I don't *think* my nephew is contagious anymore . . ."

"Pete?" Erin said from behind me. "Is that you?"

The professionally stern face startled. "Lady? I mean—Erin?"

"Ná hinis faic dhó," said the naked man on my couch.

I sighed and stood aside. "Never mind, Michael. Either someone here has some very odd karma, or God is feeling playful. It seems Agent Rawlins is in Erin's coven."

Chapter 5

⊰✦⊱

"THANK you, ma'am." Pete took the mug of coffee I held out. He was sitting on one of the bench seats at my dinette, looking uncomfortable. "Lady—Erin—I need to know why you're here."

"So do I," she said, accepting her mug from me.

He blinked.

"You performed a truth spell on Michael," I told her, settling cross-legged beside Michael on the couch—which put me next to Pete as well, since my couch butts up against the dinette on one side. My quarters are small. "He has amnesia, too, but rather more thoroughly than you."

"You learned I was telling the truth about that," Michael said.

I nodded. "And then you took the spell deeper, trying to

unearth those buried memories. But something went wrong. He broke the circle—"

"I was trying to stop the—the—I can't find the word," he said, frustrated. "It slapped Erin away and she passed out. It's supposed to protect me, keep me from being read without permission."

Erin's brows drew down. "I had your permission."

"You remember!" I cried.

"Some of it," she said grudgingly, and sighed. "Most of it, I suppose. I'm pretty sure he's not evil, not inherently. But he's barricaded like crazy. I never saw such shields." She sipped from her mug. "Molly, you make the best coffee. The fumes alone are curing my headache."

"I helped." Michael was pleased.

Pete was lost. "Who are you?"

"Michael."

"Last name?"

"Not yet." He looked at me inquiringly. "Do you wish to gift me with one?"

"We'll worry about that later. Pete—"

"I'm here as Agent Rawlins."

"Don't be stuffy," Erin told him. "We have a situation here. We could use some help. Probably it would be best if you started by telling us why you're here."

Pete frowned at his coffee. "I can't tell you that."

"You're putting him in a difficult position, Erin," I said. "He owes you truth and all reasonable assistance, but he has a duty to the FBI, too. Pete, perhaps you could ask me whatever you came to ask, and I'll be a difficult witness or informant or whatever and insist on knowing more before I answer. Then we can trade information. Will that work?"

He started laughing. It transformed his face, waking a spark of interest in me. I hadn't supped, as Michael put it, in a couple days. Not long enough to be a problem normally, but my appetite had been roused by Michael's presence. And Pete was really quite attractive when he forgot to wear his official face. . . .

Erin poked me in the ribs.

Pete shook his head, still smiling. "I've fallen down the rabbit hole, haven't I? Okay, we'll give it a try, though I can't promise to tell you everything."

"That's all right." I leaned towards him and patted his hand. "I doubt we'll tell you everything, either."

PETE was quite forthcoming about himself. He'd been born into a Wiccan family, but had inherited only a modest Gift—little more, he said, than many people unknowingly possessed. But that little had been well-trained, which made him valuable to the FBI. All of which Erin already knew, so his frankness didn't earn him any return information.

He was much vaguer about his reason for knocking on my door. He was speaking to everyone at the Village, he said, because of a report of possible sorcerous activity. He glanced at Erin when he said that, troubled.

"For goodness sakes, Erin didn't do it," I said. "As you ought to know. Not that there has there been any sorcery— at least, a node was involved, which I suppose is what you mean. But that isn't sorcery in and of itself. The current legal definition is absurdly broad."

"How is sorcery defined?" Michael asked curiously.

Pete cleared his throat. "Sorcery is magic that is sourced outside the performer."

I grimaced. "An accountant's way of seeing the world. Follow the funding, ignore everything else." Technically, the law would consider me a sorcerer—if it admitted I existed, which it doesn't. Which is ridiculous. My abilities and disabilities are innate, not learned.

"There was a time when all forms of magic were illegal," Erin said dryly. "As certain of my relatives could have testified, had they survived the flames. It's hard to argue against outlawing sorcery, though."

"All of it?" Michael was startled. "You mean that all forms of sorcery are illegal here?"

"Sorcery is black magic," Pete said firmly. "The blackest."

Michael looked confused. Apparently the bits of knowledge he could remember about our world didn't include much in the way of history.

"Most people associate sorcery strictly with death magic," I explained. "Which, of course, some sorcerers have practiced, especially since the Codex Arcanum was lost during the Purge, preventing them from—"

"Lost?" He sat bolt upright. "The Codex?"

Pete's eyes narrowed with suspicion. "Schoolchildren learn about the Purge in the third grade."

Michael didn't answer. His face was blank, his attention turned inward like one who has been dealt a great shock.

"He isn't from here," I told our FBI agent, and went on to explain, sorting out what needed to be shared, what kept close, as I went. For example, I didn't mention my nature. That was none of his business—and I doubt he would have believed me, not without proof. According to the best authorities, I'm not possible. Nor did I tell him about the snippets Erin had unearthed before she passed out. Which left Pete with the story of a man who appeared out of nowhere, naked, amnesiac, and wounded. A man not from our world.

He didn't buy it. He saw the wounds, so he accepted that part. He also accepted that Michael wasn't lying, because Erin had tested him. But he considered most of our account a mixture of conjecture, confusion, and delusion.

Michael was less offended by this than I. "Delusion is a reasonable explanation, from your point of view. You are interested in facts, not subjective analyses of the situation."

"But there's more than opinion involved," I objected. "There *was* a burst of nodal energy when you arrived. The Unit must have noticed that and—"

"Wait a minute," Pete said sharply. "I didn't say anything about a unit."

He'd just confirmed my suspicions. That vague "report of sorcerous activities" had come from the tiny branch of the FBI charged with investigating magical crimes. "I forgot," I said apologetically. "The Unit is supposed to be hush-hush, isn't it? I shouldn't have said anything."

"You shouldn't *know* anything."

"I meet a lot of people." I waved a hand vaguely.

"I don't know about a unit," Michael said. "I'm not sure what the FBI is, either, but I've made some guesses. It seems to be a bureaucratic entity which investigates sorcery, espionage, terrorism, and the Mob. But why is the Mob identified by a definite article? Is there one mob that is distinct from all others?"

Pete undertook that explanation. I went after more coffee, thinking hard. I'd been too forthcoming. While Pete might discount most of our story, he'd report it—and that report would find its way to the Unit. I didn't know much about that small, secretive group, certainly not enough to wager Michael's life on their good intentions. Besides, even good intentions can misfire.

Well, I could seduce Pete. Men are extraordinarily suggestible when I turn up the power. But that would embarrass my friends and cause problems for Pete later, when the effect wore off.

Maybe I should crank up the disbelief factor. A few comments about flying saucers, for example, or the entity I'd been channeling . . . "What?" I said, my head swiveling back towards the others. "What did you say about the Azá?"

"You've heard of them?" Pete was surprised.

"Who are they?" Erin asked.

He shrugged. "A cult. Bit fanatical. They're new here, though they've been around in England and Ireland for awhile. They've been known to source their rituals on death magic—animal, of course, but a nasty habit and quite illegal, so we keep an eye on them. Like most cults, they claim to possess ancient wisdom. Theirs is a mishmash, supposedly Egyptian in origin, but they dress up in black pajamas like a bunch of ninjas. They worship some goddess no one's ever heard of, name of—"

"Never mind that," I said quickly. "Why did you mention them?"

He really was a nice man. He smiled, and it was meant to be soothing, not condescending. "No need to be alarmed. I just need to be informed if any of them show up. Someone in their organization is sensitive to node activity, you see. They believe their goddess speaks to them that way. So whenever there's a disturbance, they hustle out, try to set up their rites on the spot. Which, as I said, sometimes include illegal practices, so we want to know if they turn up."

My choices had narrowed drastically, so I did what I had to. "Pete," I said, letting my voice turn softer, slightly breathy. "I think they're already here." I gazed into his eyes. Such a rich, pretty brown they were behind the lenses of his glasses. I'd seen them alight with laughter and I remembered that, and how attractive he'd been then. "Are they dangerous?"

He moved towards me. "It's all right." His voice had gone husky, but I doubt he noticed. "You're not in any danger, Molly."

Erin's voice came sharply. "Stop that."

"Let her be." Michael's voice surprised me. It was firm, the kind of voice one automatically obeys. "She knows what she's doing."

Pete started to turn, frowning. I turned up the power, but carefully—I wanted him protective, not ravenous—and laid a hand on his arm. "I'm frightened."

He put his hand over mine. "You're safe, Molly. I won't let . . . ah, tell me why you think they're here."

I described two odd-looking fellows in black pajamas who, I said, had been lurking around the Village earlier this morning. I was frightened, but willing to be reassured. He was captivated.

A little too captivated. He scarcely knew the others were present—Erin with her disapproving frown, Michael with an expression of extreme interest. "You'll want to let your superiors know right away," I suggested, looking up into Pete's eyes.

"Yes . . ." He was holding my hand, and started to stroke it. "Molly—"

"About the Azá," I said firmly, and pulled my hand away. "You need to make your report about *them*." I stressed the last, hoping he'd forget to report about everything else—at least for a little while.

He blinked. "Yes. Yes, of course. Molly, I . . . this is sudden, but I'd like to call you."

I smiled sadly. "Of course, Pete. You have my number."

I got him to the door. "Don't worry about the Azá," he said gently, worried that I might be worried. "We've checked them out thoroughly. Their rites are harmless—except to the animals, of course. The energy they gather that way is all directed towards their goddess, who doesn't exist."

I had to try. "They aren't harmless, Pete. Be careful. Please be careful. And don't say Her name."

"Her?"

"Their goddess."

He didn't believe me, of course. "We'll be watching them," he assured me. "Don't worry."

As soon as I shut the door on him, Erin demanded, "What the bloody blazes did you do that for?"

"I had to," I said wearily. "The effect will wear off in a day or so."

Michael spoke. "What about these Azá you saw? They are trouble?"

"They are very much trouble, but I didn't see any of them." I headed for the galley, poured out the last of the coffee, and rinsed the pot. My eyes fell on the little yellow pot that held my thyme. I picked it up and saw a face . . . a little girl with pigtails, glasses, and a smile wide as the Mississippi. I've never had children and never will, but three times I've taken one to raise. The first time it was war that killed my borrowed son, and grief nearly destroyed me. I did things then I'd rather not think about. My second child was broken by age, crippled in body and mind while I was still young and strong.

I'd vowed never to raise another child.

Ginny had made me break my vow. Her parents had been killed in the Great Storm, the hurricane that leveled Galveston in 1900, killing over six thousand people. They had been my neighbors and my friends, and I'd been unable to save them.

But I'd saved Ginny. I'd taken her to raise as my own, against all better sense. And had never regretted it.

She was gone now—grown up, grown old, and buried.

But I still had the pot she'd made me when she was ten. The pot and the memories. And, I thought with a smile, a dear friend in her great-granddaughter.

Who was appalled with me. "Tell me you didn't just lie to the FBI," Erin demanded.

"Can't do that without telling another lie." If I'd known the Azá had crossed the ocean . . . well, I know now. I rinsed the coffeepot. "Erin, I'm sorry. I have to leave."

Erin's face is so expressive. I saw anger fade to irritation, puzzlement, distress. "You don't mean that you need to run to the store."

I shook my head. "I have to leave Galveston. Could you pick up some clothes for Michael? Jeans, a couple t-shirts, shoes, underwear." I cast an experienced eye over him. "Thirty-thirty-one for the jeans, I think."

"I'm going with you?" Michael rose from the couch and stood there in all his glory.

"Yes," I said. "Oh, yes. They'll be after you."

He scowled. "You are leaving because of me?"

"I've been planning to leave for some time. This just moves up the timetable."

Erin grabbed my arm. "Why? We don't know if anyone's even looking for Michael. This isn't the way to handle things. It's not like you to rush off half-cocked, Molly. I know you've talked about moving on soon, but not like this. Not this fast."

I looked at her dear face and let the hurt rip through me. Partings have never gotten easy. "I have to," I told her gently. "The goddess Pete almost named? She's quite real. I've met her, though it's been awhile . . . about three hundred years. She's the one who cursed me."

Chapter 6

✢

MICHAEL and I left the island shortly after seven o'clock that evening.

The causeway stretching between Galveston and the mainland is man-made. Like a long umbilical cord, it holds fast to its feckless offspring—a mother refusing to release her child to a separate fate. The bay was a ruffled blue mosaic on either side as we crossed from child to parent, and the sun rode low in the sky on our left. Traffic was light.

"Do you realize," Michael said, awed, "that this was all done without magic? All of it—the bridge, the roads and buildings . . . everything."

"Ah—yes. I knew that." I didn't look at him. Michael wasn't quite as distracting clothed, but his thighs gave the crisp new jeans a lovely form, and the t-shirt Erin had bought him was the color of his eyes—a paler blue than the ocean, but just as unfathomable.

Best to pay attention to driving my rig. It handled beautifully, but I'd driven it very little since purchasing it last year to replace my old one. Not that I'd bought it in my own name. I'd been planning to leave for some time, but I'd kept putting it off. . . .

"I should have realized that," he muttered, his attention fixed on the Powerbook in his lap. Michael liked my laptop even better than television. "Sorcery is illegal here, you said." He shook his head. "Strange. Very strange."

"I guess magic is pretty easily come by in your realm."

"Mmm," he said, lost once more to cyberspace.

Michael had so much to learn about this world. After Erin left to buy clothes for him, he'd done another healing on himself. He'd come out of that popping with questions. More questions than I had time to answer—or the patience, frankly—and many I couldn't answer. So I'd handed him my laptop and shown him how to Google. He'd picked up the basics quickly, though he had to hunt-and-peck on the keyboard. I'd warned him not to believe everything he read, and he'd vanished into cyberspace while I packed up my life.

He was connected through my cell phone now. Yesterday I would have worried about the charges he was piling up; Molly Brown didn't have much money. But I wasn't Molly Brown anymore.

My fingers drummed once on the steering wheel. "For heaven's sake, shut that thing off and look at the ocean before it's a blue smear in the rearview mirror. Who knows how long it will be before you see it again?"

Suddenly those eyes were focused entirely on me. He closed the laptop. "Will it be a long time before you see it again, Molly?"

"Probably." A very long time. I'd returned to Galveston once, and doubted I would ever go back again. It hurt too much. Places changed. People changed even more . . . except for me.

"Your friend was upset by your leaving."

"I told her." Already we'd left the causeway. Bayou Vista, a subdivision with all the houses on stilts, was on our left. Ahead lay wetlands. "I told Erin a long time ago that one day I'd have to leave. People grow suspicious if you don't age."

"You'd be in danger if people suspected your nature. I understand that. Yet you told Erin about yourself. And me," he added thoughtfully.

"You needed to know, and you have to hide your nature, too. You aren't likely to give me away. Erin . . ." Already the memory hurt. Time would soften that, I knew. Eventually. "I didn't tell her. She figured it out."

"How? You're careful. You must be, or you wouldn't have survived. I've read some history now," he said, giving the laptop a pat. "This world has been hard on anyone able to use magic, but especially on those of the Blood."

I snorted. "True, but I'm not of the Blood."

"Of course you are. You may not have started out that way, but you are now."

"But those of the Blood *do* start out that way. They're born to it."

He was amazed. "You don't know, do you? I didn't find anything on the Internet about it, but I thought surely . . . some things are such common knowledge that no one bothers to write them down."

"What are you talking about?"

"Molly, originally you were completely of your world. The curse changed that. Now you're of more than one realm. That's really all it means to be 'of the Blood'—that you're inherently of more than one realm."

"You are not making any sense."

He shook his head, as baffled by me as I was by him. "What do you think magic *is?*"

"I . . . the Church teaches that it's evil, a contravention of God's laws. Most people don't believe that these days, but . . . I guess I don't know," I admitted. "It's like sunlight. It just is."

"Yet people in your world study sunlight and try to discern its nature. They're called physicists."

"You've absorbed an awful lot from the Internet in one day."

"I am an excellent researcher."

"Modest, too."

"Pardon?"

"Never mind. I suppose there are people who study the nature of magic?"

"Yes. They're called sorcerers. Not the most trustworthy beings," he admitted. "Though there are exceptions, sorcerers are known more for obsession than altruism. They can cause great havoc. But so, too, have your physicists caused havoc with their splitting of the atom."

"True. So what is magic?"

"One theory holds that it is the stuff between the realms, the current they swim in. Others believe it's the energy created by the realms' interaction. That magic is the friction caused by their, ah, rubbing against each other."

"But they're pulling away from each other, not rubbing up together!"

He made a disgusted noise. "I should expect that sort of thinking from a place that outlawed all sorcery. The realms shift, yes. Constantly. There are theories about this movement, but no one truly knows how or why they move. For some reason, your realm seems to connect to very few others. I believe it must be in . . . call it a backwater. A stagnant place."

"I think you just called my world a swamp."

He flashed me a grin. "I wouldn't dream of it."

That grin startled me. Aroused me, too, but everything about him aroused me. Grins are different than smiles. Smile can mean all sorts of things, but a grin is an offer of friendship.

A male friend . . . oh, there was temptation more treacherous than any sexual pull. I jerked my mind back to the subject. "Wicca is based on the magic of *this* world. It doesn't tap into other realms, or the space between the realms, or whatever."

"Magic continually seeps into all the realms, is absorbed, and can be used. Systems like Wicca use this kind of magic, which is part of the natural processes of each world. It's much weaker than using nodes directly, but safer."

I nodded. It fit what I knew. "And nodes are places where this world used to connect to others?"

"More or less. You might think of them as spots where the fabric between realms is weaker, making connection more likely."

"You mean that connection can happen elsewhere? It's possible to travel between realms without a node?"

"Theoretically, yes—ley lines carry node energy, after all. But it would be rather like crossing the Alps on foot instead of in one of these automated vehicles of yours." He patted the dash and added, with something of the air of one complimenting a backwards child, "Quite ingenious, really, the way your people have overcome this realm's condition."

"Wait till you see Houston." Light was fading even as traffic thickened, with all the little road tributaries emptying their currents of cars onto I-45. We'd left Texas City behind, and were passing an undeveloped stretch. I put on my headlights.

Two things occurred to me. Michael had distracted me quite nicely from my grief at leaving my home and my friend . . . and he knew an awful lot about magic. Things he must have remembered.

I planned my next question carefully, hoping to stir more of his memories. "When I was young—and that was a very long time ago—"

"How long?" he asked, interested. "You mentioned something about three hundred years."

"I was born in Ireland in 1701."

He nodded, apparently finding nothing odd about that. "And you were cursed when you were . . ." He cast an appraising eye over me. "Not quite fifty?"

A laugh sputtered out. "Michael, never guess a woman's age so accurately. It isn't diplomatic. But no, I was twenty."

"You are a very attractive fifty," he assured me. "But you shouldn't be. Fifty, that is. Your body should have been fixed at twenty."

"We're getting off the subject."

"But if something is wrong, if you are aging when you shouldn't be—"

"I did it on purpose, all right?"

He considered that a moment. "You can change your physical appearance?"

"Not exactly. I can grow older, if I choose. It isn't easy." A gross understatement, that. I prefer to avoid thinking about how I'd acquired the crow's feet by my eyes. There's only one way to age a body like mine. Starvation.

"Why did you want to look older?"

"You ask more questions than a two-year-old!"

"I want to know about you, Molly."

Heaven help me, but he softened me in a way I couldn't seem to fight. I sighed. "For one thing, I could stay in one place longer if I looked older. People notice if you stay twenty. They don't notice so much if you always look middle-aged."

"And the other thing?"

I grimaced. He was both perceptive and persistent— useful traits, even appealing at times. But annoying at the moment. "I wanted . . . friends. Women friends. I missed that rather badly." I glanced at him, wondering if he could understand. "When I looked twenty and oozed sex, men wanted me and women disliked me. Now . . . well, I use a touch more power to get what I need from men, but not much. Half of seduction is simply wanting the person you're with. So most women don't see me as a threat, especially the younger ones. They don't think of a woman of my apparent age as sexual."

He chuckled. "The young always think the world was born when they were."

"Oh, listen to the graybeard. You're what—twenty-six? Twenty-seven?" I held my breath.

"Hardly," he said dryly. "You ought to know better than . . ." His voice drifted into silence. I stole a glance at him. He was staring straight ahead, stricken. "It was there," he whispered. "For a moment it was all there, but it melted away."

Impulsively I reached for his hand and squeezed it. His fingers closed around mine tightly. "But that's good," I said gently. "That means your memories aren't gone. They're just hiding for some reason."

He drew a ragged breath. "Yes. Yes, of course. And I have been remembering some things. Nothing about my-self," he said with a lack of emotion that, by its very dearth, revealed much. "But facts, concepts, theories— they float up when I'm not watching."

"Then you'll have to spend most of your time not watching, won't you?" I gave his hand another squeeze and, reluctantly, let go. I needed both hands to drive.

"That makes sense, but it's easier to decide than to do."

"Like being told not to think of the number ten," I agreed. "I've got a couple of ideas, if you want to hear them." I paused long enough for him to object. He didn't. "First, I wondered if I was wrong about you being a sorcerer. You know so much—"

"I am not a sorcerer."

My eyebrows climbed. "You're very sure about that."

"I can't be a sorcerer. It . . . isn't allowed. And I don't know why I just said that, so don't ask. But it feels true."

Interesting. "Well, what about a scholar?"

I felt more than saw his head turn towards me. "A scholar?"

"You said you were a good researcher, and I think you must be. You've picked up an amazing amount in such a short time. You read very, very fast. You know languages and theories of magic and odd facts, and just have that manner—as if you've always loved facts for their own sake, not for what you can do with them."

"Truth. Not just facts—truth."

I smiled.

"A scholar . . ." His voice was musing, but with a lift to it. He liked the idea. And that was all he said, but I was content to let him follow his thoughts. I had a few of my own demanding attention.

Neither of us spoke again until the sun was well down. We'd reached Houston's greedy, spreading fingers—not the city proper, but Friendswood, one of the many small towns that lay in its path. People sometimes compare big cities to anthills, but I think they're more like mold.

Anthills will only grow so large, but mold keeps right on spreading.

I'd slowed to accommodate the heavy traffic when, out of the blue, he asked, "How did Erin figure it out?"

"What?"

"You said you didn't tell Erin what you are, that she figured it out."

"Good grief. You have quite a memory." I winced. "I mean—"

"I know what you meant. And yes, I think I normally have an excellent memory."

"Do you remember everything?"

"No, but what I do recall is accurate." He paused, as if considering something new. "It seems that either emotion or intent can fix things in my memory."

"Hmm. Works that way for most of us. I wonder if emotion or intent could also make you forget."

He shifted in his seat, looked out the window, then back at me. "What an uncomfortable thought. Why would I do such a thing to myself?"

I didn't know, either. "So, what was the first thing I said to you?"

"You hoped that I spoke English. Molly," he said, and amusement ran through his voice, a silvery ripple in a dark current. "You might distract me, but I'll remember what I asked, and ask again. In that way I am rather like that two-year-old you mentioned. They persist, too. Do you not want to tell me how Erin figured out about you?"

"Not really." The habit of secrecy was strong . . . as was a sneaky little wish that he would think well of me. Foolishness. Both the wish, and the desire to base it on misdirection. I was what I was.

So why not tell him? "All right," I said, signaling that I

meant to take the next exit. I wasn't hungry—well, not for food. But he must be. It was nearly eight. "I . . . used to know Erin's great-grandmother. So when I moved back to Galveston—"

"You'd lived there before?"

"I was there for the Great Storm. Anyway, I knew about Erin and I was curious, so I sort of kept an eye on her. She liked to walk on the beach at night."

"So do you."

"Yes, but I'm hard to hurt."

"She came into danger?"

"There were two of them that night," I said, remembering. "Two pond-scum bastards who followed her, just as I was. One had a knife. He grabbed her, held the blade to her throat. The other ripped open her shirt."

His breath sucked in. "Did you kill them?"

"You're more bloodthirsty than I realized."

"Perhaps you preferred to let the law kill them."

He was certainly clear on how rapists should be treated. I couldn't say I disagreed. "They had heart attacks. One lived, one didn't."

"How? What did you do?"

"Just a minute," I said, easing the big Winnebago onto the access road. "I want to pull in at that gas station and top off the tank. The sign says they have diesel."

"Are you avoiding my question again?"

"It's easier to show than to tell, that's all."

"I'd rather not have a heart attack."

"You keep asking questions, you can't complain if some of the answers aren't comfortable."

Chapter 7

⁂

IT took some maneuvering, but I got my rig tucked up next to the pumps. I shut off the motor, unfastened my seat belt, and turned to Michael. "Do you want something to eat?"

"I want you to show me what you did to Erin's attackers."

All right. No more delay tactics. I took a deep breath, got my focus, and reached out.

I was wearing a t-shirt—a pretty Caribbean blue, one of my favorite colors—so my arm was clearly visible. But as I stretched it towards him, my hand went fuzzy. Translucent. I kept reaching—and slowly, carefully, put my hand inside his chest.

He stared down at his chest, eyes wide. "A most peculiar sensation."

That was it? That was his total reaction? I gave a shaky laugh, pulled my hand back, and let it go solid again. "It

was more than peculiar for Erin's attackers. I went a little
more solid and tickled their hearts."

"You showed great restraint. You could have ripped
them out."

"I've done that, too. But not . . ." My breath hitched. For
a moment I could smell the smoke of the guns, hear the
screams of men and horses, feel the shudder of the ground
as the canons fired, and my own desperation as I hunted for
the one soldier who'd mattered . . . but he'd already been
dead when I started looking, my beautiful, bright-eyed
Charlie, my son, lying butchered in the blood-soaked earth
while I searched and searched. Too late.

Quietly I said, "Not for a long time."

"You don't like killing."

"No one should like killing. There's nothing brave or
glorious about it."

"No. Yet sometimes it's the only way to stop a great
evil."

"You're sounding more like a warrior than a scholar."

"Is it not possible to be both?"

"Maybe." My heart was beating hard. I didn't know
why. His eyes were luminous, intent on me . . . I wanted so
much to touch him. I pulled my gaze away. "You've seen
what I can do. Most succubi—those who started out that
way—are naturally insubstantial, and take on form only
with effort. It's the other way around for me, but . . ." I
shrugged. "Other succubi are from Dis. Hell, in other
words. I'm originally of Earth, even if I do partake of hell
now, too."

"Molly, you aren't of hell."

My eyes flew to him. "But—you said that I was. That
the curse made me of both realms."

He shook his head. "Your memory is faulty. I said you
were inherently of two realms. I can't tell which other

realm claims you," he said apologetically. "I can't read that deeply. But it isn't hell."

"But succubi are from hell. You saw what I did, going fuzzy that way. That's what demons do."

"There are other realms where matter and energy aren't as sharply divided as they are here. I . . . I think I come from such a place." He smiled slowly, sweetly. "So do demons, yes, though that's not my realm, or yours. And so do angels."

Without my willing it, my hand reached for him, to touch his face—and a car honked right behind us. I jumped. "I-I'd better get filled up." In more ways than one, but there wasn't time to hunt now. Soon, I promised myself, and opened my door and climbed down. "Want to learn how to pump gas?"

"Yes." He didn't move, though. "One more question."

I waited.

"Where are we going?"

"I wondered when you'd ask that. We're going to see an acquaintance of mine. You need help I can't give you." I closed the door and moved to the pump, selecting the "credit" option. My wallet was in my pocket. It's too easy to be separated from cash and other important items if you carry a purse. The credit card I used, like my rig, belonged to NMN Corporation. That was my little joke. NMN stands for Not My Name.

Michael got out and came around the front of the rig, frowning. "You said acquaintance, not friend."

"I call very few people friend. Cullen is . . ." I shrugged and took out the nozzle. "Among other things he's one of those who study the nature of magic. The two of you should have a lot to discuss."

"He's a sorcerer."

"Yes."

"No. No sorcerers."

"Go buy yourself a Coke," I said, handing him a five. "When you come back, we'll talk about it."

MICHAEL loved Coke. He bought a six-pack and drank three. He did not love the idea of seeking help from a sorcerer. He had the idea that he wasn't supposed to do that—but of course couldn't say why.

It's hard to argue with someone who has no reasons, only feelings. I did my best. We debated it off and on all the way around the loop—when he wasn't asking about engineering, building codes, the water supply, and all sorts of other things I couldn't answer. He was desperately curious about the city, and looked wistful once it had receded behind us.

"Maybe you can go back later," I said. We were on I-10, headed west. Headlights chained the highway on either side, orderly fireflies lighting the dark at seventy miles an hour. "There are a lot of other cities to see on our route, though. Big ones, little ones, all sorts." San Antonio, El Paso, Las Cruces, Tucson . . .

"This sorcerer of yours lives where?"

"In California."

"That's on the west coast.

"Yes."

"A long drive for little purpose, since I can't go to a sorcerer."

"You can't go home until you know where home is."

"I'm not sure I want to go back." He slid a long, level glance my way. "I like it here. Besides, we know someone there wants to capture me. We don't need a sorcerer, Molly. We can wait for my memory to come back on its own."

"And if the Azá find you first?" I shook my head. "Someone here wants to find you, too, and I can't protect you from them."

"I don't need your protection," he snapped. "Your help, yes. I don't know this world. But I can protect myself."

"Now you sound like a typical male."

"I am male."

I'd noticed. Oh, I had noticed. . . . "The FBI thinks the Azá's goddess doesn't exist, and that they only use animals for their death magic. I know better."

"They won't kill me. I am . . . valuable."

"I think so, too, but will they?"

"I don't know what I am," he said, his voice low and tense. "I don't know my name, or where I come from. But I know this much: they will not want me damaged."

"What if they don't know what you are, either?"

He was silent for several minutes. "An unsettling idea," he finally said. "One that should have occurred to me. It would depend on this goddess of theirs, wouldn't it? On what she knows and where she is."

"She's certainly not from these parts," I said dryly. "Nor does she have a strong connection here, thank God. Her followers have been trying for three centuries to find an avatar for her. I'm happy to say they haven't had much luck."

"For three centuries, Molly?"

I glanced at him, nodded. "They had me picked for the honor, yes. I didn't know it, though I'd, ah . . . dabbled a bit with their rites. I was a wild child for awhile, or thought I was. I'd been raised in the Church, but God and I had a falling out after my parents died of smallpox. I thought He should have handled things differently. Well." I shrugged. "I was young."

"What happened?"

"They were trolling for converts, and they had a good spiel. The idea of worshiping a goddess appealed to me—seemed like men had had things all their way too long." I'd been in London by then, a little lost . . . make that a lot lost, but sufficiently insulated by the arrogance of youth to pretend otherwise. "They put on a good show, too. Magic was a major crime back then, so it didn't take much to dazzle, make it seem like they knew what they were talking about. And what adolescent doesn't like a secret society? Wisdom hidden from the masses, with a select few admitted to the mysteries." I snorted. "I was easy for them. Easy."

"But you got away."

"At pretty much the last minute, and not through any planning on my part. They'd tested me, though I didn't know it, and I fit Her. That's why avatars are hard to locate, I found out later—body and mind have to be matched up in some arcane fashion to Her. I, ah, got myself unmatched."

He nodded. "Just as with crossing between realms, so must an avatar be congruent with the entity wishing to posses it. How did you unmatch youself?"

"Well . . ." I smiled. "Accidentally. Mostly I was just doing what came naturally. The night before the big ceremony—which I thought was to initiate me into their mysteries—a sweet boy named Johnny McLeod performed another sort of initiation. Her avatar must be a virgin, you see."

He laughed.

"She was royally pissed about Johnny, though." A little shiver travelled through me.

They'd brought me to Her when they realized what I'd done—brought me weeping, cursing, fighting. They hadn't been gentle in their disappointment, and I'd learned what they'd planned. Then I saw Her . . . or, rather, what was left of her old avatar. Centuries old, it was, kept more or less alive by Her power. It—I've never been able to think of that husk as female—had looked like a mummy. Dead everywhere but the eyes . . .

"She crumbled," I said. "After She cursed me. That little temper fit cost Her."

"I'm sorry." He reached for my hand and held it. "I've called up bad memories."

The contact was good. Steadying. For a few minutes, I let myself enjoy holding hands. But as memories faded, that simple pleasure was lost in the rise of hunger. With a sigh, I pulled my hand back.

He was silent a moment longer, then said,

"You were right to warn me. These Azá may not know why their goddess wants me. She won't be able to tell them much."

"Why not? She *is* a goddess—or one of the Old Ones who calls herself goddess, which amounts to the same thing. Can't she tell them whatever she wants?"

"Communication across the realms is chancy." He sounded distracted. "And yours is so distant from most . . . I doubt she can convey actual words. Images, perhaps."

"Visions."

"Yes, and it's devilishly hard to get precise information across in a vision."

He sounded as if he knew from personal experience. A sudden thought chilled me. "Michael, there isn't any chance that . . . I mean, you aren't . . ."

"Aren't what?"

I bit my lip. "One of the Old Ones?"

Startled silence, then a sharp bark of laughter. "Gone senile, maybe? Considering my memory problem? That's good. I'll have to tell—" He stopped short. "Dammit. Dammit, dammit, dammit."

"You remembered something."

"Someone. For an instant I had a face, a name. A friend. I knew he would enjoy the joke, and . . ." He shook his head. "He's gone now."

A tightness beneath my breastbone told me I was already too involved with this strange, uprooted man. Still I reached for his hand. "You have a friend here, too."

His fingers closed around mine. Then, slowly, he lifted my hand to his lips. I tried to pull it back—and couldn't, for he wouldn't release me. He pressed a kiss to my fingertips, and his breath was warm. His mouth was warmer.

Then, thank God, he dropped my hand. I gave a little laugh that sounded far too nervous. "You've picked up some odd things on the Internet."

"I didn't read about that." He was pleased with himself. "Perhaps it was instinct. I like the way you taste."

"Yes, well, you taste in a different way than I do. I'm trying not to jump your bones here, Michael. You are not helping."

"Jump my . . . oh. But I would like very much if you jumped my bones, Molly."

Now the hard thud of my heart made sense. So did the way my pulse throbbed in tender places, and the hunger rising, rising . . . "I can kill that way, too. If I take too much."

"But you wouldn't."

"That doesn't make it safe." For either of us.

"You couldn't drain me."

I snorted. "Oh, the sublime confidence of youth."

"The nodes," he said patiently. "I draw what I need from the nearest node, either directly or through a ley line. You can't drain them."

The nodes? Was that what I'd felt—that sparkling, delicious energy that had flowed when he was healing? Oh, gods, but I wanted to taste that. And *him*. I wanted Michael. If I could—"Shit."

"What is it?"

"A cop, the state version. He's on my tail, flashing his lights."

"What does that mean?"

"He wants me to pull over. I'm not speeding," I said grimly. "I haven't broken any traffic laws. So he has something else in mind, and it probably isn't good news."

I had no choice, though. I sure couldn't outrun him. There was plenty of shoulder, but I don't put my rig on the shoulder when I can help it. I flashed my lights to let him know I'd seen him, then waited for an exit to come along. While I waited, I briefed Michael on the various other law enforcement agencies, and suggested he let me do the talking.

"You think he is stopping us because the FBI told him to?"

"It seems likely. Unless there's some other player we don't know about in this game." There was an exit for a rest stop coming up, which was perfect. I signaled. The fuzz didn't bother with a turn signal, just stayed on my bumper as I slowed.

"There may be many players we don't know about. There were . . . I'm almost sure there were two."

I stole a glance at him. Sweat gleamed on his forehead. He was staring straight ahead, his gaze fixed on nothing his eyes could see. "Two?" I said softly.

"Who came for me. She—the one who wounded me—and another. At least one other."

"Do you think *she* might be the Azá's goddess?" There was no traffic on the access road. I pulled up into the curve of the rest stop and eased to a stop.

He shrugged. "How can I tell? I don't remember her clearly, and I know nothing about the Azá's goddess."

"I'll fill you in on her." I glanced at the side mirror. My

tailgating cop was getting out of his car. "Later. Michael, I've made some assumptions for you. Maybe I shouldn't have. The FBI might be able to keep you safe from the Azá. You might not mind it if they found you."

"No. You are right. I can't let myself be taken by any government. I'm . . . too much temptation."

True, but I suspected he didn't mean it the way I did. "Open the glove box, will you? Oh—it's this." I showed him. We had the registration and insurance papers out by the time the cop turned his flashlight on us through the window.

I hit the button to roll it down. "Yes, officer? Would you mind—" I held a hand up. "The light. I can't see you at all."

He lowered the flashlight enough for me to see that the face beneath the Smokey Bear hat was young, but he had his cop face down pat. He looked as friendly as stone. "Are there just the two of you in there, ma'am?"

"Yes, me and my nephew." I held out the papers that proved me to be a law-abiding citizen.

He ignored them. "I need you both to step out of the vehicle, please."

This was not good. Officers never ask middle-aged ladies to step out of our vehicles for a traffic violation. "What's wrong?" I made my voice breathy, as if I were frightened. It wasn't difficult.

"If you'll just step outside the vehicle, ma'am."

I glanced at Michael—who had the most peculiar expression on his face. His upper lip was pulled back as if he were about to sneeze, and his eyes were fixed on the officer demanding our exit. "All right," he said in a thin voice. "I've got him."

"Got—" I swung my head back. "Oh, my." The stone-faced cop was truly stony now. Frozen.

"What should we do with him?" Michael asked. "I can't hold him very long."

Chapter 8

⁂

I took a slow breath. *Steady,* I told myself. *You've seen stranger things* . . . but at the moment I couldn't think of any. "What did you do to him?"

"I froze him. You can ask him things," Michael said helpfully. "He won't remember later, if I tell him not to. But hurry."

"Ah . . ." I looked at the poor, frozen young man and asked, "Why did you stop me?"

"There's an APB out," he said. It was bizarre. His mouth moved, but nothing else. His eyes stayed fixed on a spot near my left shoulder. "For your plate number."

Great. "Why is there an APB out on my license plate?"

"You're wanted by the FBI."

Pete, the rat, had not been sufficiently charmed. He must have made a full report, and now someone in the government wanted to get their hands on Michael. The Unit?

Some other corner of the bureaucracy? "This is not good news. Michael, can you make him do more than forget this conversation? Could you make him think he misread the license plate and that I'm someone else altogether?"

"I believe so. He has no shields." Michael sounded professionally disapproving, like a dentist whose patient hasn't been flossing.

A couple of long minutes later the trooper spoke again, his gaze still fixed over my left shoulder. "Sorry to bother you, ma'am." Then, suddenly, he came unstuck. He gave me a brisk nod and headed back to his car.

I slumped back in my seat. "That was weird. That was so weird." I watched in the rearview mirror as the trooper's car pulled away. "If I'd known you could do that, I would have gotten you to take care of Pete."

"I . . . didn't know I could, either, at that point."

His voice sounded funny. I straightened and looked at him. His head was tilted back against the headrest, and he was almost as pale as he'd been when I first found him. "Are you okay?"

"It always gives me a headache to do that," he said absently. "A real mother—"

"Whoa. That's considered a very rude phrase."

"Oh. Is the word fuck offensive?"

"Yes, unless you're actually doing it, or about to do it."

"Odd. There are several words with a primary or secondary meaning involving copulation that do not offend. At least I don't think they do. Screw, lay, sleep with, mate, ball—"

"It's all in the context. Michael? You said 'always.'"

"I remembered . . . a little more." He turned his head to look at me. In the muted light from the dash, his eyes had an odd sheen, almost reflective. Like cat's eyes. "I performed the same spell on myself just before I came here. I

didn't know if my transit would be successful, and I
couldn't let them . . . learn from me. So I told myself to
forget. But I was rushed. Something went wrong."

"You forgot too much?"

"I forgot how to get it all back." The twitch of his lips
might have been meant for a smile. "There are seventeen
versions of this saying in the various realms: whatever can
go wrong, will."

"We call it Murphy's Law. You look wrecked." I un-
buckled my seat belt and stood. "I'm going to get you some
ibuprofen."

"This is a remedy for pain?"

"Yes."

"Good. The nearest ley line is thin, hard to draw from
with my head pounding. And the Houston node is too distant to reach directly."

"Houston has a node?"

"Of course. So many people could not live so closely
without one. They would become insane. Though that node
is well below the land surface, and the energy is badly scattered. I suspect electricity . . . ah." His eyes lit up. "You
brought me the Coke to drink."

He had the oddest gaps in his knowledge. I had to show
him how to use "the Coke" to swallow pills. Then,
abruptly, I shut off the engine and told him I was going outside to think.

THERE'S so little real night left in the Western world.
Here, halfway between Houston and San Antonio, the sky
was hazy, the stars thin. But the moon was fat and profli-
gate with its borrowed light. I started walking along the
curve of road that defined the rest area.

There were trees. I could hear a dog barking somewhere, far in the distance. And all those noisy fireflies on the interstate swishing by, making good time on their way to wherever. The grass was soft beneath my feet and the breeze held a pleasant, green scent, but I missed the smell of the sea.

I ached.

Lord knows I should have been thinking about the fix we were in. I tried, but my intentions kept scattering, then re-forming, lined up behind one thought like iron filings obedient to the pull of the magnet.

I could have him. I could have Michael. He was willing, and I hadn't seduced him into it. I didn't have to worry about hurting him.

Not physically, that is. I moved slowly, watching the restless branches of an oak nibble the moon into lace. But that had never been my real worry, had it?

I'd long ago learned control. Whatever vital force I consume—and it's not the soul; that's a ridiculous superstition—a healthy body can easily replace it as long as I don't drink too deeply. Rather like a dairy farmer, I like to think, I dine on what other bodies make naturally, without having to kill for my dinner.

But the worst hurts—the ones that don't heal—aren't physical.

I stopped and looked up at the hazy sky. I've had plenty of time to puzzle out the moral limits of my condition, and ended up with something similar to the Wiccan code. I try to do no harm. This means I leave married men alone. Also those who show signs of real emotional involvement, those too young to make responsible choices, and men too old or infirm to afford the loss of what I would drain from them.

Michael wasn't depleted by his wounds anymore. He was young, but not so young he had to be protected from his own choices. I stared up at a moon a few bumps past full, tucked my hair behind my ear, and admitted the truth. I wasn't worried about the consequences for Michael. I probably should be, but mostly I was afraid for myself.

I was so tired of leaving. That didn't mean I'd like to be the one left behind . . . and this wasn't his world.

Dammit. Dairy farmers don't fall in love with their cows.

The light in the rig came on behind me. I turned and watched Michael step down, close the door behind him, and restore the semblance of darkness. He walked towards me and my mouth went dry. "Is your headache better?"

"Almost gone." He spoke low, as if someone might overhear. "Have you finished your thinking?"

"I haven't accomplished much." I hugged my arms to myself, though the breeze wasn't cold. "I guess we could steal a license plate, if we get a chance before the next cop spots us."

He moved closer. "It's the numbers on the license plate that give us away? I can fix that."

That jolted me. "You can do that? Change the plates?" Transformative magic was supposed to be impossible for anyone short of an adept—and there hadn't been any adepts since the Codex Arcanus was lost, long before even I was born. But Michael wasn't from here, was he?

"It would be easier to throw an illusion over them. I can cast one that will fool almost anyone here." He put his hands on my arms. "You are chilly?"

"No. Yes." *Step back,* I told myself. And didn't move. "You're remembering more."

"Pieces." He stroked his hands up and down my arms slowly, looking intently at my face. "Are you warming?"

Oh, yes. "Could you cast a bigger illusion? Make the design on the Winnebago beige, for example, instead of blue?"

"Yes. And then we could continue on our way. But I

don't want to." His hands slid up to my shoulders. He moved even closer.

Those iron filings were all lined up, pointing right at him. I suspected my nipples were, too. My body longed for him. I was firm with it—firm enough, at least, not to reach for the sweet, serious face so close to mine. "You don't understand the dangers. We—we need to—Michael? What are you doing?"

"I like looking at your hair. I've been wanting to touch it." And he was, drawing his hands slowly along the length of it, then tucking his fingers in so that he cradled my head in his hands. "So cool and soft . . . you have smiling hair, Molly."

It was getting hard to remember to breathe. "Smiling?"

"Every little hair smiles itself into curls." Yet he abandoned my hair for my face, tracing it with the tips of his fingers, leaving tingles in his wake like the phosphorescence that trails a ship. "Your skin is soft, too. But much warmer."

"Michael." I tried to sound indignant. It came out husky. "Are you seducing me?"

"God, I hope so." And he bent his head.

His mouth was a little sweet, a little salty, and wholly inexperienced. With a sigh, I abandoned all my shoulds and shouldn'ts. Reason floated away with them, carried off on a warm, gentle tide. I tilted my head, slid my arms around him, and showed him how well we could fit.

As always, Michael was a fast study. And he adored kissing.

He had no inhibitions, no cultural context for a right way and a wrong way to touch. So he touched me everywhere. My back, my breasts, my shoulders—every part of my body fascinated him. He nuzzled my hair and licked the tip of my nose, making me giggle. Then he kissed me as if he had no thought of doing anything else, ever again.

If there's anything more seductive than a man who knows how to kiss, it's a man who puts his whole heart and soul into learning. Finally I pulled my mouth away. "There's a bed." I whispered that, hoping to hide the way my voice shook. "Back in the rig."

"Mmm." He was sniffing along my neck, pausing now and then to lick or nibble. "I don't require a bed. Oh." He raised his head. "Perhaps you do?"

My laugh was breathless. "I'm not sure I could make it there. Here is fine." I tugged on his hand, urging him to the earth with me. "Here is wonderful."

I have all the arts, every skill a woman can use on a man. I was as giddy and awkward as a girl being tumbled in the meadow by the young man she's been walking out with. Together we rediscovered the mysteries of zippers and shoes, removed socks and t-shirts, and made a nest in the long grass on the side of the road.

Then we were skin-to-skin, and hunger turned from a sweet tide to a roaring torrent. His body was a dream and a delight, but I had no patience left to savor it. Energy rose from his flesh like mist around a waterfall, swirling, tempting, teasing without filling me. My own skin was hot and desperately sensitive. When he licked my nipple I arched up, then pulled him fully over me. His weight pinned me, anchored me. His cock was thick and blunt, uncircumcised. It twitched against my stomach. "Now," I said. "I need you. I need you inside me, Michael."

"You have me. Take what you need. All that you need." He propped himself up on his elbows, staring down at me, his face tight with his own need. "Tell me what to do."

"Like this." I opened my legs, using my hands to urge

his hips forward. His body knew, even if his mind didn't. The swirling energy sucked at me, setting up answering tremors in my body, as my blood, bones, and flesh answered the call of an unseen tide. "Come in. Come inside."

He thrust. Came into me. And the currents entered with him, and swallowed me.

Sex is God's way of reminding us not to take ourselves so seriously. There are a thousand ways to arrange two sweaty, straining bodies. Each has its own pleasures, and each is as absurd as it is delightful. Passion—real passion—is different, and rare. It grabs you by the throat and shakes you like a terrier with a rat. Then it flings you off, across the abyss.

If you're lucky, you don't break when you land. If you're very lucky, you don't land alone.

I landed sobbing . . . held safe in Michael's arms.

He was stroking my hair, my side, my hand as I came back to myself. It took a moment for his quiet murmurs to settle into words. "I'm sorry. I'm sorry. Please don't . . . what is wrong, Molly? Tell me, *querida, mío tesoro, a chuisle mo chroj*. Let me make it better."

I turned my head, which rested on his shoulder. "It's nothing. I'm all right."

"I have heard of happy tears, but this . . ." His thumb rubbed some of the dampness from my cheek. ". . . is not happiness."

It wasn't so hard, after all, to smile. I shifted, propping up on one forearm so I could see his face. "Have you ever been around an overstimulated two-year-old?"

He shook his head. "I don't know."

"They burst into tears for no reason." I traced his lip gently. "Now you've seen an overstimulated three hundred-year-old do the same thing."

He considered that. "This is a compliment, I think."

"Oh, yes. And you were wrong. Part of the overload is happiness." I spoke true. I've lived too long to spurn the good God's gifts—and moments like this were just that, gifts of grace that fall like sunshine, unsought and unearned.

He smiled slowly. "Good." And he urged my head back onto his shoulder, and stroked my hair.

How strange, I thought. Here I was, lying on my side with a stick digging into my hip and my lover's heart beating beneath my ear. I was sated and sticky, my muscles lax and warm, my skin cooling. None of the physical sensations were new to me, yet everything was new, fresh-minted.

How long had it been since I took a lover? Not a sex partner. A lover. I ran my hand over his ribs, marveling. There would be grief later. I didn't care. Loving was gift enough.

After awhile I asked, "What do you think of the name Sarah?"

"It means soul in one of the Indian languages, princess in Hebrew. Why?"

I shrugged my free shoulder. "I need a new name."

"I like the one you have."

"So do I. But I can't be Molly Brown anymore. I'm having trouble settling on a new name, though."

"Names are important. I will give it some thought. Do you want . . ." His voice drifted into silence even as his body tensed.

I've hunted, and I've been hunted. I didn't cloud the silence with questions but, like a hare in the bush, went still myself, straining to sort the night sounds. Cars continued to whoosh past on the highway. The breeze ruffled the leaves in the trees. Grass rustled . . .

Michael sprang to his feet, yanking me up with him. "Run!"

They came at us out of the darkness. Four, five—I don't

know how many there were. They seemed splinters of darkness themselves, clothed as they were in black, their faces smeared with black. We were in full flight when we saw them, our hands clasped, bare feet slapping on the asphalt. They raced out of the trees—from in front of us. Between us and the RV.

Moonlight gleamed on metal. A gun barrel, raised—the shot cracked out even as Michael jerked me to the left. The highway—yes, they might not want to shoot us where so many witnesses streamed by. There were trees between us and the interstate, too. Cover.

There were also two more of them, rising from the brush like shadows. One with a rifle, one with something large and ominous held to his shoulder and pointed, oddly, off to the right.

But the rifle was pointed at me.

I felt the power jump into Michael. He bellowed something. A word. It slid through my brain like melted butter— hot, ungraspable. And the one with the rifle burst into flame.

And so, with an explosion that rocked the earth, did my Winnebago.

Michael jerked. Stumbled. Threw his arms around me, hugging so hard that all the air whooshed out of me. And the universe tilted in an impossible, sideways slide, and burst into bits—into motion—then stillness.

I was lying on my back on something hard and rough. It was hard to draw breath. Something heavy and warm pinned me, covered me, all but smothered me. Heavy and warm and ... "Michael," I breathed, and ran my hands over him. He was unconscious, but alive. My questing hands found a dart in his back.

Anesthetic? I blinked, gathering thoughts with care and piecing them together much more slowly than the universe had re-formed itself around me. As gently as I could—he was very heavy—I eased Michael off me, sat up, and looked around.

And began to laugh. I couldn't help it. We were back in the Village, plopped down naked on top of the node where Michael had first appeared.

Chapter 9

⁓⁓⁓

"IT'S certainly different," Erin said, dabbing at the graze on my cheek. "Not that you don't look great. You do. But it will take some getting used to."

"Mmm." I was sitting on the closed toilet in the downstairs bathroom of Erin's house, a cozy two-story in Galveston's historical section. I knew the house well, though it has been through a lot of changes. A little over a hundred years ago, the debris from the storm surge had mounded two stories high only a block from here.

I glanced at the mirror over the sink . . . which had showed me a face I hadn't seen for some time. A face ten or fifteen years younger than the one I'd seen the last time I looked in a mirror. A face surrounded by red hair, not white.

Sex with Michael hadn't just made me *feel* young again.

All that power . . . apparently a glut could undo what star-vation had wrought.

"Ouch! Be careful. I might need some of that skin."

"Hold still."

"I don't know why you're doing this. I'm perfectly ca-pable of cleaning up a couple scratches."

"Maybe I need to."

That silenced me. She slid my robe—well, it was hers, but I was wearing it—off my shoulder so she could clean the scrape there. I don't know where the abrasions had come from. Maybe I'd skidded a bit when Michael brought us back to the one spot he knew well enough to aim for, even as the drug took him under.

I'd used Theresa Farnhope's phone to call Erin, which would have amazed Theresa, had she known. But she takes out her hearing aids to sleep, which was why I'd chosen her trailer for my entering-without-breaking. I'd gone fuzzy, of course; walls aren't a problem when I'm like that. Erin's husband Pete had arrived with her and helped us load a bleary Michael into her Toyota, where he'd passed out again.

He was awake now, though still dopey. I'd left him in the kitchen drinking coffee. Pete, bless him, had made a pot, walked Michael around until he wasn't staggering so much, then left to try to find us some clothes. "Your hus-band is a miracle," I told Erin.

"True. Are you sure this lawyer of yours can be trusted?"

"For this, yes." I'd called NMN's only employee, an at-torney with interesting connections. He was sending cash and another credit card by courier. I expected them in a couple hours. He'd get us identification, too, but that would take a little longer. I'd sent him digital photos of both

Michael and me after borrowing Pete's camera and computer.

It takes a good deal of money to acquire such things after midnight, as well as those connections I mentioned. But NMN has a good deal of money. Around twenty-six million, last time I checked. Almost anyone can get rich if they live long enough.

"Getting fake ID for a client isn't part of most attorneys' job descriptions," Erin said, capping the peroxide. "So either this guy is a sleaze, or he works for sleaze. So how can you trust him?"

"The sleazes he works for—aside from me, that is—don't encourage questions. And they value loyalty. I imagine he'll tell them, but he won't tell the FBI or the Azá." I shrugged. "I don't plan to use the IDs he sends for long."

"Good grief. You're talking about the Mob."

"I didn't say that." I stood and studied myself in the mirror. I could pass for thirty-five, which was unsettling, but useful. They'd be looking for the fifty-year-old me, not this one. I touched my cheek.

"I liked your old face," Michael said from the doorway. "But this one is pretty, too."

I turned. His face hadn't changed. It was still beautiful enough to break hearts. He wore a pair of Pete's jeans, rolled up at the ankles. They were too big at the waist, too. "How wobbly are you?"

"I can walk," he said grimly. "I had better not try to run or work magic. They knew what they were doing. Sedating me was the best way to render me useless."

"They went to a lot of trouble not to damage you. Just as you suspected they would." Either the Azá knew who and what he was, or they had pretty clear instructions from their goddess.

"Instead they destroyed your home."

I wanted to tell him it didn't matter, but my throat closed up. My pot, my little yellow pot, the one thing I still had from Ginny . . .

"It's my fault," he said bitterly, pushing away from the door. "My fault that you lost everything."

"Not everything." Just the things that mattered. I still had heaps of money.

Erin was worried, but trying to be matter-of-fact. "You couldn't have known what would happen. Probably couldn't have stopped Molly, either, even if you had known."

"Perhaps not. But I should have realized . . . they traced me through the nodes and ley lines. Through my use of them. They must have."

I thought with dismay of my own use of node energy—through Michael. "Is that possible?"

"Theoretically, maybe." Erin was frowning. "Michael's energy is so distinctive, even I could pick it up when I studied the node. But I don't see how anyone could trace his location that way."

"It's possible," Michael said grimly. "Probably not humanly possible, but it can be done."

"The goddess, you mean." Dismay ripened to fear. "But she isn't here. She can't cross. I don't know why, but she can't. But if she's found an avatar here—"

"I don't think so," he said, a frown creasing his brow. "No, if she had an avatar she would have taken me herself. If only I could remember more!" He ran a hand over his face as if he could rub away the weariness. "I think, if she could reach a world heavily congruent to yours, or plant an avatar in one . . . Dis or Faerie are the closest."

Much too close, I thought.

"Dis, probably," Michael went on. "Faerie doesn't care for outsiders, and they have strong defenses. Dis is more chaotic. She might have made a deal with someone there."

Erin's eyes widened. "My children. God, Michael, my children are asleep upstairs—"

"They're safe," he said quickly. "I haven't used magic since I brought us here. I have a low-level connection to whichever node is nearest, yes. I can't sever it. It—it isn't possible. But even an Old One would have trouble finding me this quickly when I'm not drawing power."

I felt cold. "But she could find you? Even if you don't use magic?"

"I don't know. I think . . . eventually. If I stay in motion . . ." He shrugged, helpless to offer certainties when so much was unclear. "It would take tremendous power to locate me when I'm not using a node. A goddess has great power, but if she is in Dis, either personally or through an avatar, she must reserve some of that for defense. They are not friendly in Dis."

The sheer understatement of that made me strangle on a laugh.

Erin didn't see anything funny in the situation. She was looking at Michael with something close to fear. "Who are you, that a goddess would go to such lengths to capture you?"

"It's not who I am, but what I know. Or am supposed to know." He grimaced.

I sighed. "I need coffee. And then, I think, Michael and I had better leave. Just to be sure."

There were no lines around Michael's eyes, but when they met mine just then they looked old. Old and terribly sad. "No, Molly," he said gently. "I must leave. Not you."

WE adjourned to the kitchen. It's possible to break a heart in the bathroom, but a good argument demands a better setting. "You're limping," I told him severely as we headed down the short hall.

"It's nothing. An ache where she wounded me."

Apparently even Michael couldn't mend perfectly what a goddess had ripped up. "If you think that hurt," I muttered, "wait till you see what I can do."

"Molly." He stepped a pace into the kitchen and put his hands on my shoulders. "I do not want to part. You know that, don't you? But my presence has already cost you too much. Your home, your belongings—"

"Things. Just things," I said fiercely. "And they're gone now, so it's too late to worry about them. Some of them did matter, yes. Sometimes I hold too tightly to things. That's because I can't hold on to people." They died, they left, and now Michael wanted to leave. It was too soon. I wasn't ready.

"I understand your fear," he said quietly. "But I am more of a coward. I don't think I could stand it if I cost you your life."

I closed my eyes for a second. "Michael. You're forgetting something." I looked at him again and held out my hand . . . and made it go fuzzy.

He stared. "I didn't . . . God. I didn't have to do it, did I? I forgot. All I could think was that he was going to kill you." Abruptly he pulled away.

Erin tapped me on the shoulder. "Here. Want to tell me what you're talking about?"

She held out a mug of coffee. I took it and watched Michael pace. "They herded us," I said. "Kept us away from the RV. I think they used a bazooka on that, but heaven knows I'm no expert. Maybe it was one of those one-man rocket launchers."

"They blew it up so you couldn't escape," Erin said impatiently. "You told me that. What did Michael do that has him upset?"

"Saved my life."

"How?"

"I'll fill you in later," I said, though I wouldn't. Not about everything. Words of power are a myth, a legend, like the alchemist's stone—a tantalizing shortcut people have dreamed over for centuries. They don't exist. All the experts agree on that.

I wasn't about to try to change anyone's mind.

I was beginning to think Michael was something of a walking myth, himself—but a confused, unhappy myth-man at present. I gave Erin back the coffee mug and went to him.

He stood with his back to me. "It's forbidden, what I did," he said very low. "Except in the last extremity of self-defense. I wasn't in danger, but you . . . I didn't think. Perhaps the one I burned had knockout darts, too. Even if you hadn't dematerialized, he might not have killed you."

"And the others?" I put my hands on his shoulders, which were tight and tense. "Do you think they would have left me alive to tell the authorities what they'd done?"

"They couldn't have hurt you if you'd stayed immaterial."

"Their goddess could. She cursed me. She could remove the curse, or just ignore it. I don't know how much knowledge and power she's invested in her followers, but I wouldn't want to bet my life on the chance that they couldn't touch me."

"They came for us with guns, not magic."

"Because you could have stood off any magic they were likely to possess. You were their target, so they used what would work against you. If we'd hung around, we would have found out what they could do to me."

After a moment his breath sighed out. He turned his head to look at me. "All the more reason you shouldn't come with me. They may be the only ones who could truly harm you."

"Define 'harm.'" My hands wanted to tighten on him, to clutch at him and hold him. My voice wanted to plead. I wouldn't. Not for the sake of my pride—a costly indulgence, pride. Sometimes worth the price, but not this time.

But tears and pleading have a price, too. One Michael would have to pay, along with me. "I've granted you the dignity of making your own decisions," I said levelly. "Even when I disagreed, or didn't think you knew what you were getting into. What gives you the right to take this choice from me?"

He said nothing, just looked at me. I tried to stay with my breath the way the Buddhists say, but my chest was squeezed so tight with waiting that every breath hurt. If he understood, even a little, what mattered, what had kept me sane all these years—

All at once his mouth quirked up. "Do you ever lose an argument?"

I laughed—or meant to; it came out more like a sob. Then my eyes were shut tight against the tears and his arms were tight around me. He rubbed his cheek against my hair. "We'll go to your sorcerer, Molly. And pray he knows how to fix things, because I don't."

Chapter 10

❖

As soon as our clothes, cash, and Visa arrived, we left. I called my attorney collect and changed the location for the courier to deliver the ID; I'd meet him at a nearby McDonald's in about five hours. Then we walked. For hours, we held hands and walked around Galveston, sometimes talking, sometimes in silence. As it grew light we attracted some glances, but mostly smiling ones. I didn't look that much older than him now.

We'd decided against a hotel, though we were both tired. We didn't want to be separated, but passion was too new between us. It made us unsteady, and Michael couldn't draw from a node. Easier to live with exhaustion than temptation.

At ten-thirty that morning, we were on a plane headed west. I'd called Cullen and told him enough to whet his curiosity. I slept most of the way. Michael slept some, too, but he was wide awake and back to his usual self by the time we landed. Full of questions.

"Are all airports ugly?" he asked, pausing to frown at the boarding gate we disembarked into. "This could be decorated."

"Parts of them are. The people behind us don't want to stop and study the walls, Michael."

"Oh. Of course." He started moving again. "I would like to have a closer look at the way they connected this tube to the airplane. Most ingenious. Not now, I know," he said, favoring me with a smile sweetened by amusement. "Maybe later?"

I couldn't help smiling back. "Maybe."

We made it to the concourse with only a few questions along the way. "I think I didn't travel much, before," he said as we headed to baggage claim, where Cullen would meet us. "But I wanted to. So now I want to absorb everything, all at once. Were you and this sorcerer lovers, Molly?"

I stumbled over nothing.

His hand was instantly there, steadying me. His eyes were oddly gentle. "Am I not supposed to ask?"

"You startled me, that's all." I shook my head. "Unlike you, I don't always tell the truth. But I'll try to, with you. Cullen and I have had sex, yes. But we were never lovers."

He studied my face a moment, then nodded as if he understood the distinction. "I would like it if you did not kiss him. Sexually, that is. I realize that kisses are not always sexual. Would that be difficult for you? I feel . . . uncomfortable when I think of you kissing others the way you kiss me."

"Michael." I cupped his cheek in my palm. "While I'm with you, I won't want to dine on other men." Though I might have to, if we couldn't find a way for Michael to safely use node energy . . . but I wasn't going to think about that, not now. "I certainly won't kiss them."

A smile broke over his face. "Thank you, Molly." He reclaimed my hand and started walking. A little boy on the plane had taught him how to whistle—somewhat disturbing my sleep, I might add—and he did that now, whistling happily and without any discernible tune.

My heart was thumping as if we'd just negotiated some dreadful precipice. I cleared my throat. "You need to remember to call me Sandra."

"That isn't your name."

"It's the name on my ID."

"I will think on it," he told me.

CULLEN Seabourne is the most physically perfect man I've ever known. He's blond, slimmer, and taller than Michael, with a pleasant but unremarkable tenor voice. But people don't listen to Cullen. They stare at him, startled out of courtesy by such sheer, masculine beauty. He's well aware of his effect on others and capable of using it to get what he wants, but looks don't really matter to him. Magic does.

I didn't trust him, not completely. But I liked him, and, oh, but he was a pleasure to watch. Heads turned in baggage claim as he approached us. Among other things, Cullen is a dancer, and he moves like music made solid.

"Hullo, darling," Cullen said as he sauntered up. "Still in one piece, I see, in spite of ninjas and bazookas and such. But you have a new look. Nice," he said, reaching out with lazy grace to stroke one finger down my cheek. "But surprising." He leaned toward me.

"No kissing," I told him firmly.

"No?" He pulled back, quirking one eyebrow. Sometimes I think everyone in the world can do that except me. "How interesting. I have a few questions."

"I'm sure," I said dryly. "But not here, I think. You brought your car?"

"You don't think I'd trust my delicate skin to a taxi driver, do you? And you indicated a need for privacy." Deliberately he turned to face Michael. "This would be the mystery man."

"Yes. This is Michael."

Who was staring. "You," he said, "are most unusual."

Cullen's eyes narrowed. After a moment of study he said, "So are you. Though I'm damned if I can say what you are. Not quite human, I think?"

"No. But then, neither are you. I've always wanted to meet one of your kind." Michael turned to me with a smile. "Did you know this is the only realm with Lupi?"

Oh, yes. That's another thing that Cullen is. A werewolf.

CULLEN was currently living in a dilapidated little shack in the mountains outside San Diego. At least, that's where he took us. I'm not sure he actually lived there. It looked ready to fall down, but it sat almost on top of a node.

"Quite small," he told us as he pulled his dusty Jeep to a stop in front of it. "No more than a trickle, really. But enough for my purposes, since I'm the only one using it. I'm trusting you rather a lot," he added, sliding me a glance as he climbed out. "I never bring people here."

"I'm paying you rather a lot. Besides, you're eaten up with curiosity."

"True." He flashed me a grin, then turned to Michael, who was studying the land around the cabin. "See anything interesting?"

"Just your wards. Nice work," Michael said politely. "That low one—it's to keep out vermin? Insects and such?"

Cullen went very still. "Oh, yes, I am definitely curious. Shall we go inside?"

The inside didn't look any more solid than the outside, but it was slightly cleaner. There was only one room.

"Sit," Cullen said, rooting around in a cupboard. "I originally trained in Wicca, if that means anything to you." He took out an athame, two vials, and a small silver bowl.

"Yes," Michael said, seating himself at the small wooden table. It looked sturdier than the walls of the shack. "It means you're grounded in the basic energies of your realm, which is the best way to begin. With sorcery, though, I assume you're self-taught?"

"Mostly. Now and then I run across a tantalizing scrap, or cut a deal with one of my reclusive compatriots. We don't trust each other, of course, but we're equally desperate for knowledge. There's a man in Africa doing good work, a woman in Singapore . . . I've a contact or two in Faerie, as well, though they're a closemouthed lot." He gestured with the hand holding the bowl. "Sit down, Molly. I'm going to try a little creation of my own in a minute, a combination of truth and seek spells. First I have questions."

I sat. All of a sudden I wasn't at all sure I'd made the right decision, coming to Cullen. But what choice did we have? "I've told you how I found Michael."

"Questions for him, love, not you." He sat in the third chair, put his tools on the table, and looked at Michael. "You say you don't remember who and what you are, where you came from."

"I remember pieces. Not the whole."

"Yet you saw what I was right away. You saw my wards—and knew what they were, too."

"I gather that most people in this realm do not see the *sorcéri*." He gave the word an odd pronunciation I hadn't heard before.

"No. No, they don't. You really aren't from this world, are you?"

"That much I'm sure of."

Cullen drew a deep breath, let it out slowly. "I have a feeling you know a helluva lot more than I do about magic. Why come to me?"

"My knowledge isn't always accessible. I want to see if you can hide or disguise my use of the nodes. They—the Azá—track me that way. Molly hopes you can restore my memory."

"You sound doubtful."

"I am. I can tell you the spell I used to forget, but I don't know if you will be able to devise a counterspell. I cannot, but being self-trained, you are accustomed to creating your own spells."

"That will help." Cullen's eyes glittered with excitement.

Michael gave him an assessing look. "You'll get nothing from me without my cooperation. Even with it, there is some danger."

Cullen gave a bark of laughter and leaned back in his chair. "Danger? For what you could teach me, I'd risk hurricanes, lightning bolts, and an IRS audit."

I was feeling worse about this all the time. Cullen glanced at me. "Don't worry, love. If my conscience—an elastic creation, admittedly—snaps under the strain, you can still count on my sense of self-preservation. I know very well you'd make a bad enemy."

"So would I," Michael said mildly. "But we won't be enemies, will we?"

"I hope not." Cullen's grin was little short of feral. "Oh, I do hope not."

* * *

TRUTH spells were not safe to use on Michael. This time, the backlash lifted Cullen off the ground and slammed him against the west wall. Boards cracked, broke. He landed half-out, half-in, sprawled in the debris of the wrecked wall.

My ears were ringing, though I hadn't heard a thing except for the wall breaking. I jumped to my feet. "Cullen!"

Michael's hand snatched at me. "Wait. The roof . . ."

I looked up. Things were leaning alarmingly. "Hold it," I told him, and hurried to Cullen. He was pale, motionless, and slightly bloody—but blinking thoughtfully at the sky now overhead instead of rafters. "Your boyfriend packs a punch, love."

I exhaled in relief. "At least you don't have amnesia."

"No, I remember well enough what happened." He pushed up on one elbow, winced. "At least one rib. It's a good thing I'm Lupus."

There were scraping noises behind me, and a grunt. "I think that will hold." Michael sounded dubious. "The blow was unintentional, Cullen. I am sorry."

"You have amazing reflexes, then." He took the hand Michael held out, grunting as Michael pulled him to his feet, and rubbed his side. "Or maybe . . . not reflexes. Defenses. Put there by someone else."

Michael was very still. "You're talented. Given the tools you have to work with, extremely talented."

"You're a construct, aren't you? Made, not born."

"Yes."

That one word dropped into the well of silence it created even as it was spoken. *So many words have power,* I thought dimly, *not just the magical ones.* My voice, when at last I broke the silence, was small. "Michael?"

"I am sorry." His voice was remote. He didn't look at me.

"And you've remembered more than you're admitting." Excitement radiated from Cullen like heat from a stove as he moved closer to Michael. "I only caught a glimpse—but there's so much inside you! Knowledge—vast amounts of knowledge. Power—"

"Knowledge is power," Michael said sadly.

Cullen stopped in front of Michael. *What are you?*

"I cannot tell you." At last Michael turned to me. There was grief in his eyes, old grief and fresh, the raw mixed with scars from other earlier woundings. "Not *will* not, Molly. Cannot. The way I am made, some things are not possible for me."

"You could have told me more than you have." I made it a statement, not a question. I was already sure.

"When we met the state cop, much came back to me. Not everything—I am still in pieces, and they don't all fit together. But that I was made, not born . . . yes. I could have told you that."

"You didn't trust me?" I whispered.

He lifted one hand as if he would touch me, then let it drop. "The place where I've lived is a good place. Not a world as you are used to worlds, but there is much beauty, much to learn. But it is remote. Few are able to cross, and the others who live there are further from human than I am. I was . . . lonely."

I swallowed hard. "Did you think I wouldn't understand loneliness?"

"I wanted you to see me as a man. Not a thing."

My breath huffed out. "Good grief, is that all? You *are* a man."

"This is not the body I wore before I came here. Things there are much more fluid. I . . . borrowed the pattern for this body from a friend."

I shook my head. "Great Mother of Heaven! You think

I'm fooled by that delicious body of yours? I was pretty sure that wasn't your original form. Good grief—you scarcely knew how to walk when you first arrived."

Hope woke in his ocean eyes. "You were supposed to assume it was my wounds hindering my movement."

"I did, at first. But this is my area of expertise, Michael. If anyone in this realm or any other knows about men, I do. Made or born, you are definitely a man."

"Then—you do not mind what I am?"

"I started out human, then became something else, too. You started out something else, then got some human mixed in." I shrugged. "What's to mind? You're Michael."

He whooped, grabbed me, and whirled us both around, kissing whatever part presented itself—my hair, forehead, shoulder. Quick, peppery kisses that stung life into me. Laughing, I seized his face in my hands, and kissed him back.

Until hard hands thrust the two of us apart.

"Good lord," Cullen gasped, one hand still on my shoulder, one on Michael's. "It's not that I wasn't enjoying the show. I can't remember when I've gotten this hard watching others kiss, being more interested in participating than spectating. But you were drawing down hard from the node, Michael—and Molly, I thought you couldn't *take* without intercourse?"

I gaped at Michael, appalled. "I'm sorry. I didn't—I don't know how I did that."

He shook off Cullen's hand, and ran his own hand through his hair. "It's my fault. I'm supposed to control when I draw. If *she* was watching . . ."

"Well." Cullen shrugged. "It's a small node. Wouldn't be easy to spot, even drawing like you were, and I stopped you fast enough. I'd say it's unlikely anyone could have located you, but we don't have guarantees, do we? You'd better not do it again. However . . ." His eyes gleamed. "We do have an idea. At least, I do."

He stopped there, dragging it out. "Well?" I snapped.

"I think I know how to hide Michael's, ah, signature, when he draws. But I want to renegotiate our terms."

"You want more money?"

"Money?" He made a disgusted noise. "What use is that? I was going to use what you paid me, Molly my love, to try to acquire more scraps. I don't have to settle for scraps now."

"What do you want?" Michael's voice was ominously low.

"As much as I can get, obviously." Suddenly Cullen laughed. "If you could see your faces! I haven't turned into an evil wizard before your eyes, scheming to steal your souls and take over the world. I don't want them, for one thing. For another," he said wryly, "Michael could squash me like a bug if I tried anything. No, I want to learn. I want Michael's time for, say, a month. I want to ask questions, learn from him."

"I'm not allowed. No," Michael said to Cullen, holding up a hand. "This isn't negotiable. I thought at first that your realm had just drifted apart from the others, but it's more. You're under interdict. I don't know why, or who established the ban. Those pieces are missing. But I am not allowed to give you the knowledge you want."

Cullen's face tightened. "A week, just a week, then. I could spend a lifetime studying my scraps and not learn as much as I can from you in one week. Do you know what that's like? All right—one day, man!" He was fierce in his need. "Just give me one day."

"One spell." Michael's face was granite. "One spell, of your choice—within reason. No transformations."

Cullen spoke flatly. "Not enough."

"We don't have to deal with you," I said mildly. "If the idea is any good, chances are one of us will think of it, sooner or later. More likely Michael than me, I'll admit."

Cullen wore an odd little smile. "I doubt this particular notion would occur to him. Even if it does, he'll need help. Because he isn't much at creating spells. Are you?" he said directly to Michael. "You've got more facts lodged in your head than NASA's mainframe, but you don't know much about building from scratch."

"I wasn't made to create, but I can do it."

"Well enough to trust Molly's life to a homemade spell?"

His eyebrows pulled down. His gaze darted to me, then back to Cullen. "Explain."

"Not until you agree to my terms."

"Then I suppose we must leave. And then, sooner or later, the Azá will find me. They will either kill Molly, or not. And I will either kill more of them, or not—but eventually they will have me, and turn me over to their goddess. Then she will have access to all that you covet."

Cullen flung up one hand—a fencer's gesture, acknowledging an opponent's coup. "And civilization as we know it will come to an end? All right, all right. One spell. You'll give me a little time to think of what I want, since I'm to get just the one?"

Michael nodded. "And your idea?"

"Is simplicity itself, in principle. Probably not in execution." He threw me a roguish glance. "It's right up your alley, sweetheart. All you have to do is make love."

Chapter 11

❖

IT wasn't simple, of course. Michael and Cullen spent the rest of the afternoon discussing the details, arguing, now and then pausing to draw a glowing symbol in the air. But the premise was fairly basic.

Not that I understood it. Michael and I would change places, as far as the nodes were concerned. Instead of me drinking from him, he'd draw power through me. Only I'd still be tapping the magic through him, which is what I didn't understand. Somehow, though, the nodes would "read" my pull, not his. And I was mostly human, natural to this realm, so no one would be able to get a fix on me.

"Your energies are already muddled up together, love," Cullen had told me when I expressed bafflement. "Not that I have a clue how you did that, but that's what I saw when you went into a liplock. It's why you were able to begin feeding short of, ah, the usual ritual. We're just going to muddle things a bit more thoroughly."

There was a catch, of course. Isn't there always? Once we were joined this way, I would have to feed through Michael. And only him.

It was a long afternoon. The sun was low by the time they agreed on the basics and finished their preparations. Michael took me aside. "I'm not sure I should do this," he said, smoothing my hair back. I couldn't read his expression, but his body was tense. "I know you agreed, but you don't—you can't—understand exactly what you're agreeing to."

I smiled tenderly. "You didn't know what you were getting into last night, did you?" Then laughed at my accidental pun. "Well, maybe you knew, technically. Me. I'll trust your experience in sorcery, just as you trusted mine last night."

A smile eased, but didn't erase, the tension around his eyes. "Then we are ready."

"Good," Cullen said from behind me. "I'll start walking, then, and give the two of you a little privacy. I hope you won't linger in the afterglow too long, though. I'm eager."

They'd agreed that Michael would give Cullen his spell—one involving illusion—after our ritual was completed, when Michael could safely draw from the node. "You are considerate," Michael said, turning to face him. "But that won't be necessary."

"Won't be . . ." Cullen's face worked. The blood drained from it. "Damn you!" he whispered—and his eyes rolled back.

Michael caught him before he hit the floor, and lowered him carefully. "I am sorry," he said to the unconscious man.

My heart was hammering in my throat. "What did you do to him?"

"He will sleep for many hours. When he wakes, he'll remember very little ... that you brought a fellow sorcerer to visit him. That he and I exchanged spells, discussed some things, then you and I left. It won't be perfect," he said, straightening Cullen's legs so he could rest comfortably. "I can't build a memory as vivid as the real thing. But I've also planted an aversion in him. He won't want to examine his memories of this day."

"But why?"

"The spell he requested was the smallest part of what he learned today." Michael shook his head, looking with rueful admiration at the man he'd felled. "We had to collaborate, and in the process he learned more than anyone in your world has known in several hundred years. Which he was counting on, of course. Did you not think he gave in too easily?"

I sighed. I'd been too relieved to be suspicious.

"I will give him what we agreed upon," Michael said, "but must take away the rest." He settled, cross-legged, beside Cullen's body, and touched his forehead.

I didn't interfere. Should I have? I've never been sure.

It didn't take long. After a few moments Michael shook himself like a dog come in from the rain, and stood. "It's done." Regret rang through his voice like a low, sad bell. "I left him a gift."

"What kind?"

"Shields. No one will be able to do to him again what I have done this day."

I sighed. "He wants to learn so much."

"And I understand his need, better than he knows. But he is too hungry." Michael looked at me. "I've dealt with seekers like him for a very long time. Their hunger can't be sated, like yours can. Better if he forgets. It would be unkind to let him remember only a little, knowing that so much more was somewhere in his world."

"Not kind, no," I said quietly. "And maybe not safe for us, either. Michael?"

"Yes?"

"Just how old are you?"

His eyes crinkled as amusement banished the shadows. "You have been determined to see me as very young, haven't you? Though you claimed not to be fooled by my body. My delicious body?" He quirked an eyebrow at me.

I laughed and held out my hand. "Male vanity crosses all realms. You didn't answer my question."

"Soon," he said, taking my hand, "you will know that, and more. But we had best hurry. Cullen was counting on my unwillingness to use magic and draw the goddess's attention."

I swallowed. "She has to work through human agents, and we're pretty remote. Even if she spotted you, it will take them awhile to get here."

"Yes. But I am unsure how long we will be . . . occupied."

I tried for a cocky smile. "Doesn't usually take *that* long."

"This will not be as usual, Molly."

THE node lay just east of the shack, its perimeter less than ten feet from the wall Cullen had gone sailing through. In another land it would have been called a fairy circle. The San Diego hills—I refuse to call them mountains, they lack the stature for that—are arid, though, so the grass was scruffy, bleached, and brownish. But though sparse, it grew in the distinctive spiral pattern common to nodes.

The two men had set wards earlier, using four black pillar candles, one at each of the cardinal points. Michael used a gesture rather than an athame to open the circle so we could enter. A quilt awaited us.

We were to enter sky-clad—nude, in other words. This was both ritually necessary and convenient, considering why we were there. I stripped, stepped into the circle, and knelt on the quilt.

Michael left his clothes in a neat pile and joined me. With another gesture, he set flames on the candles' wicks. He knelt in front of me, taking my hands. "You're nervous. You know what to do?"

I nodded. They'd briefed me on my part—which was, basically, to control my appetite, not letting myself dine until Michael told me to. And to set the sexual pace. Most of the time, simultaneous orgasm is overrated. This once, though, it was essential. "One of these days we'll have to try this in a bed," I said, trying to lighten the mood. Mine, mostly.

"I count on that. Molly? Time is short."

I nodded again, leaned forward, and brushed my lips across Michael's—and sprang to my feet. "I'm sorry." I squeezed my eyes shut. "I can't do this. I'm sorry."

Silence. Except for the wind and a distant locust, I heard nothing at all. I opened my eyes. Michael just sat there, his face nearly as frozen as the state cop's had been.

"It's wrong," I said, miserable. "You were worried I didn't know what I was letting myself in for. Well, I knew. I was thrilled, if you want the truth. You couldn't leave me once it was done, could you?" Everyone left—over and over, they grew old and died . . . "I wanted to keep you. Because you won't die." The wind lifted my hair, pushing it in my face. I shoved it back.

He tilted his head back so he could look at me. His voice was dead level. "And is that the only reason you want to keep me? Because I won't age and die on you?"

"Well, I love you, of course. But—"

"Holy fuck."

I blinked at him.

"You said the word was not offensive when one is about to do it." He rose to his feet and gripped my shoulders. "Didn't you wonder? Of all the nodes in the world, didn't you wonder how I happened to land on yours?"

"I—I supposed it was the closest, or something like that."

"I've been watching you. What you call the Great Storm was the physical expression of a realms-wide disturbance. It opened a small . . . call it a viewing spot. I saw you save Erin's great-great-grandmother. I bent several rules to watch you raising her. Then you left Galveston, for years and years. I was so happy when you came back." His fingers tightened. "So happy."

"Watching me?" I couldn't take it in. "You've been watching me since 1900?"

"Only when you were in Galveston. I couldn't follow when you left. You were so beautiful. I watched, and I fell in love."

My mouth was hanging open like a fish's. I closed it, then said, stupidly, "But I've been fifty years old all that time."

"Molly." His smile was tender. "You shine. I wish you could see your own colors."

Something tight and small inside me was unfurling. "You love me. It isn't just the sex. You loved me before that."

He nodded, solemn again. "I didn't think you could love me. Not this fast, maybe not at all. But I could feed you, I knew that. Only, of course, I forgot. Forgot everything— you, me, why I'd fled." He shook his head. "I really am bad at creating spells. In my defense, I can only say that I was in a hurry. They'd broken into my place."

"They?"

"They shouldn't have been able to. Even Old Ones have limits. But two of them cooperated with—with—it's gone." The familiar frustration roughened his voice. "Something has changed in the realms, but I don't know what. Not anymore."

"Never mind," I said, and the unfurling reached my face, bringing a smile. "This isn't the time for talk, is it?" I put my arms around his neck. "Make love with me, Michael."

In the end it was simple, after all.

We sank to the quilt together, kissing and touching as if we had all the time in the world. This time I could be patient, thrill myself with his body, because the other hunger wasn't so great. This time, I could share a little of what I'd learned in the last three hundred years.

I explored him. His toes. The backs of his knees. His scrotum—oh, he was sensitive there, no surprise, but his response nearly tipped me over. I sat back on my heels, breathing heavily. "Give me a moment."

"No," he said, and pulled me over him like a blanket.

"I think you've forgotten who's in charge," I said as he licked my nipple. He smiled and blew on it. I shivered.

Passion was no less strong, but it built more slowly. Maybe because he and I both had to keep track of other things—he was watching the energies I couldn't see, manipulating them in ways I couldn't guess. But I could feel them, oh, yes, feel the power rising, swirling between us, yet I had to keep us paced to each other.

Finally I rose over him, guided myself down and sighed with pleasure at the fullness. I ran my fingernails over his chest. "I am *very* happy with the body you chose," I said, leaning forward and all but purring. "If you see your friend again, give him my compliments."

Michael laughed. He gripped my hips and thrust up. And undid all my care. The fall towards climax hit so fast I couldn't stop it. "Michael!" He thrust again and the swirls seemed to reach for me. "Wait!"

"No, Molly, it's now. Now! Reach for me, go deep—"

I reached. Gripped him tight with my inner muscles even as I bore down, drank deep—convulsed. And screamed.

It wasn't pain, though something ripped me open. It wasn't pleasure, though I spun on the wheel of a climax, caught in a vortex that was intensely physical, and not physical at all. It wasn't dark or light, warm or cold, or anything I have names for.

And then, for a timeless period, it wasn't me anymore.

Not just me.

Then I was myself again, the only one in my body. Which ached all over, and not just in the usual places. Michael was a warm, lumpy mattress beneath me. His breath was warm and moist against my cheek.

It was dark. The candles had burned down. One was flickering, nearly out. "Well, sailor," I whispered, "you do know how to show a girl a good time."

"Ahh," he said. "I don't think I have the breath to laugh." He paused. "I can't feel my left hand."

I realized I was lying on it. I moved. "It's asleep. Be prepared for some fierce pins and needles."

"Pins and . . . ow!" He held it up, glaring at it. "Bizarre."

"Returning circulation." I managed to roll off him. "Whew." I turned my head to smile at him. "About eight hundred, if I've figured it right."

His brow creased. "What?"

"You. You're something over eight hundred years old. Though you weren't entirely *there* for the first three or four centuries, were you?"

I hadn't experienced all of Michael, nor had he, I think,

blended with all of me. Partly because, as he'd said, he was still in pieces, with large gaps in his memories. Partly because some of what he'd lived I had no context for, so it hadn't stuck.

I had enough. "Poor Cullen. If he'd known he was entertaining the—"

"Shh." He laid a hand over my lips. "Not even in teasing, Molly. Not even here. It isn't safe."

I nodded, understanding. Understanding so much more than I'd expected to. My lover, my mystery man really was a myth of sorts.

Michael was the missing Codex Arcanum. The Book of All Magic.

His creator . . . I had only shadowy images of the one who'd conceived him. An adept? One of the Old Ones? I didn't know, nor did I understand why he'd done it. Perhaps the same desire that led humans to build libraries, the need to keep knowledge from being scattered or destroyed. For centuries, whatever the sorcerers and magicians of many realms had written in their spell books—which weren't always books, nor was the recording always writing—had also been "written" into Michael.

He'd been created here, though. Here on Earth, that is. Not on this continent, but somewhere in my world. Shortly after being made, he'd been sent to another realm, a place where magic ran wild.

Later, he'd developed a sort of homesickness for this world. At the time, though, he hadn't cared. He wasn't alive then.

Had his creator planned for him to come to consciousness? Michael himself didn't know, and I wasn't about to guess. But the place where he'd been stashed was much smaller than our universe, with magic spilling all over itself. Anything that held on to a stable form there for long achieved life. Anything living and sufficiently complex become sentient.

Michael had been built to last. And he certainly wasn't simple.

He shifted beside me, propping himself up to look down on my face. He traced my lip with a finger. "You are well, Molly? You are all right?"

"I'm well." I kissed his finger. "Unbelievably tired, but well. Um . . . shouldn't we be getting out of here?" I glanced around. "No sign of ninjas yet, but—"

"We can leave in a hurry if we need to. Of course, I only know one place to go." He smiled. "Back to Galveston."

"In that case, I want my clothes. I'm not arriving there naked again."

The two of us creaked to our feet. I was giddy with exhaustion . . . and happiness. "What about Cullen?"

"They won't bother him if we are gone. Why should they?" Michael lifted his hand to clear the wards, but paused. "One more thing before we go. I have been giving your name some thought."

I leaned against him, smothering a yawn. "I'm not sure I can give your suggestions the proper attention right now."

"I was hoping you would let me name you, as you did me."

I straightened, looked him in the eye. After a moment I said softly, "All right."

"Then I would like you to remain Molly. And I will give you a new last name."

I nodded solemnly. "That's traditional. What did you have in mind?"

He kissed the tip of my nose. "You are my gift of grace. I name you Molly Grace."

I closed my eyes, checking the fit. And smiled, and opened my eyes. "All right . . . Michael Grace."

His eyes lit. "You gift me with a last name, too."

"It *is* the twenty-first century." Another yawn overtook me. "Michael? Can we go home now?" Because that's what Galveston was, I realized. I might leave it again, maybe many times. But I'd go back. And I wouldn't go alone.

Michael lifted the wards, banished the guttering flames on the candles, then swung me up into his arms to carry me out of the circle. I found that very funny, especially when he stumbled and nearly dropped me.

"Is this not tradition? The carrying over the threshold?" he asked.

"Close enough." I handed him his jeans and stepped into my panties. "I love you."

"Good." He said that with great satisfaction, then fumbled his way into his clothes while I pulled mine on. I finished first, and told him I wanted to check on Cullen. "Just to be sure."

His brows twitched down, but he nodded. "I will wait for you."

It was a leave-taking I needed, I realized as I tossed a blanket over Cullen's sleeping body. Something new had begun, but other things had ended. I folded up a jacket and placed it under his head for a pillow, then knelt beside him and kissed him lightly on the lips. "Good-bye," I said softly.

It wasn't really Cullen I was bidding farewell to, of course.

Michael was waiting by the node, as he'd said he would be. I walked into his arms. "You are happy?" He whispered it, as if the question was too large to say out loud. "You do not regret giving up all the beautiful young men like Cullen?"

Oh, he did know me. That was going to take some getting used to, but . . . "I'm happy," I told him, and grinned. "Besides, sometimes all a woman my age really wants is to curl up in bed with a good book."

Michael grinned, too. And took us home.

BURNING MOON

Rebecca York

Prologue

❖

SOME people glory in the warmth of the afternoon sun. Antonia Delarosa had learned to seek the shadows of the night.

On this November evening, she sat in the midnight-dark lounge of the old Victorian where she lived, her narrow hands not quite steady as she shuffled and cut the tarot cards, then laid them on the table in front of her.

No light illuminated the images. But she didn't need to fix her gaze on them. As she laid each one on the table and ran her finger over the upper left-hand corner, a familiar picture came to her.

"The Empress," she murmured, seeing in her mind a woman wearing flowing robes and a twelve-star crown, seated on lush red pillows.

The next card she turned over was the Knight of Cups— coming to save the day, no doubt.

As a teenager, she had been drawn to the tarot, and she had worked with the cards for more than fifteen years, using many different decks.

Tonight, she held her old favorites, the Rider-Waite. The one that most people thought of when they pictured the cards whose origins went back to ancient legends and religions.

As always, she felt herself tapping into a combination of memory and awareness—her own unconscious.

Shuffling through the deck, she turned over one more card. It showed a man and a woman standing naked under the arms of Raphael, the angel of air, who was giving them his blessing.

"The Lovers," she breathed. That card had come up for her again and again over the past few months. Of course, it didn't always refer to a romantic relationship. Maybe she was going to mend her fences with Mom.

"Right. And hippos will fly," she muttered.

Her hand went back to the Empress, touching the surface lightly, and she uttered a small sound that was part distress and part wonder.

There was another image intruding into the picture now—something that didn't belong. To the left of the woman, an animal sat ramrod straight, his mouth slightly open, his tongue lolling out between white, pointed teeth.

"The wolf." Antonia felt a prickle of sensation travel down the back of her neck. The animal's fierce eyes stared from the card, challenging anyone who dared question his right to be there.

She had first become aware of him weeks ago on the Magician card, his outline hazy among the greenery that festooned the underside of the sorcerer's table. She had doubted her vision then. And when she had focused her inner eye more closely, the wolf had vanished.

But he came back the next night—on the five of Pentacles, in front of the two homeless people. The card represented bad luck or loss, but it had been upside down, which wasn't quite as bad—because it might indicate a reversal of bad fortune.

The wolf had refused to relinquish his position under the church window, even when she had muttered "begone," and lain the card facedown on the table.

He had returned again and again, and she couldn't guess what his presence meant.

"You're close now, aren't you? Come out and show yourself," she challenged. "Or are you a coward?"

"I am no coward."

The answer echoed in the darkened room. She had spoken the words with her own lips. But she sensed the wolf's truth.

Chapter 1

＊

A wolf mates for life. And what if his mate is killed? Does he slog through existence without her? Or does he find a way to end his misery?

Grant Marshall turned the question over in his mind as he drove down the two-lane highway toward Sea Gate, New Jersey.

He had opened the window partway, and a cold breeze off the ocean blew back the dark hair from his forehead. He knew he needed a haircut. He'd get one at the barber shop in town and hopefully get the locals talking about last month's murder.

He wasn't the kind of man who naturally started conversations with strangers, but necessity had changed his habits.

Once, he'd built houses. Now he was a vigilante—dedicating every moment of his existence to finding the man who had killed his life mate.

And when he had sent the devil's spawn back to hell, he would plunge into the cold sea and swim away from shore—until his strength gave out and he could join Marcy.

That is, if they let werewolves into heaven.

He dragged in a lungful of the damp air, imagining that he could catch the scent of evil drifting toward him. Did the killer live in this town? Or was he only passing through—as he had passed through so many communities in the last eight years.

Marcy hadn't been the killer's first victim. Or his final one. But Grant was close on his heels now. He knew the signs. Knew the kind of woman he preyed on. He knew how to search the Internet and newspapers for the creature's spoor. He would track down the monster and make sure it never took another life.

He reached the town limits, then cruised down Atlantic Avenue, which was a block from the ocean. It featured a commercial district overflowing with art galleries, real estate agencies, and t-shirt shops, most of which were closed for the season. But the all-year-round establishments like the drugstore, grocery, and cleaners were still open for business.

At the far end of the main drag and on several side streets, he saw Victorian-era houses in various states of repair. Some rivaled the decorative splendor of New Orleans's famous painted ladies. Others were worn by salt, wind, and rain.

He found the murder house on Maple Street. A blackened wound in the flesh of the town, much like the remains of the home where his wife had died.

Seeing the charred remnants of the structure made his throat close, and he gripped the steering wheel to steady himself.

He should drive on past and wait until tonight to poke

through the ruins of Elizabeth Jefferson's life. A wolf could pick up more clues than a man.

Yet he couldn't stop himself from pulling to the curb, then climbing out.

He walked around the foundation of the structure, breathing in the scents of burned wood and a crowd of people. The place had been a regular sideshow attraction. He was halfway around the blackened derelict when his sharp ears told him he had made a tactical error.

A car was gliding slowly to a stop in back of his SUV. Turning, he saw it was a patrol car.

Shit.

He kept the curse locked in his throat as a cop climbed out of the cruiser, wearing a blue uniform and an attitude. He appeared to be in his late thirties, with close-cropped blond hair and piercing gray eyes. The black plastic tag on his chest said his name was Wright. Probably he thought he always was.

"Mind telling me what you're doing here?" he said, his voice lacking any touch of warmth.

Grant stood with his hands at his sides, hoping his body language made it clear that he wasn't going to pull out a concealed weapon.

"I read about the incident here. I thought I'd stop by the house where it happened."

"Why?"

"Because I'm considering buying property in town," he answered, giving the cover story he'd been using for the past two years when he came to investigate one of the murder sites.

"Let me see your driver's license, please," the cop said.

Grant pulled his wallet from his pocket, fished out the plastic card, and handed it over.

Wright studied the license, comparing Grant's dark eyes

and hair to the man in the photograph. And his six-foot height, hundred and ninety pounds to the written description. He'd lost some weight since Marcy's death, and he'd never gained it back. But the license was otherwise accurate.

"You're from Pennsylvania, Mr. Marshall?" the cop said in a flat voice.

"Yes."

"What are you doing down here?"

"Like I said, I'm looking to buy a home in a town on the ocean."

"Why here? Are you some kind of vulture?"

"I'm a prudent investor."

Wright walked to his cruiser. Grant followed, standing back as the cop checked his name on the onboard computer.

Even though he was sure nothing was going to come up, he could feel his heart drumming inside his chest.

"You're clean." The officer sounded sorry about that as he handed back the ID.

"Yeah," Grant agreed, glad that his license didn't have "werewolf" stamped across the front.

"We don't need outsiders coming in and taking advantage of our . . . tragic circumstances."

"Thanks for the advice," Grant said, using the mild voice that worked best with aggressive small-town cops.

He felt the man's eyes on his back as he got into his SUV and started the engine. The cop followed him to Atlantic Avenue, then sped away with his lights flashing, probably racing home for a late lunch.

SWINGING back the way he'd come, Grant turned onto Norfolk Street. He intended to stay in town until his business was finished. Now he knew from the get-go that he'd have to watch out for the law.

As he turned another corner, a sign caught his eye. It said BED AND BREAKFAST, CLOSED FOR THE SEASON.

Under it was an additional line that said TAROT CARD READINGS.

He made a snorting noise. He had never gone in for mumbo jumbo like fortune-telling, and he had no intention of starting now. No intention at all. But some impulse caused him to stop for the second time since reaching Sea Gate.

Pulling up beside a neatly trimmed hedge, he studied the house and grounds. The Victorian's clapboard siding was painted dove gray, with darker gray trim. Neatly tended gardens surrounded the structure, and several bird feeders hung from the lower branches of large, old trees.

What the hell, he thought. *Maybe she can tell me if this is the week I get lucky.*

As he rang the bell, he was picturing a stoop-shouldered crone wearing a shapeless dress and knit shawl over her plump shoulders.

"Yes?"

The woman who answered the door uttered only that one brisk syllable, then went very still.

He fought to quickly rearrange his thinking. Instead of a housedress over a dumpy figure, she was wearing gray wool slacks and an emerald-green sweater that showed off her slender curves. She looked to be in her late twenties, although a streak of white at her forehead split her shoulder-length dark brown hair, drawing attention to her lush, shiny curls. But he was more interested in her blue eyes. Though she seemed to be focusing on his face, there was something strange about the way she regarded him.

It took several seconds for him to realize that she was blind.

"I was looking for the tarot card reader," he said.

"You found her."

"But . . ."

ANTONIA fought a sudden sharp stab of panic. He might leave. And she couldn't let that happen. Hoping her face showed none of the tension coursing through her, she said, "I've been working with tarot cards for a long time. I don't need to see them to read their meaning."

An eternity elapsed as he considered the statement. Finally, he answered. "Okay."

She had to gulp in a breath of air before she could manage to say, "Come in."

Then she waited with her pulse pounding while he stepped into the front hall and closed the door.

Hoping she didn't look like a nutcase, she led the way to the table in the corner of the lounge with its comfortable upholstered chairs.

She didn't need to see where she was going. She knew the landscape of this house as well as she knew her own body. Every piece of furniture was where she had placed it. Every cup and saucer was put away where she could find it.

She needed that order in her life. And usually her control of the environment left her feeling calm and confident.

Not now—because she sensed something unsettling and at the same time compelling radiating from this man.

She had learned to form quick impressions of people. That was more difficult when you couldn't see their eyes. But she liked the deep timbre of his voice. Liked the clean, woodsy scent that clung to him. Not from aftershave, but from some unnamed quality all his own.

Yet it wasn't voice or scent that commanded her to keep him here. It was fear—that he would leave her and do something that could never be set right.

She didn't really know what that meant. She only knew she had to find out what was troubling him—for his sake and for hers.

She sat down, then listened for the small sound of chair legs scraping across the rug. When she heard it and knew he'd joined her at the table, she let out a small sigh.

The cards were sitting where she'd left them. She picked up the deck and shuffled.

"I should have introduced myself," she said. "I'm Antonia Delarosa."

"Grant Marshall."

He didn't offer to shake her hand, but she knew he must be watching her, probably deciding whether to go through with a reading. Should she offer to do it for free? No. Instead of reassuring him, that would probably drive him away.

She wanted to study his expression, judge what he was thinking. She'd been sighted for the first twenty-five years of her life, and she wanted to see this man. If she couldn't do it with her eyes, she wanted to use her hands. But that would step over a social boundary she couldn't cross, so she kept her fingers on the cards.

"I guess you're wondering if you've made a major mistake by coming here," she said, struggling to keep her voice steady.

When he didn't answer, she went on. "I charge fifty dollars for a reading, and I can refund your money if you're not satisfied. But I think you will be. I've had psychic abilities since I was a little girl."

He cleared his throat. "Like what?"

She had stories waiting at her fingertips. Setting down the cards, she said, "I'd know things—things that I couldn't explain by normal means. I remember when I was seven, waking up crying—worried about my parents. My baby-sitter couldn't calm me down, and it turned out Mom and Dad had been in an automobile accident. She broke her shoulder and collarbone, and my dad had a concussion."

Into the silence from across the table, she went on. "That's just an extreme example. I knew other stuff. Not necessarily anything monumental. Like maybe whether a friend was going to call me on the phone. When I grew up, I did tarot card readings in New Orleans, before I lost my sight. People came back to me again and again. And they recommended me to their friends."

"How did your parents react to your making a living that way?" he asked, and she sensed that the answer to the question was important.

"The talent has been in my family for years. It was something we all knew about and accepted."

"So you can see the future?" Again, tension infused the question.

"You want to know your future?"

"I want to know . . ." He stopped, swallowed, drumming his fingers against the tabletop.

She never pushed people to reveal more than they were willing to tell her. She always let a querent—a person who came to her for a reading—give her information at his own pace.

Breaking one of her own rules, she reached across the space that separated them and found his hand. It was large and warm and strong, with a hint of callus between his thumb and index finger. When she stroked her own thumb along his palm, she couldn't hold back a strangled exclamation.

Chapter 2

✦

"WHAT?" the man across the table asked sharply, pulling his hand away.

"It wasn't your fault. The fire."

He made a low, angry sound. "She didn't die in the fire. Whoever killed her poisoned her first."

Antonia gasped, but Grant Marshall was already speaking again. "I should have been home with her!" The words came out as a menacing growl that would have sent her running in the other direction if she hadn't been glued to her chair.

She and this stranger were speaking a kind of shorthand now. They'd met only minutes ago. He hadn't told her that someone had burned up his house with his wife inside. She'd pulled that terrible image from his mind. And more. The fire had left him with scars. Not physical marks but guilt and unbearable pain that ate at his soul.

"You didn't know anything bad was going to happen."

Antonia had uttered that phrase many times in the past. Sometimes it gave comfort. Not now. There was only one thing that would give Grant Marshall any kind of cold comfort. And he didn't want her to know about it.

He stood up. "This is a mistake," he said, sounding angry.

Desperation came out as a plea. "Don't leave."

"You . . . see too much."

"Maybe I can help you find him," she said quickly, then sat with the breath frozen in her lungs.

He stood a few feet away, but she imagined she could hear his heart pounding.

When the chair scraped back again and he sat down, she allowed herself to breathe.

"You got that picture of the burned house from my head," he said in a voice that told her he didn't want to believe her insight.

"Because you've been focused on it for a long time."

"What else are you going to see?" he asked.

His wary tone made her tread carefully. *More than you want me to see,* she silently admitted. She was still frightened. Not of him, although she knew violence was not far from the surface of his mind. That should worry her. Yet she was more worried that she would drive him away if she said too much.

"Let's use the cards," she said, wondering what she was going to do now. She couldn't be dishonest with him. That would violate her personal code of ethics. Yet she'd learned to soften bad news.

"I've never asked for a tea leaf reading. Or anything else like that. Maybe you'd better tell me something about these cards," he said, buying them both a little time.

"Well, I don't mess with tea leaves." She laughed. "All I'd get from them is wet fingers."

Ignoring her attempt at a joke, he pressed for more information. "Then how do you read the cards?"

"Braille markings. After that, because I know the pictures so well, I see them in my head." She went on quickly, "The tarot deck has seventy-eight cards. They're divided into the twenty-two Major Arcana, cards which reference the archetypal passages in our lives, and the fifty-six Minor Arcana which deal more with day-to-day life."

Sensing that he was listening intently, she pushed the deck toward him. "Take a look at them. Each one is full of symbolism. Some go all the way back to Egyptian mythology or the Hebrew Cabala. But it's all open to interpretation. And no card is either good or bad. It's all in context."

She heard him shuffling through the deck. "What about this one? With Death riding a white horse."

She heard the strong emotion in his voice, emotion he was struggling to hide. She knew why he had pulled out the card. He was contemplating his own demise, but she didn't need to tell him that.

Instead, she said, "It looks scary, but it's not so bad. It can symbolize transformation or rebirth. The king is dead! Long live the king! It can come up when people are going through lifestyle changes. It can signify that it's time to move on. It can mark new beginnings rather than endings."

It seemed he was too restless to stay seated across from her. He put the cards down, got up from the table, and paced the room.

"You know why I came here?" he asked.

"To my house? Or to Sea Gate?"

"Sea Gate."

She swallowed. Again she wondered how much to say. "You know there was a similar murder here. You think it's related, and you hope the person who did it is still in town."

"Yeah."

Unspoken words hung heavy in the air between them.

Under the table, she squeezed her hands into fists, considering her next move. She knew she was taking a chance when she said, "In the summer, I run this place as a bed and breakfast. Well, I have people who do the actual work. There are plenty of rooms. You could stay here."

"I wouldn't be very good company."

"I'm not looking for company. And I could use the money," she added, not because money was really an issue, but because it might help him make up his mind. "I can give you a winter discount, a hundred dollars a night. For the room and breakfast."

Again she held her breath, waiting. When he said, "All right," she felt almost dizzy with relief.

"You can bring your luggage in," she said quickly.

When he walked toward the door, she wasn't sure whether he was walking out of her life. And she'd never been more frustrated in her blindness. She wanted to follow him to the car and see that he was getting his suitcase. But that would surely send him away.

Her own anxiety shocked her. She was desperate to keep this man from killing himself. More than that, she ached to make him realize that life was worth living. But she couldn't force him to see things her way, so she pushed back her chair with deliberate slowness and walked into the hall.

When the door opened again, she wiped her damp palms on her slacks. "Grant?"

"Yes."

"The room at the end of the hall is one of my best, and it has a good view of the ocean," she said. As soon as the words were out of her mouth, she wished she could call them back.

He had thought too often of the ocean, of the cold, black waves swallowing him up.

She longed to go to him then, to wrap her arms around him and give him the blessing of simple human contact. The warmth of her body could help take away the chill that had sunk into his bones.

But she wasn't going to fool herself. There was more she had glimpsed in their brief encounter. Things she didn't dare name because admitting her desires and seeing them crushed was worse than never acknowledging their existence. Once her life had been full of possibilities. After she'd lost her sight, she'd learned not to ask for too much.

Did she dare to open herself up to the pain of rejection? She didn't know whether she had a choice.

GRANT set his duffel bag on a luggage rack near the bedroom door and looked around. The room was charming, with refinished mahogany cabinet pieces, a four-poster bed, and blue and white curtains at the double-hung windows.

Had Antonia given directions for the decorating? Had she bought the furniture at country auctions? He could picture her wanting to know every detail.

Striving to put her out of his mind, he crossed to the bedroom window and stood staring out at the ocean. It was a block away, but from the second floor of the house, he could see the swells rising and falling. The view soothed him because he knew the sea would set him free.

He told himself he should leave this dwelling. He was used to being alone with his mangled heart and his quest for justice. He had mated for life, and Marcy's death had ripped away a part of himself that could never be returned.

But over the past two years, the sharp edge of grief had

dulled. He saw that as a betrayal of his wife. And he saw his response to Antonia in those terms, too.

Not a physical response, he told himself. It was nothing sexual. He had shared dark secrets with her. And none of it had sent her running from him.

But she saw him only as a man. She knew only the human part—the part about the stranger who had lost his wife and was searching for her killer.

She didn't know about the wolf who had indulged his raw grief by roaming the woods of western Pennsylvania hunting animals and ripping out their throats. She didn't know that wolf was upstairs in her house.

He had come here for a tarot card reading. But he hadn't let her go ahead with it. Was he afraid she would see through his carefully cultivated veneer of humanity?

What if he took off his clothes, walked back downstairs, and said the ancient chant that changed him from man to animal? She wouldn't see the wolf. But she would sense his presence. And that would be the end of whatever relationship she was thinking about.

He could end this anytime he wanted. Very dramatically. And that made him feel safer.

So he left his duffel bag in the room while he went back to the business district to have a look around. After driving slowly up and down Atlantic Avenue, he pulled into a space near Bridges Dry Goods Store, Ernest Bridges, Proprietor, and got out.

As he walked inside, he saw that several people were standing around talking to the man behind the counter, presumably Ernest Bridges himself, who looked like he'd been planted there for the past seventy years.

The conversation stopped, and Grant watched the crowd eyeing him speculatively, although not with the earlier hostility of the cop. Apparently this was one of the town gathering places—regardless of class or profession. One man was wearing a business suit. Another had on overalls. A woman was in jeans and a pullover. Even in human form, Grant could pick up their distinctive scents. All of them had something in common. They'd all been to the murder house.

"Help you?" Bridges asked.

Grant pulled his focus away from the olfactory analysis and scrambled for an answer. "Toothpaste."

"Second aisle on the right. Halfway down."

He ambled past shelves crammed with lipsticks and boxes of graham crackers, dishwasher detergent and beach towels on deep discount.

"You passing through?" the old man behind the counter asked as Grant came back with his purchase.

"I might be interested in vacation property," he said for the second time that afternoon.

The guy in the suit perked right up. "Well, I can surely help you out. Charlie Hastings. I own the real estate office a few doors down." He held out his hand, and Grant shook it.

When he'd started his quest, he'd thought about whether to use his own name and decided that it might be an advantage—if his goal was to flush out the killer.

"Grant Marshall. I'll stop by in the next day or two," he said, thinking that the man probably knew how long all the residents had owned their homes.

Stepping outside, he lingered under the shade of the porch, pretending he was just enjoying the sea air. Although the door closed behind him, his hearing was excellent, and he could still pick up the conversation from inside the store.

"You think he knows property values have gone down?" Bridges asked.

"Maybe. Maybe not," the real estate guy answered.

"Sell him a fixer-upper and I'll get some business out of it, too," another voice said, and Grant figured the guy in overalls must be the town handyman.

The group laughed.

"So, do you think I should put in another cabin in the back?" the woman asked.

"The tourist business will pick up in the warm weather. Leastways if we can do something about the hole in the ground that used to be the Jefferson house," Hastings answered.

When the talk metamorphosed into a deep discussion of Sea Gate property values, Grant left the porch for a walk through the business district, following the scent trails of people who had been at the murder house and also in the shopping area. Many of the paths led to a bar and grill several blocks down Atlantic called the Seagull's Roost. But he didn't go inside, because he knew the alcohol fumes would make him sick.

Instead he drove back to Antonia's bed and breakfast. She wasn't around when he stepped inside. Relieved that she was making herself scarce, he went back up to his room.

Sleep had become something he grabbed in snatches. But the bed was comfortable, so he lay down on top of the covers for a short nap. When he woke, it was dark outside.

His watch said six thirty. Later he would go visit the burned house. But he needed fuel, and his stomach told him he hadn't eaten much that day.

After a quick shower, he changed into a fresh shirt and went downstairs. He was thinking he'd go out and get some fast-food hamburgers. But the aromas coming from the back of the house stopped him.

He smelled homemade beef stew, and a wave of nostalgia swamped him. His mother had made thick stews, filled with chunks of meat the way his father liked it. Marcy had gotten the recipe, on one of their brief trips home.

There hadn't been many visits because all the were-wolves he knew—his father and his brothers—were alpha males, and they fought for dominance when left in a room together.

His father had a couple of brothers he hadn't seen in years. Just the way Grant had stayed away from his own adult male relatives. But he'd looked up his cousins on the Internet to find out if they were still alive. One was a pri-vate detective. A guy named Ross Marshall. They'd ex-changed a few e-mails. And he'd thought for a split second about asking him to help track Marcy's killer. Then he'd figured they'd only end up at each other's throats. So he'd kept to his private quest.

He hesitated in the front hall. He should stay away from Antonia, but he found his feet taking him to the kitchen.

When he stopped in the doorway, he saw her stirring a large pot on the front of the stove. The light was low, giv-ing the kitchen a cozy feel. The simple domestic scene made his chest tighten.

"That smells good," he said, hearing the thickness of his own words.

She turned to face him. "Cold weather makes me want to fix a big pot of something hearty. Are you hungry?"

"Yes."

"The stew is about ready. We can have a salad, too.

He watched as she opened the refrigerator and took out tomato, lettuce, celery, carrots. She washed the produce in the sink, then brought it to a small cutting board resting in what looked like a large cookie sheet with low sides.

"Can I help you?"

"You could set the table." She gestured toward a sideboard. "The cutlery is in the drawers. And the salad bowls are on the shelves just above."

"And I see the napkins in the basket."

As he worked, he watched her preparations, admiring her efficiency. The cookie sheet kept any vegetables from skittering away as she carefully cut them up, then tossed them into a bowl with the lettuce.

It was a strange experience, not having to pretend that his attention was elsewhere. And he found he wasn't just watching her cook. He was taking in interesting details, like the way her lower lip pursed as she concentrated on her task, and the way she'd tied back her mass of brown hair with a green ribbon, exposing the tender curl of her ear.

His gaze traveled lower, to her nicely feminine curves. He hadn't noticed a woman's breasts in a long time, and his jaw tightened. He didn't want to focus his attention on boobs. But hers were high and rounded, and he could make out the small buds of her nipples beneath the tce shirt she was wearing now. When he found his body responding, he bit back a curse.

"So—you weren't always blind?" he said in a gruff voice.

She kept busy with the salad. "I got something called uveitis when I was twenty-four. By the time they made the diagnosis, it was too late to save my vision."

"That must have been . . . devastating," he said, thinking about how he would have reacted.

"I did a lot of crying and screaming. Then I made peace with it. But I wanted to live as independently as I could, so I went to a school where they taught blind people basic skills."

"You didn't want a guide dog?"

"The school encouraged independence. I've got a white cane that I use when I go out. But I know my way around in here. If you put things back where they belong," she added with a note of firmness in her voice.

"I will." He cleared his throat. "A dog would be good protection."

"I didn't think I needed protection, until . . . Elizabeth."

"You felt safe in Sea Gate?"

She turned to face him, then carried the salad bowl to the table.

"Yes. That's why I came back to this house where my aunt lived. I used to spend the summers here with my parents. Sea Gate is about the right-sized town for me. I can walk to just about anything I need—the grocery or the dry goods store or the pharmacy."

He'd given himself the perfect opening to talk about the murder. Instead, he asked, "And you ended up with the property?"

"Yes. My mom and dad separated when I was in my teens. My aunt never had any kids. So she left me the house."

"And your mother?"

"Mom was bent out of shape about my getting Aunt Minnie's inheritance. She's in Colorado—working as a fortune-teller in Manitou Springs. It's an old hippy community, so she fits right in."

He was wound up in her narrative, when her sudden sharp exclamation sent him striding across the room.

He could see that while she'd been ladling hot stew into bowls, she'd splashed some on the side of her hand.

Quickly he turned on the water, then thrust her hand under the cold stream, holding the reddened skin upward.

"So much for walking and chewing gum at the same time," she murmured.

He wasn't sure how to respond.

"That's supposed to be a joke," she said in a quavery voice.

"Yeah." He was trying not to focus on the feel of her small hand in his large one. It was small-boned and graceful. He should turn her loose. She could take care of the emergency by herself. But he kept the hand cradled protectively in his.

"How does it look?" she asked.

The question startled him, because he'd forgotten she couldn't see for herself.

"Red. But I think it's only first degree."

She sighed. "Burns are a problem for me in the kitchen. I've got some salve."

When she started to step away from the sink, he cupped his palm over her shoulder. "Keep your hand under the water. I'll get the salve."

"It's in the drawer right under the microwave."

He let go of her, then crossed to the drawer and found the tube.

Turning off the water, he took her hand again. When she swung toward him, her breast collided with his outstretched arm, and neither of them moved for several seconds.

The contact was innocent, yet the pressure of that soft swell made his breath catch.

She angled away, tried to snatch her hand back.

But he wanted to prove he wasn't reacting to her, so he kept hold of her, blotting the water with a paper towel. Then he stroked on some of the burn medication. When he was finished, he let her go and deliberately stepped back.

"THANK you," Antonia whispered.

He answered with little more than a grunt, and she knew that she hadn't been the only one affected by the innocent contact.

She wanted to say something like, "You're not being

unfaithful to your wife by responding to me." But she kept that observation locked behind closed lips.

"Maybe I should just go out and grab something for dinner," he said.

"Dinner is already made. And it's better than anything you're likely to get in town at this time of year."

"Yeah." After a moment's hesitation, he moved to the stove, and she heard him ladling stew into a bowl.

Which left her with the other bowl. She wasn't sure now where she'd set it down, and she had to fumble around on the counter, wondering if he was watching the blind woman make a spectacle of herself. She almost stuck her fingers into the stew, but the heat warned her before she had to start over again with the cold water and the salve.

Nervous now, she wondered if she could make it across the room with the food. But she carefully counted the steps and ended up at the table, where she sat down.

While she'd been cooking, she'd imagined the conversation she and Grant might have at dinner. She'd thought she would offer him some wine. But that seemed out of place now. They both ate in silence until he said, "Do you have any salad dressing?"

She'd completely forgotten about dressing, and she felt her face heat. "I'll get it."

"I can do it. Where do you keep it?"

"The bottom shelf in the refrigerator door."

He brought two bottles and set them down on the table. She waited while he poured dressing on his salad. No point in any part of their bodies colliding again. When he was finished, she reached for a bottle and felt the plastic label she'd fixed to the side. It had the letter P, for Pepper Parmesan.

"You were right. The stew is good," he said.

"Thanks."

The conversation ground to a halt again, and she bent toward her bowl, thinking that her social skills had certainly deteriorated.

When a noise from outside invaded the silence, her head jerked up. A car had stopped out front.

"Are you expecting company?" Grant asked.

"No."

"Let me take a look." She heard him get up from the table and crossed to the window.

"Shit." He made a small coughing sound. "Pardon the language."

His exclamation sent a sizzle of alarm traveling up her neck. "What's wrong outside?"

Chapter 3

❧

ANTONIA waited for Grant's answer. Finally he said, "I don't want to worry you, but whoever was out there split as soon as he saw me standing at the window."

"Or maybe it was someone looking for a bed and break-fast who saw I was closed for the season."

"Is the sign lighted?"

"Not in the off-season."

"Well, they probably didn't see it in the dark, then." He cleared his throat. "Does this happen a lot? Someone stopping by your house—then driving away?"

"What? Do you think someone is stalking me?"

"I didn't say that. I just didn't like seeing a car speed away as soon as I showed my face in the window."

Wondering what to say next, she finally settled on, "It could have been Scott Wright. One of the local cops."

"He comes by to check on you?" Grant asked.

"You've already met him?"

"How do you know?"

"From your voice."

"Yeah, well he pulled up right behind my car when I stopped to have a look at the Jefferson house."

"He's protective of the town."

"And of you?"

She snorted. "That's what he says. But what he really wants is to . . . relieve the blind lady's sexual frustration."

"Oh yeah?" he asked, temper flaring in his tone.

She hesitated for a long moment, thinking that maybe the way to get Grant to open up with her was to share her own secrets. "I knew Scott when I was a teenager. And when I came back to town, he was . . . solicitous, so I made the mistake of telling him too much. He knows my fiancé left me when he found out I was losing my sight. He thinks I should be an easy lay. But I'm not attracted to him. And if I were, knowing he has a wife and kids would stop me cold."

"Nice guy."

She wished she could take back the part about Billy walking away from her. But it was said.

"Watch out for him. He likes to use his official position to intimidate people."

"He probably wondered why you were interested in the Jefferson house."

"Or he has something to hide."

"What?"

"Maybe I'll find out." Grant didn't sit back down at the table. "I figured that tonight might be a good time for doing some exploring."

"In the dark?"

"I have very good night vision," he said.

"Do you want some coffee before you go out?"

"I don't drink it," he answered at once, and she wondered if he was making an excuse to end the conversation.

"Tea?" she offered.

"Not now. But herbal tea would be good in the morning."

"I've got peppermint and cranberry."

"Either one."

He crossed to the sink, and she pictured him emptying out stew he hadn't eaten.

She pushed back her chair, then reached for her own unfinished bowl.

"You cooked. I'll clean up," he said. "If you trust me to put things were they belong."

"I trust you," she said, meaning more than kitchen cleanup. "The dishes go in the dishwasher. Plastic wrap for the salad bowl is in the drawer under the cutlery. Put the salad and the stew in the refrigerator."

When she'd finished the short speech, she turned and left the room, before she said anything else she regretted.

Not far away, Shadow Man got out of his car and walked toward the sound of laughter and rock music coming from the Seagull's Roost.

"Hey," Hank Horngate greeted him.

"Hey yourself," he answered.

Others around the room repeated the salutation, and he gave everyone a friendly smile and a wave. He was a fixture in town. One of the gang. An upstanding citizen whom no one would suspect of murder. Which was why he thought of himself as Shadow Man. Like the guy in that movie who called himself The Shadow. He'd learned to cloud men's minds so they saw only what he wanted.

He ordered a Bud Light and relaxed on one of the stools

at the end of the bar. The Seagull's Roost was a good place to pick up information, so he came here pretty frequently before calling it a night.

He'd made a mistake a month ago. He'd known it pretty quickly. Fouling your own nest wasn't the smartest idea in the world. Always before, he'd traveled away from Sea Gate to murder the damn bitches who reminded him of Helen. But he hadn't been able to resist Elizabeth Jefferson. Not after her husband Bob had come into the bar night after night talking about her. She'd had MS. She was in a wheelchair part of the time. And she never stopped complaining about how life wasn't fair.

Like Helen. The harpy who had ruined his life. It wasn't his fault a drunk driver had jumped the signal and plowed into them. But Helen had never let him forget he had sped through the intersection a split second after the light had turned from yellow to red.

Since they'd been kids, she'd told him how stupid he was and how he'd never make anything of himself. Then she'd spent the last two years of her miserable existence dragging him down to her level. Finally he'd had enough of playing the loving brother atoning for his sins.

He'd fed her arsenic day after day, and the doctors had thought her pain was just part of her incessant complaining. Before he'd burned her up in an "accidental" fire, he'd had the pleasure of telling her what he'd done and hearing her plead for mercy. He'd laughed in her face.

With the others, he had to use poisons that acted quickly. But that didn't dampen the satisfaction of killing women like Helen. Women who were handicapped and who made the lives of the people around them a living hell.

"What's new?" Shadow Man asked.

"I hear Bob Jefferson is going to sell the property."

"Good luck," someone else answered. "Nothing like murder to knock the price down."

"Yeah," another voice chimed in.

Shadow Man was thinking that he'd done Bob Jefferson a big favor.

"You hear about the guy at Antonia Delarosa's place?" someone else asked.

"What guy?"

"Looks like she's got a boarder."

"In the winter?"

"Maybe they're having a little fun together. She's got a nice set of titties on her. A shame to let them dry up from disuse."

That brought a laugh from some of the men.

"She needs some fun."

Another laugh.

Shadow Man joined the chorus, but privately he didn't agree.

GRANT lay on his bed with his hands behind his head, staring at the ceiling. He was still thinking that staying here was a mistake. But that car stopping in front of her house had given him a bad feeling. It might be the nosy cop. Or it might be someone else.

Had Officer Wright put his hands on Antonia? Really, he shouldn't be dwelling on that. He had his own business to take care of. But he couldn't get the picture out of his mind of the scumbag "accidentally" brushing against her breast.

He'd like to make the guy sorry he'd ever thought of touching her—except that her life was none of his business.

Around midnight he got up, dressed in black sweats,

and slipped out the back door, then hesitated. He might have driven away from the house, but he liked the idea of leaving the car where it was visible, so anyone checking up on the place would think he was still there.

AFTER Grant left, Antonia went back into the kitchen and got a deck of cards from one of the drawers. She had about five different decks scattered around the house, the way her mother had cheap drugstore reading glasses. Even then, Mom had trouble finding a pair. But Antonia knew where she kept every deck of tarot cards.

Simply holding them in her hand helped steady her roiling emotions. After shuffling, she drew a card. It was the Knight of Wands. A man on a quest. Well she already knew that was true of Grant Marshall.

The Knight of Wands never did anything halfway. He could be a generous friend—or lover. His arrival might herald a major life change.

Her chest tightened. Scott Wright might want to fuck her. Probably that was how he thought about it. A mercy fuck. And a convenience for himself. But it wasn't Scott Wright that she was thinking of making love with.

In her mind, the card flickered, and she saw a wolf running along next to the knight.

The wolf was connected with Grant. In some way that she didn't understand. The image had come to her again and again in the cards. And then he had arrived in person. And the two had merged in her mind.

The wolf must represent some part of his personality that she didn't yet understand. All she knew was that there was something different about him. An indefinable aura that set him apart from other men. And not just the shroud of sadness that he used like a suit of armor.

She wanted to rip off that protective layer. She wanted to give him back the will to live.

She knew that any intelligent woman should be frightened of him. But she wasn't afraid. She wanted to help him. And she wanted to help herself.

She turned over another card and made a small sound. It was the Ace of Cups—a symbol of new beginnings, of new love.

It heralded joy and happiness. Hers? His? Both of them? Or was she simply finding what she wanted to find in the cards tonight?

GRANT walked to a deserted stretch of beach on the outskirts of town. Behind a sand dune, where he wasn't visible from the road, he took off his clothes and stood shivering in the cold wind blowing off the ocean. Then he closed his eyes, gathering his inner resolve before calling on the ancient ritual that made him different from other men.

"Taranis, Epona, Cerridwen," he said in measured tones, then repeated the same phrase and went on to another.

"Ga. Feart. Cleas. Duais. Aithriocht. Go gcumhdai is dtreorai na deithe thu."

The first time he'd changed from boy to wolf, he'd thought his brain was going to explode. It didn't help knowing that two of his older brothers had not survived the experience. But none of them had had any choice about it. It had happened to each of them at puberty.

He'd learned to anticipate disorientation as the physical changes gripped him. He felt his jaw lengthen into a muzzle, his teeth sharpen. Long ago, he'd learned to ride above the pain of bones crunching, muscles jerking, cells transforming from one shape to another.

Thick gray hair formed along his flanks, covering his body in a silver-tipped pelt. As he dropped to all fours, he was no longer a man. He was an animal far more suited to the hunt.

A wolf.

One of the few of his species, because nature had not been kind to those who carried his genetic heritage. There were no female werewolves, as far as he knew. And half the boys died the first time they made the change.

He'd thought he was lucky to survive. He'd long ago given up that notion. Still, the freedom of the wolf grabbed him by the throat as he sniffed the wind with new clarity. He smelled salt and seaweed and small animals hidden in the dunes.

Even now, the wolf's persona filled him with a kind of excitement no ordinary man would ever know. Though legend gave the full moon power over werewolves, it wasn't true of him or any of the men in his family. Any night was his. Any day, for that matter.

Another time he might have hunted prey. Tonight he had more important business.

Staying away from the highway, he trotted toward the residential part of town, toward the charred remains of the house where Elizabeth Jefferson had lived and died.

His body might be that of a wolf. But his mind had not changed. He was thinking about staying out of sight and thinking about Mrs. Jefferson as he wove his way through the shadows.

She'd had MS. He'd found that out from his research. She'd been disabled. Like Marcy. Only his wife's problem hadn't been permanent. She'd broken her leg falling on the ice. And while she was still limping around with a cane, the bastard murderer had spotted her. Or maybe he'd seen her earlier, in her cast.

Grant didn't know. He'd racked his brain, trying to identify some time when he'd seen the guy, but he always drew a blank.

Reaching the house, he prowled around the foundation, taking in the smell of charred wood. But that wasn't his main interest. He focused on the men and women who had come here since the fire. He caught his own scent. And that of Scott Wright. And the locals from the dry goods store.

There were many others, too. One could be the killer—if he'd come back to admire his work. If he lived in town, he might have risked that. And Grant had reason to think that he might live here, because this town was so centrally located in the territory where he'd murdered in the past.

As he often did since he'd dispatched Elizabeth Jefferson, Shadow Man drove through the night toward the blackened ruin of her house. There was a certain satisfaction in visiting the site again and again, knowing he was the only one who got the secret joke of his presence at her house. He was her killer, living only a few blocks away. He had a lock of her hair in his keepsake chest, along with hair from the other bitches he had sent to hell.

Nobody else was ever going to see that chest. And if anybody wondered what he was doing near the murder house, he was just heading home.

In the moonlight he saw the blackened ruin. And he saw something more. A form moving in the darkness.

A dog?

What the hell was it doing poking around the house?

The animal raised its head, staring toward the headlights. Then it faded into the shadows. But a flash of movement gave away its location, and Shadow Man turned off the car lights and drifted forward.

As Shadow man watched, the dog dodged into a drive-
way between two houses. The animal was obviously intelligent. Was it a tracking dog? Did some big-city law
enforcement agency know about the murder?

Suddenly worried, he reached for the gun that he kept in
the glove compartment, then sped up, looking for the animal.

Chapter 4

✦

WARY of the car with its headlights off, the wolf backed farther into the shadows, thinking it would be easy to make a wrong move.

Someone was interested in the murder scene. In him.

After ducking around the side of a house, the wolf considered his limited options. He could race back to the place in the dunes where Grant Marshall had left his clothing. But that wasn't such a great idea. If somebody managed to follow him, he'd be too exposed on the beach. Better to hug the shadows near the houses.

He wove through the residential district, keeping his profile low. Stopping in the shadows, he realized several things almost simultaneously.

As far as he knew, he had lost the car. He was near Antonia's house. And all the lights were off.

It was late, and she was probably sleeping. Which meant he could slip inside, change back to human form, and wait a few hours before retrieving his clothing.

The wolf had learned to turn a doorknob with his teeth. Opening the back door, he slipped inside.

As soon as he'd crossed the pantry and entered the kitchen, he stopped in his tracks. He wasn't alone.

Antonia was sitting in the dark at the kitchen table. The sound of her breathing mingled with his. The woman scent of her body reached out toward him.

He was caught in a snare of his own making, and he had time to wonder if he had wanted to be trapped.

He heard the click of his claws on the wood floor as he backed away.

For an eternity, that was the only sound besides the beating of his own pulse in his ears.

Then she spoke into the darkness, her voice carrying just the hint of uncertainty. "Grant?"

The sound of his name startled him into absolute stillness. She must know an animal had walked into the kitchen. Yet she called out to him.

Even if he'd wanted to speak, he couldn't do that now. Not as a wolf. And as a wolf, he didn't dare approach her. Instead he made a wide circle around her chair, blood roaring in his brain. She didn't move, didn't say anything more.

Without looking at her, he walked on past, then into the hall and up the stairs. When he reached his room, he quietly closed the door. In his mind he said the words that would reverse the process of transformation.

Once again, his limbs lengthened and contorted. Once again, animal fur changed to human flesh, and his eyes lost some, but not all, of their keen night vision. He stood naked in the darkness, breathing hard, his pulse still pounding.

She had called his name. How much did she understand? More than an ordinary woman might.

ANTONIA sat in the darkness, longing to doubt her own senses, yet knowing that she would only be fooling herself. Her hearing was quite good. The click of claws had told her that a four-legged animal was crossing the kitchen floor, staying as far as he could from her chair before reaching the hall.

An animal. A large dog. Or a wolf.

She might have gotten up and run screaming from her own house. But she was no coward. And she was trained to interpret what she saw in the tarot cards. So she stayed where she was, working her way patiently through layers of logic.

She could throw that logic aside. Or she could accept the evidence of her own senses.

This evening, she had been trying to unravel the puzzle of Grant Marshall. And she had sensed he was the human aspect of the wolf who had been invading the cards for weeks.

Then the real wolf had somehow opened the back door and walked into the kitchen like he belonged there.

There were two more possibilities, of course. She could be losing her marbles, or she had made it all up out of her own needs and desires.

But she didn't think either one of those was true.

Which left her with Grant Marshall and the wolf.

Was he really some creature beyond normal human experience?

Falling back on old habits, she laid out the cards again. Her practiced fingers could identify each one from the braille markings, but her mind was too scattered to call up the pictures.

One thought drove everything else from her mind. She had heard a wolf in the kitchen. And if she was right about that, and if she was sane, she should be terrified of the man upstairs.

Yet he had awakened feelings inside her she had long suppressed. And now she wondered if she had recognized his death wish because she was half dead herself and hadn't wanted to admit it.

She didn't feel half dead now. Her heart was thumping inside her chest, and her ears strained for some sound from the second floor. Standing, she walked to the bottom of the stairs and clutched the newel post, her head raised toward the second floor. She could hear him moving around. Was he going to cut and run?

She wanted to influence his decision. But the ball was in his court now. So she turned and went into the lounge where she sat down in one of the comfortable armchairs.

GRANT climbed into jeans and a tee shirt, then paced the room, wondering what he was going to do next. Pack his bag and leave? Confront her?

Since Marcy's death, he had been afraid of nothing because nothing could happen to him that was worse than what he'd already experienced.

He was afraid now. Afraid of facing the extraordinary woman who was waiting for him to come downstairs.

Thinking he might as well get it over with, he pulled on socks and running shoes, then opened the door again and descended the steps.

"I'm in here," she said from the shadows of the sitting room.

The quaver in her voice told him she was no steadier than he.

She was still in darkness. Maybe to make the confrontation easier for him. Or maybe because light was the last thought that entered her mind when she was nervous.

He stopped in the entrance to the room and cleared his throat to make sure she knew he was between her and the door.

Now he could see her rigid shape in one of the chairs.

"Do you want me to leave?" he asked.

"Is that what you're planning?"

For months, there had been only two plans in his mind. Kill the monster and end his own pain. Suddenly he could see a glimmer of light beyond the monster's death.

He shoved his hands into his pocket. "How did you know that was me?"

He heard her drag in a breath and let it out in a rush. "For weeks, I've seen the wolf."

"How?"

"In the cards. He invaded the pictures, like he had every right to be there. He crept into the scenes where he shouldn't be. And I didn't know what it meant. But I knew he was coming here."

"Were you frightened?"

Instead of addressing the question, she stood and came toward him, and he felt his whole body vibrating with awareness of her.

"You should be afraid of . . . me," he answered for her.

"Well, you can call me too stupid for that. Or too reckless."

"I would never call you stupid."

"I was waiting for the wolf." With no hesitation, she reached out and took him in her arms. The shock of that first contact knocked the breath from his lungs.

He gulped in a strangled gasp of air as she lifted her

arms and cupped them around the back of his head, her fingers winnowing through his shaggy hair.

The pressure was gentle, not a command but a question. With his excellent night vision, he looked down at her for a long moment. Then his eyes focused on her lips.

As if she knew where his gaze had landed, her tongue flicked out, sweeping across the fullness of her lower lip.

He would have pulled away from any other woman. But not this one. With a sound low in his throat, he lowered his mouth to hers. The first touch of that intimate contact was like a bolt of lightning, sizzling along his nerve endings.

And when she made a small exclamation, he was pretty sure that she felt it, too.

He would never have reached for her on his own. Not in a thousand years. But all at once he was too needy to stop himself from devouring her mouth with his lips, his tongue, his teeth.

And she accepted what he offered and gave in return, her response frantic and subtle and overwhelming by turns, making his head spin and his body come to life.

Her controlled exterior had vanished. She was a creature of pure sexuality now. He forgot where he was. Forgot time and space. There was only the woman in his arms, giving to him and taking anything he was willing to give her.

When his embrace tightened around her, she made a small, needy sound.

Or had he been the one to voice that strangled exclamation?

Her hands stroked over his back, then under his tee shirt, her fingertips sending shock waves over his hot skin as he angled his head, first one way and then the other, greedy to experience her every way he could.

Kissing wasn't enough. He was ravenous for more. One

hand slid down to her hips, pulling her lower body against his aching cock, so that he wondered if he was feeling pleasure or pain.

When she moved against him, he thought he might burst into flames.

With undisguised greed, he slipped his other hand between them and cupped one breast, taking the weight of it in his hand, and he knew he had been wanting to touch her like that since he had secretly watched her in the kitchen.

As he stroked his thumb over the hardened tip, she made a low, pleading sound. Pulling up her shirt, he dragged her bra out of the way, then lowered his head, circling her nipple with his tongue before sucking it into his mouth. The taste, the texture of her made him drunk with need. And her little sob and the way she arched into the caress told him how much she liked what he was doing.

He pictured himself pulling her down to the floor, striping off her clothing, then stripping off his so that he could enjoy the feel of her naked skin before he plunged into her. The anticipation of her sex clasping hot and tight around his cock made him tremble.

Somehow, that erotically charged image brought him to his senses.

He had lost his wife—his life mate. And now he was in the arms of another woman.

Stiffly, he thrust her away from himself. "This is wrong," he growled.

He heard her swallow, watched her blink as though she was trying to orient herself again. Her cheeks were red, marked by the imprint his day's growth of beard.

Swaying on her feet, she fumbled her clothing back into place, then reached out a hand and steadied herself against the doorway. Slowly she raised her head and stared straight in his direction. "You aren't betraying your wife. Do you think she would want you to live with no hope of human contact?"

"She and I . . . made solemn vows." The words sounded hollow, after the way he'd just been acting.

"And you kept them. Long after most men would have given up."

He wanted to shout that he wasn't most men. Instead he turned and left the house. Left her standing in the darkened room. He ran down the sidewalk, then across the street and toward the beach. But he couldn't outrun the honeyed taste of her on his lips or the feel of her middle pressed to his erection.

A cold wind blew off the water as if trying to hold him back. He fought against it, fought toward the sound of the waves crashing on the sand.

Beyond that, he barely paid attention to his environment. His mind was focused on what had happened between himself and Antonia.

He had responded to her as he had never expected to respond to a woman again. The way he had with Marcy, he thought as he clenched his fists in denial.

But he couldn't lie to himself. It had been sharp and fast and all-consuming. When he'd touched Marcy, he had known he must have her or go insane.

And he had felt that sharp rush of desperate sensation once again.

Why? Because he had experienced it before? Because he couldn't live without it? Well, he hadn't been prepared to live at all. He had been preparing for his own death for months. And Antonia had yanked him back into the midst of life.

He resented that. Resented her power over him. Was that what had happened? She had told him she had psychic powers. Was she using them on him?

She had said she had been waiting for him. What the hell did that mean? Waiting for him tonight? Or had she drawn him to her?

Had she used otherworldly powers to enslave him? Bind him to her the way he could be bound to no other woman besides his lost mate?

He wanted to clutch at that explanation. He wanted a reason why he had betrayed his marriage vows—a reason that had nothing to do with his personal failings.

He had been running toward the beach; he stopped short when the beam from a flashlight suddenly stabbed him in the eyes.

"Hold it right there. Put your hands up where I can see them."

Chapter 5

✦

HE might have a death wish, but there was enough reason left in Grant's brain to make him stop in his tracks and raise his hands. He knew that voice. It was Scott Wright, and he knew the guy could blow him away if he made the wrong move.

"What do you know about this clothing on the beach?" the officer asked in a grating voice as though he were confronting a suspect who had returned to the scene of the crime.

If he hadn't been standing with his hands in the air, he would have smacked himself on the forehead.

"That's my stuff," he finally said. "I was swimming." Carefully he shifted one of his arms so that it partially blocked the light shining in his eyes.

"Swimming? In this weather?" Wright demanded.

"I like a nice cold dip in the ocean."

"So why are you dressed now?"

"A big dog scared me off," he said, keeping his tone even, wondering if Officer Wright had been the man in the car with its lights off. "I got the hell out of here—then came back for my stuff," he added.

The light lowered, as though Wright accepted the dog story without question. Interesting.

"Mind if I take my belongings?" Grant asked, cautiously bringing his hands to a more normal position, then reaching to pick up the clothing he'd discarded earlier.

The cop fixed him with a displeased look. "Why are you still hanging around town?"

"I told you. I'm looking for property where I can build a house."

"I think you're up to something else."

Grant turned his free palm up. "Like what?"

"You tell me."

"There's nothing to tell."

They stood confronting each other for heartbeats. Finally he asked, "Is it okay if I take my clothes home?"

Wright kept him waiting, then finally muttered, "Go ahead."

Picking up his belongings, Grant shook out some of the sand and rolled the items into a ball in his arms. Then he turned and left, feeling the cop's eyes on him as he walked toward the road. He kept imagining the impact of a bullet hitting his back, but Officer Wright let him go—for now.

ANTONIA sat in the darkness, trying to ignore the hot, aching sensations pulsing through her. But pretending nothing had happened was impossible because every cell of her body still throbbed with the aftershocks of Grant's touch.

It had been a long time since a man had reached for her with sexual intent. Well, excluding Scott Wright. He had put his hands where they didn't belong. He had played games with the blind woman because she couldn't see what he was doing.

She would never label the encounter with Grant as play. When he'd touched her, something strong and scorching had leaped between them. Something they had both felt.

Raising her hand, she slid her fingers lightly against her lips, bringing back the sensuality of his kiss.

She had thought she understood passion. She knew now that nothing had prepared her for the wild, out-of-control ardor she had felt in Grant's arms. Still felt, because there was nothing she could do for herself that would come close to satisfying the all-consuming need he had aroused. She ached for sexual release. It was all she could do to keep from sliding her hand down her body, to the throbbing place between her legs. It wouldn't take much to push herself over the edge. But she knew that masturbation would be a pale substitute for what she craved.

Her mind and body still rocked with needs she hadn't known existed. And she knew it had been as powerful for Grant, knew it from the way he had devoured her whole, then wrenched himself away and fled into the night.

When she had some control over the sensations clamoring inside her body, Antonia reached for the pack of cards on the table and began to shuffle them.

They had been at her side for years, and handling them brought her a measure of calm. At first, she simply shuffled them, letting the hard rectangles slide against her skin. Then she went through the deck more slowly, stroking the corner of each card, reading the name. Usually every one brought her a vivid image. This evening, the pictures barely registered in her brain.

All she knew was that the wolf was gone from the cards because he didn't need to be there anymore.

He had come to Sea Gate—in person. And, again, she knew she should be frightened. Any normal woman would be.

Well, not any woman. He had been married to someone else—someone who had gotten past the fear of a man who could change himself into a wolf.

Or was that the wrong assumption, she suddenly wondered. Had he been married to someone who was like himself—able to change into a wolf whenever she wanted?

She longed to know the answer to that question. She had to know if the only woman he would consider for a mate was like him.

A shaky laugh bubbled from her throat. She was certainly getting ahead of herself here. She should be running away from the man. Instead, she was worried about how she would cope if he walked away from her.

Would he?

Fanning out the deck, she reached for one of the cards, pulled it out, and laid it on the table.

There were many ways to do a reading. For a client, she might lay out a Celtic cross, the most common pattern. For herself she preferred to simply turn over individual cards.

Five years ago, she had asked questions about her life and gotten answers that had turned out to be true.

Would she regain her sight? The cards had told her that was unlikely. They had also reassured her that she would be able to make a life for herself despite her handicap. They had said she was well rid of her fiancé, Billy Raider.

He wasn't the right man for her. But she'd known that as soon as he'd started worrying about how he was going to cope with a woman losing her vision.

Still, it had taken her months to get over her hurt and anger. Conversely, it had taken her only hours to know that Grant Marshall was more important to her than any man she had met before him.

Or was she making that up because she wanted it to be true?

Her own sense of confusion made her pulse pound as she stroked her finger gently against the ten of Swords. The card showed a graphic picture of a dead man lying on a desolate plain, ten swords sticking upright in his back.

She grimaced. He represented the effects of war and strife and by extension major trauma in someone's life. It wasn't hard to get that from the image. But the extent of the card's meaning was unclear to her now. The picture could signify a deep sense of loss. Her own? Or Grant's? But it could also mean a cycle in her life or his had come to an end—which implied a new beginning. She wanted that to be true. But she couldn't force her own meaning on the card. And as she sat fingering the raised braille dots, she knew it was impossible to decide what the image meant.

Frustrated, she turned over another card, then felt a shiver go through her when she realized it was the nine of Swords. It wasn't a card she usually got. Which said something about her present circumstances all by itself.

The picture showed a woman sitting in bed, hiding her face in her hands, probably crying. It represented loss of hope, depression, bad dreams, desperation.

"Oh great," she muttered.

If someone else had gotten that card, she'd think that they needed medical or legal help. At the very least, she would assume the woman was in big trouble.

But maybe that was just her view of the situation—not reality, she added, trying to make herself feel better and succeeding only marginally.

She turned over another card. The six of Wands—a horseman wearing a laurel wreath on his head and coming home to victory. That was better. The card could herald upcoming good news. Or guests arriving.

Well, her guest had already arrived. The question was, would he stay?

More possibilities turned themselves around in her head. The card could predict a journey. Did that mean Grant was leaving?

Her thoughts were in too much turmoil to give a clean interpretation of anything.

"Have you fallen completely apart?" she whispered, hearing the tears in her voice.

In frustration, she clenched her hand around the deck, thinking about throwing it across the room. What stopped her was the image of herself crawling around on the floor trying to find all the cards.

Instead, she sat where she was, clenching and unclenching her hands, her thoughts going back to Grant.

He had lost his wife, and he had focused all his energies on finding her killer.

He had made no plans for himself beyond that. He had wanted nothing more than the satisfaction of ripping out the throat of the man who had robbed him of his reason for living.

But when they'd kissed and touched, she had reminded him that he was still living and breathing, and that had shaken him. Probably it had also made him angry—at her and at himself.

Angry enough to make him walk out on her?

She had only met him a few hours ago. Yet fear of his loss clawed at her insides.

GRANT'S feet carried him toward Antonia's house. He walked slowly now, trying to reach back into the past of a few hours ago and find the steady center of his being—of his purpose.

The exercise proved to be impossible, because something inside himself had shaken loose and was twisting around in his gut.

Deliberately he brought up scenes from another life, scenes that would help him remember why he had come to Sea Gate, New Jersey.

He hadn't thought for a long time about making love with Marcy—or anyone else. In the darkness he called on very private memories—of a time when they had driven to the state park near their home and slipped in after dark. He'd left her sitting on a rock by a stream that wound its way through mature trees and tangles of honeysuckle.

He left her wearing a simple cotton dress. When he returned, a gray wolf moving through the darkness, she was naked. Sensing his presence, she pushed off from her seat, smiling as she came down on a bed of soft moss. He moved silently to her side and stood looking down at her.

Slowly, slowly, she raised her arms, then circled the wolf's neck and drew him close, scratching behind his ears and under his chin where he liked it, then stringing kisses along his muzzle.

Since her death, he had ruthlessly kept memories like that out of his mind. Now he focused on her slender body, on her scent, on the way she touched him—the way she told him she wanted more than just to stroke and kiss him.

With a groan, he cut off the scene before it could go any further. He had deliberately brought back memories of Marcy to wipe away the heated scene with Antonia. But the two had become entwined, and both had the power to make him hot and hard.

"Jesus, no!" he denied. He hadn't asked to get tangled up with another woman. Hadn't expected it.

With a growl of anguish, he changed the picture. Maybe he had some vague idea of proving to himself that he could resist Antonia—that he could control his reactions to her.

His fantasy had her sitting outside in the moonlight, not by a stream, but on a blanket in the dunes. In his mind, he made the location far out of town, where nobody would disturb them. He was a gray wolf, standing twenty yards away, but he knew she couldn't see him, which added to his excitement as she lifted her face to the wind, drawing in a deep breath. That same wind blew her long cotton shirt against her body, making her nipples stand out against the thin fabric. He liked the view, but it wasn't enough.

Unconsciously, he clenched his jaw as the fantasy continued—as he had her come up on her knees and unbutton the shirt. Her fingers weren't quite steady, and it took a little time, drawing out his anticipation.

She was naked now. He hadn't seen her body, but he had felt it pressed to his, and he could imagine her smooth skin, her womanly curves and a dark triangle of hair at the juncture of her legs. As he trotted toward her, he waited for her to turn and run. It had taken months before he'd dared to come to Marcy as a wolf. Dared to trail his long, wet tongue over her breasts and down her woman's body. Dared to taste the rich, female part of her.

But in his imagination, Antonia didn't flee the animal stalking her. She stayed where she was, as he knew she would. It wasn't her lack of vision. She would feel the coarse fur of the wolf. Feel his sharp teeth if he delicately pressed them against her neck or her shoulder or her breast.

She wouldn't fear the wolf. She had waited in the dark for him. When he had walked into her hallway, she had called out his name.

And now, as he watched, the back door of the house opened, and he went still, seeing her emerge from the interior as though he had called out to her.

She was holding a white cane that he hadn't seen in her hand before. She'd moved so confidently through her own house. But out here, she must feel less assured.

She stood for a moment and lifted her head, the silver streak in her dark hair drawing him like a beacon.

In an unconsciously sexy gesture she swept back her hair with one hand, then swung her cane along the landing and each step before she walked down and stood at ground level. Raising her head, she sniffed the wind, much as she had in his vision of her on the beach. She was silent for several heartbeats, then she turned her head toward him.

He felt goose bumps prickle his arms. If he didn't know better, he would swear she was staring at him.

In a voice that wasn't quite steady, she asked, "Are you there?"

Chapter 6

❖

GRANT cleared his throat before answering, "Who were you expecting?"

"I hoped it wasn't Scott Wright out here."

"Why?" he challenged.

She delicately lifted one shoulder. "I don't like him."

"What if I came back to pack my things and leave?" he asked roughly.

He saw her swallow. "Why? Are you afraid of a blind woman?"

He managed a gruff laugh. "Don't use your lack of sight as a shield."

"It's not a shield. It's a handicap."

Shoving his hands into his pockets, he answered, "Not for you."

She gestured with the white cane in her right hand. "Because I work pretty hard to hide my defects."

"And you compensate very well. You see things other people miss. That can make the rest of us uncomfortable."

He watched Antonia lick her lips. She'd done it before. Probably the gesture was unconscious, but he couldn't take his eyes off the pink tip of her tongue.

"Yes," she said in a soft voice. "The cards give me insights about people. But that's not the major thing that's bothering you—where I'm concerned."

SHADOW Man sat in his car, watching the scene unfold at the back door of the bed and breakfast. He hadn't seen the man until the guy had started talking to Antonia. Somehow he had walked up to the house in the darkness, then appeared like a creature out of the mist.

That was spooky. But it wasn't the only thing about this fellow that worried him. His name was Grant Marshall, and that was a very bad piece of news.

Two years ago, Shadow Man had killed a woman in Fairfield, Pennsylvania, with the last name of Marshall.

The husband had gone missing not long after the murder—which had made the cops suspicious. Then he'd come back looking like he'd been living in the woods and explained that grief had driven him a little crazy.

The cops had investigated him up the wazoo. Too bad he'd been out of town with people from his company—and there hadn't been time for him to drive home and poison his wife, then make it back to his associates.

But more importantly, too bad he was in Sea Gate now.

That couldn't be a coincidence. He must be here because he knew too much for his own good. And maybe he was telling Antonia things unfit for a woman's ears.

Very quietly, Shadow Man rolled down the window and leaned forward. The wind had shifted, making it easier for him to hear the conversation. He wanted to pick up more, but he couldn't get any closer. He couldn't risk them knowing he was there.

His gaze absorbed Antonia. She was standing near the door with the moonlight shimmering off the silver streak in her hair. It made her look weird, and she didn't even know that.

Tomorrow or the next day, he could get close to her. No problem. He knew her habits, because he'd studied her; the way he'd studied a lot of the women in town. She went to the grocery store a couple of times a week—and brought her purchases home in one of those rolling carts that old ladies used. He could come sweeping around the corner and mow her down when she was crossing the street, if he wanted. That would be his fallback plan. But it would be better to get rid of Grant Marshall and Antonia Delarosa together—and make it look like Marshall had come to town, wigged out, and killed them both.

"OH yeah? What do you think is bothering me?" Grant asked Antonia.

"Do you really want to talk about it? Out here?"

He had built up lifelong habits of secrecy. Now *she* was reminding *him* of what he should have remembered.

"You're right. Let's go back inside," he said.

He walked up the steps and into the house, making sure that no part of his body brushed against hers. Then he waited, with his pulse pounding, for her to follow him.

Silently, she folded up her white cane and placed it in one of the pantry drawers, then walked into the kitchen.

"What do you know about wolves?" he asked, following her through the doorway, wondering what it would take to make her as uncomfortable as he felt. He hadn't talked to

Marcy about wolves until after he'd ruthlessly seduced her. Now he was doing the exact opposite.

"Not much," she answered, sounding calm, yet he detected a quaver of emotion below the smooth surface of her demeanor.

"I read a lot about them when I was a teenager. When I was nineteen, I took a trip to Wyoming," he said in a conversational voice. "I watched a pack for a few days."

"As a man?" she asked in a steady voice.

"Yes. For some reason, they let me get close."

"They must have sensed you were no threat to them." She looked like she was about to say more, then stopped.

He nodded, realized she couldn't see the automatic gesture, and went on quickly, clutching the shirt and pants from the beach that he was still holding in his arms. "They had one leader—one alpha male. And all the others were subservient to him." Before she could comment, he plowed ahead. "That was true of me and my brothers when we were young. We obeyed our father automatically—until we hit our teens."

She interrupted him with a question he assumed she wouldn't be bold enough to ask. "That's when you first . . . changed."

"Yeah. That's when we do it. A couple of my brothers didn't make it. They died in the process."

"I'm sorry."

"It was hard on my mother," he said bluntly.

She didn't ask why he was being so specific—and so stark. Probably she knew why he was presenting the reality of his life in the darkest possible terms.

"We leave home when we're old enough to challenge the leader. Like my own dad did when he was a teenager."

She bent her face away from him. "You mentioned your brothers. What about sisters?"

"My mom was lucky enough to have only one girl—because they die at birth. That's another fact of life in my family."

Still with her face averted, she asked, "You mean, there are no women—like you?"

"No."

"That must be hard. I mean about your sister dying," she said with a hitch in her voice.

"It's hard on the woman who marries one of us," he clipped out. He would have met her gaze now if she could have looked at him. He'd thought the conversation was going to make her back away. Instead, she was still standing there, acting like they were discussing some ordinary dysfunctional family.

"Grant . . ."

"I'm sorry. I can't do this any longer." He flung the last part of the phrase over his shoulder as he made for the stairs, fleeing the woman standing inside her back door.

He strode into his bedroom and leaned against the door, feeling as though he'd run a ten-mile race.

He needed to think of Marcy. Of her amazing hazel eyes that had smiled at him with such warmth. Of the bouncing golden curls that he'd twined around his fingers. Of her long, silken neck that she'd arched for his kisses. Of the way she looked in a chenille robe fixing eggs for herself in the morning and rare steak for him.

To his horror, he found that the images were not as sharp in his mind as he wanted them to be.

His father had told him that once he found his life mate, no other woman would satisfy him. That was the way it was among the males of his species. Probably they bonded with one woman so strongly because they had to stay around to coach their sons through the first change from man to wolf.

He hadn't been looking for a mate. He'd met Marcy Hammersmith by pure chance. Although she'd had a degree in biochemistry, she'd been working as a county site inspector, and she'd come out to certify some lots where he was planning to build. He'd known from the moment he saw her that she was the woman who was going to change his life forever.

He used every ounce of charm he possessed to ruthlessly seduce her. Then he waited weeks before he could bring himself to tell her the truth about his dual nature. She hadn't run from him, maybe because she no longer had a choice.

He'd had six months of honeymoon bliss with Marcy. Then a sadistic killer ripped his joy to shreds.

He wanted to step out of the bedroom now and shout at the woman who thought she could accept the wolf so easily.

He wanted to tell her every dark, horrible thing he had ever done. *You think you know me, but you don't. You should have seen me after my wife died. I went crazy. I rampaged through the woods bringing down Bambi. How do you like that image?*

He sucked in a sharp breath and let it out, then pushed away from the door. In the bathroom, he splashed icy water on his face, the small punishment a reminder of why he was here.

To stop a killer. And then to end his own pain.

And he couldn't let Antonia Delarosa take his attention from that purpose.

GRANT considered staying in his room the next morning until the shops in town were open. He'd start with the real estate office, then try the dry goods store again. The plan lasted until the smell of peppermint tea wafting up the steps lured him out of his bedroom.

When he walked into the kitchen Antonia was dressed in a flowing silk bathrobe, and he wondered who had picked the blue and green paisley print, since the color looked so good on her.

She was tending a pan, cooking corned beef hash. A bowl of applesauce sat on the kitchen table.

He lingered in the doorway again, observing her efficient movements, feeling guilty that watching her gave him secret pleasure.

"Did you sleep well?" she asked, half turning.

"Yeah," he answered, matching the neutral tone of her voice. If she could act like they hadn't been on the verge of making love the first time they'd kissed, he could do it, too.

"Do you like hash? And applesauce?"

"Yes," he answered, thinking she wouldn't know if he didn't take much of the fruit.

He poured himself a mug of tea and got out cutlery, staying out of her way. But a question kept turning itself around in his mind. Into the silence, he asked, "Can the cards tell me who murdered my wife?"

"I don't think so."

"Why not?" he pressed, then immediately regretted the sharp tone of his voice.

"I'm not a fortune-teller. I can see things in the tarot. But I'd be unlikely to identify a specific individual."

"You said you knew the wolf was coming."

She moved her spoon around in the hash. The degree of resistance must have told her it was done, because she took the pan off the heat, then reached to turn off the burner. After it gave a faint click, she raised her head toward him.

"Because he invaded the cards," she answered, her voice telling him she didn't want to elaborate. After dishing some hash onto two plates, she carried them to the table.

They sat across from each other, pushing food around, neither eating much.

"When I first got here, you said you could help me find the killer," he finally said. "I'd like to see if the cards give me any clues."

Her shoulders stiffened, but she said, "All right."

He cleared away the half-empty dishes, and she carefully wiped off the table and dried it, then washed and dried her hands, and he wondered if she was stalling. But finally, she got a deck of cards out of a nearby drawer.

"We can do a Celtic cross," she said in a strangely detached voice. "Or a seven-card spread."

"Whatever you think is best."

She kept her gaze down as she handed him the cards, and their skin touched for the first time since the night before. Quickly he pulled his hand back.

"You shuffle," she said, her voice tight.

"How much?"

"As much as you want. Until you're satisfied."

He did as she asked, then set the pack down. She turned over the first card and he saw a man poling a small boat with two shrouded figures in the front. A bunch of swords were in the background. The next card said Ace of Wands and showed a disembodied hand holding a branch with leaves. The name was at the top, but the picture was upside down. The next was called the Star and showed a naked woman kneeling by a pool pouring water from two jugs. Next came the five of Cups, featuring a mournful-looking figure.

Antonia kept her head bent, touching the braille markings on each card as she laid it out, working slowly and carefully.

When she'd arranged all seven, she sat with her shoulders hunched.

"What does it mean?" he finally asked.

She didn't answer, and he felt his heart rate accelerate. Reaching across the table, he cupped her shoulder to get her attention.

"Just say it," he demanded.

Slowly she raised her face, and he saw tears glistening in her eyes.

"What? Am I going to fail? What?" he demanded, giving her shoulder a shake because he couldn't cope with the idea that she was holding back information for his own good.

Chapter 7

"LORD, I don't know," Antonia answered in a barely audible whisper. Then more sharply, her voice cracking, "I don't know! It's all a blur in my mind."

She stood up abruptly, sending her chair flying. "I'm just going through the motions," she whispered. "I can't tell you a damn thing because the cards have stopped working for me." The last part came out in a sob as she tried to flee from the room. But the chair had landed on its side, with its legs sticking out like a fence. When they tangled in the skirt of her robe, she lost her balance and started to pitch forward.

Grant was already out of his chair. Surging around the table, he reached for her, and she landed heavily against him, with a small sound of surprise.

"It's okay. I've got you," he murmured.

"Let me go," she cried out, the plea thick with anguish.

When she tried to push away, he gathered her closer. "Don't."

She was still protesting, but he could barely hear her words above the roaring in his ears. He had forgotten why she was in his arms. The part of his mind that was still functioning told him he should loosen his grip on her. But it had become impossible to break the contact, as though the flowing folds of her robe had magically twined themselves around his legs, holding him where he was.

She was shaking, and he tried to comfort her, stroking his hands over the silky fabric on her shoulders.

"It's all right. It's all right," he whispered, not sure of what he meant.

But the light touch of his hands on silk abraded his fingertips, sending sensual messages through his body. And he found that she wasn't the only one shaking.

"Grant?" She spoke his name, but the word was muffled against his shoulder.

Her scent, the feel of her body, the taste of her skin as he pressed his lips to the side of her face had seeped into his senses, driving him beyond reason.

She raised her head, her eyes still glistening. He knew she couldn't see him, yet he felt the intensity of her gaze.

One of her hands lifted, and slowly, slowly touched his face, stroking over his cheeks, his brows, his nose, then down to his lips, the light touch holding as surely as a magic spell.

"I wanted to know what you looked like," she whispered, "So badly. The worst part is that I can't see you smile. Do you ever smile?"

"There haven't been many reasons to . . . recently," he answered.

The look of anguish in her eyes tore at him.

"I've lost my gift," she said with a terrible finality. "I

see the pictures on the cards, but I can't sort out what they
mean. It's . . . gone."

"No."

"What would you call it?" she asked in a broken voice.

"You're upset. By me."

"By your pain," she said.

He wanted to transform every drop of her sadness to
rays of sunshine. And it hurt to know that nothing he could
say would make a difference.

But there was something he could do to wipe the despair
from her face. Telling himself he had no other choice, he
lowered his mouth to hers.

Did he mean to give her comfort, or gratify himself? All
he knew was that her taste was intoxicating. A heady combination of wisdom and power and sweetness. And he recognized at the instant of contact that one draft would never
be enough. Not near enough.

He was instantly hot and hard and needy. On a surge of
hunger, he increased the pressure of his lips on hers, deep-
ening the kiss, drinking in her eager response.

She murmured something incoherent, sliding her hands
up and down his back and into his hair.

Tensions held too long in check clamored for release.
Taking a step back, he brought her with him, leaning
against the counter so he could equalize their heights,
bringing his straining erection into the cradle of her hips.

She made a fevered exclamation, rocking her body
against his, even as he devoured her mouth, using his
tongue, his lips, his teeth.

When she pushed at his chest, he thought his heart
would stop.

His hand clamped around her shoulder, holding her
where she was. She covered the hand, stroking her fingers
against his. To soften her rejection?

When she started to speak, her voice was thin and breathy. "Grant, this is going too fast. I mean—I want to be naked when we make love. I want to feel my breasts pressed to your bare chest. I want you inside me when I come."

"Jesus!"

She gulped, then made an attempt at a laugh. "I'm telling you all that because if I keep standing here with that wonderfully hard penis wedged between my legs, I'm going to explode."

"The explosion could be mutual," he managed.

"Maybe we can hold off for a couple of minutes."

When she knit her fingers with his, he clasped her hand.

"Where are we going?"

"Not far. I don't think I can walk far."

"You've got that right."

She led him into a small, comfortably furnished room. Stopping when they reached a thick oriental rug, she turned to face him. The intensely sexual look on her face scorched him as she yanked down the zipper on her robe. Tossing it out of the way, she tugged the tee shirt she was wearing over her head, then skimmed her panties down her legs.

He had never experienced anything so erotic as the sight of her standing naked and glorious in the center of the rug.

"You are so beautiful."

"Probably I'm starting to sag . . ." she tried to say. The sentence ended in a gasp as he reached to capture the fullness of her breasts, lifting them in his hands, then stroking his thumbs across her hardened nipples. She stood with her eyes closed as he caressed her, her breath fast and shaky.

"You, too. I want you naked, too," she murmured.

Her hands reached out, connected with his midsection, and lowered to his waist, where she slid open his belt buckle, then lowered the fly of his jeans so she could reach inside and push his briefs out of the way. When she took his swollen cock in her hand, he made a strangled sound.

"God, your erection feels so good," she murmured, stroking his length, exploring his size and shape with her hands. In danger of free-falling over the edge of a cliff, he lifted her hand away, bringing it to his mouth, kissing the hollow of her palm.

Barely able to breathe, he wrenched off his shirt before kicking away his pants and shoes.

When he pulled her naked body against his, both of them cried out. He held tight for a long moment, trying to catch his breath, then moved her in his arms so that her breasts slid across the hair on his chest.

She made small, urgent sounds as her hands ran up and down his back, over his buttocks, cupping him, gathering him to her. And when she spoke, her voice trembled. "Grant, I can't wait any longer."

Tugging him down to the rug, she rolled to her back as she pulled him down on top of her.

He found the slick folds of her sex with his free hand, found her hot and wet and ready for him.

"Come inside me. Quickly," she begged, her legs moving restlessly against his. "Deep inside me."

There was no way he could deny her throaty invitation.

When he slid into her, she made a small, sobbing sound.

"Did I hurt you?" he asked urgently.

"No. Oh, no. It's just that I wanted you so much."

Her face was turned toward his, and he lowered his mouth to hers, kissing her as he began to move inside her.

She clasped him to her, matching the rise and fall of his hips, her frank sensual enjoyment making it impossible for him to hold anything back.

He came like an explosive device detonating, calling out her name, even as he felt her inner muscles contract around him and her nails dig into his shoulders.

He drifted for long moments, feeling more relaxed and content than he had in years, his eyes closed, soothed by the feel of her hand stroking through his hair and over the damp skin of his back.

With his eyes closed, he thought that Marcy had come back to him, and he smiled. Then he realized she didn't smell the way he remembered.

The realization brought a spurt of panic, and he rolled to his side. When he tried to scramble to his feet, a woman's hand flailed out, scrabbled against his side, then clamped around his wrist.

"Grant, it's all right," she said.

"No."

"Were you planning to make love with me, then walk away?" she asked in a voice he knew she was struggling to hold steady.

The frank question was like a blow to the chest.

"I wasn't planning anything," he said.

Her mouth twisted. "I guess not. You touched me, and it was like being on a runaway train."

"Yeah."

He watched her swallow.

"I think it was meant to be," she said. "But I think you still can't accept that. I mean, you can't accept the concept of being happy again."

He didn't answer because he didn't have a comeback.

He watched her fingers press against the rug fibers as she said. "Do what you have to. But don't pretend that wasn't . . ." she paused, then said softly, "wonderful."

"It didn't last long," he answered with the first thing that came into his head.

"Because we were both too turned on to wait. But it was what we both needed." Again she paused. "Well, at least I did. I've been aching to finish what we started last night."

"Are you always so blunt?" he asked.

"No. I'm never this blunt. With clients, if I have bad news, I try to soften it."

"And with me?"

"With you, the stakes are too high to play around. Either you're going to stay with me—or you're going to convince yourself you made a mistake. I want you to stay. Very much. Not just for great sex. For everything we could give each other. But after Billy left me, I realized I couldn't count on having the things other women take for granted."

It was a relief to turn the spotlight away from himself. "This has nothing to do with your being blind!"

She raised her face toward him, and the illusion of her sight was so strong that he wanted to turn away from her piercing gaze.

"I wasn't trying to make you feel guilty about walking away from a blind lady. You came here thinking you were going to rip out the throat of the man who murdered your wife and then kill yourself," she said, finally stating what neither one of them had yet discussed. "But I hope I've given you a choice. I hope you can admit that you might have something to live for."

He struggled for breath, wondering what he might say if he managed to fill his lungs.

"I want you to make the right choice," she added softly.

"We've known each other less than a day."

"I know. But that doesn't mean we haven't . . ." She turned her hands palms up. "I want to say bonded. Is that the right word?"

"Don't you dare say that!" he fairly shouted. "I bonded

with someone. With my wife." He looked around the room, feeling the walls closing in on him. "I have to go out."

Snatching up his clothing, he ran from the room, ran from the woman who had seduced him into forgetting his marriage vows—into forgetting his purpose.

ANTONIA felt around the rug and found her robe, then her panties. After she'd pulled them on, she remembered she'd been wearing a tee shirt, too, and searched until she found it.

After putting herself back together, she stood. But her legs were unsteady, and she sat down heavily on the sofa. When she was feeling more in control, she walked out of the room and up the stairs, hardly daring to think about what had happened. She had made love with Grant, and the emotional and physical joy had been more than she had dreamed were possible.

But he hadn't accepted what their joining meant.

She thought back over what she had said. Maybe she had been too blunt. Maybe she should have pretended she didn't know exactly why he had come to Sea Gate.

Pretended? No. She would have been lying, and she wasn't going to lie to him.

So she took a shower, then came back down and began to clean the kitchen.

She was in the middle of loading the dishwasher, when a knock at the door made her heart leap.

Was Grant back? Had he come to his senses?

On her way to the front hall, she realized Grant probably wouldn't have knocked.

"Yes?" she called out through the closed door.

"It's Charlie Hastings, ma'am."

"From the real estate company?"

"Yes."

Wondering what he wanted, she pulled open the door and aimed her gaze toward where the man's face should be. "What can I do for you?"

"I'm going around town, telling people what they can expect to get for their property—should they be interested in selling."

"I'm not."

"Are you positive? This is a pretty large house, for someone on her own."

"But I run a bed and breakfast in the summer."

"Well then, I could advise you on modernizing."

"I'm fine," she said, wondering why he'd picked today of all days to come around with his offer—until she thought about the man staying at her house. Obviously the town would be interested in Grant. Probably they'd be wondering what was going on in the house with the two of them alone here.

As she thought about what she and her houseguest had been doing less than an hour ago, she felt her cheeks heat, then hoped Hastings wasn't studying her face.

"I could take a look around," he said, and she flashed on the scene in the den. Had she and Grant left any telltale evidence?

She was thinking the real estate agent might shoulder his way into the hall when she heard booted steps just before another voice said, "The lady told you she's not interested."

Antonia recognized the boots and the authoritative tone. It was Scott Wright. He must have been doing one of his drive-bys, seen Charlie, and decided it was his duty to stop.

"I was just trying to be helpful," Charlie answered, addressing the cop. Somehow they had both made it into the front hall.

"She said she doesn't need your assistance," Scott answered, moving closer to her. She could feel his breath against the top of her hair, and she wondered which man she least wanted in the house. She decided it was the cop.

"Uh, maybe I would like an opinion on modernizing my kitchen," she allowed.

She could practically hear Officer Wright bristling. "It sounded like he was bothering you," he said.

"I'm fine."

When the pushy lawman had left, she wished she could just tell Charlie to forget it. But she'd trapped herself now. "The kitchen is a little outdated. Maybe you can make some suggestions for quick fixes."

"Of course."

She led the way back down the hall, then waited, hearing the real estate agent walk around the room. When he opened the refrigerator door, she wondered if there were any spills inside.

But her mind was going down a different path as well. Maybe being alone in the house with this man wasn't such a good idea.

She didn't know she'd shaken her head until he asked, "Did you have a problem?"

"Uh no."

Just then, the doorbell rang.

"I'd better answer that," she said quickly, wondering who it was this time.

The man who called out to her was another familiar voice. Dwayne Shipley. Relieved that she was no longer going to be alone with Charlie, she opened the door.

"Ms. Delarosa? I had some time, and I thought I'd look at that loose paneling you wanted me to take care of. And see what else needs doing, like that wall socket in the pantry."

"Yes. I appreciate it," she said, thinking that her house was turning into Newark Airport. What other small-town busybody was going to show up with an excuse to look around?"

She was leading Dwayne down the hall, when she stopped short, remembering where the paneling was. In the room where she and Grant had made love. Not long ago.

"Maybe you should just do that socket," she said.

"And you wanted some painting done in some of the upstairs rooms. The off-season is a good time to take care of that."

"I've got a guest now."

"Grant Marshall," he said promptly.

"How do you know?"

"From the other day at Bridges."

"Oh."

Footsteps approaching from the kitchen told her Charlie was coming to join the conversation.

"Morning, Dwayne," he said.

She would have given a lot to see what kind of look the two men exchanged.

"Odd for you to take in lodgers in the winter," Charlie observed.

"Well, he . . . needed a place to stay," she said lamely.

"You call me if you decide to sell," the real estate agent said, using his hearty, friendly voice. Or you can do some easy updates. The kitchen needs painting, for example."

"I'll keep that in mind. Just let yourself out," she added, thinking that she should start keeping her door locked.

"I'll just get my tool kit and fix that socket," Dwayne said.

"Yes."

She busied herself with the rest of the dishes. Then got out of Dwayne's way by going into the lounge and sitting

with her cards. But if her concentration had been bad earlier, it was worse now.

To her relief Dwayne announced he was finished with
the wall plug about a half hour later, and he could come
back to do the painting another time.

She locked the door behind him. Then went back to her
useless cards, shuffling them and turning them over, hoping that the jumble of images would tell her something
important.

They only confused her more.

Hours crawled slowly by before she heard the doorbell
ring.

Stumbling into the front hall, she called out, "Who is it
this time?"

Chapter 8

❖

"GRANT," his now-familiar voice answered.

Relief flooded through her as she unlocked the door. When he came inside, she wanted to reach for him, but she only stepped back as he locked up again. He stayed near the door, and she raised her head toward him.

"Thank God. I've been worried about you," she said, uttering the understatement very calmly before adding, "I've been listening for your car. I didn't hear it."

"I left it in the parking lot at the 7-Eleven and came across the back way."

"Why?"

"Yesterday I thought it might be an advantage to let people know I was here. Now I'm thinking there's too much damn interest in me in town. I couldn't even get my hair cut without stopping all conversation at the barbershop. I figured it might be better if it looked like I'd gone somewhere else."

Her mind focused on the part about his hair. He'd gotten it cut? She hoped it wasn't too short now. Would the length still feel good against her fingers?

Her attention switched abruptly when she heard him suck in a breath and let it out in a rush.

"What?" she asked.

"Why was your house full of people?" he demanded, his tone suddenly sharp.

"How do you know that?"

"I know you had a bunch of guys in here, because I can smell them. Everyone has a distinct scent. And I can sort them out. That's one of my talents."

"I should have figured that out."

"They're all men—men that I've met in town. Scott Wright, for one." He paused for a moment, then said, "Also a real estate agent named Charlie Hastings and a fellow wearing overalls. They were both at the dry goods store yesterday."

"Dwayne is the one in overalls."

"What—were they having a convention here?"

"Well, Scott thought Charlie was hassling me."

"Was he a problem?" Grant pressed.

"Only mildly. In that pushy way salesmen have." She cleared her throat. "He kindly offered to appraise the house. And Dwayne Shipley, who does handyman stuff for me, suddenly decided to fix a broken wall plug he's been neglecting for months."

Grant's tone turned fierce. "One of them could have been the murderer, looking for an excuse to check the place out. I mean, including your friend Scott."

"No! And don't call Scott my friend. I can't stand him."

She turned and walked through the wide arched doorway into the lounge.

Grant followed but stopped near the doorway. "Did anybody else give you . . . bad vibes?"

She sighed. "All of them, actually. That's why I locked the door. You need a key. I'll show you where I keep them."

"Not now." She was so tuned to him, that she thought she could hear him shifting his weight from one foot to the other. "While I was poking around town, I had time to do a lot of thinking."

Suddenly sick with tension, she waited for him to say he was leaving.

"My getting involved with someone now isn't fair to her."

She raised her chin. "If you mean me, say it straight out."

"I came to Sea Gate with a purpose. I have to see it through. I have to find out who murdered Marcy." He made an angry sound. "And Wendy Spencer in Baltimore. Cara Boston in Williamsburg. Laurie Carmichael in Morristown. Donna Dunn in Princeton. Phyllis Nelson in Camden. Tracy Porter in Rising Sun. Ginnie Gold in Washington, D.C."

"So many," she whispered.

"That's not the whole list. And until I nail the bastard who poisoned them, then burned up the evidence, I can't . . . think about myself."

She considered the implications. "You mean, find him and rip out his throat, don't you?"

"You're still being pretty direct."

She pressed her hands against her hips. She longed to argue that tearing the killer to shreds wasn't a great prelude to the rest of his life. But she was pretty sure he didn't want her opinion on that subject.

Walking to a wing chair, she gripped the back and asked, "You said one of the men who came over could be the murderer. Why do you think so?"

He made an angry sound. "Because I put you in danger!"

"How? Just by staying here?"

"Unfortunately, yes. When I first started looking for the killer, I didn't give a shit what happened to me. So I didn't bother to use an assumed name. I even thought it might work like a lure. If the guy is in town, he probably knows I'm the husband of one of his victims. Probably he's got a whole book full of press clippings. For me, his interest is an advantage. But not for you."

"You could find somewhere else to stay," she murmured.

"That would be worse. Now that I've called attention to you."

"Maybe, over dinner, you should tell me what you know about the killer."

"It's not great mealtime conversation."

"But necessary," she said briskly. She hadn't thought about food in hours. Now she started considering what to fix. "Um, since we haven't been drinking coffee, I have some cream I need to use up. How does salmon chowder sound?"

"Don't go to any trouble for me."

"Right. You can always go out and catch yourself a couple of rabbits."

He made a strangled sound, and she wished she could see his face.

"That was a poor attempt at a joke. I guess because I'm nervous."

"Marcy never joked about the wolf," he said very quietly.

"Well, if I were an entirely sober-faced, respectable citizen, I wouldn't be reading tarot cards for a living, would I?"

"I haven't noticed any other customers beating a path to your door."

"Wait until this summer."

The sentence hung in the air between them. Would he still be with her in the summer?

When he didn't answer the unspoken question, she took a step toward the hall. "The soup should be ready in about half an hour."

"Okay. Thanks."

She knew he was still lingering in the wide doorway. It took all her resolve to keep from stopping and cupping her hand over his shoulder. Or touching his lips with her fingers. She craved the physical contact. She longed to hear him say something—anything—about their future. But he'd said he was still stuck in the past. So she walked by him and into the kitchen, where she went about assembling the ingredients she'd need for the soup. Glad to focus on cooking, she chopped onions and garlic, then melted the butter in a small pot and added the vegetables.

When they felt nice and soft against the spoon, she turned down the heat and stirred in flour. Slowly, she added a little chicken broth, stirring until the mixture was uniform. Then she opened the cream.

It smelled a little off, and she didn't want to ruin the soup. So she got out another spoon to have a taste. She was lifting it to her lips when Grant's sharp exclamation rang out from the doorway.

"Don't!"

Frozen in place, she heard running feet, then an arm lashing out and knocking the utensil out of her grasp.

Chapter 9

⚜

"WHAT? What's wrong?" she gasped as the spoon clattered to the counter.

"It's poison."

"Poison," she breathed, wondering if he'd lost his mind. "How do you know?"

"The same way I know who was here. By the smell. I can smell something dangerous coming off that cream."

"Grant. Are you sure?"

When she reached toward the carton, he snatched her hand away, wedging it against her side as he dragged her into his arms.

She could feel his heart pounding as he held her to his chest, feel him shaking.

"How . . . how . . ." she tried to say. But her brain wasn't working all that well.

"It looks like one of your visitors left you a present. Either Charlie or Dwayne or Scott," he said in a grating voice.

"One of them?" she asked, hardly willing to follow the logic of it.

He clamped his hands on her shoulders. "It has to be one of them. They were here today."

"Somebody else . . ."

"I'd *know* if somebody else had been in the house."

As she struggled to rearrange her thinking, he went on, "And one of them is using the killer's MO. Like I told you, he poisons his victims, then sets their houses on fire."

"You're sure?"

"Of course I'm sure! I've made a study of the bastard. Not only that, he picks women who have some . . . handicap."

"Marcy had a handicap?" she gulped out.

"She had broken her leg." His fingers dug into her shoulders. "He went after her. Now I've brought him to you."

"But . . . but you stopped him."

"And the bastard doesn't know we've caught on. He's probably waiting around for you to use that cream."

"You mean he could be . . . waiting for it to happen?"

"Oh yeah. Do you usually have a cup of coffee after dinner?"

"Yes." She struggled to think logically. "But if he's outside watching, he can see you knocked the spoon out of my hand."

Grant answered with a sharp laugh. "I don't think so. In case you don't realize it, you were cooking in the dark. I'm the only guy who could have seen what you were doing. I'd been standing in the doorway for a while—watching you."

"I didn't know."

"I can be pretty quiet."

She felt his body tense.

"What?"

"I . . ."

"Say it!"

"If he's waiting to see what happens, we can trap him."

"No. We can call the police."

"If it's Scott, we'll tip him off."

She thought about that. Thought about what might happen next. Swallowing hard, she asked, "What would you want me to do?"

"You have milk, right?"

"Yes."

"And you didn't put any of that damn cream in the soup?" he asked very carefully.

"No. I'd just opened the carton. I've got a better than average sense of smell, too."

"You would." He held her a few feet away from himself, and she imagined he was looking into her eyes as he issued clipped directions. "Put some milk into the soup pot. But leave the cream carton on the counter right next to where you're standing," he went on rapidly. "Then you'll turn on the light, pretend to be cooking, and taste the soup. Act like you've drunk his damn poison. Maybe you can start gagging—then fall to the floor. And lie there."

"What kind of poison is it?" she murmured. "What are the symptoms?"

"I don't know. But probably he'll be so excited that you took the bait that he won't be real particular."

She made a strangled sound. She wanted to tell him they weren't in the middle of a made-for-TV movie. Instead she asked, "And where will you be while I'm lying on the floor?"

"Waiting for him," he said in a low, hard voice that sent a shiver down her spine. And she knew that he was thinking this was his chance to get his claws and teeth into the man. Could she keep the worst from happening? She didn't know. But she had to try.

Her arms slipped around him and she hung on tight, pressing her lips against his shoulder, wondering if it was the last time she would ever hold him.

Then she eased away. "Let's do it, before I chicken out."

"Are you sure ?" Now he was the one who sounded uncertain. "Maybe it's too much of a risk."

"Is the wolf turning tail on me?"

"No!"

"Then help me get ready."

With the light still out, he carefully washed down the counter where the spoon had landed, while she unlocked the back door. When he had left the kitchen, she crossed to another drawer and got something she thought she might need. With her private preparations made, she turned on the light and fussed around the kitchen for a few minutes before pouring some milk into the soup, keeping the carton shielded with her body before returning it to the refrigerator.

As she stirred the mixture, she wondered if she had lost her mind by agreeing to this crazy scenario.

Resolutely, she shoved her doubts aside and focused on making it look like she was in the midst of cooking poison soup.

First she found the can of salmon she'd put into the pantry and marked with a braille label. Then she carefully removed the skin and bones from the fish, before breaking it into chunks and adding them to the soup, working slowly and carefully, giving anyone outside in the darkness time to get a good look at what she was doing.

She was glad she couldn't see the carton of cream, because the idea of touching it again made her stomach roil.

Somewhere in the house, she could hear the sound of

Grant's voice. He was speaking strange syllables, words she didn't understand, but they raised the hair on the back of her neck. She was pretty sure that the next time she encountered him, he'd be a wolf.

Desperate not to lose her focus, she dragged in a deep breath, stuck a large spoon into the milky soup and took a sip.

Wondering if the killer was really watching her performance, she went for melodrama. Face contorted, she pretended to cough and gag, then dropped to the floor where she made a show of writhing in agony before going limp.

Once she was still, she wished she'd gotten herself into a more comfortable position. Her leg was twisted, but there was nothing she could do about it except lie on the floor with her pulse pounding.

Eons passed, and the leg began to ache. But she stayed still as death, fighting the horrible sensation that she'd lost control of the unfolding drama.

Her mind screamed for her to scramble up and run. But she stayed where she was. And finally, finally her straining ears caught the sound of the back door opening.

When someone crossed the pantry and entered the kitchen, her stomach knotted painfully. The worst part was that she had no way to know who was there.

Was Scott looking down at her? She'd bet on Scott.

For heartbeats, the man remained very still, then he walked toward her.

"How was your dinner, bitch?" he asked, and she knew then who it was. Dwayne Shipley, who had come to fix her broken electrical plug and left a little present in her refrigerator.

She felt him bend over her. When he jerked on a lock of her hair, she gasped.

"What the fuck?" he growled.

* * *

THE wolf who had been waiting in the shadows saw the man hover over Antonia.

It was Dwayne Shipley. The hayseed in the overalls. He was the monster who had killed Marcy.

In a blinding rage, the wolf leaped through the doorway, landing on the killer's back, bringing him down. A knife went flying from his hand, clattering across the tile floor, as he fell forward so that his head hit the corner of the cabinet before he sprawled in a heap on the floor.

Even as the wolf stood over the unconscious man, ready for the kill, he heard Antonia's desperate voice.

"Grant, don't. Don't!"

Turning his head, he saw her crawling blindly forward across the kitchen floor.

She couldn't know that Shipley was down, as she scrambled toward them. And Grant couldn't tell her. As a wolf, he couldn't speak. He could only give a warning snarl.

She ignored him and kept coming, still crying out as she closed the distance between them.

"Grant, don't do it. Don't kill him. You'll regret it for the rest of your life."

The rest of his life? He had dedicated the rest of his life to killing this monster. And now she was trying to stop him.

He wanted to howl at her to back off, so he could take care of his own business.

But it seemed she wasn't going to give up easily. She reached his side, half falling over the inert Shipley as she grabbed the wolf's shaggy coat, tugging on him. When he tried to shake her off, her grip on him tightened.

"You asked me to help you trap him. I did. Now turn him over to the police." As she spoke, she came up on her knees, finding his muzzle with her hands and locking his mouth closed with her fingers.

"Grant, I love you. I love you," she cried.

The declaration reverberated through him, even as she kept shouting.

"I want us to have a life together. Don't kill him. If you love me, don't do it."

He went very still, his head spinning, partly because she was making it hard for him to breathe. He was so close to achieving satisfaction. He could kill the monster. Remove this obscene scar on the body of humanity. And now Antonia was telling him to give up that pleasure? That necessity.

The wolf lusted for revenge. The man inside him knew that something fundamental had changed since he had met Antonia.

He had lived to kill the fiend who had taken his mate from him. Now he wanted something more. And he knew with a burst of insight that the woman on the floor holding on to him with such courage and determination was more important than revenge.

With that realization, something new and tender bloomed in his heart. He had been trapped in the freezing winter of his life. Now green shoots dared to poke through the sheets of ice.

He couldn't tell her any of that. He couldn't even use his eyes to convey what he wanted her to understand.

All he could do was tell her with his body. Wordlessly, he bent one leg and bowed to her in a gesture of submission, hoping the posture told her some of what he was feeling.

She must have been waiting for a sign from him, because she loosened her grip on his muzzle.

"Thank God," she breathed.

Delicately, he stroked his tongue against her cheek. He wanted to remain close to her, but he couldn't stay in wolf form now.

Slowly, he eased away. The man on the floor lay without moving. But Grant couldn't take a chance on leaving him alone with Antonia. Changing shape was such a private act for him. Still, he stayed in the room, backing up a few feet and saying the ancient chant of transformation in his mind.

As soon as his body was under voluntary control again, he ran back to Antonia. Pulling her to her feet, he wrapped his arms around her and held on tight.

"Grant. Thank you Grant," she whispered, as her hands swept over his naked back and shoulders.

"No, thank you." He let himself hold her for a few precious seconds, then he loosened his hold. "Got to put my clothes on."

"Yes."

He dashed out of the room, picked up his discarded sweatpants and shirt, and brought them back to the kitchen. After dressing, he used a length of rope he'd seen in a kitchen drawer to bind the man's hands. By the time he had secured the killer, Shipley was stirring.

He put himself between Antonia and the bastard. "Why did you kill my wife?" he asked.

"I don't have to tell you nothin'." The man lay there looking pale and sick.

From the corner of his eyes, he saw Antonia edging closer. When he tried to hold her back, she gave him a savage shake of the head.

Then she faced the killer, staring at him with a gaze fierce enough to pierce flesh and bone. "No, you don't have to tell us anything. I can read it in the tarot cards. I know all the women you murdered," she said in a low, menacing voice.

"Oh yeah? I say you don't know squat."

"I know . . . from the tarot," she insisted. "The cards tell me people's secrets."

"You're lying," he answered, but he didn't sound so sure of himself.

"The cards showed me your victims. Marcy Marshall in Fairfield. Wendy Spencer in Baltimore. Cara Boston in Williamsburg. Laurie Carmichael in Morristown." She stopped and took a breath. "Donna Dunn in Princeton. Phyllis Nelson in Camden. Tracy Porter in Rising Sun. Ginger Gold in D.C., Wendy Spencer."

"Ginnie!" Shipley snapped.

"Thank you for correcting me," she answered.

Grant blinked. He had given Antonia those names and places only a few hours ago, but somehow she'd memorized them.

"How . . . how do you know all that?" Shipley asked in a shaking voice.

"From the tarot. From their ancient wisdom," Antonia intoned. "The cards told me who you killed. The cards tell me everything."

"No. I was careful."

"I know you poisoned them. I know you burned their houses to destroy the evidence."

"You can't *know!*"

"I know everything," she corrected him. "Shall I tell you how you're going to die? In the electric chair? Or by lethal injection?"

"No. I'm not going to get caught. They deserved to die. Every one of them."

"What poison did you use? I don't know that. What poison did you put in my carton of cream when you were in here this afternoon?"

"Strychnine," he gasped out.

"Thank you for the information," Antonia said, pulling out the small tape recorder from her pocket.

"You blind bitch. You taped me," Shipley screamed.

"That's right. And Grant didn't even have to beat a confession out of you."

"Yeah," he muttered, then took the recorder from her and clicked it off before giving the bastard a swift kick to the chin. Once again, Shipley went still.

"What did you do?" Antonia gasped.

"Mr. Shipley is taking another nap," he told her, "So we can talk. As soon as I call 911."

After telling the cops that they were holding a murderer, he turned back to Antonia. "We'd better get our stories straight."

"You mean that I asked you to help me trap Dwayne because I smelled something funny in the cream and remembered I'd left him alone in the kitchen?"

"You remembered that?" he asked sharply.

"Well, not till just now," she answered, then plowed on, "And we agreed I'd have a tape recorder in my pocket because I was pretty sure I could get him to confess."

"That, too." He cleared his throat. "And I grabbed him from behind when he tried to cut off a lock of your hair."

She sucked in a sharp breath. "That's what he was doing?"

"Yes. The knife is still on the floor under the edge of the counter. Don't touch it—we don't want to smudge those nice incriminating fingerprints."

"And we won't tell any shaggy dog stories," she murmured.

"No."

A police siren in the distance told them that the law was coming.

THEY were at the state police barracks for hours, telling their stories separately so that the cops could make sure their accounts matched. While they were there, a judge issued a search warrant. Shipley's journal was at his house. And he'd taken a lock of hair from each victim before he burned them up. Which should make a pretty good case—combined with the knife and the poison the police had collected from the kitchen, along with the taped confession.

Finally, one of the officers drove Antonia and Grant back home.

The moment the door was closed, she felt his hand on her shoulder, and sensed his tension. "I only told you those names and places once. How did you rattle them off like that? Did you really see that in your cards?"

"No. Not the cards. If you're blind, you have to memorize stuff. I'm good at it."

"Good at a lot of things," he said in a thick voice.

"But not too independent to scare you off?" she asked, hearing her own uncertainty. "I mean, I didn't tell you what I had planned when you asked me to let Shipley see me drink the soup. I wasn't sure you would agree on doing it my way."

"I wouldn't have," he said, and he let her sweat for another twenty seconds before he shifted his grip and crushed her to him. "But it was the right way to go."

"Grant. Oh, Grant."

Still holding her tight, he said. "I thought my life was over when I lost Marcy. You gave it back to me."

"Thank God."

"I love you. I thought I could never say that again. But it's true. And I have you to thank for that miracle."

"I knew you were afraid to trust your feelings. Afraid to trust us."

"It happens fast with my kind. We meet our mate and bond."

She heard him swallow. "But the bond is supposed to be for life. I didn't think it could happen for me a second time. I thought there could never be joy in my life again."

"I know. You were so . . . focused on death. His . . . and yours."

"You saw *that* in your cards?"

"Yes. And I knew that if I could save you, I had to do it."

"There is no way I can thank you for that."

"I think you'll figure something out." Reaching up, she pulled his head down to hers.

The touch of their lips sent a sensual shock wave through her. And the way he groaned into her mouth and deepened the kiss told her that he felt it as strongly as she.

"How about if we make love in bed this time?" he asked in a voice he couldn't quite hold steady.

"For starters."

Taking his hand, she led him up the stairs to her bedroom. He had been passionate with her. Wild. Thrilling. This time, he was tender as he began to undress her, murmuring soft endearments while he unbuttoned her shirt.

And as he removed her clothing, she did the same for him, delighting in the slow buildup of need as hands brushed intimate places and lips trailed over warm skin.

This time was so different from the last, she marveled. This time, she knew they were sealing a commitment to each other as they touched and kissed.

Last time there had been no way to slow down their out-of-control desire. Now he drew out the pleasure for both of them—pleasure beyond anything she could have imagined.

And as he brought her up and up to a high peak where the air was almost too thin to breathe, she felt much more than sexual pleasure. She felt the sure and certain knowledge that she belonged to this man in every way that a woman could belong to her mate.

When he was inside her, he went still above her, kissing her lips and stroking back her hair.

"I love you," he said, in a strong sure voice.

"And I love you," she answered.

"In case you can't tell, I'm smiling," he murmured.

"I can hear it in your voice."

He began to move, then, with long, slow strokes that lifted her beyond the clouds and brought her to a soul-shattering climax.

She gasped out his name—and heard her own name on his lips as he poured himself into her.

"Thank you," she whispered.

"Thank you. For so much," he answered.

Emotional and physical exhaustion claimed her then.

Some time later, she woke and knew from his breathing that he wasn't sleeping.

"How long have you been awake?" she asked.

"A while." He moved his lips against her eyebrows. "I've been waiting to ask for a reading."

"What do you want to know?"

He cleared his throat. "First, do you think the cards will work for you again?"

"I hope so," she said, praying it was true as she reached into her bedside table and pulled out a deck.

"What—you have them in every room of the house?"

"Just about." Sitting up, she dragged the sheet over her breasts, then shuffled.

After taking a deep breath and letting it out, she pulled a

card from the deck. "The two of Cups. Harmony and partnership. Two people about to enter a wonderful relationship."

"I like that one."

She pulled out another. "The ten of Cups."

"What does it mean?"

"Family ties. Joy. That we're going to have the happiness we always wanted."

He pulled her close, nuzzling her ear with his lips. "So is it in the cards for you to take on a partner in this bed and breakfast? I mean, a husband who could do the heavy lifting and the repairs."

"That's what I was hoping. I was thinking a beach town might be a good place to raise your children."

He went very still. "You're not afraid of . . . the consequences?"

"I think there are ways to make it more likely we conceive boys."

She felt him nod against her cheek. "In my family, we live our own lives. But I've talked to some of my cousins. Ross Marshall married a woman who's a genetics specialist. Ross told me she's studied how to better our odds." He lifted her fingers to his lips and kissed them. "For a long time I didn't care about that. Now I do."

"Good."

"You're not sorry you got tangled up with a . . . werewolf?" he said, his hand tightening on hers as he used the word for the first time.

"Well, if someone had said, 'You're going to meet a tall, dark, handsome stranger, and by the way, he changes into a wolf when it suits his purposes,' I would have been a little worried. But the moment I met you, I knew . . ."

"What?"

"I knew I cared about what happened to you."

"Thank God."

He stroked his hand over her bare shoulder and down under the sheet to her breast. And she snuggled against him, reveling in the warmth of his body and the sensuality of his touch. They could finish the conversation later. At the moment, she simply wanted to enjoy the pleasure of being with her life mate.